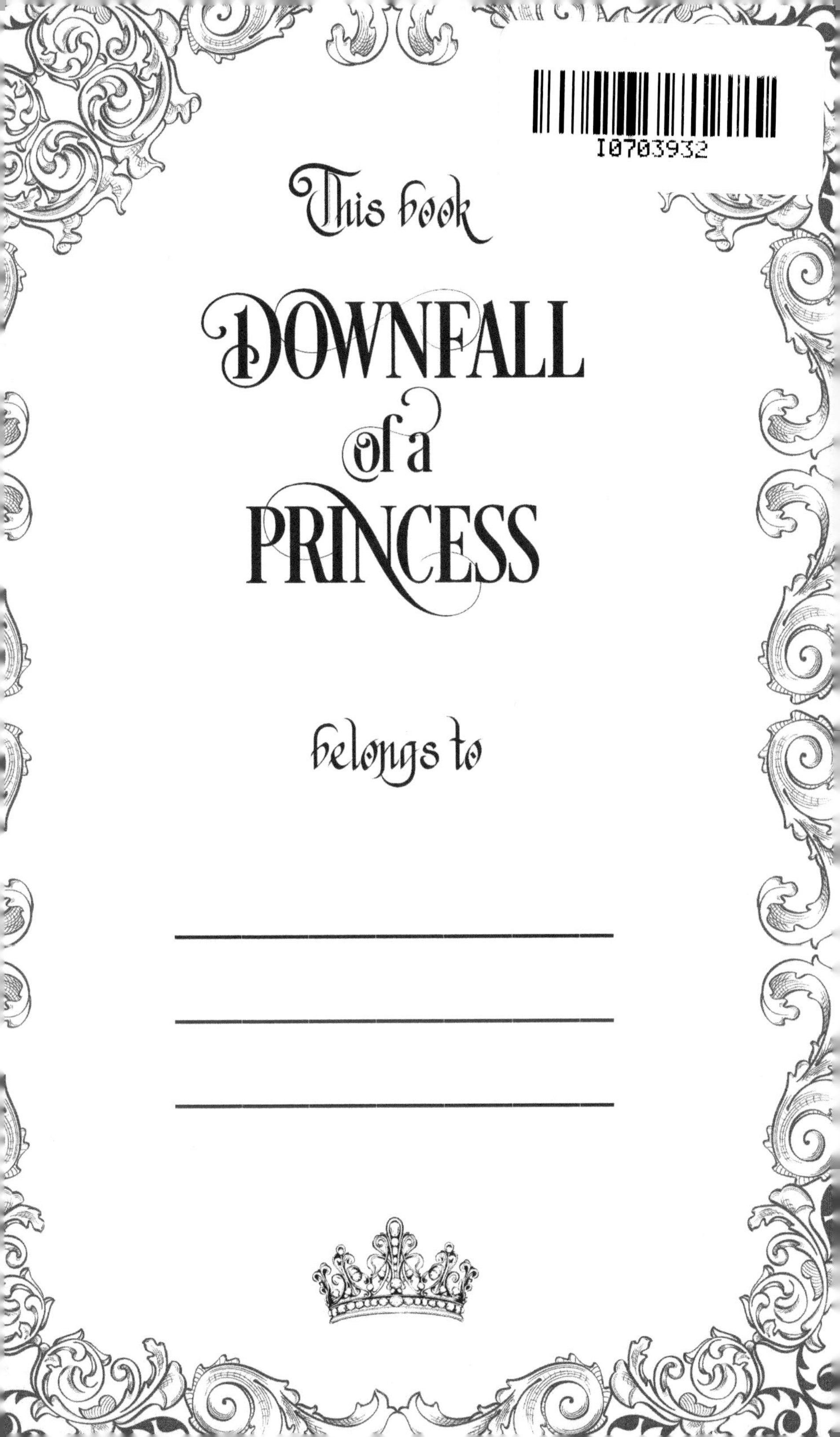

This book

DOWNFALL of a PRINCESS

belongs to

____

____

____

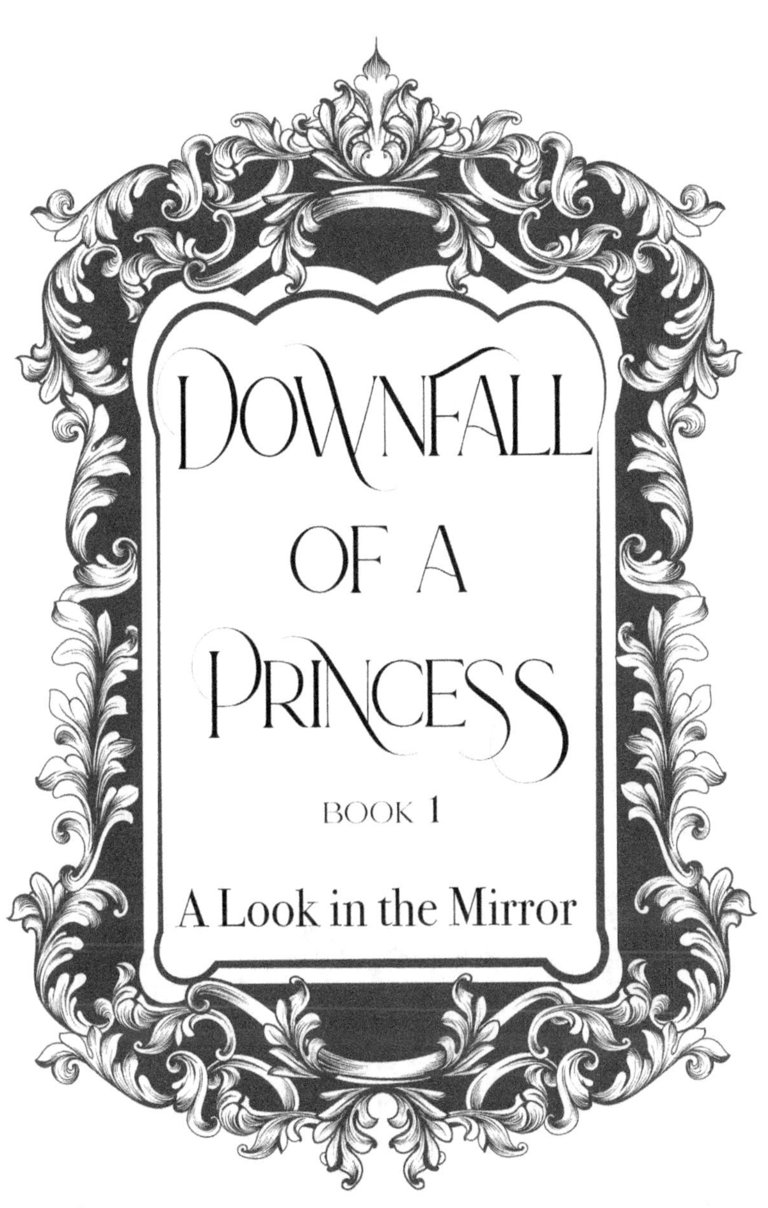

MARINA SIMCOE

Downfall of a Princess

A LOOK IN THE MIRROR
BOOK ONE

MARINA SIMCOE

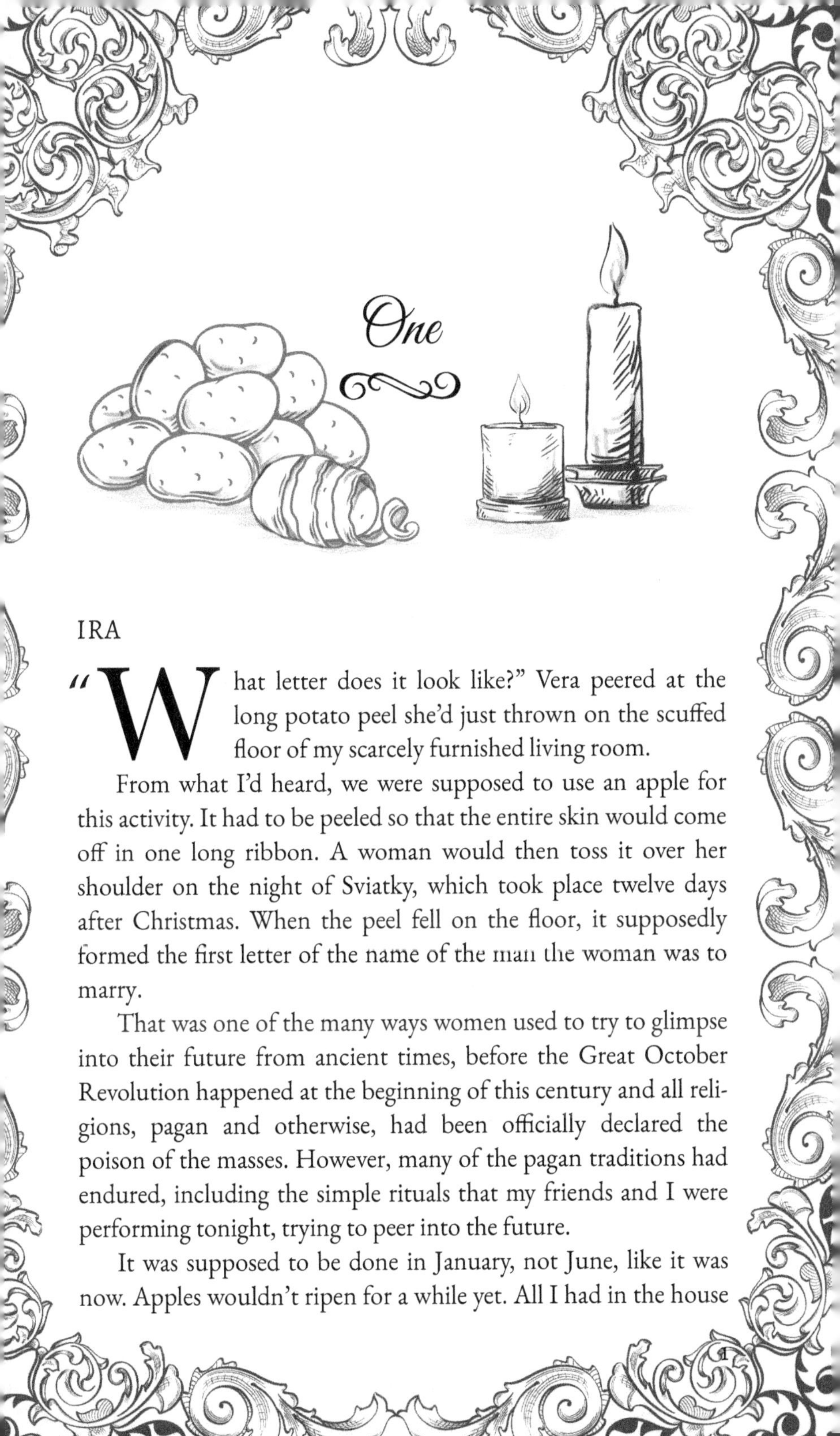

One

IRA

"What letter does it look like?" Vera peered at the long potato peel she'd just thrown on the scuffed floor of my scarcely furnished living room.

From what I'd heard, we were supposed to use an apple for this activity. It had to be peeled so that the entire skin would come off in one long ribbon. A woman would then toss it over her shoulder on the night of Sviatky, which took place twelve days after Christmas. When the peel fell on the floor, it supposedly formed the first letter of the name of the man the woman was to marry.

That was one of the many ways women used to try to glimpse into their future from ancient times, before the Great October Revolution happened at the beginning of this century and all religions, pagan and otherwise, had been officially declared the poison of the masses. However, many of the pagan traditions had endured, including the simple rituals that my friends and I were performing tonight, trying to peer into the future.

It was supposed to be done in January, not June, like it was now. Apples wouldn't ripen for a while yet. All I had in the house were potatoes. So, the results couldn't be true anyway. But school had been out for a week, and we were looking for something to do other than chores.

Tanya tilted her head and squinted at the potato peel. "It looks like an 'I,' I think."

"I... Like in Igor? Igor Petrenko?" Vera cringed. "Fuck, please no. He has like no teeth."

"He won't grow old enough to marry," Tanya said matter-of-factly and shrugged in response to my questioning glance. "Mama said his teeth are rotting because of some shit he and his stepdad are cooking and taking to get high. She said it'll kill them both soon enough."

Alcohol was expensive, so people were constantly in search of substitutes. For as long as I remembered, my parents' poison of choice had always been moonshine. My dad distilled it from potatoes or from birch juice in our kitchen, making the whole house stink. Mama never minded the stench because making and selling moonshine was the one reliable thing Dad did that brought money.

Dad hadn't made any moonshine for a while, though. But somehow, he'd managed to get drunk even more often lately. The morning when Mama disappeared, about a month ago, I'd found him passed out on the front porch with his face down in his own vomit. By some miracle, he'd survived. He'd slept for a day, cleaned himself up a bit, then left again. He'd been in and out of the house ever since, leaving me to fend for myself.

Not that he'd ever looked after me even when he was around. I'd been pretty much on my own most of my life, even before Mama left. Since I was eight, I'd been helping Baba Nadya with her huge garden in exchange for fresh milk and potatoes because Dad sold the only cow we used to have. I had also maintained our garden after Mama gave up on it years ago. I collected seeds every fall and got some manure from the Kolenchiks for helping them clean their barn.

"Maybe the "I" is for Ivan?" Vera said hopefully.

"You mean Baba Masha's grandson?" I asked.

Ivan would be a much better choice than Igor. Years ago, his parents had moved to the city and taken Ivan along. His dad even got a car. Ivan only came to our village in the summer now. It'd be great for Vera if she married Ivan and moved to the city. Except that like Baba Masha often said, Ivan's parents wouldn't want a "dirty village girl" for a daughter-in-law.

Vera knew it. She wrinkled her nose in a doubtful expression.

"Ivan would be good," Tanya agreed. "He's cute."

"Whatever." Vera kicked the peel along the floor. "All boys are gross and stupid, anyway. Let's do the one with the mirrors now."

A shiver of apprehension ran down my back. "That's a scary one."

"What's so scary about it?" Tanya propped the mirror from Mama's bedroom against the back of the couch.

It was an old foggy mirror in a thin metal frame that was bent and rusty in places. It wasn't big enough to have it on the floor, so we had it on the couch, with an even smaller mirror in a white plastic frame positioned in front of it.

"It doesn't stay on its own." Vera shoved the smaller mirror into my hands. "You'll have to hold it."

"Me? Am I going first?" I gripped the plastic frame of the mirror so hard, my knuckles turned white.

"Don't be a scaredy cat," Tanya scoffed.

Vera struck a match to light two short candles. "This one is not about boys. You'll get to see your future, Ira."

"But they say you may see ghosts too," I muttered softly, as if the ghosts could hear me. Chills spread through my chest, and I gripped the frame even harder to stop my fingers from trembling.

"What's so scary about ghosts?" Tanya shrugged. "It's not like they can hurt you. They're dead. Oh, what if you see the ghost of your mama?"

My heart ached at that. I'd just recently stopped crying at night, and now tears prickled behind my eyelids anew. I bit the inside of my cheek until the coppery scent of blood hit my tongue. The sting of physical pain helped to keep the tears at bay.

"My mama isn't dead, stupid," I snapped. "How can there be a ghost of her?"

"Oh yeah? But why did your dad dig in the old potato field behind the bus stop the night she was gone? Nastya Kolenchik saw him."

"Nastya Kolenchik wags her tongue a lot, everyone knows it. She makes up shit." I shrugged, trying to look calm, even as everything inside me screamed.

Mama left weeks ago, and no one was looking for her. No one ever would.

People disappeared sometimes. Both men and women. It must be normal, I assumed, since no one particularly worried about them or searched especially hard. Vera's grandpa, for example, had gone fishing five years ago and never came back. They said he must've fallen into the river drunk. They said Mama might've found a new lover and left with him, but some said she was dead. Either way, no one would investigate it. The only *melicia* station was two villages over, and they had a lot to do as it was.

The villagers would gossip for a while, then they'd settle on a version of the truth that suited them the most and move on. And so it would remain, unless my mama came back one day and proved them wrong, or her dead body was found.

"Whatever. Let's just do it. It's dark enough outside already." Vera dripped some hot wax from the burning candles on two chipped saucers, then stuck the candles into the wax. "Or I'll just go home."

Tanya glanced at our curtainless window in a wooden frame with peeling white paint. "It's really dark out there. If you leave, I'm coming with you, Vera. I'm not walking at night alone."

Vera smirked, like a badass that she really wasn't. "What? Are you afraid to get raped or something?"

"Aren't you?"

"It's not rape if you don't fight it," Vera said flippantly. "Like my mama always says, 'If it happens, just lay back and enjoy.'"

Tanya cringed. "What's there to enjoy?"

Vera lost her virginity last year. How and with whom, she wouldn't tell. But by her own brazen admission, she'd been with a lot of men since. Villagers shook their heads, lamenting she grew up to be a whore just like her mama. Like Tanya and I, Vera was only thirteen, but people had already labeled her a whore, blaming her for the actions of the men she'd been with.

Tanya told me in secret that she'd also already had sex with the boy she was dating. The boy was also seeing an older girl, who would "give him what he wanted," and Tanya was hoping that now that she gave him that too, he'd stop seeing that other girl.

I hoped for Tanya's sake that he would. But then what did I know? I was still a virgin, and the more I learned about sex, the less I wanted to have anything to do with it, if only it was up to me.

"If you fight them," Vera continued with the practicality beyond her age, "you're gonna end up with a black eye, like the one that Ilyinishna is sporting. Have you seen her lately?"

I rubbed my upper arms. "She said she fell."

"Yeah right, fell and landed on her eye." Vera smirked. "It's a good thing you wear glasses, Ira. Boys don't like girls with glasses, anyway. That's why they don't bug you."

Except that they did "bug" me. My thick, cheap glasses might've deterred boys from asking me out, but they didn't make me immune to being groped behind the school building or being spied on in the bathroom. I hadn't even been kissed yet, but I had already fought my way out of a few situations where the boys wanted far more than just kissing.

"So," Vera prompted. "Are we doing it or not? Because if not, I'm leaving."

If they left, I'd be alone. During the day, I didn't mind it, but nights could be scary, especially after the drunk older boys had broken the glass in my bedroom window two weeks ago. They scared me so much that night, I'd been sleeping on the couch in the living room ever since.

If I could keep Vera and Tanya here longer, hopefully, I'd be tired enough to fall asleep quickly, instead of lying on the couch and listening to every noise this old log house made at night.

"No, guys. Stay," I said. "I'll do it."

I propped the smaller mirror against my shoulder while Vera and Tanya held a candle on each side of it.

"Now make a corridor and wish to see your future," Vera instructed.

I straightened the smaller mirror, making it reflect in the bigger one. The reflection bounced from one mirror to the other, back and forth to infinity, forming a long dark corridor of shadows lit by the two candles on each side.

"What do you want your future to be like?" Tanya asked.

"I...I don't know. I just want to be happy, I guess?"

Except that I couldn't even define what "happy" meant. To me, happiness was just an abstract idea, where I wouldn't be cold, or hungry, or alone. My imagination didn't reach far beyond that. In the thirteen years I'd been alive, I hadn't seen a single example of true happiness.

My parents weren't happy. They screamed at each other when they were together and couldn't care less if they were apart. Everyone in our village had their share of problems that they tried to drown in drinking, or fighting, or both.

The only adult I enjoyed having around was Natalia Borisovna, my Language and Literature teacher. She was young, just out of university. She came to our school through a contract with the government that had granted her admission into the university under the condition that after graduation, she'd work a year in a rural area like ours, where few teachers wished to live permanently. But Natalia Borisovna's year was up. She left at the end of May and returned to the city.

Maybe that was where happiness resided? In the city?

"So? What do you see?" Vera shifted at my side impatiently, making the flame of her candle flicker.

The light bounced back with a gazillion reflections, forcing the shadows to shift and lurch down the endless, dark corridor inside the mirror. At the end of it, all I could see was darkness.

Was that what my future held? A dark nothingness?

It was a grim realization for a thirteen-year-old. But we all matured early here, and maturity meant looking at things realistically. Nothing bright or shiny waited for me in our village, only a dead-end life.

As if sensing my somber thoughts, Tanya heaved a sigh. Her candle flickered, nearly going out. The mirror tunnel darkened, momentarily turning into a black abyss. The shadows solidified in the middle, looking impenetrable.

The flame of Tanya's candle burst back to life, mirroring the one on Vera's side. The two lights stretched down the corridor until the reflections turned from gold to silver.

Then, I saw a face.

A pale, beautiful woman stared back at me from the mirror. Her silver-gray eyes studied my face, moving from my eyes to my nose to my mouth, then back again. She was dressed in a dark long robe over a white shirt. And she *saw* me.

"Ahh..." My mouth fell open.

I shrank back from the couch. The mirror slipped from my shoulder and crashed to the floor. The old glass cracked, breaking into four jagged pieces.

"Fuck, Ira!" Vera leaped back, narrowly avoiding a cut to her bare knee. "What did you do that for?"

"Hey, what did you see?" Tanya asked softly. "Was it your mama?"

The woman in the mirror had luminous pale skin, raven-black hair that blended with shadows, and silver eyes that glistened like stars. She couldn't be any more different from my mother who had ruddy skin, a bulbous nose that was permanently red from heavy drinking, and light-brown hair that I'd inherited.

"No. It wasn't Mama."

"Then who was it?" Vera asked.

"I don't know."

I had no idea who the woman was. I had never seen anyone like her before. But she looked real, and I wished she had stayed.

I LAY on the couch in our living area with the kitchen just behind a partial wall.

The girls left shortly after the mirror had broken. I'd walked out with them to use the outhouse. After returning to the house, I locked the door, made sure all the windows were also locked, then propped a chair under the handle of the closed door to my bedroom. I put a plate on top of the chair, then an upturned glass, and finally balanced a fork on top of the glass. This way, if anyone were to climb through the broken window in the bedroom to get to me in the living room, they'd tip the chair with all the dishes and hopefully make enough noise for me to wake up and run. A heavy sleeper like me needed a lot of noise to wake up.

Only sleep wouldn't come to me tonight as I lay on the couch, clutching the knife I'd kept under my pillow ever since Mama left.

The wind howled in the rafters somewhere. A mouse scratched inside a wall. The miraculous vision of the silver-eyed woman in the mirror tunnel didn't stay in my thoughts for long, replaced by real-life concerns I faced.

Mama was gone. Dad said she left us. If so, I didn't blame her, I just wished she'd taken me along.

If the rumors were true, however, then she hadn't run anywhere at all but lay dead in the old potato field. Maybe I should borrow a shovel from Baba Nadya and dig behind the bus stop tomorrow. I'd look for Mama since no one else would.

The front door screeched open, then slammed shut. I jumped on my couch, pulling the knife out. Then realized it must've been

Dad coming home since he was the only one who had the house key. His stumbling footsteps and grunting noises confirmed it. At least he didn't crash on the front porch this time, managing to get inside on his own.

I stuck the knife back under the pillow and lay down, pretending to be asleep. Hopefully, he'd just go straight to his bedroom without trying to speak to me. Listening to his mumbling rants would be a waste of time. But at least when he was too drunk to stand upright, he couldn't punch hard enough to hurt.

Instead of the bedroom, however, Dad stomped into the kitchen, mumbling, "I've got nothing, man... Nothing. The bitch left. Took everything. But I need it. I'll pay you later. I'm good for it, man... I swear."

He wasn't talking to himself. Someone came with him, as another set of footsteps followed him into the kitchen. Then, the light flicked on, illuminating the space behind the partial wall and out of my view.

"You really think she's left, huh? You don't remember anything at all?" a male voice replied. I didn't think I'd heard that voice before.

"What's there to remember? She's gone. Took everything. Now, I've got nothing."

"You've never had anything, you idiot. You've long traded for booze anything worth something. But booze is cheap, and the potato piss you distill is even cheaper. But this here..." A chair screeched, being shoved aside, then a plastic bag crinkled. "This shit is expensive, dude. I told you before, it was gonna cost you."

"I know, I know... But I need it now..." Dad's voice dissolved into blubbering. "Take it. Whatever you want. Take the house..."

"This old shithole?" The man laughed. "What am I going to do with this rat-eaten log shack in Bumfuck Nowhere? Huts like this one are abandoned and rotting into the ground all over the place around here."

"It's a good house. Warm... big enough..." Dad was trying to talk up our "shithole," which only made him sound even more pathetic.

"Hey, you have a daughter, don't you?"

The stranger's words shook every idea of sleep from me. I sat up, my eyes flying wide open.

Why was he talking about me?

"Yeah... Sure..." Dad mumbled. "I do. I do. Ira is her name. Ira, Irina," he repeated, as if proud that he still remembered my name.

"Yeah, I saw her at my aunt's house another day. She did some weeding. A young thing, isn't she?" The male voice flowed lazily, like warm bacon fat, making me feel greasy just from hearing it.

Now, I recognized the man. He was Baba Nadya's nephew, the one who lived in another village and came for a visit every now and then. I'd seen him smoking a cigarette on the back porch of Baba Nadya's house as I was weeding her expansive tomato patch. At some point, he'd put the cigarette out and headed my way, but I was pretty much done with the weeding by then, so I just hopped the fence and ran home before he had a chance to get close. He was at least three times my age, fat, and bald, and I had nothing to talk to him about.

"I'll take the girl for a bag of this," the man said.

My insides froze, the chills spreading through to my limbs.

"The girl?" Dad sounded confused, not angry. Why was he not angry at that asshole? "What girl?"

"Your daughter. Ira."

"Right. Ira... What do you want her for?"

"Just a little fun, buddy. Nothing you probably haven't done with her yourself."

My dad hadn't touched me. Sometimes, I questioned whether he was my dad at all. I didn't look like him. He was tall and lanky, with dark wavy hair. I was tall but more solid, with my mama's lighter hair that held no curls whatsoever. My eyes were gray green, like bog water on a cold November day. Nothing like my parents, who both had blue eyes.

I wondered if Mama told him that I was his because it was the only way she knew how to protect me from the man I had to share the house with. Or maybe she did it to protect herself?

Either way, it'd worked so far. He never touched me, not in *that* way, anyway. He'd hit me plenty with a fist, or a belt, or whatever happened to be close by when I misbehaved or when he was in a bad mood. But that was it. Until now.

Now, he was trading me for drugs.

"Like... a night with her? For this whole bag?" He was considering it. No, he sounded like he'd already decided. He was just trying to figure out the price.

Deep inside, I knew that the man he was negotiating with could simply walk in here right now and take what he wanted for free. Dad would do nothing to stop him.

"A whole night?" The man laughed again. What a derisive sound that was. I hated it. "An hour would be more than enough, dude. For now, anyway."

"Do I get just one bag?" Dad whined.

I didn't listen to the rest of their negotiations. I slipped out from under my tattered cover, crossed the creaky floor as quietly as I could, removed my makeshift alarm system by the door, and tiptoed into my bedroom.

Here, I threw on a pair of sweatpants and a sweatshirt, stuffed more clothes and whatever money I had saved by doing chores for others into my schoolbag, then climbed out of the broken window.

They'd be looking for me soon enough, but they didn't even know whether I was in the house to begin with. With any luck, I'd have plenty of time to put a good distance between me and this place before anyone would notice my absence.

After a few days, Dad probably wouldn't even remember he had a daughter at all. Just like he didn't remember what happened to Mama.

I had a vague plan but a clear destination. I'd walk about

fifteen kilometers to the next village. Then take the bus from there to the town. From there, I'd take the train to the city.

Quite a few people from our village had moved to the city. No one had ever come back. I figured the city was where happiness lived. And if so, that was the place where I should be too.

How badly I was mistaken. The city, at least the version of it that I got to experience, held not a trace of happiness. On the contrary, with the larger number of people, the misery seemed to multiply here as well.

I lasted a few days on my own, sleeping behind garbage bins outside of an apartment complex at night and shoplifting food during the day. After an attack by the local gang during a *melicia* raid, I stopped hiding and let the authorities arrest me.

Afraid they would send me back to live with my dad, I faked memory loss, claiming I didn't know who I was. It proved easy enough to do because I didn't wish to remember it anyway. Once they'd determined I was underage, they sent me to an orphanage until my next-of-kin came forward to claim me.

As I'd expected, no one had come for me in the three years that followed. By now, I assumed both my parents were as good as dead. Even if they weren't, they'd probably be glad I was someone else's responsibility.

One morning, about three years after I'd become the ward of the state, I woke up to the sound of someone crying.

The girls' bedroom was illuminated by the muddy yellow light of an early spring sunrise. It was time to wake up, but the day nurse hadn't come in yet. Actually, she wasn't called "a nurse" anymore, but "a sister." Since the orphanage was privatized two years ago, its ownership went from the government to a charity organization that was funded by a church. Girls had been separated from the boys, which I didn't mind at all, and instead of nurses and a supervisor, we now had sisters and a head mistress to look after us.

Thankfully, they had kept most of the teachers. I happened to like the school here. Some of the teachers I even liked more than Natalia Borisovna, more so because thinking of her made me remember the village where I came from, and I did not want to remember.

Another muffled sob came, prompting me to sit up in bed. The metal bed frame creaked as I turned around to my neighbor on the left. She was a few months older than me and belonged to the group of girls who often made others cry with their bullying and teasing. However, seeing her vulnerable like this stirred compassion in me.

"Vika? Are you okay?"

She quickly wiped her eyes with the sleeve of her nightshirt, then turned with her back to me. "Fuck off."

Her response didn't offend me. Rudeness was so common in my life, it almost felt like a norm. The appropriate response was to either be rude in return or just ignore it. I chose to ignore it. It was easier that way. The less people noticed me, the better off I was.

The morning shift sister finally swung open the door to our huge common bedroom.

"Wake-up time!" She flicked the lights on.

I squinted in the bright light of the long fluorescent tubes under the ceiling. It bounced off the glaringly white walls, making the space appear even brighter.

The girls climbed out of their beds. There was close to a hundred of us in the senior girls' bedroom where I was moved to when I'd turned fourteen. I took the stack of my clothes from the nightstand next to my bed, the only piece of furniture each of us had to store all our worldly possessions in.

Life in the orphanage wasn't too bad. The building was warm. They fed us three times a day. The food was bland and the menu boring, but I didn't complain because despite my best efforts to forget, I still remembered what it was like going without any food at all.

We went to school Monday through Saturday, and after classes, we worked in the factory next door.

I didn't mind being here. I accepted the monotonous routine, the inevitable bullying by the older girls, the yelling and the occasional slap from the staff, the rules and restrictions that often made little sense, and the unfair punishment that came from breaking them. Despite all of that, I felt safer here than back home or out on the streets. And safety was all that mattered.

As I was growing older, however, concerns started invading my mind. Next month, I'd be turning seventeen. And a year after that, I'd be graduating school. Then, like the other girls put it, I'd be "kicked out" for turning too old to stay in the orphanage.

I'd get my high school diploma and some money, then be "sent out into the world." The money was barely enough for a few meals. The job we held with the factory was contracted through the charity organization; we lost it the moment we left the orphanage. And the high school diploma was of little use in the country where university graduates had to compete for table-waiting jobs to survive.

After *perestrojka*, the new way of life came with many sporadic changes. The government-owned companies went under. The privately owned ones couldn't keep up with job creation. Unemployment was sky-high, and nepotism flourished.

I racked my brain about what to do next.

The older girls whispered about finding a "sponsor." That was a fancy English word that came into our language along with other terms of capitalism. The girls talked about affluent men securing jobs and renting apartments for young women. In exchange, of course, the women gave the only thing they had —themselves.

I still hadn't tried having sex, and not just because of the orphanage's strict rules against dating. The idea of having a man's hands on my naked body made my skin crawl with tiny imaginary spiders. From everything I'd learned about sex, back home and later in the city streets, it was always about the man's pleasure. A woman was just a tool, a device for him to use.

But if a woman's fate was just to serve as a device, then why not be the device that men paid to use? From that point of view, getting a sponsor made sense. Maybe my repulsion of sex would go away once I actually started doing it?

Except that to attract a sponsor, one had to be pretty. And I wasn't sure if I made the cut in that department.

On my way back to our bedroom that night, I paused in front of the large mirror on the stair landing and took a good look at my reflection.

I was tall, maybe even too tall, one of the top ten tallest girls in our group. My body had gained some curves over the past few years, unfortunately not in all the ideal places. I had boobs. The buttons on my chest struggled to hold my dress closed with my breasts pushing against them as if trying to burst free. My belly protruded slightly both above and below my belt. My stomach was never completely flat even when I'd been starving. What remained flat, sadly, was my ass. My relatively narrow hips made my waist look wider, which was far from the classic feminine hour-glass shape that men seemed to prefer.

My hair was too dark for a blonde but too pale for a brunette. My eyes seemed too round to pull off a sultry look, and my lips too thin for a naturally sexy pout. I had freckles. And of course, I had my glasses in an outdated plastic frame that didn't help.

Personally, it didn't bother me how I looked. I was strong and healthy. This body had enabled me to weed a field all day and to work a mind-numbing assembly line at the factory six days a week. I was capable and willing to work hard. Except that the world didn't seem to value these abilities enough for me to earn a living. Someone like me—with no family, no money, and no connections —had to at least be beautiful in order to survive.

A shadow fell across the mirror. The thought of the silver-eyed woman flashed through my mind. Every now and then, I'd think about her pale face and the surprise in her eyes that turned to kindness as she looked at me. By now, however, the vision of her had faded in my memories, becoming nothing more than an echo of a dream.

Instead, the face of the night-shift sister appeared in the mirror next to me.

"Time to go to bed," she reminded me.

I'd hardly spoken to her before now, but the anxiety about the future prompted me to ask, "Do you think I'm pretty?"

She gave me a surprised look.

"Vanity is a sin, Ira." The reprimand came out flat, with no passion behind it, as if the sister had grown tired of her own mantra. She heaved a sigh, then said in a more animated voice, "You know what they say, 'Don't be born beautiful, be born happy.'"

Happiness remained an abstract concept to me. I still associated it mostly with safety and security, nothing more.

"Or lucky," the sister added. "One needs a lot of luck to be happy." She sighed again, then ushered me into the bedroom along with the other girls coming up the stairs.

I changed into my nightshirt. The bedroom had no privacy partitions, but I'd long gotten used to undressing in the open, like other girls did.

The bed on my left remained empty even after the sister gave the first warning about the lights being turned off soon.

"Where is Vika?" I asked Vika's neighbor on the other side of her bed, but she just shrugged with no answer before getting under her covers.

The girl on my right, Dina, hissed behind me, "You're such an idiot. Don't you know anything? The *melicia* was in the Head Mistress's office this morning. They said Vika ran away."

"She did? Why?"

"She must've had enough."

"Enough of what?"

Dina gave me a long, disgusted look.

"Didn't you hear?" she asked.

I shook my head. "Hear *what?*"

The sister clapped her hands together.

"Lights off!" she yelled before hitting the switch.

Her keys rattled as she locked the plastic box over the light switch so that we, heavens forbid, didn't turn it back on to have a party after she'd left.

"Hey, Dina," I whispered from under my covers the moment the sister's footsteps died down outside the bedroom door. "What do you mean? What was I supposed to hear?"

"You really sleep like a log, stupid," she scoffed, turning with her back to me.

I'd always been a heavy sleeper, now especially so, since I no longer had to keep a knife under my pillow. Between work and school, we barely got eight hours for sleep, which never seemed enough. I fell asleep the moment my head hit the pillow, and I rarely woke up before the lights went on in the morning. Because of that, I often ended up as the target of pranks. The girls would paint my face with toothpaste while I slept or pour a glass of water under my covers to make it look like I peed myself.

The night that followed, however, something did wake me up.

My legs felt cold with the covers off. Without opening my eyes, I patted around in search of my blanket. Instead, someone's hands slid up my legs and under my nightshirt.

Terror shot through my chest like an electric charge, startling me wide awake. With a gasp of horror stuck in my throat, I sprung upright.

"Shh, keep still." Mihail Pavlovitch, the representative of the charity organization, the highly respected member of the church, and the major benefactor of the orphanage, gripped my hips, digging with his fingers in my underwear.

A picture of him with his smiling wife on his arm during a publicity tour of the orphanage last year flashed through my mind, just before I kicked him into his protruding belly.

"Fuck!" he cursed, then slapped my face with a heavy hand.

The blow rang in my ears, making his next words sound as if reverberating inside a giant bell.

"Lay still, little bitch, or it'll be worse." He plopped on top of me, making the metal springs of the bed whine.

He smelled of sweat, tobacco, wool of his suit, and the cologne that made me gag. The thin mattress sank under his weight, pressing me into the trap under his heavy body.

Panic blinded me. Whatever he'd meant by "worse" couldn't be any worse than this.

He leaned back to open the zipper of his pants, and I used the chance to scramble from under him. I fell to the floor, hitting my knees, then crawled between the beds to the main aisle.

"You stupid bitch." He stomped after me. The menace in his voice left no doubt that I was not getting away.

Finally finding my voice, I screamed for help. Only no help came. Someone must be awake in the bedroom, but the girls didn't dare intervene. What could they do against him, anyway?

Helplessness amplified my terror. Every fear I'd ever felt snowballed, rolling over me and threatening to crush. Slamming the bedroom door open, I ran out onto the landing.

The sister was rushing up the stairs, her shape blurry without my glasses. The moment she spotted Mihail Pavlovitch behind me, she stopped in her tracks.

"Go back to your bed, Ira," she said in a hollow voice. "And keep quiet."

"If it happens, just lay back and enjoy," the "wise" advice I'd heard before rang through my head.

Only I always knew it wasn't about any actual enjoyment.

It was about resignation, giving up when there was no more hope. When one lost all control over her body, the only thing left to do was to separate her heart and soul from it. To save the little she still could.

Except, I wasn't there yet. I could still fight.

Run.

Do something.

The sister was blocking the stairs. I turned on my heel, but he was right behind me, reaching for me. I lurched aside to evade him, tripped, and fell against the massive mirror on the wall. My chest and both hands hit the cold smooth surface.

Panic shook me. There was nowhere to run. I wished the glass would melt like ice and the darkness behind it would take me.

"Fucking skunk," he hissed behind me, grabbing my hair. Yanking my head back, he slammed my face into the mirror.

The glass was supposed to break under that blow. The shards were supposed to hurt me, cutting my skin and disfiguring me for life if I survived. Blood was supposed to splash over the mirror and the wall.

But none of it happened. The hard surface suddenly felt soft. The shadows from inside the mirror reached out. Two arms embraced me, pulling me in.

The beautiful face of the woman with silver eyes was right above me, guiding me like a full moon on a dark night.

A voice sounded, soothing and kind, "Come to me, child. Here, you'll be safe."

Two

ARI

10 YEARS LATER

Drawing in a long breath of warm early-summer air, I turned my face up to the afternoon sunshine. Summer had been slow to come to Rorrim Queendom this year, but it seemed finally here.

Gem caught up with me, lining her horse up stirrup to stirrup with my mare Revlis.

"Nice day, isn't it?" Gem said, opening all the buttons in the front of her dress.

I'd done the same already, unbuttoning my light cotton dress down past my bra to help me keep cool. We rode side by side along a wide paved road out of Egami, the capital city of Rorrim, in the world behind the mirror that I had accidentally discovered ten years ago and never looked back.

"Thanks for dragging me out of the palace today, Gem."

"Someone had to." She tossed back her long ponytail of thick, chestnut hair.

Five years older than me, Gem had been my unofficial guide in the palace, helping me learn and adapt to my new life. She seemed to always be in the know about everything and everyone at the queen's court, which made her the perfect woman for the job of lady chamberlain, the position she'd held for over three years now. As the niece of Queen Anna, who'd become my adoptive mother, Gem was also my cousin.

"If I didn't physically drag you out every now and then, your butt would've long merged with the chair in your study by now," Gem quipped.

That was true. I spent a lot of time indoors. But mostly because I constantly felt the need to catch up. I didn't grow up in Rorrim, yet as the queen's daughter and the crown princess, I was expected to govern the country one day. There was a lot to learn, and the more I read, studied, and observed, the more things I found I needed to know.

Queen Anna, my silver-eyed savior from the mirror, proved to be kind, intelligent, and just—everything my birth mother never was.

That night when I'd barged into the queen's life, sobbing, terrified, and confused, she sat with me on the floor in front of the ancient mirror in the palace's grand throne room. She held me, stroking my hair and whispering words of comfort no one had ever said to me before.

She'd assured me that I was worthy of love, that I deserved a good, peaceful life, and that she was going to give it to me.

"You are of my bloodline," the queen had told me. "You must be. The blood of my ancestors is flowing in you, child. That's why I was able to see you through the mirror. A miracle brought you here. And now, nothing and no one will ever hurt you again."

The queen was married. For years, she'd tried to have a child of her own and failed. She said my anguish must've opened the portal for me to escape my world, Fate had led me to her. But I also believed it'd been her compassion that guided me into her arms that night and for that, I was forever grateful.

In Rorrim Queendom, I became Aniri, the Crown Princess, or Ari for those close to me. Ira, the frightened, helpless, struggling to survive girl of my past, was long gone. I buried her along with the memories of that world that I loathed to revisit.

A farmer's wagon rattled down the road toward us. I steered Revlis to the right to let the wagon pass. The farmer sat in the front, holding the horse's reins in her hands. She waved at me with a smile.

"Afternoon, Your Highness."

The farmer's husband rode with the kids in the back, among the baskets of green onions they must be delivering to one of the grocers in the city. The man tipped his head to me in greeting.

"I'm surprised people still remember who you are," Gem teased. "They probably just recognize the crown, not your face. When was the last time you showed your face in public?"

My crown, the circlet of golden stars, was so delicate, I hardly felt it upon my hair. However, it shone brightly enough in the sunshine to be spotted from a distance. Gem might be right; it was the crown that gave away my position. But I also wasn't as much of a hermit as she was making it out to be.

"Oh, come on." I waved her off. "I do get out. I went to the Games last week, didn't I?"

"The Games are a given." Gem lowered her eyelids, shading her blue eyes with her long, dark eyelashes. A smile spread on her lips, slow like melted butter. "Ever since the Games Master acquired Falo, the new gladiator from the South, a woman must be dead to miss the Games."

I'd seen Falo in the arena. Like most people from the cold southern parts of the country, he had blond hair and blue eyes. His long locks and the golden armor he wore in the arena made him look like Yarnus, the son of the Rorrim's Great Goddess Nus.

I arched an eyebrow. "Don't tell me you've slept with him already."

Gladiators belonged to the crown. However, I'd never heard of Queen Anna visiting the men's quarters for private time with any of them. Her court ladies, on the other hand, liked frequenting the fighters' rooms after the Games. The married women tended to be more discrete, but Gem was single, not even engaged yet, and therefore had the freedom to do as she pleased.

"Not yet," she said with a disappointed groan. "You know the rules, no sex for the gladiators during the first month upon their arrival to Egami."

That particular rule was in place to protect the women of Egami and to give every new gladiator time to adjust to his new life in the arena. Only after the Games Master had fully assessed the new fighter's character and deemed him safe to be left alone with a woman was he allowed to have a private audience with a lady.

"I've put a request to the Games Master for next month. But she says the line to see the new boy is pretty long. Can you believe it? He's that popular already."

The "boy" was in his twenties, but gladiators were often referred to as boys, regardless of their age. It didn't surprise me that the new man was so popular with women. His act in the arena was amazing. He'd scored a few impressive victories already, and victors tended to enjoy more attention from both the crowd and the court ladies.

"He did pretty good during the last Games," I admitted.

"He was magnificent!" Gem swooned. "He's so beautiful. I can't wait to have that gorgeous face between my legs." She tilted her head with a sly glance my way. "You should come with me to the gladiators' quarters next time. As the crown princess, you may even gain a favor with the Games Master, and she'd move you up in line for a private visit with Falo."

I'd been to the gladiators' quarters just once. When I turned twenty-one, Gem took me there on a visit that was supposed to be an unofficial rite of passage of sorts. By that age, I was considered an adult in every aspect. I was allowed to drink and gamble. I got a seat on the Royal Council. Since then, I was also not only allowed, but encouraged to have sex, which Gem probably hoped for me to do when she took me on a tour of the gladiators' private living area five years ago.

Each man had his own room upstairs, but the main area downstairs served as a large living space with dining and gambling tables. Here, they held parties after the weekly Games. I remembered the gladiators' quarters as a cheerful place, filled with music and laughter. Expensive wine flowed freely, with the finest food being served. The noble court women sat on the couches with the gladiators of their choice at their feet. Some couples danced, others gambled.

I'd had a glass of wine with Gem before she got distracted by a young gladiator with both his shirt and chest armor gone.

Another young man came over and sat on the floor at my feet. He smiled at me and hugged my leg through my skirts. He seemed friendly and acted respectfully, waiting for a sign from me that would allow him to go any further. His hand had never strayed higher than my knee, but the contact alone proved sobering.

The world had tilted then, as if slipping off its axis. The music had suddenly sounded false and the laughter derisive. My vision had focused on the other men's hands in the room. I saw them sliding under the women's skirts and into their necklines. The touching had been fully consensual of course. No man in Rorrim would dare touch a woman without her explicit permission or he'd lose his head by law.

I knew it, but my mind had leaped elsewhere that night. It had reached back to that dark place inside me that I wished I could rip out of my soul and burn. I'd yanked my leg away from the man, jumped to my feet, and ran back to my carriage. I rode all the way to the palace and didn't remember how I got to my room.

Then, I'd made a clumsy excuse about my coming down with a sudden sickness for the Games Master so that she wouldn't punish the poor gladiator responsible for my flight. It wasn't his fault that my mind viewed any physical contact with a man as a threat.

I never visited the gladiators' quarters again. The aftergame parties reeked of sex. And sex was clearly out of the question for me.

"I'm good," I said to Gem, steering Revlis off the road and onto the path around the city wall.

She pursed her lips. "I'm afraid nothing is *good* about this situation, Ari. You're twenty-six. And as far as I know the closest you've ever come to being with a man has been a leg hug. You'll need to marry one day. How are you going to know what to do with your husband to conceive an heiress?"

I raked my hands through the silver-white strands of Revlis's mane. "I still have time. You're older than me and aren't married."

"You can't compare me to you," she retorted. "The future of a country doesn't depend on me. I can stay the way I am for the rest of my life if I so wish. My older sister is married, with three daughters. There are more than enough heiresses to our mother's lands and title. You, however, are the only daughter of our queen. I hate to pressure you, but you are our only hope for the continuation of the current ruling line."

I tightened my fingers in the horse's mane. "Do you think I don't know that?"

Gem wasn't the first or the only one to bring up the subject of a marriage. My future husband hadn't been chosen yet, but the buzz about possible candidates had been going around the palace for years. The talks of marriage had mostly been delivered to me in the form of veiled comments and gentle nudging. Gem was the only courtier who ever dared speaking frankly with me like that.

I narrowed my eyes at her suspiciously. "Did my mother put you up to this?"

"Would you blame her if she did?" She jerked her head, her ponytail swaying behind her. "After so many years of anguish with the queen trying and failing to conceive, you were our miracle. You arrived here by magic, as an answer to our prayers. No one questioned your right to her crown. Now, you're our only hope for the peaceful continuation of the current ruling line without the risk of a war for succession, but you act like you couldn't be bothered." She spread her arms aside, holding the reins in one hand. "Pardon me, Your Highness, but that's selfish."

When she put it that way, I felt rotten inside. Rorrim had become my one true home. I cherished the trust and love of its people, learning diligently how to become the ruler they deserved.

"Gem, I never said I didn't care. I know what's expected of me, and I have no intention of running away from my duty. But I'm not even married yet. How can we talk about an heiress already?"

She perked up. "Just say a word, and the queen will marry you in no time. You know she and the king have been compiling a list of suitable candidates for years now. You can have a husband within weeks if you wish. But then, what are you going to do with your pure, innocent groom when the time comes to consummate your marriage? Trust me, it helps to know in advance what's supposed to happen in the bedroom between a woman and her husband."

Just thinking about the wedding night made me break out in sweat. I rubbed my arms to chase the sudden chills out of my skin.

Oblivious to how uncomfortable this conversation made me feel, Gem continued in an upbeat tone, "Ari, sweetie, you can't expect a young gentleman from a good family to know anything about sex. A wife teaches her husband the ways in the bedroom. That's how it is. But what can you teach him if you've never been with a man yourself?"

The question hung between us, unanswered.

Gem was right, of course. The continuation of Queen Anna's line was important. Her ancestors had ruled Rorrim Queendom for over a millennium. During their reign, there had been so few wars in the country, the detailed account of all battles fit in one medium-size book in the Royal Archives. The people of Rorrim treasured peace above all and enjoyed the prosperity it brought. I couldn't be the one to jeopardize it all now. But the very idea of a man touching me made me want to run as far away from all men as possible.

We turned around a bend of the city wall. The Egami's execution site lay on our way to the forest path where Gem and I were heading for our ride.

As my lessons on governance had taught me, every law had to be enforced in order for it to be respected. The wooden scaffolding had stood in this very spot for centuries. As the wood rotted and deteriorated, it was replaced again and again, keeping this spot for punishments ordered by the queen.

The spot had been chosen outside of the city so as not to upset the city dwellers with gruesome views. Though judging by the crowd gathered around the platform now, some of the dwellers chose to travel all the way out here specifically to watch.

Gem winced. "There is a flogging here today."

If it were a beheading, I would've known about it. But flogging was normally a punishment for crimes too small to warrant notifying either the queen or the princess about.

A man was being whipped on the platform. Even from a distance, he appeared huge, dwarfing the brawny helper of the executioner who was delivering the flogging.

The punished man's arms were spread wide, tied with ropes to two poles on each side of the platform. With his shirt off, his wide back was turned to me. His skin had already been covered in red welts from the whip. It broke in a few places, blood dripping down onto his worn brown pants.

I stiffened as the whip hissed through the air. The wet sound of broken skin and splattered blood followed.

"Let's just ride past it quickly." Gem nudged her horse to go faster.

The man must've done something to deserve it. He wouldn't be punished otherwise. Still, I winced and held my breath as the executioner's helper raised the whip again.

As I rode by, I couldn't take my eyes off the man on the platform. Something seemed unusual about him. Something I couldn't quite figure out... Until I realized, he didn't *reflect*.

People of the world behind the mirror wavered under pressure of fear or shame. If felt strongly, those emotions would make their bodies reflect their surroundings, making them look nearly invisible, as if they subconsciously tried to escape the scary or shameful situation they were going through.

I squinted through my glasses. The royal jeweler, working with my mother's personal healing witch, had created special crystal lenses for me set in a gorgeous frame of golden filigree and tiny gems. With the glasses on, my vision was perfect, but I couldn't see anything changing about the punished man's body. It remained large and solid. With not a single ripple of *reflection* on his skin or clothes.

That meant he wasn't scared or ashamed while being punished. Did he even care? Or could it be that he was innocent?

The last idea stuck in my throat at an uncomfortable angle. If an innocent man was being whipped, then our laws had failed him.

We'd circled the crowd around the platform on our way to pass it. The man's face now came into my view. His tangled, russet hair fell over his eyes. A full beard of the same color covered the lower part of his face.

"Ari," Gem hissed beside me. "Let's go."

"Wait." I stirred my horse closer to a couple standing by. "Greetings, good people."

The woman turned to me, then bowed. "Greetings, Your Highness."

The man glanced up at me, then dropped his gaze. It was considered impolite for a man to stare at a woman he wasn't married to. He bowed silently, letting his female companion speak.

"Do you know what that man is being whipped for?" I asked. "What's his crime?"

"They say he started a fight." The woman pointed at the city official who stood by the platform holding the scroll with the verdict. "Some slaves quarreled while fixing the road to the palace. He then beat them up or something."

"Slaves? Is he a slave too?" I turned to the man on the platform.

My breath hitched as my gaze crossed with his. His brown eyes watched me from under his sweat-soaked tresses. He wouldn't look away, holding eye contact firmly even as his body convulsed from yet another hit of the whip. I found no fear or remorse in his expression, no emotions at all, just resignation. He'd accepted his punishment, even though this whole situation didn't sit well with me.

"He's one of the slaves who've been working on the palace grounds this spring," the woman explained.

Gem moved her horse closer to mine.

"You can't intervene, Ari," she warned quietly. "Not without undermining the law. The verdict had been delivered by the judge appointed by the queen."

Curiosity flashed in the stranger's eyes, like a spark of light breaking through the fog of apathy. Once he realized who I was, I expected a plea for help, but he didn't ask me to intervene. He probably just wondered what I was doing here.

"Is he guilty?" I asked, finding it impossible to simply move away.

Gem shrugged. "He must be. No one gets punished in Egami City unless proven guilty."

So much was true. Crime didn't happen often. When it did, it was thoroughly investigated, and every accused got a fair trial. I might not like what I was witnessing, but that gave me no reason to challenge the system. The law that leveled the punishment on this man was the same law I swore to uphold. As the crown princess, I represented the law of the crown.

I couldn't possibly stop this now...

But the look in the slave's eyes haunted me. I recognized that blank expression, and now I knew why he wasn't afraid of the whip. He'd reached that place where his body separated from his heart and his mind. As the whip tore into his flesh, his mind had already grown numb. He felt no pain, no fear, and no shame. Just resignation.

I knew it because I'd been close to that state too before, in the world I didn't wish to remember but could never forget.

The executioner's helper raised the whip once again, and I could no longer stand back.

I didn't remember how exactly I got off the horse or how I got on the platform, but the raised whip never came down again. The helper's arm jerked and dropped to his side, as I stood in front of him between the whip and the slave.

"Your Highness?" the helper muttered, blinking at me in shock. "I'm so sorry, I almost hit you..." His skin turned ashen from the horror of that realization, then a ripple of green from the grass and brown from the weathered wood of the platform *reflected* through his entire body.

"Princess Aniri, greetings." The executioner stepped in, followed by the city official with her scroll. "I beg your pardon, but the verdict hasn't been fully executed yet."

They all stared at me now. The people around the platform

moved closer too. Gem jumped off her horse and stepped toward the platform, chewing on her bottom lip. Her inner battle was obvious to me. As my older cousin, she often bossed me around in private. In public, however, she didn't dare reprimand the princess, holding back to see how much of a scene I would cause before she had no choice but to intervene.

"Is there a problem, Your Highness?" The official twisted the scroll in her fingers, looking ill at ease.

The punished slave stared over his shoulder with undisguised interest now, waiting for what I'd do next. But I had no plan. I'd interrupted an execution of the law for no good reason and with no excuse whatsoever. The best thing to do would be to apologize and leave, but I knew it would haunt me if I did so.

I cleared my throat. "Every verdict can be appealed. Has this man had a chance to bring his case in front of the Royal Council?"

The city official's eyebrows rose high to her blonde hair pulled up into a tight bun.

"Um... He's just a slave, Your Highness, being flogged for starting a fight. It's a minor case that hardly warrants the attention of the council."

I grabbed on to that one single straw. "The law is the law. An accused has the right for an appeal heard by the Royal Council."

"I doubt this man has the means to take his case that far," the city official replied tentatively.

"Well, then..." I glanced back at the punished man behind me.

He was no longer looking at me, his head dropped between his shoulders, his mangled back turned to me with his arms stretched wide in the restraints. But I knew he heard every word. His muscles stiffened as if he was afraid to move and miss what was happening.

I faced the official again. "Then, I'll personally review his case and present it to the council."

Both women, the city official and the executioner, gaped at

me in shock. The executioner's helper grunted, scratching the back of his head.

"It's just two more lashes left, Your Highness," he said. "Hardly worth your time to bother."

Two lashes.

Was it enough for me to step aside and let them finish?

I glanced back at the prisoner again. This time, he met my eyes, but I found no guidance in his expression. Just like before, he didn't seem to care about what was happening to him. He simply watched what I would do.

I stretched my hand toward the scroll with the verdict.

"I will personally review his case," I insisted.

If the man was indeed as guilty as he'd been charged, the two lashes could always be delivered at a later date. However, he might not have fought against the verdict hard enough. If so, I might be able to find something to at least reduce his punishment to the lashes already given.

"As you wish, Your Highness." The official surrendered the scroll to me. "I'll have the rest of the paperwork on his case delivered to the palace by my clerk."

"Thank you." I shoved the scroll under my arm.

The executioner collected the bloodied whip from her helper. With a bow and a goodbye, the official headed back to the city gate. The crowd started to disperse, too, as the city guards untied the prisoner.

"He should return to his life," I told them. "Until the decision by the council."

Freed, the man straightened to his full, impressive height. His wide shoulders blocked the sun. A couple paces of distance remained between us, but I already had to tilt my head back to see his face.

Rubbing his wrists where the restraints used to be, he rested his gaze on me.

"Thank you." He spoke softly, but his deep voice reverberated far and wide, requiring no strain to hear him.

"I... I didn't do much." My words suddenly tripped on a lump inside my throat.

Facing him like this, on even ground, unsettled me. Standing tall, he no longer looked in need of my compassion, and it wasn't exactly just compassion that I felt. My chest warmed from the inside. Heat radiating through my entire body, including my face.

Was I blushing?

I must be, I realized with a flare of mortification.

Except for my father, King Trebor, I hadn't been this close to a man for years now. *That* had to be the reason for my flustering state. Men had been largely unfamiliar species to me.

"Well..." I blinked, trying to collect myself, which wasn't easy with the prisoner's eyes focused on me so intensely. "It's too early to thank me. The appeal hasn't happened yet. Let's see what the council will say."

"I didn't thank you for the appeal," he replied, leaving me speechless.

What did he thank me for then?

I learned to hold my own in the most difficult of conversations with high standing officials, court members, and foreign dignitaries. Why did I feel like I was losing ground here, after exchanging only a handful of words with a slave?

"Your Highness." Gem rushed to my rescue. "What an excellent handling of the situation on your part," she gushed in a voice that anyone who knew her less than I did would undoubtedly take as a praise. However, the veiled sarcasm in her words didn't escape me. Gem was clearly annoyed by the interruption of our ride and by my meddling in things she didn't think I should've meddled in. "Shall we proceed with our day now?"

There was nothing left for me to do. Eager to escape the confusing feelings taking over me in this man's presence, I nodded and went back to Revlis.

Gem and I rode in silence until the execution platform remained far behind us and the canopy of the forest obscured the blue sky above.

The thoughts of the punished man wouldn't leave me.

"Since when does Mother own slaves?" I asked Gem sharply.

"You know she doesn't. We just contracted their owner to help with the garden work. The spring was short this year, with too much work left to do for the palace gardeners. The stone paths behind the east wing were badly damaged during the winter. The head gardener asked for help, and I couldn't deny her. The one thing that slaves are really good for is the heavy manual labor."

I said nothing to that. I didn't feel like talking at all. The sun shone just as brightly. The day remained as lovely as ever. Only nothing felt as pleasant as before.

Clutching the verdict scroll in my hand, I almost wished to find nothing that warranted a reduced sentence for that man. Then, it'd mean the laws worked exactly how they should, and nothing was wrong with the world I'd grown to love as my one true home.

Three

ARI

"Good morning, Your Highness," the guards greeted me as I approached my mother's breakfast room the following day.

Mother sat in her usual place at the head of the table opposite her husband King Trebor, the King Consort. Dressed in a flowy lavender dress that reached down to her flat-soled velvet shoes, she stirred cream and sugar in her cup of coffee.

At fifty-two, the queen was still the most beautiful woman I'd ever seen, and to me, she'd always stay that way. Her dark hair was swept up into a voluminous bun inside her wide golden crown. There were just a few silver strands over her temples, which only enhanced her beauty and emphasized her years of wisdom and experience.

"Morning, Mother," I gave her a peck on the cheek, inhaling a whiff of her flowery fragrance.

"Good morning, dearest," she murmured. "Did you sleep well?"

"Yes," I lied.

Some nights had been better than others. After ten years in

Rorrim, nightmares had become rare, but I'd long lost the ability to "sleep like a log" that I had when I was younger. Last night, I'd stayed up way past midnight to pore over the paperwork of the punished slave's case, but I saw no reason to bother the queen with complaints about my insomnia.

I made my way to the other end of the table.

"Morning, Father." I placed a kiss on the cheek of my other parent, King Trebor.

He gave me a bright smile. "Good morning, sweetie."

Father was a tall man with vivid blue eyes and sandy-blond hair that was neatly cut and styled into perfect waves. Unlike the queen's, there was not a glimmer of silver in the king's locks. His team of skilled groomers made sure to maintain his youthful appearance by dying his hair regularly.

The king was wearing one of his usual dress coats with rich embroidery along the stiff collar and wide cuffs. Tall and slim by nature, Father had gotten a little wider around the middle with age and now wore a waistcoat corset for a slimmer shape. The padding of the shoulders of his coat and the slightly raised heels on his boots further enhanced the masculine form and the elegant, regal stance that was appreciated in all high-born men.

"The head chef made your favorite muffins this morning," Father informed me with his ever-present smile. "She sure loves to spoil you."

"I'm glad she does." I beamed in response and grabbed a lemon-cranberry muffin from the basket in the middle of the table, then took my place between him and Mother on the right-hand side of the queen.

Squinting at the sunshine flooding the room through the three sets of glass patio doors, Father took a sip of his tea.

"It looks like it's going to be another gorgeous day today," he said. "Any plans for this afternoon, Ari? Did you have a fun ride with Gem yesterday?"

His words brought yesterday's gory flogging scene to the fore-front of my mind. I cut the warm muffin in half, smeared a dollop of butter on it, then watched it melt. My mouth should be watering at the delicious aroma. Instead, a bitter taste lingered in it.

"Mother." I turned to her without answering Father's questions. I simply couldn't match his cheerful tone this morning. "Since when do we hire slaves at the palace?"

She glanced at me over the rim of her coffee cup before setting it down. "Technically, we don't hire them, dearest. Their work is contracted through their owner. We deal with her."

"What difference does it make? Either way, the crown is using slave labor—the work of men and women who are owned by another person."

She folded her hands on the table in front of her.

"Well, first of all, slaves are usually almost exclusively men. There are no women in the group we hired. Women tend to manage their finances in ways that don't involve signing off their freedom in exchange for money. If they do end up in debt, they usually work out a repayment arrangement other than slavery. Sadly, men are far more reckless and more emotional by nature, which often lands them in debt beyond their control." She took the cup again but didn't raise it to drink, holding it over the table. "Second, slaves are owned by another person only because they carelessly allowed for it to happen. You know that no one is born into slavery in Rorrim, and everyone can work their way out of it if they apply themselves. You see, Ari," she took a deep breath, "sometimes people fall on hard times. By providing them with employment, we actually help them repay their debt to the owner, regain their freedom, and return to society debt-free."

"They get flogged while they're at it," I muttered under my breath, staring at the muffin that I no longer had any appetite to eat.

"Oh, I see." Mother nodded. "That's what it's all about? I heard a punishment was delivered yesterday. I'm sorry you got to witness it."

"I'm sorry it happened at all."

"Ari, darling, some things are necessary to happen. You've been learning what it means to run a country, and punishment is a sad but necessary part of it." She glanced down the table at Father, who quietly ate his breakfast. "Trebor dear, I don't want to bore you with state matters. Why don't you go see to the horses? Didn't you say a mare needed attention for her hoof or something? Surely, you need to discuss it with her groomers."

"Yes, of course." Father dabbed his mouth with a napkin before getting up. "I'll see you at lunch, Your Majesty." He gave Mother a quick kiss, then winked at me with a smile. "Enjoy your morning, sweetie."

Mother followed him with her gaze, speaking only after the door had closed behind him.

"You shouldn't bring up these topics in the king's presence, Ari," she reprimanded gently. "Men find conversations about state affairs either boring or unsettling, neither is good for their volatile disposition."

Father was the sweetest and the least "volatile" person I knew, but I didn't argue with her on that.

"The punishment was brutal..." my voice broke, and I swallowed hard. The images of the man's mangled back and the blood soaking into the coarse fabric of his pants rose in my mind as vividly as when I first saw them.

"Oh, honey." Mother reached along the table to cover my hand with hers. "I'm sorry it upset you. Being a just ruler is a constant strife for balance between kindness and ruthlessness. One can't work without the other. Punishment is often necessary for justice to be served."

I didn't move my hand away. Like always, the warmth of her touch felt comforting, and I could never deny that comfort to myself.

"What did that man do to earn the punishment?" she asked. "I'm not familiar with the details of his case."

"He started a fight."

"Ah." She sounded as if she'd expected it. "The flogging seems an appropriate verdict to correct his behavior. Sometimes violence is the most effective response to aggression. Sadly, that's the only language some men understand. Men are violent by nature. Their physical strength can get out of their control, and it's our job to help them correct that. They need to be reminded that no matter how physically strong they are, there is a power that will hold them accountable for their irresponsible actions." She squeezed my hand gently. "Let's just hope that the man learned his lesson and will control his temper better from now on."

Usually, her logic, presented in a calm, even voice, made sense. However, not everything in this case fit neatly together.

The queen peered at me. "I got a report that you intervened in his punishment, Ari."

News traveled fast in Egami. The punishment of a slave might not warrant the attention of the queen, but her daughter stopping it certainly did.

"I did, Mother. I've reviewed his case, and I'd like to appeal it in front of the Royal Council."

Mother's brow furrowed in a concerned expression.

"Do you believe an injustice has been done in his case?"

This wasn't exactly a case of injustice. According to the court papers, the man's name was Salas. He did start a fight with other slaves while working on repairing a road to the palace. The fight resulted in a broken arm of one of his opponents. By law, flogging was the appropriate punishment for his crime. But one thing bothered me.

Several passersby witnessed the other men taunting Salas relentlessly. He was clearly provoked into the attack. However, when standing in front of the judge, Salas never mentioned that fact. He'd made no attempt to argue his case or to defend himself. He simply accepted the blame and the verdict as it was presented to him.

Was it enough to reopen his case and to put it on the council's already very busy agenda? At best, it would reduce the sentence by two lashes. I feared it'd sound too trivial to Mother. To the man being flogged, however, I believed that every lash was of importance.

"Some circumstances of this case caught my attention," I said. "I believe they warrant a reduced sentence for this man."

The queen patted my hand before letting go of it and leaning back in her chair. "Very well, I will support your request for an appeal."

"You will?" I exhaled with relief. Her support meant a world to me both in the council room and beyond.

"Ari, I applaud your asking questions and seeking answers. No law is perfect. Our society constantly evolves, and we should strive for improvement every single day."

"Thank you, Mother." I picked up my muffin and finally took a bite of it.

She moved her spoon on the table, then adjusted the napkin in her lap.

"Laws of the land are important, Ari," she said, looking at her cup of coffee instead of me. "But so are our traditions."

I caught a slight change in her tone of voice and set the muffin down again. "What traditions are you talking about, Mother?"

She took a long drink of her coffee before meeting my eyes. "Your father and I have been looking for a suitable candidate for the next king consort."

"Ahh, that..." I exhaled.

I knew this conversation was coming sooner or later. I'd just hoped for *later* rather than *right now*.

"Yes, dearest. You are of the perfect age for marriage—mature enough to guide your future groom but also with many years ahead of you to ensure an offspring."

"Right. The offspring," I groaned inwardly, holding my back straight and my head high.

"Ensuring the continuation of our line is one of the most important duties of a queen. You know that, dear."

"Of course I do, Mother."

"Now, that leads me to the delicate topic I've been meaning to discuss with you." She cleared her throat and tucked a loose strand of her hair behind her ear. "In order to produce offspring, usually the more experienced wife guides her innocent husband through the... um, the *process*. And I'm afraid you're not sufficiently experienced in that matter, dear."

"Right." I shifted in my seat. "Any chance I could maybe get a more experienced and slightly less innocent husband?"

She huffed a laugh, as if I'd told her a joke.

"You know a royal husband's reputation can't be anything but spotless. Your father and I have worked hard on our list of candidates. All of them come from royal families with excellent ancestry. Their mothers vouch for their purity and virtuous upbringing. Which means your duty will be to introduce intimacy to your future groom. But you can't introduce something you haven't experienced yourself, can you? From what I've heard, you haven't been intimate with a man yet." She let the silence stretch, obviously waiting for me to either confirm or deny that claim.

"You spoke to Gem, didn't you?" I mumbled, not meeting her eyes.

"I did," she admitted with a soft smile. "Daughters often share with friends things they wouldn't talk to their mothers about." She leaned toward me again. "But if there is a reason for your hesitation around men, tell me, maybe I can help? I am the queen, after all."

I clasped my hands in front of me. How exactly could a queen help?

Did I need help? Was something wrong with me?

I didn't hate the idea of sex. I had experienced the pleasure of sexual release. I just hadn't had the desire to share it with anyone yet, being perfectly content with my own hand so far.

"I really don't know what to say, Mother."

She peered at me closely. "Does the company of women possibly excite you more than that of men?"

This conversation was unlike any other I'd had with the queen before, but it wasn't the first open or sincere one. I might not have spoken to Mother on this particular topic before, but we'd shared many heart-to-heart conversations about life in general. Being honest with her wasn't difficult or new to me.

I pondered the best way to answer her question. I did feel far more at ease in female company, but that wasn't what the queen's question implied.

"No. Not sexually, Mother."

She nodded. "We can make some arrangements then."

"What kind of arrangements?"

"Whatever suits you best, dearest. I'm afraid your past may be to blame for your hesitation, but I don't want it to dictate your future." Her voice softened with compassion that made my heart squeeze with love.

Queen Anna was the best mother I knew, the *only* mother I had who was worthy of that name. It hurt to disappoint her in anything. My desire for her approval had been a huge drive behind my success both as a student and the council member.

"What will be best for you, Ari?" she continued. "I can't possibly send the crown princess to a fun house like a commoner. Any contact with the fallen men from such an establishment would cause a scandal the crown cannot afford, especially while arranging for your marriage. But I will support any other way you choose to go about it."

I adjusted my glasses, then twisted a diamond bracelet around my wrist. "Do you really think it's necessary for me to do before the marriage, Mother? Maybe... Maybe my groom and I will figure things out after? Somehow?"

I was stalling, and the queen knew it. If there really was a problem with my having physical intimacy with anyone, it wouldn't magically disappear after my marriage. If the thought of getting naked with a man made me feel like running for the hills now, what would I do when I stood in the bedroom of my groom, with the added pressure of the whole world waiting for us to consummate our marriage and give an heiress to Rorrim's crown?

There'd be no way to hide. Literally overnight, my personal issues would become the talk of all queendoms.

I understood the queen's concern, but I feared I couldn't alleviate her worries that easily.

"Trust me, it's best to know these things in advance," Mother assured me. "Your groom will be nervous during his first time. It wouldn't help if you were nervous too. You need to know what to do and guide your groom with confidence expected from your age and position. You know, if there is any doubt about your marriage being real in every aspect, including physical, it may be annulled. The groom's family may also demand a public consummation, which isn't pleasant for anyone. Luckily, there is still time for you to get the experience you need."

"Honestly, Mother, I'm not sure how. I don't know if I can..."

"You can have any man you like," she offered promptly. "Discreetly, of course, but I will allow you to bring anyone you feel comfortable with into your chambers. Perhaps, there is a gentleman of my court you find agreeable?"

Most men of the royal court belonged to my father's gentlemen-in-waiting. They usually left the room when I visited Father's parlor. I hardly interacted with any of them.

"They're all fine gentlemen, Mother. But I don't feel that kind of affection for any of them."

"It's not a matter of affection, dear." The queen smiled. "Physical attraction isn't always the same as the matters of the heart. In your case, it's actually preferable that it isn't." She gazed up, as if pondering the issue at hand. "How about the royal gladiators then? I've heard those men are well skilled in the art of pleasuring a woman. The crown will handsomely reward the one you choose if he manages to please you and put you at ease."

I huffed a nervous laugh. "You'll pay a man to have sex with me?"

"Ari, dearest, men don't need to be paid to have sex. Their urges make them crave it all the time, especially at your age. For any man of the queendom, it'd be an honor to spend a night with the crown princess. The compensation will be simply a token of our appreciation after the fact, nothing more."

I rubbed my forehead, wishing I could just disappear from this room altogether. However, that wouldn't solve the issue. Maybe it was best to get it over with, somehow.

"Does it have to be a gladiator?" I asked.

"Of course not. It's just that my gladiators are easily accessible, clean, and discreet. But as I said, it could be anyone you find acceptable." She took her chin in her hand, lost to a moment of contemplation. "Do you find the gladiators threatening, perhaps? I can understand that. The nature of their occupation requires them to be large and act aggressively."

The image of Salas, the punished slave, came to my mind once again. As far as size was concerned, that man would easily give any of the queen's gladiators a run for their money.

"Maybe I should have Gem take you to the theater this week?" Mother mulled over another idea. "There is a new production group performing this season. If a delicate, artistic type of man is more to your liking—"

"I'll find someone, Mother." Placing my linen napkin next to the plate with my unfinished muffin, I got up from the table.

The queen's support was important in this matter, but I couldn't possibly have her search for a bed partner for me. I was old enough to woman up and resolve my own issues.

More than anything, I wished to be the queen my mother would be proud of. I had studied hard for that. A queen ruled her people and ensured a smooth continuation of her line to preserve the peace in her land. If that meant I also had to know how to bed my future husband, then that was what I was going to learn too. Somehow.

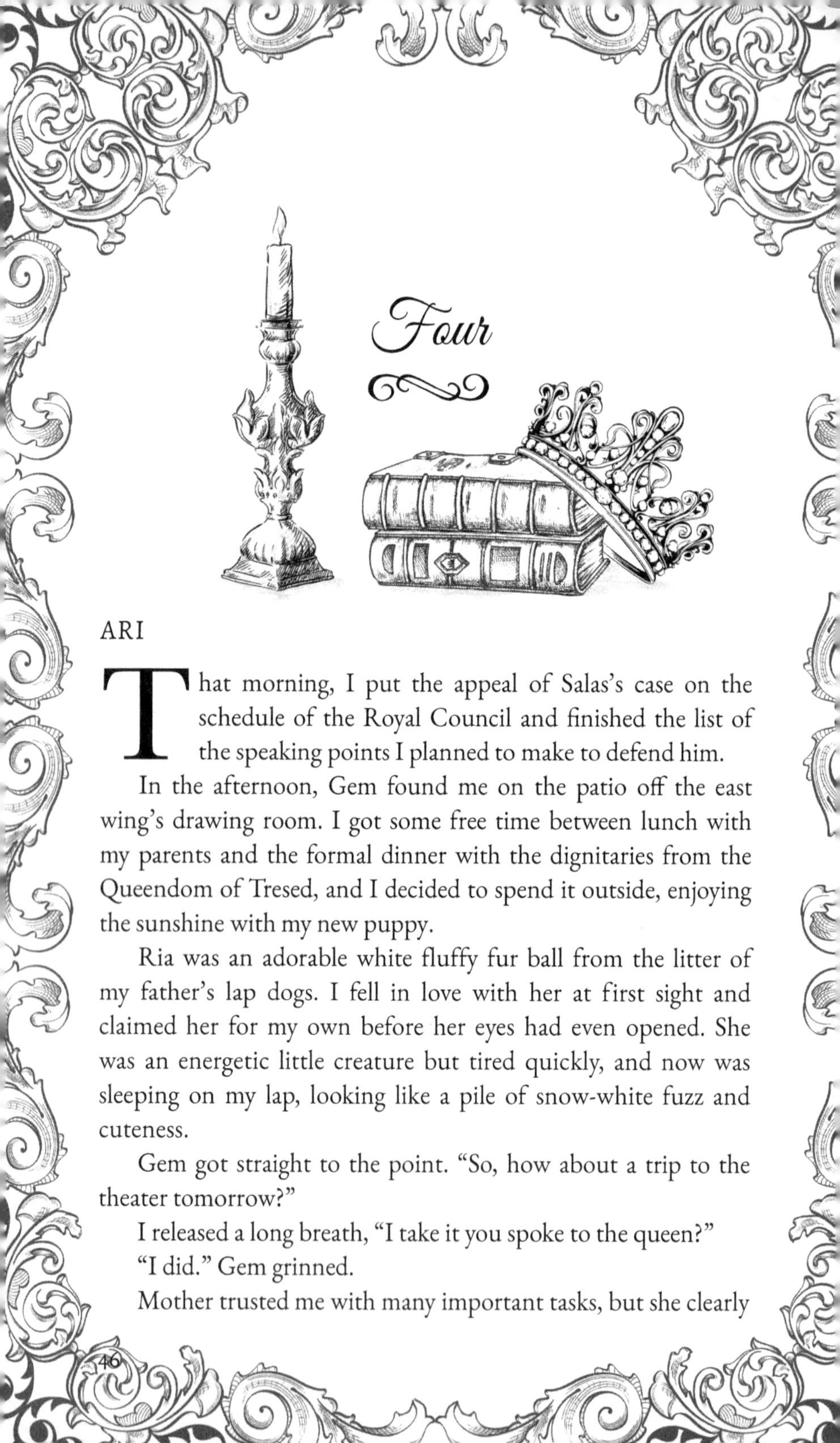

Four

ARI

That morning, I put the appeal of Salas's case on the schedule of the Royal Council and finished the list of the speaking points I planned to make to defend him.

In the afternoon, Gem found me on the patio off the east wing's drawing room. I got some free time between lunch with my parents and the formal dinner with the dignitaries from the Queendom of Tresed, and I decided to spend it outside, enjoying the sunshine with my new puppy.

Ria was an adorable white fluffy fur ball from the litter of my father's lap dogs. I fell in love with her at first sight and claimed her for my own before her eyes had even opened. She was an energetic little creature but tired quickly, and now was sleeping on my lap, looking like a pile of snow-white fuzz and cuteness.

Gem got straight to the point. "So, how about a trip to the theater tomorrow?"

I released a long breath, "I take it you spoke to the queen?"

"I did." Gem grinned.

Mother trusted me with many important tasks, but she clearly believed I could use some help with this one, sending Gem for assistance.

I splayed a hand on Ria's soft side. "All right. What play is being performed in the theater this month?"

Gem shrugged. "Does it matter?"

"Not really," I agreed.

The purpose of this visit wouldn't be to watch the play but to ogle the male actors in hopes that one of them might catch my fancy. Was Mother right to suggest that I would find "a delicate, artistic type" harmless enough to invite to bed with me?

What was my type, anyway?

No matter what man I tried to envision in my bed, unease crawled up my arms and down my back with a nasty pricking sensation.

I didn't fear an emotional intimacy with a man. I was even looking forward to finding a true friend in my future husband. In Rorrim, I finally saw what a happy or at least a content marriage looked like.

My new parents shared a friendship and a deep respect for each other. Their union was not a love match, it couldn't be, considering Mother's position. Her parents carefully selected Father from a long list of young princes. Mother had seen Father only a handful of times before they were married. Practically strangers at first, they'd grown to genuinely care for each other over the years.

I'd never witnessed them raise their voices, not to mention hands, to each other. I'd never seen Mother deny my father anything, either. Whatever he'd asked for, she made sure he had it. Though, his requests were always reasonable.

Mother clearly enjoyed spending time with Father. I'd seen them walk hand-in-hand in the park whenever her busy schedule allowed for some free time. They had separate bedrooms as their station required, but everyone in the palace knew their physical relationship remained strong. Mother visited Father's chambers regularly, and she kept no other lovers or favorites.

I wanted that—someone who'd be my best friend, to whom I could come home to after a long day of meetings and politics, someone I could trust completely and be myself with, away from any pretense or intrigue, someone I could hug whenever I needed it and who would hold and support me back. Someone I, too, could walk hand-in-hand with in the park and have conversations that flowed as easily as a brook through the soft ground in a forest.

I hoped to find that in my future husband, just like Mother had found it in Father.

But that was not what Gem had been tasked to help me with. For now, all I needed was someone to have a night of sex with.

It shouldn't take longer than one night, should it? I didn't need passion. I just had to go through with it once to know what to expect the next time. That should hopefully be enough to calm my nerves before the wedding night, so that I wouldn't embarrass the Crown of Rorrim in front of my virginal husband.

Gem dragged a wicker chair next to mine and sat in it. Hiking her long skirts up past her knees, she propped her feet onto the low parapet at the end of the patio, exposing her bare legs to sunshine.

"Don't worry, Ari," she said with an encouraging lift in her voice. "We'll find you someone who knows what he's doing. He'll teach you all the fun things about sex."

I gave her an incredulous look. "Fun? Really? At this point, it honestly feels like a chore."

"I imagine it could be. Especially when you have to worry about that pesky procreation duty. But it doesn't mean you can't also enjoy sex for what it is—pure pleasure."

"Enjoy" and "pleasure" were used in the same sentences as "sex" so often, I had to believe there must be some fun in that activity.

"Gem. Can women really enjoy sex?"

She smirked. "Why else do you think so many of us end up in the gladiators' rooms after the Games?" She leaned closer, lowering her voice. "Do you ever touch yourself, cousin?"

"Well... Sometimes." I cleared my throat, trying to sound casual, but my face heated with blush.

"That's fine, sweetie. Women can talk about things like that among ourselves. There is no harm in getting yourself off every now and then. It's pleasant, isn't it? And healthy. It helps with tension relief and such."

I stroked Ria's warm, silky fur. The gesture soothed and grounded me.

"Now imagine," Gem continued, "there are two more hands and a tongue helping you come."

"A tongue?" My mouth fell open.

"Right." She sighed with a soft moan. "Frankly, a tongue is the best body part that Goddess gave to a man. Some are also very good with their fingers. But fingering requires some added finesse not all of them possess, sadly."

I stared straight ahead, processing what she'd just said. My knowledge about sex was mostly theoretical. I'd never discussed it with anyone in such detail before. Right after my arrival to Rorrim, I was deemed too young for the courtiers to even mention sex in my presence. After a certain age, people just assumed that I already knew everything about it, even though none had bothered to teach me. All my knowledge came from the comments and innuendoes that I'd overheard while coming of age at the royal court and from the horrific experiences in my old world.

A pair of workers made their way around a corner tower of the palace's east wing and past the lily pond with goldfish. The two were fixing a garden path by laying decorative bricks into a pattern over the hard-packed dirt and gravel.

Today seemed even hotter than yesterday. Both women had their shirts off to keep cool in the heat. The younger one had a comfortable bandeau-style top to support her voluptuous breasts. The older woman had smaller chest and chose to forgo a top or a bra altogether. All she had on were loose cotton pants and work boots, in addition to a leather apron that protected her thighs and chest when she carried a stack of bricks from behind the tower.

I watched them work for a few moments.

"What kind of pleasure can a man possibly derive from, you know... licking a woman down there?" I wondered out loud.

Gem ran a hand over her chestnut hair that had already been twisted into an up-do for the upcoming dinner but without any heavy adornments in it yet.

"Why would you worry about a man's pleasure, Ari? Men are simple creatures. They like sex and reach their completion without any effort on our part. He'll be there for you, not the other way around."

"But how about my future husband? Wouldn't I have to make sure he reaches his 'completion' in order to impregnate me with the heiress to the queendom?"

She tilted her head, playing with a dangling ruby earring in her ear.

"You have to keep in mind that sex with your husband has a different purpose than sex with a lover. One is for procreation. The other one is purely for pleasure. You wouldn't do the same things with your husband that you do with a lover." She winced at such a possibility. "It just wouldn't be right."

"So, the husband wouldn't use his tongue?" I smiled through a sudden tightening in my chest.

The idea of people licking each other seemed fun, but a wisp of horror sneaked out from the dark memories that I wished I'd forgotten long ago. I shut my eyes and dropped my head down to hide my face from Gem while I trumped down on those memories, forcing them into the farthest corners of my awareness.

I'm not going to remember.
My past is not my future.
It has no power over me.
Not now, not ever.

I repeated in my head ad nauseam, until the shadows of the

past had been contained once again and all that remained was sunshine and Gem's words flowing in the warm summer air.

"...I've never been with a virgin before," she chatted. "But I've heard the young, innocent grooms can get quite confused on their wedding night. Your future husband will know nothing about sex. You'll have to show him where everything goes and how all the pieces fit together." She winked. "If you know what I mean."

"It really feels like a chore," I muttered. "I wish men would be allowed to get at least some experience too. I would've preferred to learn it all with my own husband rather than with some random man."

Gem made a face. "Ari, you don't want your husband to know too much about sex, not even after your wedding. Too much sex can turn a good boy into a wicked one, and a man's reputation is irreparable once it's been damaged. As far as your husband is concerned, it's best to focus purely on procreation with him. He'd be the father of your children. That's what he's been preparing for all his life, anyway."

"But if they knew at least a little bit about procreation, I wouldn't have to worry about all of this now."

She shook her head vehemently. "A well-raised boy saves his virginity for his wedding night. It's a man's most treasured asset. If his reputation is ruined, no woman of any importance would have him. And then what is he to do? There are very few avenues available to a man to make a living on his own. He could possibly join the army, but the competition is pretty fierce for soldiers' positions. We've had no wars for so long, there is simply no need to keep a large army permanently. If the boy is lucky to have the necessary talent, he could try to become a royal gladiator, a singer, or an actor. Gladiators receive a room and board, as well as a pension from the crown. Actors often manage to entice wealthy benefactors to take care of them. But for a nobleman, if they lose their virginity before marriage, their reputation is ruined. No one would marry a ruined man."

I knew the traditions of Rorrim's society but until now, I

hadn't dwelled on them much. These gender roles were a part of the world that had become my home, and so far, I'd been focusing on just learning them without questioning.

"Do you think it's fair to men?" I asked.

Gem stretched in her chair. "Every tradition has a reason behind it, doesn't it? Keeping men's chastity makes perfect sense. A woman always knows with certainty who her children are and how many she's responsible for to raise into adulthood. With a man, one can never be sure. It's not men's fault of course, poor things, they can't help it. Goddess created them as irresponsible slaves to their own desires. If allowed to run around freely, a man can impregnate hundreds or even thousands of women in his life-time, possibly without knowing who or where his own children are. Can you imagine what that would do to a society?" Gem's eyes opened wide at the horror of such a scenario. "Clearly, the Great Goddess intended for women to be the stronger, more responsible half to keep men under control. It's in their interests, really. With men's brains being so different from women's, they need us to guide them and look after them." She waved a hand in front of her face in an attempt to cool off. "Oh, it's so hot today." Reaching toward the side table, she picked up the bell and rang for a maid to bring her some ice water.

At the sound of the bell, Ria raised her head and blinked, waking up.

I lifted the puppy to nuzzle her fluffy forehead. "Are you awake, sleepy head? How did you get to be so adorable?"

My gaze drifted behind the puppy and out into the garden. A man was heading toward the two bricklayers. Stepping heavily, he stomped from behind the tower while carrying a huge load of bricks on his back. The stack was wide and high, propped by wood and strapped with leather belts that looped over his broad shoulders.

Unlike the women, the man had a long-sleeved shirt on. The sleeves were rolled up past his elbows, but sweat still soaked the fabric on his wide chest and under his arms. It would be highly inappropriate for a man to remove his shirt in public, no matter how hot the day was.

The man's head was down, his brown hair hanging over his face, but I recognized his tall, large frame and his long scruffy beard. It was Salas, the same man who was whipped just last afternoon. Now, he was at work again, carrying bricks on his injured back.

Gem took a long drink of her ice water delivered by the maid.

"Let's hope our trip to the theater yields some results," she said optimistically. "Because otherwise, I'm out of ideas here. It's not like I can take the crown princess to a fun house and pay for a night with a working boy there. Or even worse, bring one to the palace." She signed. "They aren't allowed to leave their brothel at night. Not to mention the scandal that would cause..." Her voice trailed off as she noticed my stare and traced it to the man with the bricks on his back.

Salas set his heavy load on the ground a short distance ahead from the women. As he straightened, the rusty streaks of blood on the back of his shirt came into view.

"Hey, isn't that the same slave who was flogged yesterday?" Gem tipped her chin at him. "They shouldn't allow a criminal on the palace grounds. I'll have to speak with his owner."

Something about that man kept drawing my attention to him. His height and size made him stand out, but it wasn't just that.

I wondered what he was thinking when he started that fight. Hadn't he known he'd be punished? Aggression like that wasn't tolerated, the law was clear on it. If he was harassed by the others, why didn't he file a complaint with his owner about the other slaves' behavior instead?

"He isn't hurting anyone, is he?" I replied to Gem's concerns.

Salas's sudden appearance in my vicinity unsettled me. Even from a distance, I felt his presence with my skin. Tearing my stare away from him, I set the puppy down. She immediately took off along the patio in chase of a large butterfly that fluttered by.

"Here, Ria." I grabbed a morsel of cooked beef liver from the crystal bowl on the table. I had it brought in, intending to do some puppy training before she'd passed out in slumber on my lap.

The butterfly flew over the low banister at the end of the patio, and the silly puppy leaped over it to follow. I didn't know she was old enough to jump over the banister already.

I sprang to my feet.

"No, Ria. Come here!"

Sadly, we hadn't quite mustered the "come here" command during our training yet, or any command, for that matter. Ria tended to do as she pleased rather than following any commands at all.

"Ria, come on, you hellion," I groaned, stepping over the banister.

Gem sat up straighter. "Ari, leave it. Let's send a maid or a footman to fetch the dog."

It'd take time to get a maid. Meanwhile, Ria was heading toward the hedge of the huge garden maze. If she made it inside, neither I nor the maid would have an easy time finding her. The puppy was so small, an owl or a fox could easily snatch her before we got to her.

"Riaaa!" I dragged out her name in frustration.

The furry rascal dashed across a flower bed, plowing a path through the blossoming tulips. I hiked up my long skirt and sprinted after her, hopping over the neat rows of flowers.

Her ears flopping, her tail wagging, the dog swerved along the gravel path and toward the man in the bloodied shirt. She weaved between Salas's feet, beelining for the lily pond next. She was still so young. What if she fell in and drowned?

"Get her! Please!" I yelled, gasping for breath.

Following my plea, Salas turned and gave chase after her. Thankfully, his legs were much longer than hers. He caught up with Ria in two long strides, then scooped her off the ground with a hand as huge as a shovel.

"Oh Goddess, thank you." I pressed a hand to my chest, slowing down on my way to him. "Thank you so much. I would've never found her in that maze..."

Somehow, my words of gratitude sounded inadequate when talking to him. This man had been through hell in the past twenty-four hours. And here I was, with such a trivial problem as my dog running away, the problem that I couldn't even solve on my own. He had to solve it for me.

"Thank you," I mumbled, suddenly having difficulty looking straight at him.

"It was no trouble, Princess."

Once again, the deep rumble of his voice startled me. I was not prepared for the weirdly pleasant vibration resonating through my chest in response.

I glanced up, meeting his eyes. They were brown, a little lighter than his hair in the afternoon sun that made them glow like two golden drops of honey.

"I...um." Gods, what was I going to say again?

It felt like I had to say something, but all the words scattered in my brain. It must be because of how big he was. He towered over me, blocking half the sky. Surely, I must find it intimidating, especially from this close.

"Your dog." He moved his hands forward.

Ria, the little troublemaker, sat comfortably in the palm of his hand. He covered her with his other hand, gently scratching the puppy's head behind her ear. Like the rest of him, his hands were massive. His knuckles were scuffed, with his fingernails cut short or broken. Fine red dust from the bricks covered his skin in a thick layer.

I had a feeling he could easily crush my head between those giant mitts of his. Yet by how carefully he handled my dog, I also believed he could cradle a butterfly between his calloused palms without so much as crinkling its wings.

Finding nothing better to say, I was about to repeat my stupid thanks, grab my dog, and be on my way when a whiff of coppery smell of dried blood reached me with the breeze from his direction. It was stronger than the smell of sweat.

"Does it hurt?" I asked, meeting his honey-colored eyes once again.

His thick eyebrows jerked up in surprise, but he quickly schooled his features into an expression of indifference. His gaze dropped to the ground, as was expected of well-behaved men when talking to women they weren't related to.

"It's nothing that Her Highness needs to concern herself with," he replied, holding the dog out to me.

If I took the puppy, Salas would be free to leave and go back to his bricks. Instead, I left Ria where she was, essentially trapping him into the conversation with me. Ria didn't seem to mind it one bit, happily accepting the ear scratches.

Should I tell him about the appeal progress of his case? I feared that would make me look like I was expecting his gratitude when, really, I didn't think he cared about his case at all.

"That fight you started..." I said instead. "Why didn't you defend yourself in court? Why didn't you complain about the other men insulting you?"

Maybe if I knew the answers, I'd sleep better tonight. If curiosity was what kept this man in my thoughts, then all I had to do was satisfy it.

He kept his gaze down. "There was nothing to defend. I lost my temper. I shouldn't have done that."

"You attacked four men—"

"Six."

"Pardon?"

His beard moved, and I could've sworn it was now hiding a smile. Or a smirk.

"There were six men, Princess. The other two ran away before the guards got there."

I held back a gasp. "You attacked six men? Alone?"

"I didn't mean to break any bones," he muttered into his beard.

I believed he didn't. He looked genuinely remorseful about that. Though, I wasn't sure whether he regretted the entire fight or just the arm that he broke.

"Why did you do it? What could they have possibly said that made you so mad at them?"

He rolled back his shoulders with a wince and shifted his weight to another foot. Yesterday, he kept stealing curious glances at me. Today, he seemed to try his hardest to avoid my eyes at all costs.

"The matter is of too little importance to trouble Your Highness with," he fired off.

His posture was humble, his voice remained respectful. Why then did I feel like I'd just been told to fuck off and mind my own business?

"Your Highness!" Gem marched over from the patio, flanked by at least a dozen guards. About half of the women carried crossbows with bolts soaked in sleeping potion. If it weren't for the crossbows, I doubted a dozen guards would be enough to stand against Salas if he chose to fight them, since six men hadn't been a match for him the last time.

Gem touched my elbow.

"We should go, Your Highness. It's time to get dressed for dinner." It sounded like a suggestion, not an order. Only the firm grip of her fingers on my arm left no doubt she meant for me to follow her without a debate.

I didn't move, looking at Salas, but he thrust out his hands with the puppy again, as if silently imploring me to take the dog and leave.

My curiosity had not been satisfied, not in the slightest. If anything, it only burned brighter now. But I couldn't keep questioning him with all this crowd here, especially since he refused to reply.

"I just want to help you," I said. "With the case."

"I appreciate your kindness, Your Highness." He bowed to me with the unexpected grace that could rival that of a courtier.

"But there really is no need to trouble yourself. I committed a crime. I accepted my punishment. The case should've been closed."

"Would you rather they deliver those two lashes?"

He frowned, shifting stiffly, but said nothing.

"You don't like attention," I replied for him. "I can see that. But it doesn't mean you should let bad things happen to you."

He jerked his head up, sucking in a sharp breath. His nostrils flared; his stare burrowed into me.

I realized how patronizing my words might have sounded. I wasn't familiar with his entire situation. He wouldn't tell me. But that didn't give me the right to pass a judgment. As a slave, I supposed he didn't have control over many things that happened in his life.

"Sorry," I muttered. "I didn't mean it like that..." Reluctantly, I reached for the puppy. "I'll take her."

"No need to apologize," he replied softly, gently placing Ria in my hands.

Our fingers touched, with his feeling warm and rough, like the sun-warmed bricks he worked with. I had a sudden feeling that a grip of a hand like that could be trusted to never let go.

"Salas!" a female voice sounded to my right. The older of the two bricklayers rushed to us, pulling on a shirt over her head.

Gem jerked on my arm, her stare narrowing on my hand on top of Salas's palm. I held Ria in one hand but forgot to retrieve my other hand from him. His touch—the touch of a stranger—caused no discomfort. On the contrary, it put me at ease, as if it were a normal thing for us to hold hands like that.

The bricklayer got closer.

"I'm so sorry, Your Highness." A ripple of *reflection* flashed across her skin, momentarily coloring her in green and blue—the colors of the sky and hedges surrounding us. It passed as she collected herself. "Is he bothering you? He's normally quiet and hardworking but, sadly, has a temper as it turns out."

"Salas was no bother," I protested, finally reclaiming my hand from him. "He helped me catch my dog."

"Oh, good, good." She flicked a thumb over her shoulder and hissed under her breath at my puppy rescuer, "Get back to work, boy."

With a bow to me, Salas turned to leave, seemingly relieved to be free of my company at last.

I stared at the dark-red spots on the back of his shirt as he walked away probably to fetch another mountain-load of bricks.

"He shouldn't be working, not until he heals," I pointed out.

The bricklayer stretched her neck with a grunt. "With all due respect, Your Highness, but what use would punishment be if slaves were allowed to take days off after?"

Ria whined, restless in my hands. I scratched behind her ear to calm her down, just like Salas had done.

"Why is he a slave?" I asked the woman.

Gem moved closer to me. "Your Highness, we really should go. I'm sure the queen—"

I ignored her, asking the bricklayer again, "How long has Salas been a slave?"

The older woman scratched her chest through her shirt. "I really don't know, Your Highness. He just carries bricks for us and doesn't talk much. His owner could answer all these questions for you if you wish. She lives in the city somewhere and doesn't come out here often. But her helper is at the barracks. He's the one who manages the slaves for her."

Gem stepped forward, clearly determined to bring me back to the safety of the palace patio.

"Thank you for your answers, good woman." She reached into the pocket of her dress, then left a silver coin in the bricklayer's hand for her trouble. "We really should be going now. I believe your dog needs to use a bathroom, Your Highness."

Ignoring the bricklayer's bows and thanks, Gem maneuvered me back to the patio, along with our escort of the guards. Here, I kissed Ria on the nose and placed her in a basket for the maid to take her away for now. Satisfied I was no longer in any mortal danger, Gem released the guards too, then she paced the patio, giving me a glance every now and then.

"What?" I asked, sitting down in an armchair in the shade.

She stopped in front of me abruptly. "Why do you have such a sudden interest in that slave, Ari?"

"I don't have any particular interest in him," I protested. "I'm... I'm just a little curious."

"Why?" She squinted at me, propping her hands on her hips. "What about him sparked your curiosity?"

What was so special about Salas?

What exactly did I want to know about him?

Surely, every one of the men in those barracks had a story to tell about how he ended up selling his freedom. Salas couldn't be unique. Yes, he'd fought alone against six. But it was safe to assume he wasn't the only one getting into brawls out there, either.

Yet something had set him apart from the rest to me.

Long ago, in another world, I lived a life that I thought couldn't happen in Rorrim. Here, I believed, I could never again feel so helpless, or hopeless, or resigned to suffer. Now, however, flashes of all those feelings came back to me, reflected in Salas. His suffering resonated with recognition in my chest.

At the same time, Salas didn't appear weak. He had stood on that platform like an oak tree in an open field weathering a storm, and I had a feeling that the storm he'd been battling was even bigger than even I could see. Yet he endured it, and that made him stronger than any storm that came his way.

I could never explain it all to Gem. She wouldn't understand. Instead, I wetted my lips and said the first trivial thing I could think of, "For example, why is he not married?"

"Maybe he is?"

I shook my head. "If he had a wife, it's highly unlikely he'd be a slave. All debts would be in her name not his. If she needed money, she would use her property as a collateral for a loan or work out a repayment arrangement with wages garnishment."

Gem tapped her chin with her finger. "Maybe he's a widower?"

"His wife's family would've taken care of him after her passing. Or if there was no living female relative, he would've been directed to a widowers' house, which is an esteemed charity establishment. There, he'd be working under the care and supervision of staff, keeping his freedom. With his size and strength, he could easily be a gladiator too."

Gem huffed. "Not everyone can be a royal gladiator, Ari. One needs a character reference from a lady of the royal court, in addition to his talent, abilities, and skills. And even then, the games master can send him away packing. That woman isn't easy to please. Besides, maybe he didn't want to become a gladiator at all. Gladiators fight in the arena, risking their limbs and lives."

"You know he isn't afraid of a fight."

"Well, maybe that's where his problem lies? No one would hire a man of his size when he's known to be violent. He sold his freedom to pay off his debt. That's how slavery usually works. Which could mean he's a gambler too."

I pushed my glasses up my nose in a gesture that was mostly just a habit. The frame fitted me perfectly, needing no adjustments.

"I don't know, Gem. There is just something about him that breeds questions. Like in the way he speaks and holds himself. At some point, I got the feeling he might've been educated."

Salas used his words to hide behind them, which I'd learned to do well myself.

"Education is useless for a man," Gem dismissed. "For a slave, it would actually be a burden. But..." she perked up, her voice lifting, "I'm glad you like him."

"Like him?" I stared at her incredulously. "I don't know the man enough to either like or dislike him."

"But I have a feeling you may want to get to know him a little bit more *intimately*." She smiled slyly.

I ran a hand over my hair and said nothing because Gem wasn't entirely wrong. I had questions about Salas. I wondered about his past. But I also knew that nothing good could come of us getting closer in any capacity. He must know it, too, judging by how eager he seemed to escape my company.

Gem pulled her chair closer to mine and leaned forward. "I'll tell you what. Instead of going to the theater, why don't I ride to the city and talk to his owner?"

"About what?"

"About letting him off work for a day or two, so I can bring him to your bedroom for a visit. Very discreetly, of course." I drew in a breath, but Gem grabbed my hand, not giving me a chance to voice an argument. "Listen, I've noticed how you look at each other. You let him hold your hand, for Goddess' sake. I've never seen you holding hands with a man before."

"It was just a random touch." I jerked my hand away from her.

"There was nothing random in how long it lasted. He didn't seem to mind it, either."

Gem darted a glance over my shoulder, where the bricklayers must've returned to their work. I couldn't see them while sitting with my back to the garden, but I assumed Salas would be working with them again, probably carrying another load of bricks on his mangled back.

"We'll clean him up for you," Gem said. "I'm sure he's handsome under all that dust and scruff."

"It would help if his back was healed," I replied quickly.

"True." Gem curled her lips, cringing. "You don't want him to stain your sheets with blood."

I didn't care about the sheets, but Gem didn't need to know that.

"He'll never heal if he keeps working like that," I pointed out.

"Maybe, but we can't tell his owner how to run her business.

If she feels he's fit for work, she's within her rights to make him work."

Salas sold himself to his owner, and the laws of ownership were clear. The crown didn't meddle in the rights of the property owners unless any other laws were broken, which in this case, they were not.

Mother often told me, *"As a queen, you can't fix injustice just for one person without considering adjusting the laws for the entire country."*

If one slave was allowed to rest and heal after being punished for the crime he committed, then others would have the right to demand the same. Otherwise, there'd be no justice, just favoritism.

However, forcing anyone to carry loads of bricks over the raw wounds seemed like an unnecessary cruelty. Salas's punishment didn't include this added torture. It didn't feel right, even if it was legal.

"If you're going to bring him to my bedroom, Gem, I want his wounds treated and him well rested. Make that clear to his owner when you're talking to her."

A smile spread on her face. "So, is that it, then? Is this the man you fancy?"

I resisted the urge to glance back over my shoulder where Salas was working in the garden. Resisting it took quite an effort on my part because he drew my attention stronger than the gravity that kept my feet on the ground.

Did I "fancy" him in the way Gem thought I did?

"Since you're so curious about him," Gem went on, not waiting for my reply, "you can ask him whatever questions you want when he's lying naked in your bed, the two of you are all sweaty and out of breath after a good fucking. You'll be amazed how chatty men become after sex, even the most silent types."

The image her words conjured in my mind sent a warm, tingling sensation through my belly. When I thought about Salas's large naked body sprawled on my bed, I wasn't sure exactly what I felt, but it certainly wasn't fear or repulsion. Quite the opposite.

Maybe I was finally old enough to crave a man's attention in the most basic, physical way? I wished so hard to move past the horrors of the world I'd left behind, and maybe it had finally happened? Maybe I was ready to desire sex?

Gem was right about one thing—I'd never felt this way about any man before. Whatever it was, I should use it. I *should* have him.

I thought about his big, calloused hands. I didn't dare imagine them on my body, but the idea of just holding them in mine made me weak in my knees. The feeling was new but not unpleasant.

The day suddenly seemed hotter. I grabbed Gem's half-empty glass of now tepid water and drained it in two big gulps.

"Gem." I tugged at the neckline of my dress to let some fresh air under the fabric. "But I don't even know him."

"Sweetie, that's not important," she assured me. "He looks old enough to know a thing or two about sex. As long as he can please a woman, it's all that matters. Now, you really should go get ready for tonight's dinner with the dignitaries. While I..." She got up, ready to jump into action, "I will have to learn a few more things about that slave before I allow him to get anywhere near your bedroom. Let's not forget, he's a convicted criminal. I need to make sure you'll be absolutely safe in his presence."

The skin on my nape prickled, as if sensing Salas's stare from behind.

What was he thinking about me?

I couldn't guess, just as I couldn't even remotely predict how he would take my proposition.

"Gem," I said, knowing too well just how tenacious my cousin could be when it came to getting things her way. "Please promise me one thing. You'll make it clear to him that it's an offer, not an order. If he wants to refuse, he can."

She scoffed. "He'd be an absolute fool to refuse you."

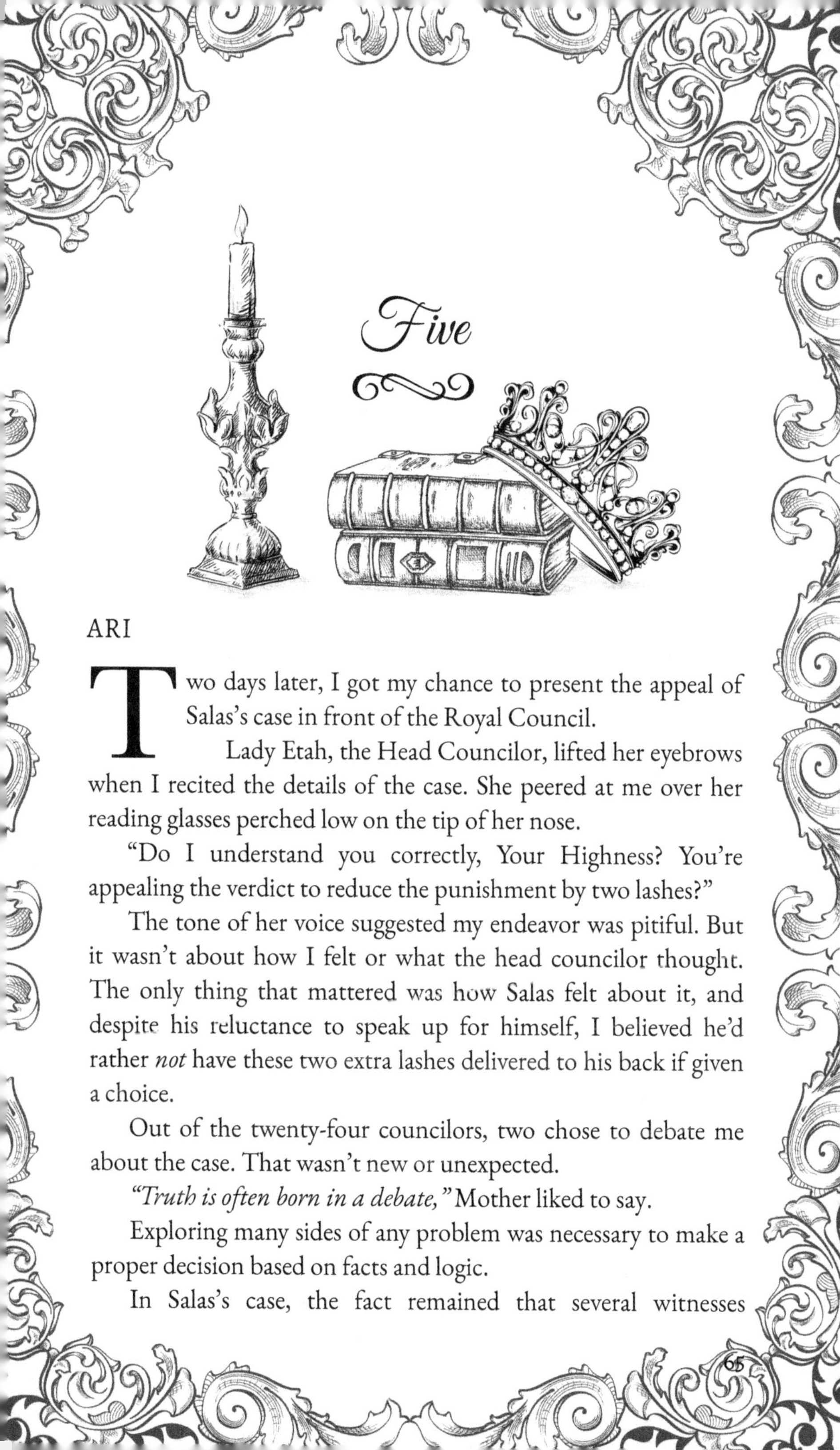

Five

ARI

Two days later, I got my chance to present the appeal of Salas's case in front of the Royal Council.

Lady Etah, the Head Councilor, lifted her eyebrows when I recited the details of the case. She peered at me over her reading glasses perched low on the tip of her nose.

"Do I understand you correctly, Your Highness? You're appealing the verdict to reduce the punishment by two lashes?"

The tone of her voice suggested my endeavor was pitiful. But it wasn't about how I felt or what the head councilor thought. The only thing that mattered was how Salas felt about it, and despite his reluctance to speak up for himself, I believed he'd rather *not* have these two extra lashes delivered to his back if given a choice.

Out of the twenty-four councilors, two chose to debate me about the case. That wasn't new or unexpected.

"Truth is often born in a debate," Mother liked to say.

Exploring many sides of any problem was necessary to make a proper decision based on facts and logic.

In Salas's case, the fact remained that several witnesses

described other men harassing him before the fight. The reports held no mention of him shouting back at them. He stoically bore the insults in silence until the moment he struck one of the men.

The reports held no information about what exactly the insults were or which particular one had finally provoked him into the attack. I wished I knew, but it proved not necessary to eventually convince the council to reduce the verdict to the lashes already served.

The satisfaction from the victory coursed through my veins with excitement as I exited the council meeting room shortly before lunch.

Gem immediately accosted me on the other side of the door.

"It's been arranged," she informed me in the discreet fashion of a seasoned courtier, keeping with my pace down the corridor.

"What has been arranged?" Lifting my glasses, I rubbed my eyes. Winning the long, intense debate left me elated, but also mentally drained. "What are you talking about?"

"You'll have that slave tonight."

Gem had kept her voice down. But to me, it came like a slam of a hammer against a church bell.

I looked around to make sure no one was close enough to hear us. However, Gem had been a member of the royal court long before I came to Rorrim. She knew how to act and when to speak. The corridor was empty, with only two guards standing at the doors to the council meeting room, both too far to hear us.

"Tonight?" I exhaled.

I didn't forget our conversation about Gem making the arrangements. But the memory of it had shifted into the background with my daily duties taking the front seat. Subconsciously, I must've been hoping for more time, which proved impossible with my super-efficient cousin.

"Yes, tonight." She grabbed me under my arm, walking with me to my rooms.

"Does it have to be tonight?"

"Why wait?" She paused. "The sooner the better, is it not?"

"Yes. Of course. It's just that..."

My heart slammed into my ribs, pumping blood so hard that a swishing sound pulsed in my ears. All that blood must've run away from my face because Gem patted my hand sympathetically.

"Oh Ari, you're nervous. That's understandable. Most people are nervous the first time, but that's why it's best to do it when at least one of the couple has done it before. Since you're attracted to him—"

"Am I?" I couldn't exactly name this unsettling feeling I experienced for Salas. I just knew I'd never had it before for anyone else.

Gem tilted her head, searching my eyes. "Don't you want him? How do you feel about spending a night with him?"

"'I... Well, I'm curious about him."

"Curious?" She pondered my answer. "Curious is good. I was curious about sex too. That was probably the strongest emotion I had before my first time. Whatever it is, we should use it. Who knows when you may feel even remotely 'curious' about a man again?"

My stomach fluttered like an empty plastic bag trapped in a hurricane. My palms felt sweaty, and my heart was doing somersaults.

Was that how attraction felt?

Until now, I imagined it'd be a warm, cozy feeling, like sunshine and fluffy puppies, not whatever wretched mess had been happening inside me.

We came to my private sitting room located next to my bedroom. Gem poured herself a glass of chilled water from the carafe by the unlit fireplace, then stretched in a chair by the open patio doors.

"Once you do it once, sex will stop being such a big thing," she said. "You'll even feel silly for stressing over it so much."

"I hope so." Too restless to sit down, I remained standing in front of Gem.

"If this slave is really good, you may even like sex enough to start visiting the gladiators regularly afterwards," she teased. "All is good, by the way. He's healthy and fixed."

"Fixed?" I echoed.

The procedure was often performed on unmarried men, especially if there was a reason to believe they engaged in sexual activities with women. It prevented them from fathering children out of wedlock. I'd never seen the procedure done, but I'd been told it was common, safe, and reversible if needed, usually performed by skilled healing witches.

"Yes, fixed," Gem took a drink of water. "A sound decision for a single man his age."

"How old is Salas?"

"He's over thirty already, way past the age to hope for a wife."

"Did you speak to him? What did he say?"

She shook her head. "I talked to his owner and sent a healing witch to treat his back and to assess his overall health. The owner agreed to give him time off work, just like you wanted, in exchange for compensation for the time lost, of course."

"Are we going to pay her?"

"Well, she owns his time and has to be compensated for it being spent elsewhere. She thinks I'm getting him for my own use, by the way."

"But does Salas know he's going to be with me? Did he agree?"

With her elbows on the armrests of her chair, Gem spread her hands aside. "It's safe to assume he'd rather be with you than hauling those bricks out there."

"So, you didn't actually talk to him?"

"It's unnecessary," she dismissed, then gave me a long, penetrating look. "Ari, like I said, it's normal to feel nervous. But I made sure you'll be safe. I've talked to his owner. He's been with her for three years now. She vouched for his character. The fight this week was the only one he's ever been involved in, and according to the reports, he was provoked, as you know. Men are primitive creatures." She shook her head with a roll of her eyes.

"They always compete for dominance, even in the groups where they are on the same level of hierarchy. They bully each other, even when they should feel camaraderie while being in the same situation."

I paced the room. Moving often helped me think. Right now, it helped my nerves to settle somewhat too.

"What did Salas do three years ago, before he became a slave?" I asked.

"He had a different contract with someone else."

I adjusted my glasses. "So, he's been a slave for more than three years?"

"Yes. At least twice as long."

"How long does he still have on his contract before he's free?"

"Three more years, but the generous compensation offered by your mother for his services would reduce that to two."

That added up to at least nine years of all his contracts combined. Salas had given up his freedom for over nine years— almost a decade or even more of not belonging to oneself. It must be terrible.

What compelled him to do something like that?

"If I go through with it, he'd be free a year sooner," I reiterated.

"Yes. A win-win situation for everyone." Gem lifted both hands with a smile.

I poured a glass of water for myself and guzzled it at once. My hand trembled either from nerves or anticipation, most likely from some crazy explosive mix of both.

Gem noticed it but misunderstood the reasons.

"Ari," she said softly, "the guards will spend the night by your bedroom door. If he so much as raises his voice, let alone raises a finger to you, he'll die. I'll make sure he knows it—"

"No." I slammed my empty glass down on the stand by the fireplace. "Promise me no matter what happens tonight, Salas won't be punished."

"Are you insane?" She stared at me in shock. "If he dares defy you—"

"Even if he does," I insisted.

"Ari. Any assault on the princess is a crime punishable by death. That's the law of our land."

"Not in this case, Gem. Salas won't be coming here by choice. He'll be brought to my rooms because I ordered it."

"So?"

Did she really not understand?

I knew way too well the emotions a situation like this might cause.

"We're putting him into a situation that's outside of his control, and he'll feel it. He may feel uncomfortable. Pressured. Helpless. If at any point he's triggered by it, if he loses his calm, I..." I heaved a sigh. "I don't want him to be held accountable for his reaction. Please, promise me there will be no consequence for him, no matter what he may or may not do tonight."

Gem gripped the armrests, flexing her jaw. "I'm responsible for your safety here. I'll take any precaution possible, but what if something goes wrong anyway? He'd need to be punished."

I thought about Salas's large, calloused hands cradling my tiny puppy ever so gently. There was something about him that made me believe he was safe, despite the fight he'd had, or his size, or his temper that the bricklayer was talking about. But I also understood I couldn't rely solely on my feelings while being alone with a man I hardly knew and who was about twice my size too.

"If something goes wrong, we'll stop it," I said. "You said there will be guards just outside of my door. I believe I'll be able to read the situation, too, and not let it escalate to the point of it becoming dangerous. Believe me, I will send him away the moment I don't feel completely safe." I was the princess, after all. Salas was just a slave. The power was entirely on my side with not a drop of it left on his. "But regardless of what happens—if he loses his temper, if he refuses to go ahead with it—I don't want him to be punished."

Gem pursed her lips, not looking convinced at all. But I held her gaze, waiting for her to confirm that my condition would be met.

"Fine," she finally conceded. "Weird, but fine. He won't be executed."

"Not executed, or flogged, or reprimanded in any way. His owner won't be notified of his behavior, whatever his behavior might be. His working conditions won't get worse. His life will not be affected in any negative way by my barging into it uninvited. Do you understand? That's the only way I'll do it."

Gem arched an eyebrow, looking baffled. I rarely spoke this categorically. Usually, I was open to discussions and negotiations as Mother had taught me. But I felt strongly about it. In this case, there was no room for negotiations.

"Ari, you're looking at it all wrong," Gem said. "Any man in Rorrim and beyond would be flattered if you invited him to your bedroom. This is a huge honor for a slave."

"Maybe. But even a slave should have a say in a matter like this. And so far, Salas has had no say whatsoever. You can't hold him responsible for his reaction to the situation he hasn't agreed to or might not have felt free to decline."

The last time we spoke, Salas hadn't looked like he even wished to be in my company. Maybe the setting had made him uneasy, not me. The bricklayers had been there. He was supposed to be working, not chasing spoiled little puppies around the gardens. But if it was me who made him uncomfortable, if he wished to have nothing to do with me, I wanted him to have a clean exit from this whole thing.

"It'd be as if nothing ever happened," I insisted. "No negative consequences to his life, whatsoever."

Gem dropped her head between her shoulders, worn out by my persistence. "All right. As you wish, Your Highness. The slave won't be punished. But he'd be an idiot if he spoiled this chance for himself."

"Well, that is entirely up to him now, isn't it?"

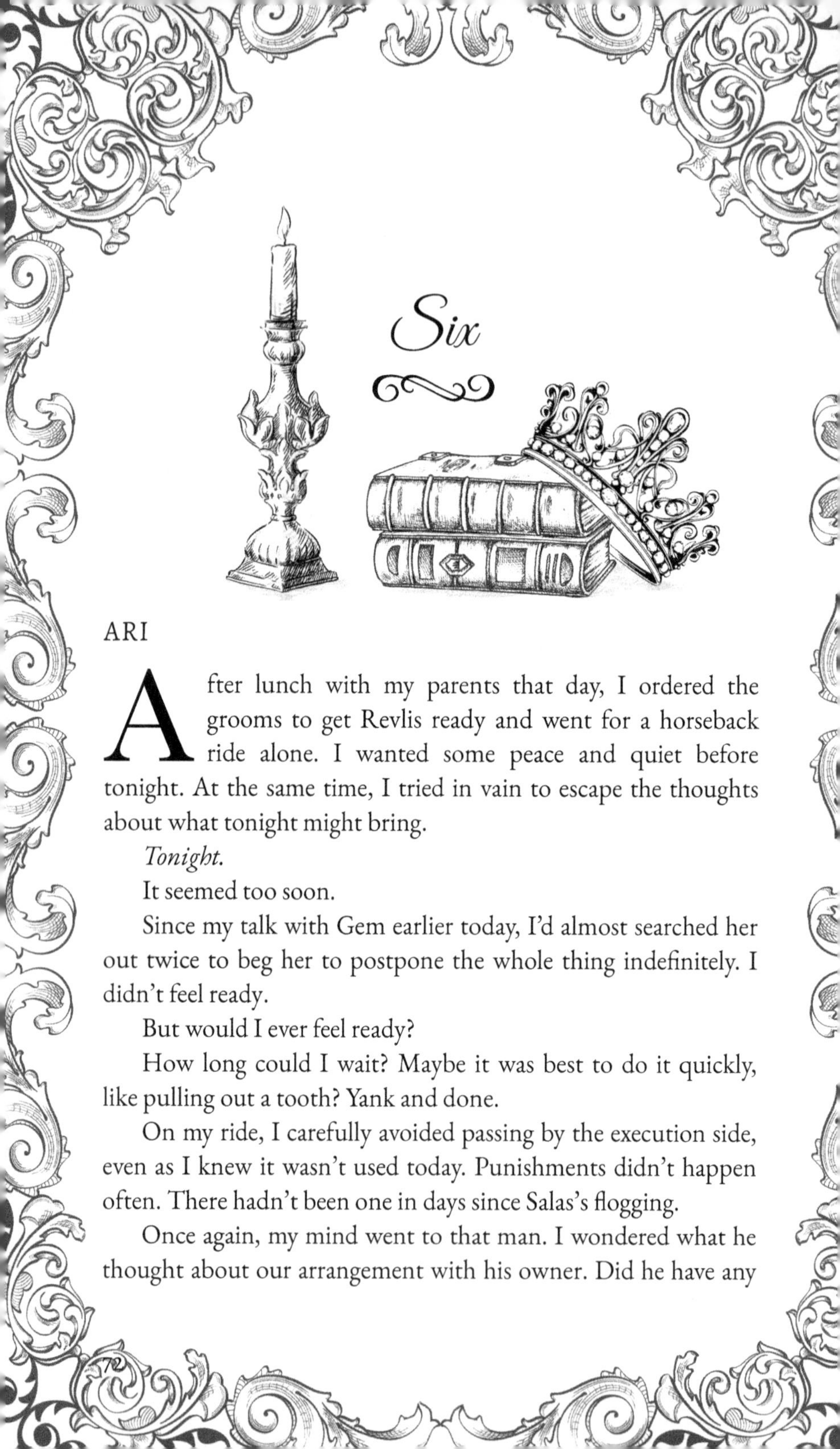

Six

ARI

After lunch with my parents that day, I ordered the grooms to get Revlis ready and went for a horseback ride alone. I wanted some peace and quiet before tonight. At the same time, I tried in vain to escape the thoughts about what tonight might bring.

Tonight.

It seemed too soon.

Since my talk with Gem earlier today, I'd almost searched her out twice to beg her to postpone the whole thing indefinitely. I didn't feel ready.

But would I ever feel ready?

How long could I wait? Maybe it was best to do it quickly, like pulling out a tooth? Yank and done.

On my ride, I carefully avoided passing by the execution side, even as I knew it wasn't used today. Punishments didn't happen often. There hadn't been one in days since Salas's flogging.

Once again, my mind went to that man. I wondered what he thought about our arrangement with his owner. Did he have any ideas about who'd requested his company tonight? Would he be relieved or resentful to discover it was me?

In all of my twenty-six years, Salas happened to be the only man, other than my father the king, who I didn't feel entirely scared of, repulsed by, or indifferent about. Regardless of how tonight went, it was already progress for me. Salas's term of servitude was going to be cut shorter too. Gem was right. Our arrangement seemed like a win-win situation.

After the ride, I left Revlis with one of her regular grooms in the stables and returned to my rooms.

Dinner was waiting for me in the cozy sitting area in my bedroom. Dishes with cold cuts, cheeses, sliced fruits and vegetables sat on a low table in front of the couch, along with a pyramid display of desserts and a tea tray.

In my bathroom, the carved marble tub with brass claw feet had been filled with steaming hot water.

In Rorrim, magic was a part of life, alongside science and technology. Running water was available almost everywhere in the country. We built sewers in the cities and used electricity for lighting, along with candles and gas lanterns where needed. To generate electricity, wind and water mills were built. There weren't many of those, but because the use of electricity remained low, it was enough.

Books and newspapers were printed. But quills and ink were still widely used for handwriting.

People of Rorrim abhorred war. As a result, the weapons here never developed past swords and crossbows.

But I knew of things not found in this world. Things like cars and guns...

Pearls of fragrant oils floated on the surface of the bath water, along with white rose petals. Several unlit candles were arranged around the bathtub with a silver box of matches laying open on the stand nearby.

Standing in the doorway to my bathroom, I stared at the delicate lily petals floating in a slow circle in the steaming water. Images appeared in my mind, floating in circles, too, faster and faster. The scenes were foreign to Rorrim yet painfully familiar to me.

Concrete and asphalt streets, filled with people. Women wearing short skirts or jeans, neither being in fashion in Rorrim. Men behaving in a way that would get them arrested and executed in this world.

A group of men emerging from the lit city streets and accosting me as I hid in a dark alley behind a dumpster. At least one of them had a gun...

The memory slammed into my brain like a punch to my head. I gripped the door frame for support and rubbed my chest against the tightness that wouldn't let me breathe.

I didn't want to remember that.

My past did not control my future.

But could I ever be truly free from it?

A knock on the sitting room door sounded through the bedroom door that I'd left open.

The last thing I wanted was for someone to find me here, covered in sweat and struggling to breathe in the romantic setting of candles and flower petals.

I drew in a long, slow breath, banishing the images from my head, then hurried out into the sitting room.

The door from the corridor opened, and Gem marched in.

"You're back!" She beamed.

"I am. I—"

My words were cut short by her opening the door wider. An entire army of royal guards appeared to spill into the room, forcing me to retreat toward the bedroom to give them all space.

A tall, cloaked figure entered with the guards, and suddenly there seemed to be no more space and no more air left not just in the room but in the entire universe.

It really was happening.

Salas was here.

They had put a dark cloak on him and pulled the hood low over his face to draw the veil of propriety over a man's visit to the princess's quarters. Gem tried to avoid starting any malicious rumors while leading him through the palace to my chambers. Only no cloak would conceal his height or his broad shoulders. I knew who he was before Gem gestured at him like a magician who'd just pulled a rabbit out of a hat.

"Well, here we are."

Maybe it was too soon. Maybe I wasn't ready for this. Maybe I should've canceled or at least postponed this.

But he was here now, and it was too late to fret over it. I was the crown princess, and I had to act accordingly.

"Greetings." I addressed the room, silently congratulating myself on how calm and collected I sounded. I turned to the tall, cloaked figure next. "It's very nice of you to join me this evening. Welcome." I gestured at the open door to my bedroom.

With a nod, he walked past me inside. An odd metal rattling accompanied his steps. I squinted at Gem in silent question. She pressed something into my hand—a small golden key.

"Use it only when you absolutely have to. He's fully functional as is." She widened her stance, crossing her arms over her chest. "I'll be spending the night here, with the guards."

I frowned at the key, then shoved it into the pocket of my riding dress.

"Good night." I nodded to Gem, then followed the man whose hands were meant to end up on my naked body tonight. My composure wavered at that thought, and I almost tripped when entering the bedroom.

Salas stood in the middle of the room. His hood pushed back, he stared at the sword displayed on the wall over my bedroom's fireplace.

Warning pulsed in me with alarm. I should've hidden the weapon earlier instead of leaving it in the open like that. But the sword had been hanging in the same spot for years. In my mind, it had become simply a part of the room's décor by now.

"The creation has outlived its creator," Salas said softly.

I didn't think he intended for me to hear that because he looked a little startled to find me standing next to him when I asked, "Do you know who made it?"

"Don't *you*? Since it's yours?"

That deep voice of his instantly made me feel lightheaded. I had to focus to muster a reply.

"My father gave it to me years ago. It came from the arsenal of the royal gladiators. Father thought it was appropriately small and light for me to practice with if I happened to have any aptitude for swordsmanship."

"*Do* you have the aptitude?"

I exhaled a laugh, adjusting my glasses. "No. No aptitude, no interest in any kind of weapons. I never used it. It's been hanging here as a decoration ever since. It's pretty."

"The hilt is." He nodded. "But it doesn't match the blade."

Father had found the sword's simple hilt with the worn leather on the grip too plain for a princess. He had the leather replaced and the pommel gilded and inlaid with gemstones before gifting it to me.

"How do you know this isn't the original hilt?" I asked, watching him carefully.

Under my attention, his expression shifted to a masterfully crafted indifference.

"I never said I knew for sure. I just pointed out that they don't match. The blade is strong, well-made, and functional. The hilt is... well, pretty."

"You know a lot about swords?"

"Just the most common things." He turned away from the wall.

His behavior didn't seem threatening. Removing the sword from the wall now would be weird and, likely, unnecessary. But I couldn't neglect my own safety either.

Walking past Salas, I unlocked the patio doors and swung them wide open. The warm evening air rushed in. The wild colors of sunset streaked the sky. But most importantly, the patio provided me with another place to escape the bedroom if things with my visitor ran astray at any point of the night. My rooms were on the second floor, but palace guards usually patrolled the gardens below regularly. They'd hear my screams for help if it really came down to that.

"I'm in control here," I repeated in my head.

Fabric rustled behind me, along with the soft clinking sound from earlier. I turned around and... found my control slipping from me.

Salas took off his dark cloak and casually tossed it over the back of the couch. Underneath, he wore a floor-length sarong tied around his hips and an equally long robe. Both were made from white material so thin, it was nearly transparent.

The robe was open in the front, revealing his bare chest. His skin was completely smooth there with a ruddy glow. The bare chest surprised me. By how scruffy and unruly his hair and beard were, I'd expected all that hair wouldn't be just on his head and face.

Realizing I'd focused on his chest for far too long, I blinked and jerked my head up. His hair had been cut and tamed into a neat style with a slight wave to it. His beard was also trimmed and smoothed. I was glad it hadn't been shaved off. It suited him somehow, though it also made him look slightly untamed no matter how much care went into his grooming.

I met his eyes and realized that the awkwardness was all mine. Salas seemed relatively relaxed and comfortable in this rather unusual situation. Not a single ripple of *reflection* ran through his large frame. Which meant he didn't feel scared or ashamed to be here. He simply appeared to hold back, waiting to see what I would do next.

"Thank you for coming over," I muttered.

The evening light darkened his honey eyes to the color of

black coffee, and they gazed at me with amusement. The corners of his eyes crinkled with a smile that his trimmed beard couldn't hide.

"Thank you for the invitation, Princess." He attempted a bow, the clinking sound finally drawing my eyes to his hands.

Wide fur-lined metal cuffs circled his wrists. The pretty designs embossed in the metal almost made them look like jewelry if it weren't for the black chain connecting them. The chain ran from one cuff to the other, then down to the similar manacles around his ankles.

Anger heated my chest and face.

"What the fuck is this?" I gasped. "I'm so sorry. I did *not* order these."

With my eyes on the chain, I pawed at the side of my skirt in search of the pocket, then rummaged inside it for the key that Gem had given me. Its purpose became very clear to me now.

Salas lifted his hands, as if to stop me. "It's for your protection, Princess."

That made me pause.

"Do I need to keep you chained in order to be safe with you, Salas? Because if that's the case, then you should leave. You've already earned your money just by coming here. I promise no one will take it away from you now. You're free to go." I motioned at the door behind him.

He turned, following my gesture.

"I swear I could punch Gem right now," I cursed under my breath.

He pivoted back to face me again. "Don't blame Lady Gem for taking measures to protect you. She doesn't know me."

"Maybe she doesn't," I agreed. "But *you* should know. Tell me, do I need to keep you in chains for my safety?"

His stare didn't flicker. He didn't flinch when he replied, "No, Princess. You don't need the chains."

"Give me your word," I insisted.

"Will you trust the word of a slave?"

"I'll trust *your* word." For once, I didn't feel awkward, holding his gaze firmly.

"Then you have it," he said. "With me, you don't ever need to be afraid. As long as I'm around, I'll protect you from any danger, including myself."

That was more than what I'd asked for. His words reached deeper than he would ever know. Without saying another word, I opened the lock that held the two ends of the chain together. The chain rattled to the ground, setting free both his hands and his feet. The cuffs remained, but they no longer restrained him since they weren't connected anymore.

He stepped over the chain on the floor. "Thank you."

"I meant what I said, Salas. You're free to leave if you want. It will not affect your compensation."

He watched me closely, a spark of a new interest twinkling in his eyes.

"I think I'd rather stay," he said.

"Really?" I felt both unnerved and thrilled by his decision as well as by his attention. "Did you know you were coming here to see *me?*"

"No. No one told me who requested my presence at the palace. But I wondered if it was you."

"You did? Why?"

"You were the only person from the royal court who's ever spoken to me or even looked at me."

"So..." I laced my fingers in front of me, choosing my words carefully. "No one talked to you about the purpose of your visit then?"

"No." He arched an eyebrow, with a new spark of amusement in his eyes. "But I've been bathed, fed, and groomed. My hair was trimmed, my nails filed and buffed, and every part of my body has been scented, and oiled. I'd be a clueless fool not to figure out the purpose of my coming here at this hour."

"Right." I squeezed my fingers tighter. "And how do you feel about it?"

"How do I *feel?*" He jerked his head. A frown momentarily crossed his features, but it smoothed out quickly. "It'd take too long to list all the emotions I've gone through today, but that's not what you're paying me for, is it?"

I winced at his bringing up the money. However, his silence

about it wouldn't have changed the fact that he was being paid for tonight and it was my mother who was paying him.

"Let's just get one thing straight, Princess," Salas continued, "our arrangement is about sex, which gives you access to my skills and my body but nothing else. There is no need to talk about *feelings*."

"Of course." I nodded. "As long as you're here willingly."

"I am." He rolled back his shoulders, tossing a look around the room. "So, where do you want me?"

"Where? Oh..." I tripped over my next breath.

Already?

Just like that?

He sounded so businesslike. But then again, what was it if not a business transaction?

I brought a hand to my mouth and surveyed the room uncertainly.

"I'm not sure... Where would be a good place?"

With a tilt of his head, he studied my face. "You're twenty-six years old, Princess, aren't you? I remember your last birthday celebration. Fireworks were shot all over the country. Newspapers said the queen released twenty-six pigeons during the parade in your honor."

"Doves," I corrected, rubbing my sweaty palms on my thighs. "They were white doves, not pigeons. And yes, twenty-six of them. I am twenty-six."

"Which is old enough to know where and how you like being pleasured, isn't it?" he said matter-of-factly.

For some unfathomable reason, the word "pleasured" sent my attention straight to his crotch. The thin material of his sarong clung to the bulge between his thighs closely enough for me to study its outline. Which I consciously chose *not* to do, jerking my gaze up to his face again.

He wasn't smiling. The amusement slowly cooled in his eyes as he took in my blushing cheeks and fidgeting hands.

"You haven't been with a man before, have you?" His voice softened. "Is this supposed to be your first time?"

I scratched my forearm, though it didn't itch, and adjusted my glasses that didn't need to be adjusted.

"I guess Gem never communicated that, either."

"Lady Gem never spoke to me," he said. "This arrangement was done through my owner who vouched for my character. There was no need for Lady Gem to speak with me directly."

A woman's word was worth more than a man's, especially since the woman was a well-respected business owner and the man was just a slave.

"Well, yeah… I mean yes, the purpose of this encounter is for me to gain experience in… um, sex. I'm sorry you had not been informed of that in advance," I rambled on. "If it's something that you have a problem with, my suggestion to leave—"

At a shake of his head, I shut my mouth.

"I already promised I'd stay," he said, then added under his breath, "and frankly, you did get the best man for the job."

What was that supposed to mean?

But I didn't ponder his words for long, still racking my brain for the best way to go about this.

Should I take him straight to bed? Or would it be easier to do it right here on the couch? Or in the bathroom maybe, for a quick clean-up? How messy could these things get, anyway?

"Have you had dinner yet?" he asked unexpectedly.

"Dinner? No." I hadn't even thought about food.

"Good. Come here then." He gestured at the sitting area by the fireplace, placing his other hand just behind my elbow as if to guide me but not quite touching. "Take a seat, so I can help you get rid of your boots and make you some tea."

"My boots?" I repeated like a dummy but plopped on the couch in the spot he'd pointed at.

"Boots aren't comfortable to wear indoors." He took a box of matches from the tea tray and lit a tea light in the stand under the pot to keep it warm. Then, he got down on one knee in front of me and lifted his hand, palm up. "May I?"

"Are you really going to take my boots off for me? You know that's not what you're here for."

"I know, but I don't mind, and it's easier for *me* to do it than calling in a maid." He snapped his fingers, urging me to surrender my foot to him, but I shuffled both my feet closer to the couch.

"I can do it myself."

"Princesses aren't supposed to do things for themselves."

"I haven't always been a princess," I blurted out before I could think better of it.

He studied me from behind his dark locks hanging over his forehead. "Maybe you'll tell me more about it over dinner?"

Oh no, that was not going to happen. Talking about my past with someone I'd just met, when I hadn't even mentioned it to anyone other than Mother, was not on tonight's agenda.

I couldn't think of a better way to divert him from that topic than shoving my foot into his hand.

"Here. Go ahead if you insist."

He pulled the boot off and placed it by the fireplace behind him, then removed my other one just as easily. After that, he hovered his both hands over my calf covered by the pant leg of my riding pants.

"May I?" he asked again.

My riding outfit consisted of a sleeveless dress from a light cotton to help me bear the heat. The long skirt of the dress was largely decorative. With the high slit in the front all the way up to my waist, its only function was to drape majestically over the croup of the horse as I rode it with my legs on either side of the saddle. The pants I wore underneath protected my thighs from chafing during the ride.

As Salas waited for my permission to touch my calf, I stiffened, wondering how far he wanted to go and whether I should allow it. My muscles strained, ready to jerk my leg away or even kick him.

Yet he'd somehow taken control over the situation without overpowering me. He'd taken the lead, leaving me the choice to follow. Even with him in charge, I still had a choice.

"Alright." I nodded tentatively.

Sitting back on his haunches, he placed my foot on his knee, then hiked my wide pant leg up past my knee. With deft fingers, he untied my garter, then rolled down my thin cotton stocking before taking it off.

He did it all slowly, giving me plenty of time to pull away if I so wished. Somehow, he also managed to get it done without touching my skin even once.

"It's not just my boots you're taking off then?" I cleared my throat, holding still as a mouse.

"Stockings are a part of it. You wouldn't be wearing them if it wasn't for the boots."

In summer, women in Rorrim normally wore just short underwear under their light dresses and sandals on their feet. Working women often switched to flowy pants made from breathable material, for practical reasons. Men usually stuck with long pants and boots or closed-toe shoes throughout the year. It wasn't customary for any self-respecting gentleman to show bare legs or feet in public.

"Do you ride horses too?" I asked, since he'd demonstrated a skill in dealing with riding boots.

"No," he replied briefly.

"But have you ever? I mean *before*?"

"Before I sold my debt to a slave owner, you mean? No. I've never ridden a horse other than in a wagon." He reached back to drape my stockings over my boots by the fireplace.

His back seemed to be healing well. There were no blood stains on the pristine white material of his robe, but the raised scars from the whip with dry blood still crusted in their crests were visible through the thin fabric.

"How did you get into debt?" I asked somberly.

Turning to face me again, he shook his head.

"Talking about me won't get us in the right mood, Princess." He took my bare foot into his hands, not bothering to ask for permission this time.

If distraction was his goal, it worked. My breath hitched as his warm palm connected with the sole of my foot. I forgot all about the question I'd just asked.

His huge hand wrapped around my foot, nearly swallowing it whole. Gently as if handling a puppy, he rubbed the top with his thumb. He traced each bone to my toes, massaging them in circles, then moved to the bottom of my sole.

"Your horse is white like snow and so is your dog," he said, his deep voice soothingly flowing through the room. "Is it intentional?"

I remembered he'd seen Revlis on the day of his flogging.

"No," I said. "A pure coincidence."

"How old is your horse?"

"She's eleven. I got her about seven years ago. I wasn't that great of a rider back then, so Father advised me to go with the most mild-tempered mare. And she was it. I still prefer her over any other."

He raised my foot a little. Cupping the heel in one hand, he applied firm, even pressure to my sole with his thumb. It felt wonderful. The tension from being trapped in a stiff boot drained from my foot with the relaxation spreading through the rest of my body.

"And your dog?" Salas asked. "Ria, the puppy."

I noted he remembered her name.

"Ria is a daughter of Father's lap dogs. He has a pack of hunting hounds like most men do. But he also has a pair of lap dogs—two little furry creatures he's quite fond of."

"I thought those were Queen Anna's dogs. She has a portrait painted of her with the two of them, hasn't she? I saw a copy of it in a store window once."

He set my right foot back onto his lap and started working on the left one.

"Right," I agreed. "They're hers." Owning lapdogs was not considered manly. Officially, Ria's parents belonged to the queen, though the king was the one who doted on them. "Father is just... um, in charge of their training since he knows so much about dogs because of his hounds."

"It looks like that little one needs some more training." Salas smiled into his beard.

"She does." I liked how fondly he spoke of Ria, even as she'd mostly been a pest the day he met her. "Did you ever have a dog?"

"Yes, a very long time ago," he said quickly, then set both my feet down. "Time for your tea, Princess. Where can I wash my hands?"

"The bathroom is right there, behind the pillars to the left." I gestured in that direction.

I appreciated how he'd used small talk about my pets to put me at ease. But it didn't escape me how persistently he avoided any conversation about himself.

As Salas headed to the bathroom, I remembered the tub with the freaking rose petals. I scrambled to my freshly massaged feet and dashed after him.

"Wait."

But he had already entered my bathroom that was finished in pale pink marble with antique bronze fixtures and stained-glass mosaics on the walls.

"Nice," he drawled appreciatively, sweeping the room with a wide glance before pausing it on the tub. "And what is this for?"

"The maids did it," I fired off, like a five-year old blaming her siblings for a mischief.

"How thoughtful of them." He approached the sink, turned on the faucet and scooped the silky soap paste from the open jar to wash his hands.

He was clearly impressed by the opulence of my rooms but didn't seem overwhelmed as could've been expected from someone who'd never been to a fine home before.

"A bath is a great idea," he said, rinsing the soap from his hands. He then dipped a hand into the tub. "It's nice and warm still, just what you need after the ride on a hot day." He wiped his hand on the end of his robe. "Come, Princess, I'll help you bathe."

"Me?"

He tilted his head. "You are the only princess here, aren't you?"

His smile was kind, letting me know he wasn't mocking, just trying to lighten the mood. While I searched for an answer, he struck a match, then walked around the tub, lighting the candles around it.

"I don't need help," I said.

He completed the circle around the tub, with all candles now lit, then stopped in front of me.

"Not even with washing your hair?" He lifted a hand to a loose strand on the side of my face, then gently placed it behind my ear.

The tickling of the hair against my cheek and the slight brushing of his fingers just below my temple sent a ripple of excitement through my chest.

Or was it an alarm?

I couldn't tell when it came to my feelings with him being this close, but I didn't shrink away.

I realized what Salas was doing. First, he'd gotten me to accept his touch by massaging my feet. Now, he was getting me accustomed to his close proximity.

He treated me like a skittish animal in the wild, with care and patience. But maybe that was what I needed all along? Patience and care. I certainly had never found even a drop of that in any man who'd touched me before.

"I already washed my hair this morning," I exhaled slowly, pulled into an odd trance when this close to him.

He smelled nice, after all the grooming they had put him through today. But it was the warm scent of his skin under all the musky perfumes that made me swoon a little.

"How about scrubbing your back then?" He smiled, gently placing a hand on my shoulder. "And maybe some other difficult-to-reach places?"

I should let him. After all, that was what he'd come here for—to take my clothes off, to put his hands on my body, to show me what happened between a man and a woman during sex.

I'd had no problem dealing with Salas in a businesslike manner. I'd found it easy to be friendly with him too. I enjoyed talking to him. But these tiny sexy sparks that he'd now brought into our interaction proved to be the roadblocks for me.

He shifted a tiny bit closer, speaking just above my ear.

"Let me take this dress off you, Princess."

His fresh breath fanned over the side of my face. My skin prickled with tiny ripples of ice and fire. His warm, potent male scent made my head spin and my knees buckle. It also made me wish to bury my face in his neck and breathe him in for eternity.

"Oh, gods..."

I staggered back, grabbing the edge of the stand behind me. The candles on it shook. I found one by touch, blew the flame out, and thrust it toward him.

"Here. Take it. Light it in the sitting room, for mood and such. Have some dinner, you're probably hungry. It must take a lot of food to maintain all of *this*." I waved my hand in front of his broad-as-a-wall chest. "I need a bath. I smell like a horse."

"Not the worst smell, believe me."

I ventured a glance up at his face again. His smile somehow had the ability to loosen the tight knot of anxiety in my chest.

"Please, let me take a quick bath on my own. I promise, it won't take long."

"As you wish, Princess." He accepted the candle from me, then left, closing the door behind him.

I dropped my shoulders, propping my butt against the edge of the tub.

What was happening with me?

Maybe I was coming down with something? The flushes of

heat and cold. My racing heart. My heightened scent sensitivity. Were they symptoms of a sickness? It would be such a nice and easy explanation if I'd just caught a cold and Salas had nothing to do with it.

I took my clothes off and got into the tub. The water was just a degree above lukewarm, which proved perfectly fine for a quick refreshing bath after a hot day.

Only after I finished bathing, I realized I hadn't brought any clothes to change into. All I had was my silk robe, printed with cherry blossoms and nightingales, that hung on a hook in a corner. I dried myself with a towel then put the robe on, making sure it overlapped tightly in the front before tying the belt around my waist.

With my hand on the door handle, I paused to collect myself.

It felt like armies of butterflies led an incessant battle in my stomach. But I had no reason to feel this way. I'd been holding my own in front of foreign dignitaries, seasoned politicians, and army generals since my first council meeting that I attended at eighteen. All of them had been smart, experienced women who'd mastered poker faces and were ready to use my every weakness to their advantage. Yet I survived and even thrived among them.

I could certainly stand to spend a night with a handsome man.

Turning the handle, I shoved the door open and entered the bedroom.

Salas sat on the floor by the table with food. At the sound of the door opening, he took the teapot from its stand and filled two cups.

"How do you take your tea?" He turned to me, then slid his gaze down my body.

I adjusted my robe over my chest, feeling an odd urge to explain. "I didn't want to put the same clothes on, and I didn't bring any clean ones to the bathroom with me."

"You look lovely, Princess." He tore his stare from me and directed it back to the table. "Tea is ready. Cream? Sugar?"

"Just cream, please."

I sat on the couch and pulled the ends of my robe closed over my knees. Salas remained on the floor, the way the royal gladiators often did when in the company of the ladies from the palace.

"I took the liberty of making you a plate." He placed a dish with different mini sandwiches in front of me. "I hope you like these."

I took a rye wafer he'd topped with pâté and a cucumber slice. He joined me by taking one too. I noted the quality and the variety of the fancy sandwiches he'd constructed.

"What do you normally eat?" I asked after we'd finished a few sandwiches and Salas had refilled our teacups.

"Whatever the owner feeds us. Usually, it's something that fills us up the most with the least impact to her wallet." He set down his cup and leaned against the couch seat sideways to face me better. "But I'm not here to talk about the far-from-fine cuisine of the slaves' barracks. Tell me, Princess, how far have you gone with a man before. Kissing? Touching? What have you enjoyed?"

I would rather stick my bare hand into an open flame than talk about my past sexual experiences.

"Nothing," I said quickly. "I've done nothing at all."

He seemed surprised by my answer, and I didn't think he believed me.

"Not even a kiss?"

"No."

"Have you ever wondered what a kiss would feel like?"

"Um, I don't really think much about things like that." Though I certainly was wondering about them now, studying his lips framed by his beard. "How does kissing work with a beard? Does it get in the way?"

He laughed. It was a rich, deep sound—hearty and genuine. As if on their own, my lips stretched into a smile in response. Propping an elbow on the seat of the couch, he beckoned me with his finger to lean closer.

"There is but one way to find out," he murmured in invitation.

I kept staring at his mouth. It was a pleasant thing to look at, especially when it was curved into a cheeky grin like that. But a kiss would bring him closer. Way too close...

"No. Please—" My hand holding the teacup jerked involuntarily, spilling the tea. I put it onto the saucer on the table a little too hard with a loud clunk.

His smile slipped away. He moved the cup with the saucer away from the edge while his focus remained on me.

"What's wrong, Princess?"

I clasped my hands in my lap, dropping my gaze to them. I should've known this would happen, that my memories would resurface and get in the way. The past few days had been intense, and I struggled to keep the darkness at bay even during the day. Now, I felt worn down and vulnerable.

"Did something happen?" he sounded somber, grave even. "Tell me. I believe I will understand."

What could I say?

How would I put all those dark, tangled memories into words?

How could I bring them out into the open like this?

As I kept silent, his large hand descended over both of mine on my lap in a warm, reassuring touch.

"Whatever happened, you proved stronger than it," he said. "You survived."

He spoke as if I'd already told him, as if he needed no words to know, and it was a relief to have someone understand it like this, without words.

"Nothing has to happen tonight," he assured me. "Sex can't be forced. Intimacy takes time to develop, even if it's just the most basic physical kind. You have to be in the right state of mind to enjoy it. Because without joy, what's the point in any of it?"

I realized the turn our situation had taken—the man who had nothing was comforting the woman who had it all. But I had no willpower to refuse his comfort, shamelessly soaking his attention and the warm sensation of his touch.

"It takes time? So sex isn't really like pulling a tooth out, is it?" I managed a smile. "Yank and done?"

"A tooth? I sure hope not." He chuckled. "I'd love to think I can make it far more enjoyable for you than that. But only when you're ready for me."

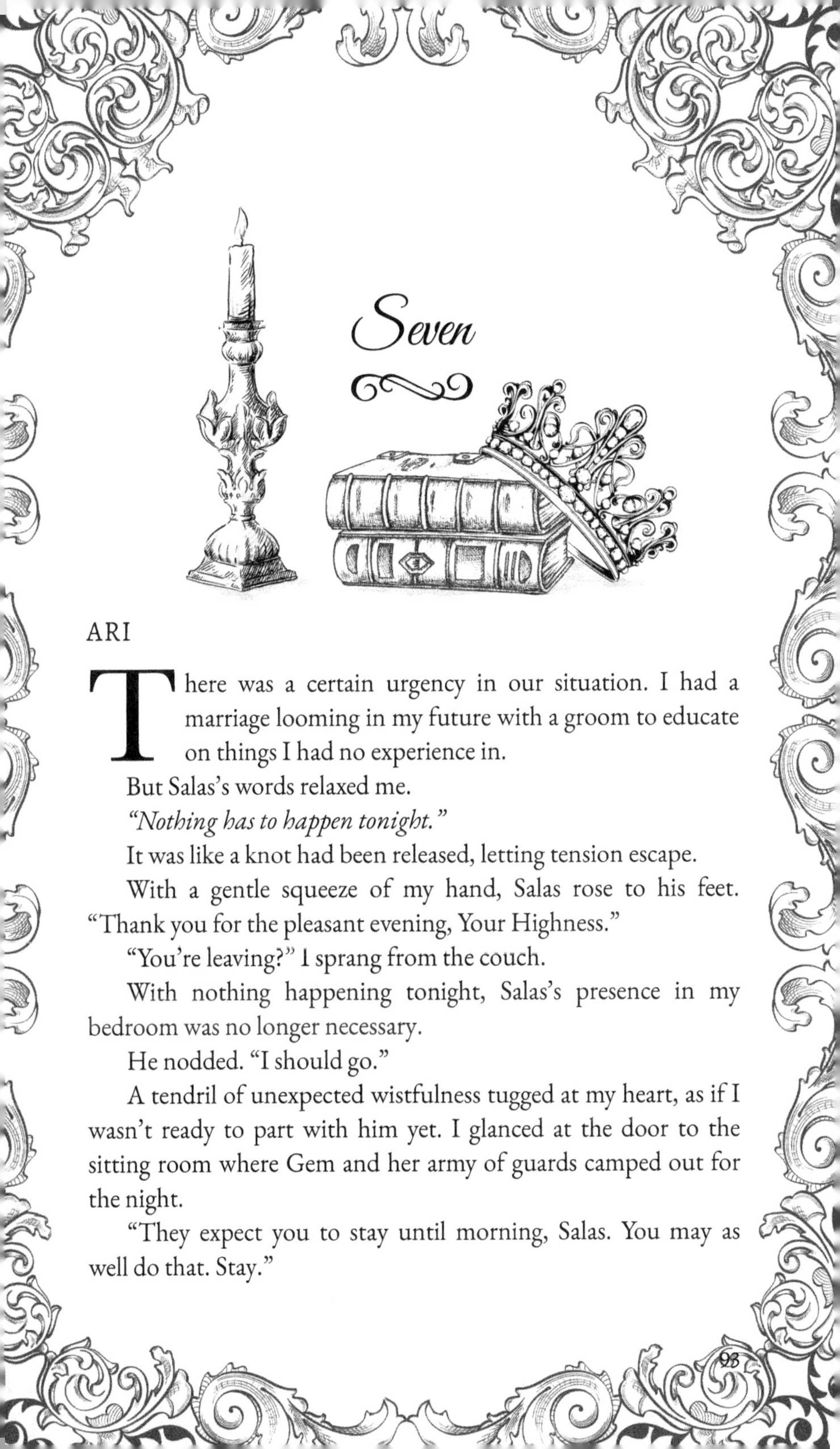

Seven

ARI

There was a certain urgency in our situation. I had a marriage looming in my future with a groom to educate on things I had no experience in.

But Salas's words relaxed me.

"Nothing has to happen tonight."

It was like a knot had been released, letting tension escape.

With a gentle squeeze of my hand, Salas rose to his feet. "Thank you for the pleasant evening, Your Highness."

"You're leaving?" I sprang from the couch.

With nothing happening tonight, Salas's presence in my bedroom was no longer necessary.

He nodded. "I should go."

A tendril of unexpected wistfulness tugged at my heart, as if I wasn't ready to part with him yet. I glanced at the door to the sitting room where Gem and her army of guards camped out for the night.

"They expect you to stay until morning, Salas. You may as well do that. Stay."

He gave me a long look, as if testing my resolve about the offer.

"You said nothing needs to happen," I hurried to explain. "We'll just sleep. I have a big bed. I don't think I have a nightshirt big enough to fit you, but you can sleep just the way you are." I gestured at his outfit from the material so thin, it could be used as a veil. "I have a spare toothbrush and an extra blanket too. And I don't think I snore. So…"

He smiled at that last statement.

"A night without listening to the snoring of a few dozen other men in the barrack sounds tempting."

"So, you'll stay?"

"Thank you for your offer, Your Highness," he said with a formal bow. "I accept it."

BRIGHT SUNSHINE WOKE ME UP. I squinted at it, confused. Why was the sun so high already? Then, I remembered. Salas stayed the night. My heart leaped with a jolt of nerves or thrill, or both.

We'd left the patio doors open before going to bed. My lacy curtains swayed in the cool morning breeze. During the night, I'd dragged the cover up to my ears and burrowed under Salas's back like a rodent, seeking warmth from his large body. He was sleeping on his side with his back to me, also completely wrapped into his own blanket.

I shifted to get my glasses from the night table, and he stirred, rolling onto his back.

"Morning, Princess," he murmured with an easy smile, as if it was a normal thing for us to wake up together.

"Morning." I rose over him on my outstretched arm.

The sunshine brightened his eyes to honey-amber once again. From this close, I could also see the golden flecks and dark streaks in his irises. It looked too pretty, almost magical, for a simple man like him.

"You have freckles," he said unexpectedly. "How have I not noticed them before?"

As I watched him, he clearly had been studying me too.

"Oh. Yeah, I have some." I touched the side of my nose.

"They're tiny. And only on your nose and here." He tapped the top of my cheek with the tip of his finger. "Hard to see, especially from a distance, but very pretty."

And now, I was blushing like a schoolgirl. What was it about this man that kicked me off-kilter so easily? I constantly had to remind myself of reality to keep my mind from floating off in a bubble filled with nothing but thoughts and sensations of him.

I dropped my gaze, and it landed on his bare chest. Once again, it amazed me just how smooth it was. His skin almost looked shiny, but the ruddy undertone was now gone.

"You're not naturally this hairless, are you?" I asked.

"Oh, this?" He chuckled, running a hand over his chest. "That would be the one thing I could've done without yesterday —them ripping out all the hair on my chest." He winced.

"Why would they do that?"

He rolled his head on the pillow. "They must've been under the impression you prefer bare-chested men."

"I really don't care either way." I hadn't interacted with men enough to form any preferences of that sort.

I placed a hand on his chest in the opening of his robe. His smooth skin felt warm and soft after the oils they had rubbed into it yesterday. He didn't seem to mind my hand, letting it rest on his chest comfortably.

"Did you have a lot of chest hair before?" I asked.

He jerked up an eyebrow, humor shining brightly in his eyes. "Like a bear hide."

I snorted a laugh. "It's a shame I never got to see it. Did it hurt to remove it?

"Like a son of a mutt."

I gasped. I never heard a man in Rorrim swear before. The fine gentlemen of the palace wouldn't utter such vulgar words probably even in their thoughts.

"Where are your manners, Mister Salas?" I teased, leaning closer. The movement made my hand slide under his robe.

"If you wanted fine manners, my princess," he matched my tone, "you shouldn't have picked your date from slaves' barracks."

His face was turned up to me as I leaned over him. My thigh pressed to his side. My hand remained on his body under his robe. Surprisingly, I wished to stay right where I was, close to him like that.

"I think I found exactly what I needed," I replied softly.

His expression turned serious, any hint of a smile was instantly gone. He rose on his elbow toward me but stopped before his lips had a chance to touch mine.

"Give me a sign, Princess," he exhaled, the sweet scent of lilies from my teeth cleaning powder still fresh on his breath. "If you're ready, give me a sign."

"A sign?"

"A look, a touch, a gesture. Anything. I need to know. I'd love to kiss you right now, but I don't want to frighten you."

If he just went ahead and kissed me, I didn't think I'd stop him. But I couldn't bring myself to take that first step, and he wouldn't do it for me, letting me move at my own pace.

I removed my hand from his chest and sat back quietly.

"Sorry. I... I can't." I looked at him in desperation, feeling deflated. "Something must be wrong with me."

He sat up next to me.

"There is not a single fucking thing wrong with you, Princess," he said with firm conviction. "Don't ever think that. Besides, kisses aren't necessary for either pleasure or procreation. Trust me, you can very well manage without them."

"Really?" I tilted my head, pondering it for a moment. "Interesting. So, you don't like kissing?"

"It depends."

"On what?"

"On several things, one of them is the person I'm kissing." He paused, before adding, "If you ever feel up to it, I would genuinely love to kiss you."

It sounded so simple, like an offer between friends. It made it easy to be straightforward with him in return.

"I'm not sure if I'll ever be up to anything, to be honest."

"Fair enough—" He opened his mouth to say more, but a loud knock on the door interrupted us.

"Your Highness?" Gem yelled from behind the door, pounding her fist against it. "Princess Aniri?"

It was late morning already. Gem must've let me sleep in, taking into account my visitor, no doubt. But now, she sounded rather panicky, her voice filled with worry.

"May I come in?"

"No!" I jumped off the bed and ran out from behind the silk screen separating my bed area from the rest of the bedroom.

I didn't want anyone to see Salas and me on the bed together like that—warm, relaxed, and comfortable. Nothing indecent was going on. We weren't even naked. He was wearing his entire outfit of the robe and sarong. I had a floor-length nightgown on. But this moment belonged to us and only us, and I felt fiercely protective about sharing it with anyone else.

"I'm fine." I leaned with my hand against the solid door, as if to hold it against Gem's invasion. "What do you want?"

"Oh, good morning, Your Highness." Worry eased from Gem's voice. She spoke loudly for me to hear her through the thick wooden door that I refused to open. "How are you doing today?"

Now, I sensed a teasing note in her voice.

"What do you want, Gem?" I replied flatly.

"Her Majesty is wondering if you'll be in a *position* to attend the council meeting this morning." The word she emphasized obviously meant to hint at all the possible positions I might be in with Salas right now.

I rolled my eyes, ignoring her baiting me. "Why wouldn't I?"

I checked the wall clock. I'd missed breakfast with my parents already. I'd never slept past breakfast. Ever. Usually, I was up before sunrise, if I even managed to fall asleep at all. Clearly, Salas proved to be a cozy sleeping partner. Warmth rushed through my body at the memory of cuddling against his back.

"I'll be there," I assured Gem.

"It's starting in less than thirty minutes, Your Highness. Should I send a maid in to help you get dressed? How about a breakfast? To restore your strength?"

"No. Just... give me a minute. I'll ring for the maid myself."

I turned around to find Salas standing on this side of the screen. He must've heard at least my side of the conversation with Gem. Silently, he walked over to the couch to pick up his cloak.

It was time for us to part. A wisp of melancholy curled around my heart once again, but I couldn't possibly keep him in my room forever.

He draped his cloak over his shoulders. Standing with my back to the door, I reached behind me and placed a hand on the door handle. Opening the door would end this night and our time together. It would burst our bubble of calm and sunshine, of just Salas and me. And I couldn't bring myself to do it.

As he bent over to pick up the chain from the floor, I snapped, "Leave it. Gem will get rid of it."

He straightened, stepping over the chain. His eyes found mine, and I saw some of my sadness reflected in them too.

"Salas..." I let go of the handle and stepped toward him, suddenly needing to be closer. Much, much closer.

I slipped a hand under his cloak and under his robe, finding his bare chest underneath the layers of fabric. I needed more. More of him. Before he left.

"This is the sign, Salas." I tilted my head back, turning my face up to his. "The sign you've asked for."

The focus in his eyes sharpened.

He leaned over me. Fast and unstoppable.

His body came flush with mine, and I whimpered, retreating to the door.

"Shh." He cupped the side of my face, promptly taking half a step back to give me space. "It's all good, sweetheart," he cooed, calming me. His thumb gently stroked along my cheekbone, his hand being the only physical contact between us now. "I'll never hurt you. I gave you my word, remember?"

I swallowed hard, enthralled by his words and his caress. He leaned closer, stealing my breath.

The touch of his lips came light and airy, like a dawn feather fluttering in the breeze. My heart fluttered, too, thrashing like a bird inside my rib cage.

He parted his lips, and I did the same, letting him deepen the kiss. He didn't touch me anywhere else. It was just his mouth on my lips and his hand on my cheek. My awareness shrank to those two points of contact between us. The rest of the world no longer existed as my mind floated in a slow circle in a universe all of its own.

Pleasure surged in me with a shudder, I gripped his shoulder in search of support. I opened my eyes, forgetting when and how I'd closed them in the first place.

The room appeared to melt out of focus. His face was the only steady point in the chaos.

"There you go, Princess," he murmured. "You can never again say that you haven't been kissed."

And so it happened.

Salas became my first kiss.

Emotionally elated, I felt physically weak, as if my bones had suddenly softened. I staggered forward, resting my forehead against his chest. He held me to him, and I trusted him to keep me upright, no matter how much I fell apart.

His heart thundered in his chest. It beat as fast as mine, as if he, too, was strongly affected by our kiss.

Needing to see his face, I lifted my head again.

"Was it a good kiss, Salas?" I had nothing to compare it to.

"It was perfect." He wasn't looking at me, staring straight at the door instead. "Probably, the best I've had."

"Have you had many kisses before?"

Shifting me to his side, he reached for the door handle.

"Salas?" I prompted, afraid he wouldn't answer.

"Yes," he replied. "I've had many kisses, Princess. Not all of them I've wanted or asked for, though."

His words came like a punch to my stomach. Chills spread through my body all the way to the tips of my fingers as the full meaning of his words seeped through every layer of my being.

"Salas." I grabbed his hand before he turned the handle. "I want to see you again."

He pushed the door open.

"Ari!" Gem jumped from the couch in the sitting room, then caught herself and sank into a bow like the etiquette demanded. "Good Morning, Your Highness."

Salas drew his cloak's hood low over his head. The moment we crossed the threshold, he stepped away from me.

The guards scrambled to their feet from where they had been sitting or sleeping in piles by the walls, around the fireplace, and on every piece of furniture in the room.

Gem leaned to my ear, speaking for only me to hear.

"I was this close," she lifted her hand with her thumb and her forefinger almost touching, "*this close* from breaking down the door this morning. The only thought that kept me from doing it was that you must be having a really good time with that slave." She arched her eyebrow in question. "*Did* you have a good time?"

I watched the guards lead Salas away. He didn't turn around, didn't wave, or say goodbye. He left, and I didn't like the hollow feeling his departure caused in me.

"I need to see him again," I said to Gem when we were left alone.

Her expression turned skeptical. "Was he that good? Or is it something else? I can't tell by your face or by your behavior whether you're pleased or pissed with him."

"I'm not upset."

"Well, that isn't much. Was he or was he not a good fuck?"

Her swearing didn't offend me. I swore and cursed too. It was perfectly normal in an all-female company. But I didn't appreciate her word choice when applied to Salas.

"What?" She spread her arms out in response to my glare. "We aren't at your mother's ball. There are no men here. You won't offend their delicate sensibilities. I can curse all I want. No need to beat around a bush. Was this slave any good at fucking?"

"I can't answer your question for several reasons," I replied icily. "One, I wouldn't know how to rate his performance since I have nothing to compare it to. And two, we didn't fuck."

"You didn't?" Her mouth fell open. "It's past ten in the morning. What have you been doing all this time?"

"Sleeping." I propped my butt on the back of the couch by the fireplace.

Gem sank into the chair by the closed patio doors, looking devastated from disappointment.

"And that's it?"

"Yes. Mostly. But we also talked and ate. He made me tea and then... he kissed me this morning."

"He did?" She perked up. "So, did you like the kiss?"

"I did, yes," I admitted.

Gem threw her hands up in the air, casting her eyes upwards.

"Thank you, Eci, the Goddess of Winter, you didn't create this woman out of ice after all!"

I shook my head at her antics.

"So." She leaned closer in her chair. "Why didn't he finish the job, so to say?"

"Meaning I'm his *job*?"

She brushed me off with a hand gesture. "You know what I mean. Why did you stop at kissing?"

"We ran out of time." I gave her the simplest of explanations. "You know I have things to do, but I slept in."

"That's absolutely fine. The queen is aware."

"Mother knows?" I had the queen's general approval, but I hadn't informed her that Salas was visiting specifically last night.

She nodded. "I had to tell her. She sent for you this morning."

"What exactly did you tell her?"

"That you had a male visitor overnight and that you needed some more time before you were ready to part from him. The queen seemed delighted. She said she wouldn't fault you for skipping the council meeting, either, as long as you attend the dinner with the ambassador tonight. However, if you insist on going to the meeting, you'll have to hurry. I'll send the maids with breakfast right away and—"

"No. I don't feel like rushing." I shook my head, getting up. "Tell Mother I'll be a little late. I need a few more minutes."

"For what?"

To wrap my mind around everything that happened and figure out how to deal with the unexplained ball of longing growing in my chest.

But of course, I couldn't tell Gem that.

"I need some time to rest."

"From a kiss?" Gem winked. "Damn, he must be good."

I said nothing to that, heading back to my bedroom.

"Ten minutes, Gem. Send the maid with a very strong coffee in ten minutes." I shut the door, then crashed in my bed face down.

There was an added benefit to having Salas spend the night in my bed I noticed when taking a deep breath in. My sheets now smelled like him.

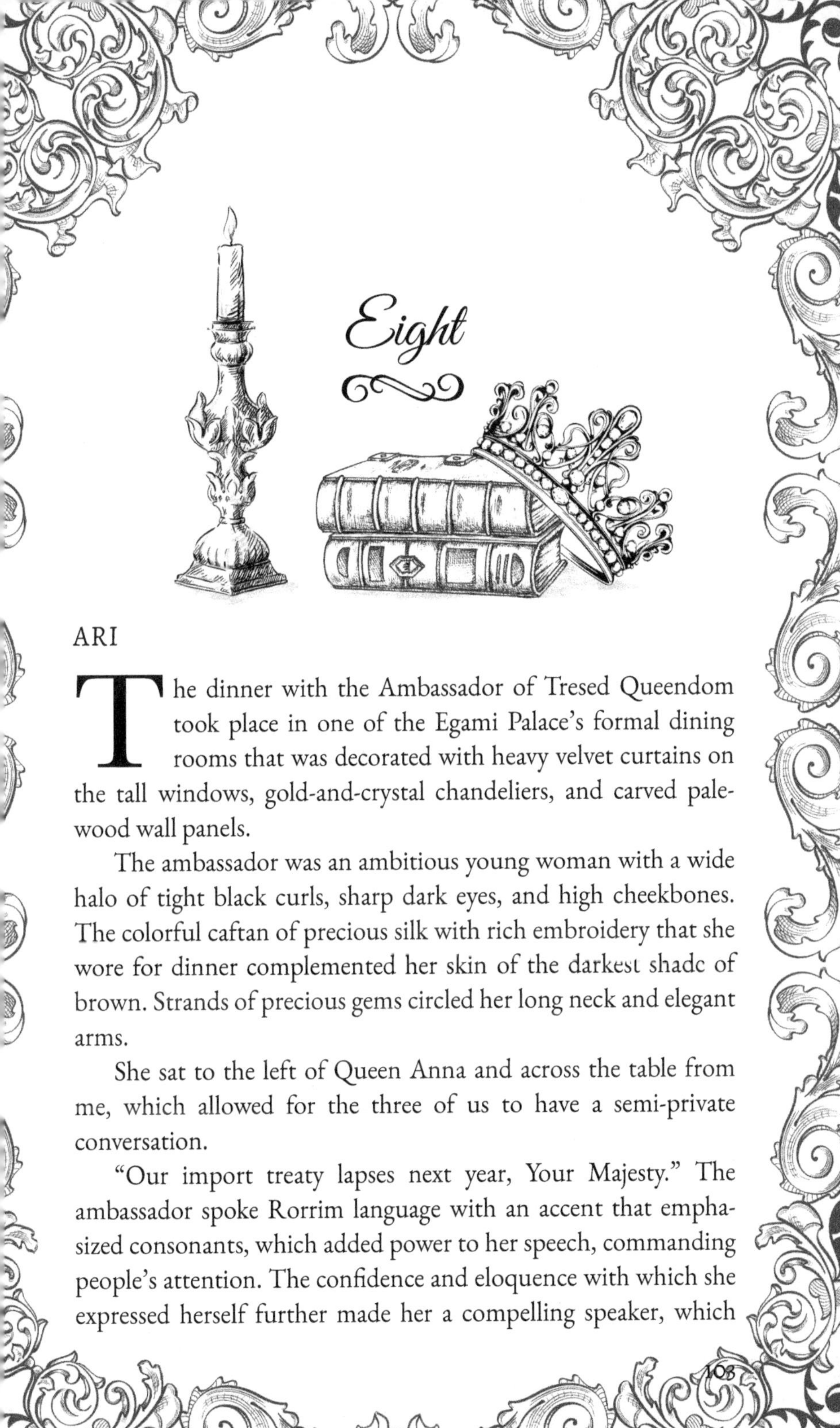

Eight

ARI

The dinner with the Ambassador of Tresed Queendom took place in one of the Egami Palace's formal dining rooms that was decorated with heavy velvet curtains on the tall windows, gold-and-crystal chandeliers, and carved pale-wood wall panels.

The ambassador was an ambitious young woman with a wide halo of tight black curls, sharp dark eyes, and high cheekbones. The colorful caftan of precious silk with rich embroidery that she wore for dinner complemented her skin of the darkest shade of brown. Strands of precious gems circled her long neck and elegant arms.

She sat to the left of Queen Anna and across the table from me, which allowed for the three of us to have a semi-private conversation.

"Our import treaty lapses next year, Your Majesty." The ambassador spoke Rorrim language with an accent that empha-sized consonants, which added power to her speech, commanding people's attention. The confidence and eloquence with which she expressed herself further made her a compelling speaker, which was perfect for her job. "My queen is willing to renegotiate the terms as soon as this year if you're up to it."

My attention spiked. That was an unexpected offer. Tresed was a big, powerful country. They didn't throw concessions like that around. Every favorable agreement we'd had with them cost us months or even years of careful negotiations.

"It may be wise to revisit it early," Mother agreed calmly. "There have been some changes in both our economies that the new agreement would reflect better."

"Wonderful." The ambassador brought a glass of wine to her lips for a sip, then added, seemingly unrelated to her previous statement, "Can you believe that the queen's nephew, Prince Elbon, has come of age already?" She sighed. "They grow up so fast, don't they? I still remember like it was yesterday the grand festivities our queen held for his first birthday. It was such a lavish, no-expense-spared celebration. And now, he's eighteen already and perfect for marriage. Our queen is so fond of that boy. She raised him like her own son. Princess Aniri?" She turned to me, and I smiled politely at the sound of my name, meeting the ambassador's eyes. "Can I have the honor of presenting you with Prince Elbon's portrait? He's such a handsome boy. His beauty serves as a constant inspiration for our poets and artists alike. With your permission of course, Your Majesty." She gave a respectful bow to my mother.

The smile froze on my face. Words proved hard to come by.

My mother cast a glance at me. "I'm sure the princess will be delighted to accept the portrait."

I lowered my fork carefully, keeping my hand steady even as my insides seemed to plummet into a dark abyss. Until now, marriage was something to worry about in some distant future. This proposition made it no longer distant but real.

"It will be my honor and my pleasure, Ambassador," I said with firm confidence I did not feel.

"The timing is fortunate," Mother noted. "Princess Aniri is of perfect age to take a husband."

The ambassador leaned in eagerly. "Prince Elbon was brought up in the queen's personal household. He's been raised to the highest standards expected of a young man of his standing. The prince is an extremely accomplished young man. He speaks six languages, writes poetry, and is unmatched in swordsmanship. He also raises his own hounds and horses. They are delightful creatures indeed."

"The crown princess loves horseback riding." Mother raised her glass as if in a toast to this match already.

"Oh, they will get along splendidly," the ambassador cheered.

Losing my appetite, I glanced down the table where my father was having a quiet conversation with the ambassador's husband. Dressed in colors that complemented his wife's outfit, the ambassador's spouse was wearing a shirt with wide, long sleeves and the front full of ruffles. He smiled politely without speaking much.

I tried to imagine a slightly younger version of him as my groom and felt no excitement at that. But I wasn't supposed to be excited.

A state marriage was a political move. In this case, it would give us leverage to renegotiate the import treaty on far better terms, in addition to everything else Tresed would offer as part of Prince Elbon's dowry.

All of it still wasn't enough for me to feel thrilled about the marriage, but I looked forward to renegotiating the terms of the treaty and to figuring out what other benefits we could gain for Rorrim in the process.

After dinner, the king took the gentlemen for a tour of the royal stables as the ladies moved to a drawing room for a glass of wine or sweet sherry.

Here, the ambassador accosted me on the patio where I'd gone for a breath of fresh air. Seizing my arm, she spent at least a half-hour listing the many virtues of Prince Elbon, who seemed to be a highly accomplished young gentleman indeed. By the end of our conversation, I was convinced the prince must be a saint who was sent to this world to serve as an unattainable ideal for the rest of the male population.

"Needless to say, the prince is virginal and pure," the ambassador added. "His seed has never been spilled, fully saved as the priceless treasure for his future wife only."

I wondered how that had been achieved.

"Thank you, Ambassador. I'm delighted to consider Prince Elbon as my future husband. He sounds... um, virtuous."

"He certainly is," she agreed with a satisfied smile. "Our queen made sure of it."

It took me a few more minutes to finally free my arm from her grip. As the ambassador moved back into the drawing room, possibly to find my mother to further drive home her idea about the prince and I being a match made in heaven, I gripped the railing with both hands and dropped my head between my shoulders.

The tall formal crown weighed down on my head especially heavily tonight. The bodice of my ballgown must've been laced too tightly because it squeezed my chest, pressing against my ribs with every breath.

Gem sidled next to me, holding two glasses of red wine.

"Here." She handed one of the glasses to me. "I thought you might need a drink after the lengthy conversation with the ambassador."

"Thanks." I took a drink, barely tasting the wine.

Gem watched me over the rim of her glass. "It looks like the marriage talks are well on the way, doesn't it?"

"Looks like it."

"You don't seem happy about it."

"What does it matter if I am or not? A state marriage has nothing to do with happiness. It's about gaining a political and economic advantage for our country. A union with a queendom like Tresed would bring all of that and more."

"But what do you think about the prince?"

I shrugged. What could I possibly think about someone I'd never met?

"I've never even seen the prince. But I'm sure he knows well what's expected of him and will make a good royal husband."

"Judging by what I've overheard from the ambassador, he is very well groomed for the role of king consort."

"Well, there you go. What more can I ask for in a husband?" I tipped the glass again, emptying it into my mouth.

"I suppose you're right." Gem casually swirled the wine in her glass. "But since you aren't married yet, a certain slave is currently waiting for you in your rooms."

"Salas?" My heart thudded with the excitement it'd sorely lacked earlier tonight. "Why is he in my rooms now?"

"You said you'd like to see him again. And my princess's wish is my command." Gem bowed dramatically with playful reverence.

"Did *he* want to see me again?"

I remember the words he'd said just before we'd parted and right after he gave me my first kiss.

"I've had many kisses... Not all of them I've wanted or asked for..."

Salas's past had not been smooth. No one ended up a slave without hitting a few bumps on the road that led them there. But I sensed his life journey might've been even rockier than I'd first thought. He seemed to be a kind man, but his tenderness and patience with me came from a deeper place than mere kindness. It came from understanding.

Gem suddenly burst with laughter.

"You're being funny, Ari. Who cares what *he* wants? He's there for you, that's all that matters."

There was no point in discussing it with her when I could ask Salas directly. He was waiting for me in my bedroom this very minute. And suddenly, that was the only place I wished to be right now.

I handed Gem my empty glass. "Please tell me you didn't drag him into my rooms against his will."

"I didn't have to, sweetie. He went through the entire grooming routine without a word of protest. Now, he's all clean and smelling nice just for you, ready to finish what he's started."

I drew in a breath and fisted my hands in the silk jacquard of my skirts.

"You better not have put him in chains this time."

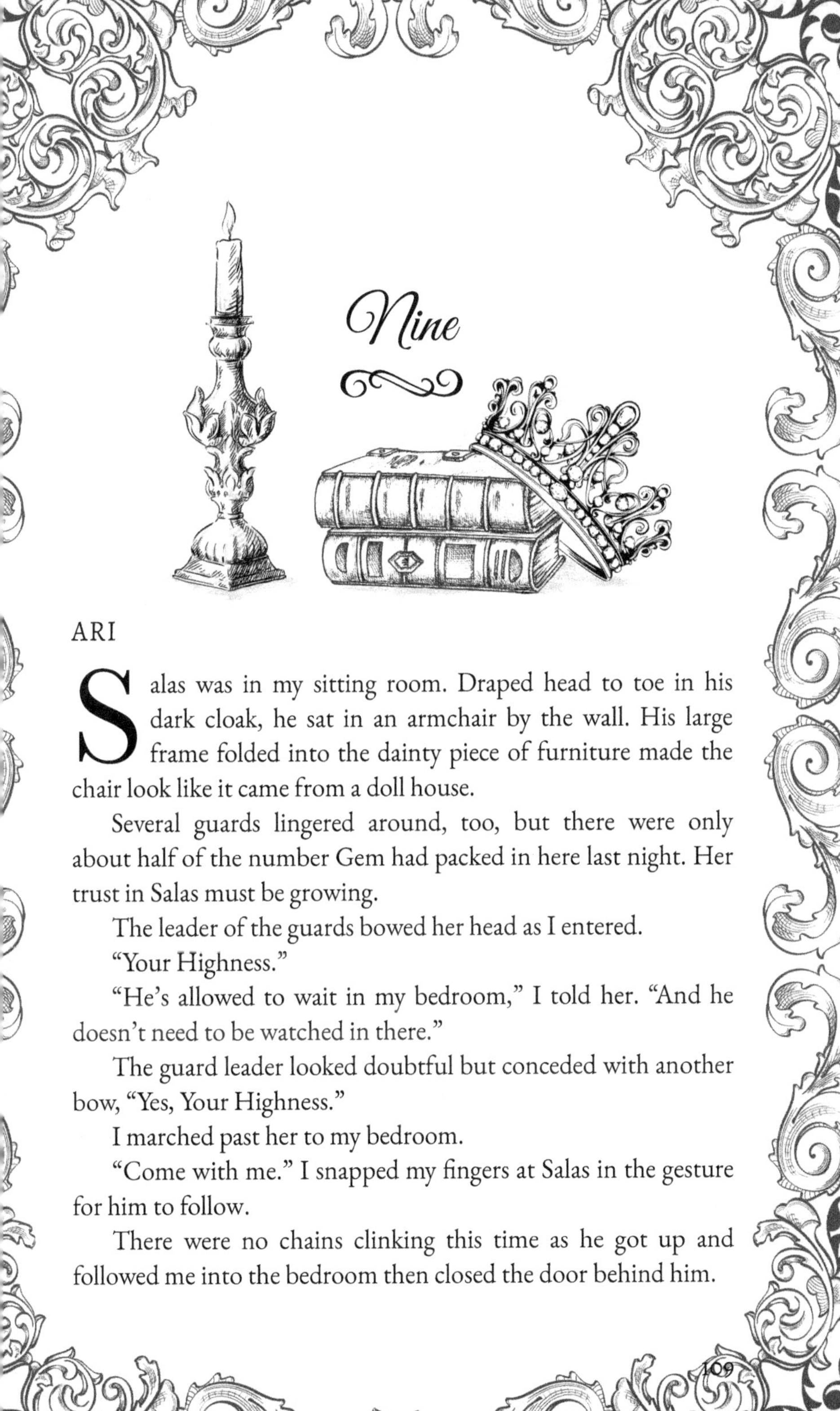

Nine

ARI

Salas was in my sitting room. Draped head to toe in his dark cloak, he sat in an armchair by the wall. His large frame folded into the dainty piece of furniture made the chair look like it came from a doll house.

Several guards lingered around, too, but there were only about half of the number Gem had packed in here last night. Her trust in Salas must be growing.

The leader of the guards bowed her head as I entered.

"Your Highness."

"He's allowed to wait in my bedroom," I told her. "And he doesn't need to be watched in there."

The guard leader looked doubtful but conceded with another bow, "Yes, Your Highness."

I marched past her to my bedroom.

"Come with me." I snapped my fingers at Salas in the gesture for him to follow.

There were no chains clinking this time as he got up and followed me into the bedroom then closed the door behind him.

I opened the patio doors wide. The evening air rushed in, and I breathed it deeply.

"You look very... regal tonight, Your Highness," Salas stated behind me.

I didn't want to act *regal*. I felt his presence with my skin. It was incredibly alluring, making me hate the distance between us.

"It's the dress." I turned around as he took off his cloak.

Faced with all his groomed and pampered glory, I drew in a shaky breath.

He studied my midnight blue evening gown stitched with golden skylines of Rorrim's major cities along the hem.

"The dress is spectacular," he agreed.

"Representing Rorrim in style in front of foreign dignitaries is a part of my duties." With my hands behind me, I fished for the ends of the ribbon that laced my tight bodice at the back. "Sadly, the more formal the outfit, the more uncomfortable it tends to be. This one is insanely tight and stiff."

"Allow me?" He came closer.

Instead of stepping behind me to find the ribbon, he brought his arms around me. Promptly finding the bow by touch, he untied it and loosened the ribbon, loop by loop.

His bare chest was right in front of me. I inhaled as deep as the tight dress allowed, stealing a lungful of his scent. He must've misinterpreted it as a sigh.

"A long evening?" he asked sympathetically.

"A formal dinner with an ambassador and about a hundred attendees."

"Sounds exhausting," he murmured into my hair. "Tired?"

"Not particularly. No." The rare, good sleep last night helped with keeping my energy up through the day. But it was nice of him to ask. "I got offered a husband." I smiled, turning my face up to his.

"A husband?"

"Yes. A very accomplished young gentleman, by the sound of it."

If I worried Salas might have any reservations or concerns about my future marriage plans, I didn't need to worry. He seemed completely unaffected, which helped me direct my emotions in a proper direction too.

Salas and I were two strangers from different walks of life. We only met because of a very specific situation, and we would part ways when it was over. In the end, Salas would get a new start a year sooner, and I'd be left with fond memories of him—the most pleasant memories of being with a man I'd have to date.

"Is he the one? Are you going to propose?" he asked, brushing a loose strand of my hair behind my ear.

Salas wasn't a hungry for gossip courtier. He didn't know which young gentleman I was referring to or even which one of the many foreign ambassadors currently stationed in Egami I'd dined with. Yet it never hurt to be cautious in matters of state importance. I didn't mention Prince Elbon's name, or country, or even his title.

"I haven't met the man yet. It's safe to say there will be more than one candidate. So, I've no plans to propose to anyone for now. Rest assured a public announcement will be made if I do."

"How long do we have?" he asked.

"For you to teach me everything you know about sex?"

"*Everything?*" He smirked. "That would take a very long time, Princess. We'll never finish the lessons before you need to claim your groom."

"Well, I'd like not to be a clueless virgin on my wedding night. How long will *that* take for you to accomplish?"

"Normally, just to get rid of virginity, one night would be more than enough. But with you..." He tugged on the lock of my hair he'd just put away and wound it around his finger instead, looking lost in thought. "Some things just can't be rushed. You need to be ready. Nothing good comes out of it otherwise."

Salas had a story. He clearly wasn't forthcoming in telling it, but I also wasn't sure anymore if I wanted to hear it.

How much did I need to know about the stranger who could

only stay in my life for a night or two? How deeply could I dive into his secrets before I risked starting to care and it would make it unbearably harder to part from him then?

No feelings involved. That had been Salas's one and only condition from the beginning. My mind agreed with him wholly. My heart, however, squeezed with subtle regret.

"I've been thinking about our kiss all day today," I confessed.

With a finger under my chin, he directed my face to his, his dark eyes flicking between mine.

"Is that a sign, Princess?" he asked softly.

I smiled, remembering his plea to give him a sign when I was ready for more. Hope pulsed in my heart, spreading through my body in a warm wave of desire.

"Will you kiss me again?"

The air moved as he shifted closer, the heat of his body enveloping me.

"You aren't the only one who's been thinking about that kiss all day," he murmured, before his lips touched mine.

My mind spun in a twister. I swayed forward, leaning onto him for support as my knees suddenly grew too weak for my legs to hold me.

He made a sound deep in his throat. Sliding a hand behind my neck, he sank his fingers into my hair, bringing me closer. I tilted my head back, parting my lips for him. His tongue found mine, robbing me of breath.

He pulled away way too soon.

Dazed, I brought a hand to my face where my skin glowed with warmth after being brushed by his beard.

"Now I felt it." I smiled. "Your beard."

"Sorry." He ran his thumb around the corner of my mouth. "I got carried away."

"This kiss was even better than the one last night, wasn't it?" Lightness elated me. Maybe it was from the wine I'd had earlier. But Salas was also to blame. His effect on me was stronger than that of any wine. Apprehension shifted far back, giving place to joy. "Admit it, I am a damn good kisser."

My head swam with giddiness. I gripped the ends of his robe to anchor myself from floating away into a happy cloud completely.

"Smart ass." He grinned.

"It's 'Princess' to you, sir." I tapped my finger against his wide, hard chest.

By etiquette, he really should address me as "Your Highness." But I liked hearing the careless "princess" from him too much to insist he follow the etiquette when we were alone.

"My apologies." He inclined his head, humor shimmering in his dark gaze. "Come here, *Princess* Smart Ass." Snaking an arm around my middle, he yanked me to him.

"How dare you?" I gasped in shock and pretend outrage. Him calling me names was a huge breach of propriety, but I was having too much fun to be angry for real.

He read me well, his moods matching mine perfectly.

"Tell me to stop, and I will. But if you don't, I'll take it as a sign you want me to go on." Gripping my hair in his other hand, he kissed me again.

I didn't stop him. I didn't want to. He stole my breath and all my words, and I didn't want any of that back as long as he just kept kissing me.

Letting go of my mouth, he trailed his kisses along my jawline, then down my neck, tugging at the bodice of my dress.

"I'm going to take this off you now," he warned, then ordered. "Arms up."

I obediently stretched both arms over my head for him to take the top of my two-piece gown off.

The bodice was ribbed, lined, and supportive enough to require no bra or undershirt. The moment he removed it, I crossed my arms over my chest to hide my naked breasts. He didn't seem to mind that, working on untying my skirts. Like everything before that, Salas did it with excellent skill.

After loosening the ties on my overskirt, the crinoline, and the underskirts, he shoved them all down to my knees. The voluminous layers puffed up around my legs like midnight-blue clouds of silk and tulle.

"Now hop out, Princess." He opened his arms for me.

"Really? Like this?" I jumped up, throwing my arms around his neck.

He lifted me out of the skirts easily, then carried me to the bed. I buried my face in his shoulder, loving a little too much how easily he carried me across the room, how strong his arms felt, and at the same time how gently he held me. He pressed his lips to my shoulder, the tickle of his beard keeping the smile on my face.

When he laid me down, I remembered that I had on only my short underwear and my kitten-heel sandals. I crossed my arms over my chest again as he carefully removed my heavy formal crown.

"Do you want your glasses on or off?" he asked.

The glasses were already kind of foggy from our mingled breath during the kissing. I also wasn't sure if I had to see every single detail of what was about to happen.

"Off, please," I said. I couldn't remove them myself with my hands shielding my breasts from view.

He took the delicate frame between his thick fingers and carefully took off my glasses. I closed my eyes as he did it. Then, I felt a light kiss on the tip of my nose and... froze.

This kiss was not necessary. It was a sign of affection. People kissed each other on their noses for fun because they liked each other. He didn't need to do it, but he did, as if he couldn't help it.

With my eyes tightly shut, I heard the sound of my eyeglasses being deposited onto the night table. Then Salas returned to kiss me where he was actually supposed to, first on my mouth, then on the side of my neck. His beard brushed my skin. I exhaled a laugh, but the sensation quickly turned from ticklish to tantalizing, sending tingles of excitement down my body.

This was new and different. Being this close to him still felt a little unnerving but with more thrill than fright now. When he slid a hand up my side, his thumb touched the underside of my breast, and I stiffened.

"Do you like this, Princess?" He nibbled on my neck gently. "Do you like it when I'm kissing you here?"

His questions distracted me from the position of his hand under my breast. A wave of warmth rushed down my body as my muscles relaxed. I stretched like a cat.

"Let me kiss more of you," he murmured against my collarbone. "Let me show you how good it can feel."

His hand skimmed down my hip, then around my back to cup my butt cheek. His thumb slipped up and under my underwear.

My breathing turned shallow. Sweat dampened the bedding under my spine. This was no longer new and exciting. His hands in my underwear brought an echo of something dreadfully familiar and highly unwelcome.

Sensing the tension gripping my muscles, he ran a soothing hand up and down my side. "It's all good, Princess. You're safe. Sex is supposed to be fun."

Supposed to. That was what they said. But now, the memories from that other world tried to creep into my awareness, soiling the light moment with darkness. Dread gripped my throat.

Salas gently traced the swell of my breast above my hand that I kept holding over it.

"How about you let me kiss just one for now?"

His voice, light and playful, bounced through the darkness like a ray of sunshine, and I followed it, letting it guide me back to him.

I even managed a smile. "You mean just one boob?"

"Hmh," he hummed, kissing my collarbone. "Just one. As a test. If you don't like it, you can hide it from me again. Which one are you willing to give up? Left or right? Which one is your least favorite?"

I snorted a laugh. It was brief and filled with nerves, but he managed to make me laugh in a situation that could wreck me with fear. I let my hand fall away from the breast closest to him.

"This one?" he purred, leaning closer. "Poor thing, why is it your least favorite when it's so gorgeous?"

He cupped the breast with a light squeeze, and I drew in a shuddering breath, struggling to keep it together.

"Not your hands, please. Just your mouth..." I begged. "Your kisses."

He paused, but only for a second. "Gladly."

His warm breath fanned over my skin before the tip of his tongue traced my areola. I tried to focus on my breathing, but all my senses quickly narrowed to that one warm, slick touch dancing on my breast.

Sparks of desire skittered through my chest, then rushed down to my lower belly. Arching my back, I pressed my breast into his mouth. He hummed approvingly, dragging his tongue over my nipple. It pebbled under his caress. Taking the tip into his mouth, he gently rolled it between his teeth.

Pleasure zigzagged with lust through my body, arousal pooling between my thighs. I bent my legs, digging my heels into the bedding.

Salas slid a hand down to my ankle and unbuckled the strap of my sandal, then took it off, and tossed it to the floor, all while sucking on my nipple. By touch only, he found my second sandal and disposed of it just as quickly.

Letting go of my breast for a moment, he lifted his head. "Will you trust me with your most favorite one now, Princess?"

A smile sprang to my lips. I removed my hand from my other breast, too, leaving it at his mercy.

He raked his gaze over it. "Just as beautiful as the first one. I have a really hard time choosing *my* favorite."

He grinned before sucking my other nipple into his mouth. Need pulsed between my legs. It thrilled me that I could finally feel it with someone else, not just when I was alone.

At the same time, the awareness of him held me back. A shiver of pleasure ran down my body, and I tensed, subconsciously trying to suppress it.

He caressed my side with his fingers, staying away from touching my breast, just like I'd asked him.

"Tell me, sweetheart," he coaxed, speaking with his face so close to my breast, his beard brushed over my erect nipple with every word. "What do you usually think about when you're touching yourself?"

"Who told you I do... that?" I wished so hard I could somehow stop myself from blushing. But the treacherous heat already flushed my face and neck.

"Don't you?" He kept stroking my side, slowly trailing his fingers along the curve of my hip then over my ribs.

A warm sensation spread through my entire body, making it hard to focus.

"Tell me your fantasy, Princess," he implored. "What do you think about when you come undone?"

What, not *who*.

He understood me enough to know there was no person I fantasized about, no man I wanted.

"A river..." I watched a beam of moonlight on the ceiling. The light undulated and ebbed in a slow dance, following the movement of the curtains in the breeze—like water in a slow stream. "Sometimes, I pretend I'm floating on my back in a warm, dark river." It wasn't easy to put into words the scenes conjured by my imagination, especially since they were mostly sensations, not images at all. "The stream caresses my body..."

"Like this?" He skimmed his hand down my side again, then over my belly and upper thigh. Pleasure rippled in the wake of his light touch.

"Yes," I exhaled. "Just like that... Hands then rise from the water. I can't see the people, and I don't care who they are. I just feel their hands. They're soft and gentle. And they are... everywhere."

His hands felt nothing like the apparitions from my fantasy.

His were wide and warm, with hard calluses that scraped my skin lightly. But their touch was as gentle as I needed. Releasing a breath, I relaxed.

"Just like that," he murmured approvingly before closing his mouth over my nipple again.

A glide of his tongue, followed by a slight press of his teeth, sent a spike of desire through my core. The throbbing between my legs ached, and I shifted my legs open.

He took it as an invitation. His hand promptly slid between my thighs. I gasped, momentarily mortified, but he quickly found the place where I wanted him so badly. A swell of pleasure flooded my body as he slowly circled my clit. My thighs trembled.

"Oh Goddess," I circled my hips, following the blissful sensation of his touch.

"Is it here where the river hands touch you in your fantasy, Princess?" Salas whispered between licks and nibbles to my nipple that sent steady bursts of arousal through my body.

How quickly he'd taken over my fantasy.

And how accurately he'd made it a reality.

"Yes, right there..." A wave of pleasure rolled through me, quickly followed by another one, longer and building up in intensity.

Salas's touch proved better than a million disembodied hands. He played my body with more skill than even my mind could direct it.

I whimpered, raising my hips into his caress.

"Harder?" He rubbed faster. "Do you want the hands to invade you, own you, rip you to pieces, then put you back together again? Do you want me to make you come, sweetheart?"

I trembled in need. My fingers fisted into the sheets, I thrust my hips into his touch.

"Salas... I..."

"I know, Princess." Kissing my breast, he set my orgasm free with his hand.

The explosion of pleasure rendered me speechless. I shut my

eyes, letting it take me. For a few blissful moments, the world fell away.

And when I opened my eyes, I found Salas watching me. A gentle smile played on his lips as his hand worked me, tenderly bringing me down from the height of climax. But despite his best effort, I didn't go down gently. I plummeted.

"Don't." I circled his wrist, yanking his hand off me.

The fog of lust evaporated. Reality rushed in, and it wasn't soft or sweet. Earlier, there had been something exciting about being at my most vulnerable with someone else in the room. Now, it felt more awkward than anything. I grabbed an edge of a blanket and pulled it over my naked body, shielding it from him.

This was the first time I'd orgasmed in someone else's presence.

Why didn't I feel elated like I did after our first kiss?

Maybe because he just watched instead of panting and sweating through his own orgasm with me? For a few moments, I lost control completely when he didn't. The feeling I had now was similar to if I were the only naked person in a crowd.

"Have the hands in the river pleased you?" He kissed my shoulder as I turned to my side, facing away from him.

Now, he also knew one of my fantasies that I had never shared with anyone before. I had opened a door for Salas that wasn't meant to be open for anyone, and there was no longer a way for me to close it.

He stroked my arm, and it took all I had not to shake his hand off me. It'd be petty and unfair to punish him for things he had no clue about.

It wasn't his fault that his mentioning of "hands" now brought forth the memories of many other hands that had touched me against my will. Rough, eager, unskilled hands that took without giving.

"Boys will be boys." It was always said with a smile to excuse even the most outrageous behavior as a "phase," a normal stage of growth.

The boys at my school always ran in packs, like hyenas. For fun. And for added courage during their attacks. They laughed like hyenas too. The sound cut my hearing, as if they were here. Or worse, as if I was suddenly transported back into the past, into the world I thought I'd left behind for good.

I pressed my hands over my ears to block the sound.

"Princess?" Salas's concerned voice reached me through the cacophony of noises in my head.

"I wasn't always a princess..." I exhaled a breath, the words trailing out of my mouth with it.

Were they loud enough for him to hear?

It didn't matter. I wasn't even sure if I kept on talking or if the memories just thundered through my brain, images morphing into words for the first time ever.

It happened practically over summer, when my body changed. I got my first period a few months earlier. I grew taller. Got boobs. It was all so new to me. My body didn't even feel like my own. In my mind, I was still the same kid I was last year, playing hopscotch and jumping rope. But they looked at me and saw someone else. Not even a someone. Just something. Something to grab and rub themselves against until they came.

I wasn't the only one. All girls had it happen to them. The teachers would yell at the boys if they got caught, but nothing was done to stop them from doing it again.

"Boys will be boys."

And the girls had to pay for that...

I didn't want to remember.

Nothing good came from those memories, only shame and disgust. But they barged in, unbidden.

They locked me in a janitor closet after school once. One of them stayed outside, letting the others come in and use me in any way they dared or knew how. A janitor, an old woman, yelled at them and threatened them with her broom, sending them scurrying away like cockroaches. I ran...

After that, I tried to be especially careful. I'd ask to use the bath-

room before the last bell rang at the end of the day, so I could run home while everyone else was still in class. I stayed away from dark hallways and ate my lunch sitting on the floor in front of the teachers' lounge. But they still caught me outside near the playground area that spring.

They ripped my dress and broke my bra. The one who did it fell backwards when the bra clasp snapped. I used the chance to run away.

Mama yelled at me for the ruined clothes and slapped me. The bra was a hand-me-down, the only one I had. There was no way my parents would buy me a new one. When I came to school without it the next day, they said I did it on purpose, that I liked being groped, that I was a whore.

That I was asking for it...

Repulsion ran through me in a shudder.

An arm hugged me gently. With his touch, the memories ebbed, and I gasped for air.

"Salas." I turned to face him, grateful for the lifeline of his hug that pulled my mind out of the past.

Did I voice any of those memories out loud? I wasn't sure. But he looked like he'd heard it all.

"It's been years..." I muttered. "Long ago. In another world. It doesn't matter anymore."

"If you want to talk more, I'll listen," he replied simply.

I shook my head.

"I don't want to talk. Don't want to remember. I left that world. I just wish it would leave me too."

He stroked my hair, gently easing the pins out of my up-do and dropping them on the nightstand.

"Sometimes talking helps. Even the darkest things are less scary if brought out into the light."

"Does it really help?" I asked. "Is that how you deal with your past? You talk about it?"

His hand stilled in my hair.

"No. I've had other ways to deal with it."

"And did they work?"

"My past has no hold on my thoughts anymore," he said with conviction.

If that indeed was the case, I envied him.

"Lucky you."

"Yes," he echoed. "Lucky."

I FELL asleep with my nose pressed to his chest and his arms wrapped tightly around me. The position was unusual for me, not even the most comfortable, but warm and safe. I used Salas's large body as a shield against the nightmares that threatened to spill from my memories into my dreams. And it worked. I got a few hours of uninterrupted, dream-free sleep and woke up to the sun already rising over the horizon.

He snored softly with his nose buried in my hair. When I moved my head, a deep rumble sounded inside his chest. He shifted closer, his hips hugging my thigh.

We shared a blanket this time. I'd never put a nightshirt on last night, and his sarong must've shifted during the night. As he leaned into me, I felt no barrier between his skin and mine. Hot, naked male body pressed against me, and one part of it felt considerably harder than the rest.

Alarm jolted me, shaking off the remnants of sleep. I slipped from under his arm, somehow managing not to fall off the bed in the process. I grabbed a nightshirt from the trunk at the foot of the bed and put it on belatedly.

Salas groaned softly, hugging my pillow instead of me. Sprawled like that, his massive body took more than half of my spacious bed. Yet he didn't look threatening. Almost a child-like serenity settled over his face. Mussed overnight, his hair fell over his forehead, and I resisted the urge to brush it away for him.

Tenderness warmed my chest. I realized I hadn't even fed him last night. Our dinner sat untouched on the table by the couch. The spreads and sauces might've gone bad overnight, but fruit should still be good.

With a platter of sliced oranges, grapes, and cut-up fresh pineapple, I padded back to the bed.

Salas stirred. His thick, dark eyelashes fluttered open. It took him a moment to gather his bearings as he stared at the silk pillow in his arms. Then he seemed to remember where he was.

"Morning, Princess." He grinned, falling back into the pillows.

I could get used to seeing this smile every morning, and I didn't think I'd ever grow tired of that greeting.

"Morning." I sat on the bed and placed the fruit platter on the blanket between us. "I should probably ring for a real breakfast, with coffee and stuff." I wondered why I hadn't done so already, but deep inside, I knew the reason.

Salas and I had no past and no future together. All we had was the present, so I tried to stretch every moment we had, trying to keep it free from any interruptions.

"It's early." Salas rubbed his eyes, hiding a yawn. "When do you usually get up?"

"Six. That's when the maids come to help me get dressed. But I'm often awake before that."

At least I woke up in time to have breakfast with my parents this morning.

I popped a grape into my mouth, then took a segment of peeled orange from the plate and offered it to Salas. Instead of taking it from me with his fingers, he lifted his head and took it from my hand with his lips, then tossed his head back onto the pillow, chewing with a blissful smile on his face.

"Am I to feed you now?" I narrowed my eyes at such audacity. His happy expression made it hard to be upset with him in earnest, however.

"Mhm," he hummed. "Spoil me, Princess."

Humor shone in his eyes. He squinted in the sunshine, rising on his elbow as I sat on my knees at his side. The shroud of his initial gloomy indifference had slid aside, allowing me to see the other side of Salas—the happy, easy-going side that loved fruit and sunshine.

Smiling, I picked up another piece of orange and brought it to his mouth. He took it from me again, lightly brushing his lips against the tips of my fingers.

"Good?" I asked, suddenly unable to tear my eyes away from his lips.

"Excellent." He grinned. "Best breakfast ever."

I ate another grape, then fed one to him.

Rising on his arm, he brought his face closer to mine.

"Why do you get up so early? You're a princess. You can sleep in whenever you want, can't you?"

"Well, I have a country to run. The queen has shifted many of her responsibilities to me over the years, getting me ready to accept the crown from her one day."

"Can't the country run on its own for a day? What's the worst that can happen?"

A lot of things could happen, some with potentially dire consequences for Rorrim. I had another council meeting this morning. Then, the head of the city guards was to deliver her report to the queen, for which I had to be present. The ambassador lunch came after that and another formal dinner tonight. My failure to meet with the foreign dignitaries could be taken as an insult to their queens, which in turn could lead to an international conflict.

I picked up another grape and brought it to his mouth again. Feeding him somehow proved more fun than eating myself. "My job comes with no days off."

"Then, you're long overdue for one." He accepted the grape. "Come on, Princess, spend the day with me—"

I stuffed a piece of pineapple into his mouth, cutting off his words of temptation, but that didn't stop me from feeling tempted. The prospect of spending an entire day with Salas, not caring about the time passing by, was too enticing to refuse outright.

We could talk all we wanted, eat breakfast, and laugh loudly the way I never dared in polite company. I had no idea what we could talk about the whole day.

Did we have enough in common to have a conversation that long?

I didn't know, but I wouldn't mind finding out.

I wouldn't be opposed to more kisses, either, and maybe to more of what he did to me last night.

"Sex was supposed to be enjoyable."

Finally, those words started making sense to me.

Holding my wrist, he casually licked the pineapple juice off my fingers. It seemed effortless, with not a drop of awkwardness or pretense, like we were long-term friends, comfortable in each other's company. I had no idea how he did it—whether he really felt this comfortable with me by now or he was just an excellent actor—but my own awkwardness had thinned too.

When he released my wrist, I moved my hand to his hair. The neat style the groomers had arranged it in yesterday had fallen apart during his sleep. His thick russet tresses with copper highlights were disheveled from sleep, making him look younger, even vulnerable, and truly adorable.

I ran a hand through his hair. "I should find you a hairbrush."

"I hate to say it, Princess, but you need one too." He flicked a long strand of my hair that hung over my face.

I giggled. The sound immediately shocked me into silence. I *never* giggled.

And suddenly I knew exactly what I wanted. I cupped his cheek, filling my palm with the slight prickle of his beard. With my other hand, I squeezed his shoulder. His body felt strong and solid under my palm. Reliable.

I shifted closer and kissed him.

He held still as I pressed my mouth to his. Tasting the pineapple on his breath, I licked the sweetness of the fruit from his lips, and he parted them for me in an invitation for more. It was like a dance, and I enjoyed learning every step of it.

My control slipping, I leaned harder against him, accidentally knocking him off balance and sending him back into the pillows while crashing on top of him with a laugh. My hand remained on his cheek, my fingers deep in his beard.

"Did I feel your beard this time?" I wondered. "I can't even tell." All I remembered of the kiss was my head spinning, the sweet taste of the pineapple, and a sudden wish for more.

He seemed to fight a smile, but it crinkled the skin at the corners of his eyes, sparks of humor dancing in his irises.

"You wish to feel my beard, Princess?"

Rising to me, he rubbed his cheek against mine. I laughed, falling backwards into the bed. We knocked over the plate with fruit, the grapes rolling everywhere.

"Now look what you've done," I squeezed out through laughter.

"Let's clean it up." He caught a grape and popped it into my mouth, then grabbed another one for himself.

I lay on my back, eating the grape and watching him. The sun shining through the patio doors behind Salas turned the ends of his hair into a copper halo around his head. The corners of his mouth lifted in a soft smile. The look in his eyes was light and easy. And I had a hard time reconciling this smiling, playful man with the one I'd seen tied to the gallows and whipped.

I cupped my cheek in some semi-conscious effort to preserve the prickly sensation of his beard pressed against it.

"Stay here today," I said, without giving myself a chance to overthink it. "I have two meetings, an ambassador lunch, and a large, formal dinner after. But I'll be back tonight. The maids will bring you breakfast and anything else you want. You can rest, have a bath, or take a nap. I can get them to bring you some books from the library. Uh... Can you read?" Literacy was not a given among the men of the lower class where many slaves tended to come from.

"I can read." He nodded. "But I won't stay."

"Don't you have a day off today? Since you spent the night with me?"

"I do. But I have plenty of things to do too."

"Like what?" I frowned, recognizing a lame excuse when I heard one.

"I just remembered that I need to tidy up my bunk in the barrack," he replied flatly. "And it's my turn to do the dishes after lunch."

"How exciting." I climbed from the bed and collected the plate with the remaining fruit.

"The life of a slave is filled with excitement," he deadpanned. "But I also remembered something that I should *never* forget, not even when your freckles manifest themselves so enticingly in the morning light."

"What did you remember?"

"That you are the crown princess, and I am who I am. You have dinners with ambassadors, and I have my contract with the slave owner. And so it will remain."

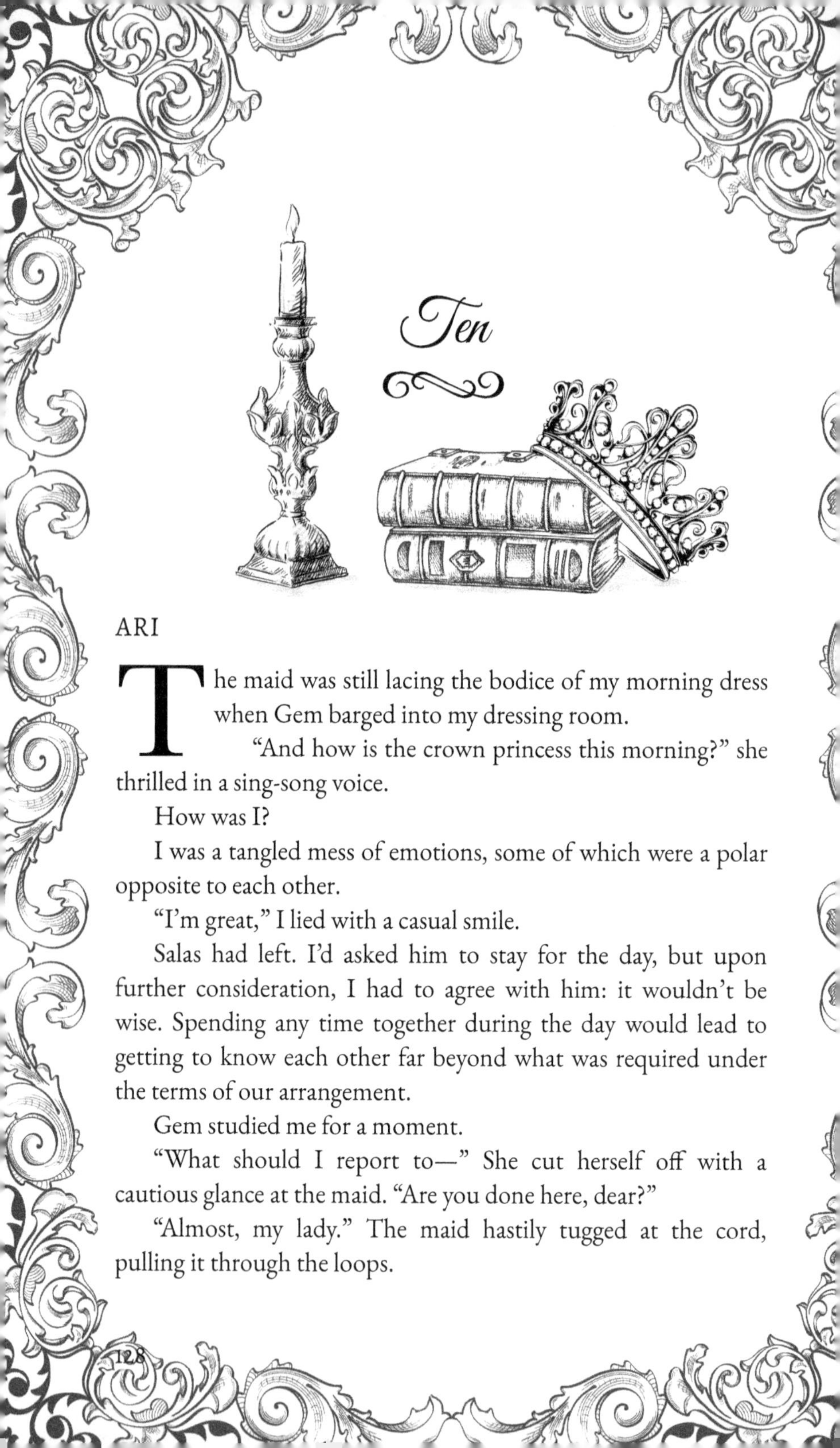

Ten

ARI

The maid was still lacing the bodice of my morning dress when Gem barged into my dressing room.

"And how is the crown princess this morning?" she thrilled in a sing-song voice.

How was I?

I was a tangled mess of emotions, some of which were a polar opposite to each other.

"I'm great," I lied with a casual smile.

Salas had left. I'd asked him to stay for the day, but upon further consideration, I had to agree with him: it wouldn't be wise. Spending any time together during the day would lead to getting to know each other far beyond what was required under the terms of our arrangement.

Gem studied me for a moment.

"What should I report to—" She cut herself off with a cautious glance at the maid. "Are you done here, dear?"

"Almost, my lady." The maid hastily tugged at the cord, pulling it through the loops.

I remembered how smoothly Salas had accomplished that process in reverse last night. He'd navigated through all my barriers with ease and achieved what no man had done before. He'd made me accept his touch. He'd made me enjoy and even crave it...

Oh, Goddess... I did crave it, I realized.

"Let me finish it." Gem sent the maid away and took over her task, lacing my dress for me. "The queen canceled your breakfast with her this morning. She's working in her study instead. But she's already asked me about how the things are going with your new 'mentor.'" Gem snorted a laugh. "Isn't it sweet she calls him that? I find it adorable how supportive the queen is of your rolling in the sheets with that slave. My mother used to scold me for bringing boys to my room. She worried they'd distract me from my studies. But then again, I was at least a decade younger than you when I started having an interest in boys. Mother must've thought they'd be all I'd ever care about." Gem yanked on the laces, tying them at my waist. "So, should I let the queen know your *mentor* has accomplished what he was hired for? It's been two nights already."

"Normally... one night would be more than enough. But with you..." Salas's words echoed in my mind.

For once, I was grateful for it taking longer. I wasn't ready to part from him yet.

I couldn't hide Salas from Gem, but I rigorously protected the feelings he'd caused in me. They pulsed warmly in my chest, like fragile saplings taking root, and I made sure not a single ray of their light shone through.

"No need." I kept my expression neutral, stepping out of Gem's reach the moment she was done with the dress. "I'll talk to Mother myself."

I found Queen Anna in her study, putting the final touches on her speech to the council. She raised her head from her work as I entered.

"Good morning, Ari dearest." She set her quill aside and

greeted me with a smile. "Is it true what they're telling me? Are things going well with your... um..."

I couldn't recall if I ever saw the queen so lost for words before.

"With my initiation into sex, you mean?" I finished for her, forcing her to blink uncomfortably. "Yes, Mother. It's going splendidly. I'll be ready to impart my new knowledge on my future husband in no time."

"Well," she cleared her throat, "that is very good to know."

I leaned forward, propping my hands on her dark cherry desk.

"I want to pay off my *mentor's* entire debt, Mother."

I wasn't sure exactly when the idea of Salas remaining a slave had become unacceptable for me, but simply shortening his contract no longer felt good enough. He had to be free. Immediately.

My demand surprised the queen. Her slim eyebrows moved closer in a frown of concentration, as she must be trying to find a reason behind my demand.

"No one should be a slave," I explained. "No matter how much money they owe."

Her expression hardened. She drew in a breath, leaning back in her high-backed, carved-oak chair.

"Are you planning to pay the debt of all slaves in Rorrim then? Because as the future ruler of the country, you can't favor any one person without considering the impact it would have on the rest."

I pushed away from her desk and crossed my arms over my chest.

"Not *every* slave was in my bed last night, Mother."

The political implications of my decision were the reason I came to speak with her in the first place. I knew what I had to do, but I needed to figure out the best way of doing it.

This time, the queen remained as calm as the surface of the pond in the royal gardens on a windless day.

"Our agreement with him stipulates the sum of one year, Ari. Why would you amend that?"

"One year is not enough. I don't want him to be a slave for even a day longer."

She folded her hands on the table. "And why is that? Do you feel remorseful about spending time with a man so much below you in station? Do you think elevating him would make you feel better?"

I groaned in frustration. How could such a highly intelligent woman like my mother get something so simple so very wrong.

"I don't want just to 'elevate him.' I want him—"

I realized I was going to say "happy."

After just two nights spent with Salas, I already cared about his happiness and wellbeing. Eventually, we'd part, and I'd never see him again. But I had to know that he was free and happy out there somewhere, living a life that he could never have if he remained property of the slave owner.

"I want him free," I said instead.

Mother studied my face. "It would take a considerable amount of money to buy his freedom, Ari."

"I know. I'll take it from my annual allowance, or I can sell some of my jewelry to bypass the necessity for council's approval." I could go without a few new dresses, and I certainly had enough diamond necklaces to last me a lifetime.

"You cannot keep a move like that from the council. It'd bring more harm if you're discovered hiding something like that from them."

"Then I will disclose my intentions at the next meeting."

"There is a strong chance they will not support it." Resting her elbows on the table, the queen pinched the bridge of her nose. "Either way, they will demand an explanation."

"I can explain—"

"How?" Mother pinned me with her stare. Her disappointment was almost palpable. It crushed my heart. "How can you possibly explain your sudden interest in this slave? How can you even admit it publicly, without inviting all kinds of questions and risking a slew of malicious rumors? Especially now, when we're facing dowry negotiations and every misstep on our part could mean a loss of valuable concessions?"

"So, having the man in my bed is not a problem. But buying his freedom is?"

"Exactly. It's perfectly acceptable for a young woman to gain some sexual experience before her marriage. Anything more than that, however, makes it look like favoritism. We don't want anyone to think you have taken a lover. Not while your marriage is being arranged and negotiated."

I huffed in frustration.

"I can fuck him, but I'm not allowed to care for him."

The queen flinched at my choice of words, but her voice remained steady when she explained, "The crown princess only cares for her country, her family, and her husband. In that exact order. Taking a lover at this time would indicate to the foreign powers that your interests lie elsewhere and that their union with us may lack commitment on our part."

"But I'm not taking a lover."

"Your action will be interpreted as if you were. Doing him favors of such magnitude implies it."

I scraped a hand down my face, disheartened but refusing to give up.

"I feel very strongly about this, Mother, enough to stand in front of the council and defend it until my voice is gone. However, if there is any other way to do it, I'll consider it."

Resting her elbows on the table, she placed her chin on her fingers laced together. "Tell me, daughter, why do you care about this slave?"

I wasn't supposed to care. I had every intention not to. But how could I send Salas to the back-breaking labor again and to any potential punishments with a whip now? How could I live, knowing what he would be going through daily for the next two years?

"He is a person, isn't he?" I said. "Born free, like all of us in Rorrim. Why is it so wrong of me to want to give him his freedom back?"

"Are you sure there is nothing more behind that wish of yours?" the queen probed.

"Yes, I'm sure. I've been perfectly aware of the purpose of our arrangement from the beginning. I've successfully avoided getting to know him more than necessary for that purpose. There is no attachment or any deep affection between us, if that's what you're implying. I am fully prepared to part from him for good. Rest assured, Mother, there is nothing 'more' that the crown should worry about."

"It's smart of you to remember that." Mother nodded. "But I didn't expect anything less than *smart* from my daughter."

"Mother, I'll never see him again. But he will be out there somewhere, living his life, and I want that life to be good."

Doubt crossed the queen's features.

"You do realize that freedom will not guarantee it for him? What made him a slave in the first place can very well bring him back to an owner again. Many slaves see their servitude as a solution, not a problem."

"I understand that. I know that I can't keep watching over him indefinitely or foresee all possible pitfalls in his future. Ultimately, Salas is not my responsibility. But there is one thing I can do for him right now, and I want to do it. I want to pay off his debt. All of it."

"I see." Cupping her chin, she seemed to consider it. "The request and the money will have to come from me," she finally said.

"From you?"

"Yes." She nodded firmly. "You've already argued on his behalf in front of the council once. Doing it again would definitely imply a connection between you and him. It is better if I champion his case instead of you this time."

Breath rushed out of me with relief.

"Will you, Mother? Really?"

"I can present buying out his freedom as a gesture of gratitude for 'mentoring' services rendered. There will be nothing personal behind us paying off his debts."

"Thank you." I pressed my hands to my chest.

She looked at me sternly.

"You will have to end all associations with this man in the future."

"That is the plan, Mother."

"Has our agreement with him been fulfilled?"

"Almost. I... I just need one more night."

Some things couldn't be rushed, like Salas said. One more night with him won't solve all my problems and magically erase all my inhibitions. I didn't believe it'd even bring me much closer to losing my virginity. But I wanted to at least say goodbye to him. I had to see him one more time.

"All right," Mother conceded. "Ask Gem to arrange it. But from then on, we shall focus on securing you the best marriage match possible. You don't need any complications that may potentially spoil things for you in that matter."

"I have no intentions of maintaining any kind of association with Salas in the future," I promised.

There simply was no form in which we could continue "associating" with each other. And once the work on the palace had been completed, the slave owner would move her group elsewhere. Realistically, there'd even be no chance for me to run into Salas ever again.

"Very well." Mother seemed satisfied with my reassurances. "Since I have you here this morning, why don't we go see your father?" She rose from her chair, putting away the speech she was working on. "I would like for you to see the portraits of the potential grooms we have selected and to hear your opinion about them. There is still some time before the council session."

This was not how I planned to spend this morning. But she

had just agreed to "champion" Salas's case for me, the least I could do was to look at those portraits.

"Alright. Let's go see Father. Where is he?"

"In his parlor, I assume."

Father's rooms occupied the gentleman's wing of the queen's palace. The front room of the wing served as his personal parlor where he received his gentlemen-in-waiting on the evenings when the queen was preoccupied elsewhere, and he was not required to accompany her.

Since Mother had canceled our breakfast, Father was spending the unexpected free time alone. We found him in his favorite reading spot in the window seat in his parlor.

He appeared flustered when we entered after only a brief knock on the door. Promptly getting off his seat, he shoved the book he was reading behind a dusty stack of volumes on duck husbandry and bird hunting. I glimpsed the title of the book he'd been reading. It was the eleventh volume of the complete political history of Rorrim Queendom. This type of reading material was considered too complex for a gentleman's brain and therefore not appropriate for men.

If Mother saw his book, she pretended she didn't.

"Good morning, darling." She placed a kiss on his cheek.

Father yanked the ends of his dressing robe closed over his modest potbelly. "Please forgive my appearance, Your Majesty. Had I known you'd visit, I would've taken care to dress appropriately this morning."

Mother waved him off gently. "You look lovely, dear, in whatever you wear."

"Morning, Father." Rising on my tiptoes, I kissed his cheek too, then adjusted the pompom of his sleeping cap over his shoulder. "You look great."

"Have you eaten yet?" Father fussed. "I shall ring for some breakfast."

He headed for the ribbon of the bell by the door.

"I have to be in a meeting soon," Mother declined.

"Maybe at least a cup of coffee with some morning bread?" Father remained hopeful.

She shook her head. "Sadly, no time to spare. I just had another item added to my already busy agenda this morning." She didn't look at me, but I knew she was referring to my request to buy Salas's freedom. "Actually, it may be good for Ari to skip the council session today if she wants to have coffee or tea with you later."

She seemed not to want me around when the council discussed Salas's case. Maybe she didn't trust me not to jump into the discussion and betray my "personal interest" in his fate.

"I'll gladly have breakfast with you, Father." I trusted Mother to fulfill her promise. If she believed it was best for me to stay away, I had no problem with complying.

The king rang the bell and sent a footman for some coffee, bread, jam, and cold cuts for us for later. Once that had been settled, he faced us with the brightest smile on his face.

"To what do I owe the pleasure of seeing my two favorite people here this morning?"

"Ari would like to see the princes, darling," Mother announced.

"Excellent," he exclaimed. "I'll get the portraits right away."

Out of his inner rooms, he brought a leather-bound case and placed it on the cigar display table.

Like most high-born gentlemen, Father didn't smoke. But a man of his standing was expected to own an expansive collection of cigars. It was believed that women appreciated a trace of tobacco in a male's scent but not the yellow teeth or foul breath that came from smoking it. As a result, many noble men carried a cigar in their breast pocket, regardless of whether they ever smoked one or not.

From the case, Father produced three frames and set them up on the table, propping them on their unfolding stands.

"Prince Nevar, Prince Leafar, and Prince Elbon, Your Highness." Father gestured at each picture gallantly as if introducing the actual live people to me.

"What do you think?" Mother looked at me expectantly.

What could I think?

The men in the pictures looked equally good. Each had a different color hair, eyes, and skin. Each styled his hair differently and wore the distinct clothing of his country. All looked like they had barely crossed from boyhood into adulthood. And none made my heart beat any faster.

"They're handsome." I nodded.

"Aren't they?" Mother agreed excitedly.

One of them would eventually become my husband. However, the warmest feeling I could imagine developing for either of them was something like an affection toward a younger brother, which would be fine if it wasn't for that pesky issue of procreation to continue the ruling line.

"They look so young," I added.

"Prince Elbon and Prince Nevar are eighteen," Father said. "Prince Leafar has just turned nineteen."

Mother brought her hands together, nodding with approval. "Just the right age for a man to get married."

"What makes it the right age?" I asked.

"They are in their prime time for procreation," Father explained. "Old enough to ensure healthy offspring, but not too old for their virtue to have been compromised."

"Men are lustful by nature," Mother commented with a sigh. "Parents of boys often face a real challenge when preserving their sons' purity. As the boys grow older, they're faced with more temptations. It's best to marry them off early, to give them the much-needed guidance and protection of a wife in a timely manner."

Father nodded as she spoke, agreeing with every word. "The families of all three princes vouch for their purity, of course."

"Of course," I echoed flatly.

I loved spending time with my parents. Right now, however, I would rather carry loads of bricks in the scorching heat outside than be here with them. The whole situation felt more uncomfortable than an ill-fitting shoe.

Now, they both stared at me expectantly, as if waiting for me to choose a husband right then and there.

When I said nothing, Mother gestured at the pictures.

"Trebor, why don't you tell Ari a little about each prince?"

"Of course, Your Majesty." Father stood behind the first picture, placing his hands on the frame. "Prince Elbon is the nephew of the Queen of Tresed Queendom."

"Right. He's the one with hounds and horses." I remembered the ambassador gushing about the prince.

Prince Elbon reminded me a little of the ambassador's husband. He had the same serene expression in his dark eyes, his mahogany-brown hair was also braided in neat rows close to his head, their ends hanging down to his shoulders.

"Yes. He is very passionate about both horses and hounds," Father confirmed.

"The ambassador has made it very clear that our treaty with Tresed Queendom would be renewed on extremely favorable terms were Prince Elbon to become your king consort, Ari," Mother said. "However, we need to keep in mind that he's only the queen's nephew. Her own son is too young for marriage, but it's safe to assume that the queen will ensure her son's dowry is much more generous when he's of age. That new union may weaken our standing with Tresed in the future."

"The other two princes are queen's sons, aren't they?" I knew enough about the current royal families to remember that.

"Yes." Mother pointed at the picture of a pale-faced young man with raven-black hair braided into a long plait. "Prince Nevar is the only son of the Queen of Western Islands." She then gestured at the picture of the blue-eyed man with his medium-length blond hair coiffured into a frame of curls around his youthful face. "Prince Leafar is the youngest and rumored favorite son of the Queen of Olakrez."

"Are they both into hounds and horses too?" I asked since it looked like some response was expected from me here.

"They are," Father chimed in. "Prince Leafar is an excellent rider. He participates in horse races and has been an undefeated champion in his country for the past two years."

"The prince has no shortage of marriage proposals," Mother added. "The queen has declined a number of them already, searching for a perfect match for him. However, I have it on good authority that our courting efforts will be favored by her."

"What is his mother offering as his dowry?" I asked.

Since the princes' appearance made no difference to me, I might as well use a more materialistic approach.

"As a part of his dowry, our peace treaty with Olakrez would be extended for one hundred years."

That made me pause. "One hundred years? Really?"

The last Rorrim war was with Olakrez. It lasted for several years and completely devastated the people of the disputed territories on both sides of the border. The historical accounts of the brutalities of that war were hard to read. I couldn't even imagine what it was like to live through them.

The peace treaty was several centuries old now, but it remained shaky and was renewed on a year-by-year basis, constantly hanging over our heads like a sword ready to drop. A guaranteed peace for an entire century would bring a lasting stability to the relationship between our queendoms.

"Mother, Father." I moved my eyes from her to him. "Prince Leafar it is, then."

"Splendid." Father clasped his hands together. "An excellent choice, dearest."

However, Mother's forehead furrowed with a deep wrinkle of concern.

"It's not a decision to be made lightly, Ari."

"I didn't make it lightly, Mother. I gave it some thought."

Granted, it was just a few moments of thought, but I didn't

believe it would make any difference if I took weeks or even months to decide.

My reassurance didn't seem to lift the queen's concerns.

"This will have an effect on the rest of your life, daughter," she said. "You need to consider the man, not just his dowry."

"But I've never met any of these men."

"True." Mother rubbed her chin. "I've been thinking about how to rectify that. I'm planning to invite delegations from each queendom for a friendly visit with games and tournaments for the princes to participate in."

"Do you think they will travel all this way just for a chance of my proposal? I can only marry one, the other two will have to return home empty handed."

"Ari, you are the most eligible bachelorette in the world right now. They'd be fools to turn down even the slightest chance to meet you and win your heart. I will put together a request to the council to come up with a program of the events and the budget. I'm sure the council will approve the visits. Everyone wants to see you happily married, and it takes more than a dowry to be happy. You'll have to meet the princes to see who you have the best connection with. Remember, he will be your spouse for the rest of your life. If you choose wrong, you'll have to deal with the consequences for as long as you live. The only thing worse than a demanding, capricious husband is an aggressive one with a bad temper." She curved her lips in distaste.

The one with a bad temper was the least desirable type of a husband.

A comparison nagged at me like a faint tapping from a distant past, striving to break through, until it finally jumped to the forefront of my mind. The way men sometimes were perceived as aggressive in Rorrim reminded me of how assertive women were quickly labeled as difficult in my old world.

For the first time in years, I allowed the memories of that world to enter my mind freely. I considered and analyzed them calmly, and it didn't destroy me.

A valet arrived with the breakfast Father had ordered.

Mother smoothed the skirts of her morning dress. "Well, it's been a delightful morning, my darlings. I hate to leave you, but I have a busy day ahead." She gave Father a parting peck on a cheek, then kissed my forehead. "We'll talk later, Ari. Matters like this shouldn't be rushed, despite how much you wish to settle down or how much I long for a granddaughter."

Father put away the portraits, and his valet served our coffee and tea on a low table by Father's favorite window seat.

"Would you like to see the dogs now, my king?" the valet inquired.

Father's eyes lit up. "Yes, please. Bring them in." He then turned to me. "I hope you don't mind them being here, sweetie."

"Not at all." I shook my head. "Could you please bring Ria too?"

While Ria's parents dozed on the velvet cushions at Father's feet, the puppy played with a stuffed squirrel. She growled, attacking it, which made me laugh.

"She's quite a vicious one."

"Lapdogs often are." Father smiled, drinking his tea. "It's good that they're small or they'd be too dangerous to keep as pets."

I draped a thin slice of a cured ham over a toast, then moved it around my plate absentmindedly.

The king gave me a close look before setting his cup down. "Are you nervous about the upcoming nuptials, Ari?"

"Not exactly nervous, just... apprehensive a little," I admitted. "I wish there was a way to postpone this whole thing."

"Well, the wedding isn't going to happen tomorrow. These things take time, hopefully enough time for you to get used to the idea."

"Hopefully," I exhaled. "Were you nervous when marrying Mother?"

His smile softened. "I was. But mostly I remember feeling excited. A woman may see marriage as an added responsibility.

Some view it as an obligation or even a trap. But for a man, it's the most important event in his life. I'd been preparing for the role of a groom my entire life. It was exhilarating to have it finally happen." He laughed quietly. "I was too excited to eat anything that morning and nearly passed out at the altar. Your mother held my hands and yanked them when I swayed backwards. I believe I would've fallen if it wasn't for her."

The many years of difference in their age had been smoothed out with time. The shared experiences during their long marriage undoubtedly brought them closer too.

"I hope my marriage is like yours, that my husband and I will become good friends."

He nodded, picking up his cup again. "I got very lucky with your mother as my wife. She is exceptional both as a queen and a woman. She's been caring and respectful toward me, which as you may know is not always a given in a marriage." He reached over to cover my hand with his. "You may or may not love your future husband, Ari, but please be kind to him. Remember he will have left his home and his family to be with you. Physical attraction is often flitting, but mutual respect provides a solid foundation for any union." He chewed on his lip as if carefully considering the subject he was about to breach. "Your mother never kept lovers, Ari, which is highly unusual for a queen, especially one who has tried and failed to conceive an heiress. No other man has ever caught her attention after our marriage, and I'm eternally grateful to her for that." He petted my hand before letting go of it. "If you show respect to your future husband, he'll pay you back in loyalty and devotion. Then the two of you can get through anything in life."

I ate my sandwich, slowly churning Father's words over in my head. I was sure he meant to support and encourage me, but his words failed to spark even the slightest enthusiasm in me for this wedding. Maybe Mother was right, and meeting my future husband would help.

"How many times did you get to see Mother before your wedding?" I asked.

"A few. Briefly. The longest one was when we danced at the ball that her mother, the late queen, gave in honor of my arrival from Olakrez. I think I left a good impression on your mother. She kissed me after the ball. That was our first kiss."

"Maybe if people were allowed to court for longer, to get to know each other a little better, it would be easier?"

He looked doubtful. "Courting is difficult between royals. It's hard to meet while living in different countries."

"How does it happen between people who aren't royals and when there are no treaties to worry about?"

"A dowry is always a consideration, regardless of one's social standing," Father explained. "But usually, a woman interested in a man can visit his family home and meet him before proposing. The meeting happens with a chaperone present, of course. Usually, that would be an older family member or the boy's tutor, depending on the future groom's age. The bride would bring gifts and have a conversation with her chosen one."

"What kind of gifts?"

"That very much depends on the woman's station and level of income as well as her desire to impress the man and his family. Not that you have to worry about any of that, dearest. We already arranged to send a prized stallion and a master-crafted sword to each of your potential grooms."

"Thanks. But what if I had to do it myself, what could I give as a gift?"

He tapped on his chin, considering his answer. "Weapons, hounds, or horses are always good choices. Once the couple is officially engaged and know each other better, the gifts can be a little more intimate. Like a piece of manly jewelry, a fashionable cravat, or a nice shirt."

In all my life I hadn't yet met a man whom I could personally gift a horse or a cravat. But a shirt? Salas would wear a shirt.

The thought hit me like a cannonball. Why did I think about Salas all of a sudden? Probably because he was the only man I'd had any kind of a relationship with, as brief and superficial as it was meant to be.

"Are you alright, Ari?" Father's concerned voice reached me. "You look rather pale. Is there something in the food? This bread seems a little stale, doesn't it? I don't think it was freshly baked this morning."

"No. The bread is good. I'm fine. Just a bit..."

"Probably nervous after all, aren't you?" he asked sympathetically. "Some fresh air should do you good. Shall we take the puppies for a walk? Or better yet," his voice lifted, "how about we go to the city? It's a market day, and I could use a new pair of gloves. What do you say? If you take me, I can leave my usual escort of gentlemen-in-waiting behind. It'd be just you and me."

There was no time for a trip to the market. Even without the council meeting this morning, I still had a long list of things to attend today. But he looked at me with so much hope and excitement, it hurt to upset him.

"Sorry, I can't do it today, Father. But I promise to make time for the next market day."

"Will you?" He grinned before placing a loud smooch on my cheek. "I can't wait. But I'll try to be patient."

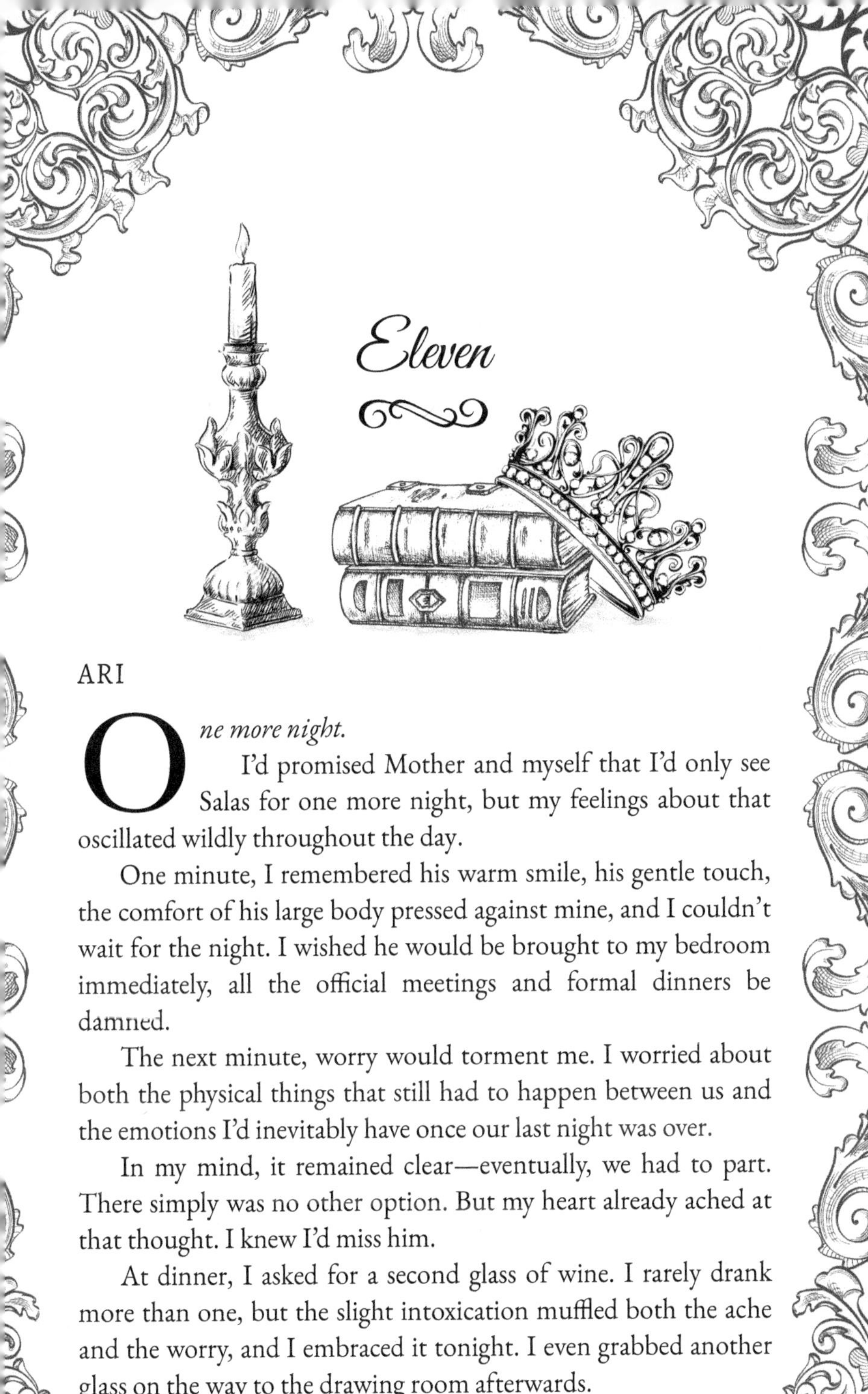

Eleven

ARI

One more night.

I'd promised Mother and myself that I'd only see Salas for one more night, but my feelings about that oscillated wildly throughout the day.

One minute, I remembered his warm smile, his gentle touch, the comfort of his large body pressed against mine, and I couldn't wait for the night. I wished he would be brought to my bedroom immediately, all the official meetings and formal dinners be damned.

The next minute, worry would torment me. I worried about both the physical things that still had to happen between us and the emotions I'd inevitably have once our last night was over.

In my mind, it remained clear—eventually, we had to part. There simply was no other option. But my heart already ached at that thought. I knew I'd miss him.

At dinner, I asked for a second glass of wine. I rarely drank more than one, but the slight intoxication muffled both the ache and the worry, and I embraced it tonight. I even grabbed another glass on the way to the drawing room afterwards.

Sipping my wine, I feigned interest in the conversation with two councilors who argued about the historical origins of the legislation titled Amendment to Guardianship. Furtively, I kept glancing at the doors of the room, waiting for Gem to arrive.

As she entered, she moved her gaze across the room and nodded slightly when finding me. That was a confirmation I'd been waiting for. Salas was here, in the palace.

My heart made a somersault, giving my mind a spin. I turned to the councilors, trying to keep my voice steady.

"The Amendment to Guardianship was signed into law by Queen Elle, Queen Anna's great-great-grandmother," I said to put their argument to rest. "Before then, it was only a tradition. The necessity for the legislation came after one of Lady Ecila's tenants passed away, and her widower argued that he should be granted the guardianship of his daughter until she came of age to take over the lease of the land. The queen ruled that in line with our long-standing Succession Law, the guardianship should be granted to the closest female relative, not the father, which then went to the girl's aunt. Now if you excuse me, ladies..." I gulped the rest of my wine, then placed the empty glass on the tray of the maid who happened to be passing by and headed for the door.

Taking a detour by the liquor stand, I grabbed an open bottle of wine and left the room.

SALAS WASN'T in my sitting room. Only the guards lingered around in their usual places. Their leader greeted me, "Your Highness."

"Where is he?" I clutched the wine bottle in my hand as if holding on to a lifeline in a storming ocean.

"In the bedroom, as you requested." The leader gestured at the door.

"Right. Thanks." I took a swig from the bottle before pushing the door open.

Salas crouched by the table in front of the couch, assembling sandwiches from bread and cold cuts. The tea light was already burning bright under the teapot, with two cups waiting on their saucers.

"Good evening, Princess." He beamed, turning to me. "Tea is almost ready."

Longing tightened in my chest, as if my heart was squeezed by a gentle hand wearing a soft velvet glove. The tension of the day with all its worries drained from me, banished by Salas's radiant smile.

The desire to come to him like this every night rushed me. For a moment, I believed I'd give everything just for him to wait for me here tomorrow and every day thereafter. But it was the one thing I could never have.

The longing in my chest changed from soft and warm to hard and hurting. I swung the bottle up to my mouth again, hoping for the fog of intoxication to muffle the pain.

Salas followed the bottle with his eyes, then got up from his crouch.

"How much of that have you had, Princess?"

I loved it when he called me princess. It sounded casual and friendly coming from him. Right now, however, he sounded unimpressed.

"Why do you need to know?" I licked my lips and shifted my weight to my other foot, swaying off balance a bit in the process.

He frowned.

"Just trying to gauge how long it'll be until I'll have to hold back your diamonds while you puke." He tipped his chin at my dangling earrings that almost touched my shoulders and the several long strands of precious gemstones around my neck.

"Ah." I plopped the bottle on a nearby stand, managing not to tip it over. "Don't worry." I took off the necklace, then slipped the earrings out of my ears and dropped them all on the stand next to the bottle. "See? No diamonds. No problems."

I grabbed the bottle again, but he sauntered to me and intercepted my wrist on the way to my mouth.

"Why do you need this, Princess? Are you nervous? Scared? Is it because of me?"

Unnerved by his probing look, I closed my eyes. The air around us permeated with the scent of the fragrant oils that had been rubbed on his skin. But with the desperation of an addict, I searched for his own scent underneath.

I'd seen first-hand what an addiction looked like. I knew what it did to people, turning them first into raging monsters, then into trembling shadows, before slowly killing them in terrible ways. I knew it could start from just one use, so I hadn't touched any drugs and never drank hard liquor. Yet I had no willpower to resist Salas. One kiss had proven enough for me to crave more of him to the point of insanity.

His hand remained wrapped around my wrist, and I made no attempt to free it.

"*Everything* is because of you, Salas," I muttered. Keeping my eyes closed made it easier to speak the truth. "What if *you* could be my everything?" I exhaled a bitter laugh, opening my eyes again. "Wouldn't that be something?"

It might've been just a play of shadows and moonlight, but I glimpsed the reflection of my own longing in his eyes. I blinked, and it was gone.

His frown deepened. He took the bottle from me and lifted it to the light, inspecting the contents that now barely reached the half mark.

"In my defense, the bottle was open when I took it. I didn't drink it all," I assured him.

"You've drunk enough."

"Are you scolding me? Even my mother doesn't do that anymore."

He lowered the bottle. "I'm not going to tell you what to do,

Princess. But if you intend to get piss drunk, nothing will happen between us tonight."

"Is that a threat?" I huffed.

"A warning. I avoid having sex with drunk women whenever I can."

"And why is that?"

"Several reasons. Alcohol often muffles sensations, including pleasure. When drunk, you may not feel things as acutely as I wish for you to feel them. If you pass out and don't remember in the morning the pleasure you had at night, then what's the point of it all? But most importantly, people often see things differently when they're drunk than when they're sober. What you think you want while you're intoxicated may be something you'll loath the next day."

"Or maybe I'll just *think* I should loath it?" I challenged. "Alcohol lowers our inhibitions and lets us finally have what we crave."

He raised his hand, as if to caress my face, but then dropped it without touching me.

"Either way," he said softly, "I don't want you to forget or regret a single moment spent with me."

Staying away from him grew unbearable. I stepped closer, resting a hand on his chest.

"How could I ever regret *you?*"

I should tell him this was our last night, but just thinking about that hurt. I should tell him that the Queen of Rorrim was personally pursuing a full buy-out of his contract, but I feared he'd think I fished for his gratitude. I didn't wish to bring the business of the day into our one last night together.

All I wanted was for him to kiss me again.

I rose to my tiptoes, lifting my face to his, and he took what I offered. His mouth claimed mine. His arms wrapped me into a tight hug. His body pressed against me.

I was exactly where I wished to be.

With a soft groan, he broke the kiss and rested his forehead against mine. I tangled my fingers in his hair, perfectly content to stay like that for the rest of the night if he so wished or for the rest of my life if Goddess let me.

Sadly, he unwrapped his arms from around me. With a long breath in, he stepped away, then grabbed a teacup from the table and a wine glass from the small curio cabinet in the corner.

"You want me to drink from a glass like a lady?" I smiled.

"No." He handed me the cup of tea. "This is all you'll drink for the rest of the night."

"Just tea?"

"Like I said, nothing will happen if you're drunk."

"But I'm not drunk."

"Good. Let's keep it that way." He tapped a finger against my teacup to emphasize his point. "We have unfinished business, Princess, and I really hope we'll do more than just kissing before the sun is up."

I brought the cup to my mouth and took a sip of tea to mask a shiver of apprehension... or was it anticipation that ran through my body? "Who is the glass for, then?"

"The glass is for me."

He placed it on the stand, then took a linen napkin from the tea tray, folded it, and wrapped it around the neck of the bottle before pouring the wine with an elegant flip at his wrist.

"You've done this before," I said, watching him.

"Once or twice," he admitted before lifting the glass. "To you, Your Highness."

"To our three-night stand," I added.

He shrugged. "As good a toast as any."

Bringing the glass to his lips, he took a long breath in, inhaling the aroma of the wine, then closed his eyes while taking a drink. He savored the scent and the taste like someone who knew how to appreciate both.

Salas served tea and poured wine with the skill that, I'd bet my crown, he didn't acquire while carrying bricks.

The royal palace served fine, expensive wine, and Salas

appeared to enjoy it. I waited for him to drink more, to empty his glass, and to refill it after. But he set it down on the stand after just one sip and moved away, seemingly uninterested.

"Dinner, Princess?" He gestured at the table.

I followed him, sitting down on the couch as he took the same place he'd had the first night—on the floor at my feet.

"Are you hungry?" I asked.

"No. I've eaten."

"What did you eat?"

He arched an eyebrow at my question, as if surprised by my interest in his persona. "Potato stew."

"How about some maple-cured red fish or smoked doe cheese?" I lifted a plate with the delicacies.

"Thanks, but I'm good." He took the plate from me and put it back on the table, closer to me than to him.

I had a feeling he could eat more despite the potato stew he'd had for dinner, just like he could've drunk more wine, or like he could've kissed me until we both panted for breath. But he seemed to hold back on everything, as if afraid to indulge before he had to give it all up and return to his life of a slave.

He interrupted my thoughts by placing a hand on my knee. "Tell me, Princess, did you think about me today?"

"Did I?" I replied with a nervous laugh.

Had there been a minute when I did *not* think about Salas? Since the first moment I saw him, this man had occupied my thoughts for one reason or another pretty much permanently.

From his easy tone, I understood Salas wasn't expecting that kind of confession. He was just trying to get me in the right mood by flirting a little.

"Yes," I said simply. "I did think about you."

He rose on his knees, positioning himself between my legs.

"When did you do it? In a meeting? During dinner?" His voice dropped a notch.

"Both," I replied honestly.

He slid his hands up my thighs. "And what exactly did you think about?"

I'd thought about how to grant him his freedom, about how hard it'd be for me to part from him, and about how I would have to go on without seeing him again. I'd also fantasized about having his hands on me again. But I chose to mention only the last part to him now because I sensed that was what he wanted to hear.

"I thought about all the best parts of our last time together. Like your kisses..."

"Hmm, you like those, don't you," he hummed confidently.

"I do."

He leaned toward me, and I met him halfway, eager to feel his mouth on mine. His kiss was gentle and sweet. The glide of his lips against mine remained measured and carefully controlled. Once again, Salas was holding back. Or maybe he was pacing himself?

My glasses fogged from our mingled breath, and I took them off. From this close, I didn't need them to see him.

"This is a gorgeous dress, Your Highness." He moved his hands up my sides, gliding them over the ivory silk of my evening gown—an A-line dress with long diaphanous scarves for sleeves. "But I'd like to take it off now."

"Do it, then." I arched my spine to give him access to the buttons on the back of the bodice.

"Way too many buttons," he complained, even as his thick, calloused fingers did a quick job of undoing the tiny pearls.

"When did you learn to remove women's clothes so quickly?" I quipped, but immediately added, "Actually, don't tell me. I don't want to know anything about your past lovers."

"I don't want to talk about them either," he echoed, promptly distracting me with more kisses to the side of my neck. "I just want to keep kissing you. Here." He pressed his lips to my collarbone. "And here." He caressed my shoulder, sliding down the fabric of my dress. "And here." He kissed the top of my breast, tugging the dress down.

My breathing turned shallow. Remnants of the past fears fluttered along the fringes of my awareness like ripples of shadows. But when Salas slid a hand inside my dress and cupped my breast, the only memories that came to mind were those of him touching me before. The gentle sensation of his hands on me had replaced any unwanted touch of others imprinted on my body.

I relaxed into his caress. He tugged my dress further down, and I freed my both arms, allowing him to push the bodice down to my waist.

He kissed the tips of my breasts, then sucked a nipple into his mouth, rolling the hardened bud between his teeth gently. Desire coursed through my veins, heating my blood. With it, a lick of darkness seeped through from my past.

I tensed, but Salas kissed my lips again and whispered sweet nothings into my ear until the shadows receded and all that remained was him, the calm night, and the moonlight.

"Let me kiss you everywhere, sweetheart," he murmured, pushing my skirt up and into my lap.

Everywhere.

His breath warmed my skin as he kissed down my body. He hooked his fingers under the waistband of my underwear, and I lifted my hips, letting him take it off.

Anticipation pulsed through me with an anxious beat. He must've sensed the tension gripping me all over again.

"You're in control, Princess," he assured me. "Remember, you can stop me anytime."

He kissed between my breasts, then down my stomach. Dipping his head lower, he pressed a kiss to my inner thigh. Heat rushed through my chest and pooled in my lower belly. At the same time, my back stiffened, and my legs strained, as if ready to bolt.

To run...

That was how I'd survived. By always running.

Memories fought to break through once again, but I pushed them away. This was Salas. He didn't belong to my past. He was here. Now. His touch was unlike anything else. Gentle and skilled, it was meant to bring me nothing but pleasure.

Sliding his hands up my thighs, he parted them. His thumb stroked me lightly, like a caress of a butterfly wing. I sucked in a breath as my inner muscles flexed, sending a rush of heat and pleasure through my core.

Circling my right ankle with his fingers, he placed my left foot on his shoulder.

"Let me kiss you here, my sweet Princess…" He lowered his head between my thighs, then glanced up before going any further.

I stared at him, wide-eyed, torn between thrill and terror.

"It's just me, Ari. You can trust me to make you feel good." He gave me a kind smile, and my heart melted.

"I'm glad it's you, Salas." I nodded. "I trust you." I lifted my right leg over his other shoulders, parting my legs wider for him.

Sweet, achy pleasure spread through my body as he flicked his tongue against me. My arms jerked. I wished to wrap them around him, to hold him to me, to fist my hands into his hair. But I clutched my skirts instead. I feared that too many sensations would overwhelm me. Too much of Salas would consume me, and I'd never want to let go of him ever again.

Tossing my head back, I closed my eyes and focused on his tongue and the sensations he created with it in my body.

He started so slowly and gently, I could barely feel his touch. The teasing grew more tantalizing, making me moan and squirm. When I thought I couldn't take it anymore, he pressed harder, even nibbling lightly.

I pushed my feet into his shoulders, lifting my hips toward him. He gripped my thighs, working me harder still, and I had no choice but to let go.

An orgasm rocked me. I gasped for air, feeling like I was falling, further and further down into a whirlpool of never-ending pleasure.

I couldn't stand the intensity. It pressed on my chest. My eyes prickled with tears.

Maybe it was the wine, after all. Maybe the stress of the day had caught up with me. Or maybe knowing that I'd have to say goodbye to him in the morning devastated me more than I dared to admit.

Pleasure broke the gates of my composure, and when it ebbed, sorrow flooded me instead. I jerked my feet from his shoulders and closed my legs.

"What's wrong?" His deep drawl vibrated with worry as he reached for me. "Ari, sweetheart, what happened?"

He used my nickname that he'd probably overheard from Gem and thought it'd help to calm me. Climbing onto the couch, he dragged me onto his lap. I wanted to melt into his body and soak up every drop of comfort his closeness often gave me, but something prodded against my thigh. Hard and persistent. His erection.

I went stiff. My muscles locked so hard it hurt.

"Calm, Ari..." He stroked down my arm. "Relax..."

"Relax and enjoy." The words echoed in my mind, triggering the memories I did not want to revisit. But with my defenses down, I could no longer hold them back. I couldn't fight the darkness.

"If it happens, just lay back and enjoy."

The words boomed through my brain like an explosion, flooding my mind with shame and horror.

"No." I scrambled off his lap and crawled to the opposite end of the couch. "Don't touch me. Don't... Please."

He sat back, lifting his hands up, his palms facing me, as if to show he meant no harm. I knew he didn't. Yet I could no longer breathe with him in the room.

"Ari?" He stared at me in shock. "Did I do something wrong?"

"Not you, Salas. But everyone who's come before you."

I curled into myself. Tears welled in my eyes. I dreaded them spilling over. Hugging my arms, I tried in vain to hold on to my composure, hating to break down in front of him.

"Come here," he pleaded. "Tell me what I can do to make it better?"

I trembled, torn between the need for comfort he offered and the instinct to run.

Run.

Always running. That was how I'd survived. Until I had nowhere to run anymore.

His erection pushed against the thin material of his sarong. He traced my terrified stare to it.

"Don't worry about it," he said firmly. "It's just a physical reaction of my body. I can't control it. But I *can* control my actions. Nothing will happen unless you want it."

His crestfallen expression devastated me. Salas had been kind to me. Patient and gentle. He'd done nothing wrong. I hated for him to blame himself for my past.

I wished to explain it to him, but I wasn't sure how.

"You wanted to know how far I've come with a man..." I cleared my throat, struggling to put into words what I'd been trying so hard to forget. "I was thirteen. I ran away from the village where I was born. You see... My parents, the people who gave birth to me, drank a lot. They fought. My dad killed my mom, then tried to sell me to feed his addiction."

The shock on Salas's face should've stopped me, but I'd finally found the words for things I never spoke about, and it was impossible to hold them back now.

"I escaped and ran to the city."

There wouldn't have been a happy ending to my story if it wasn't for Queen Anna, I firmly believed that. Happiness had stayed away from me, even as I'd searched for it with the desperation of a woman obsessed.

How naïve I'd been, thinking that life in the city would be better. Many changes had happened in the country at that time, and changes always meant someone came up on top and someone was left behind, unable to adapt. Desperation reigned among those on the very bottom.

"I had no place to go and ended up sleeping in an alley," I recalled. "I had no money. During the day, I wandered the streets in search of something to eat. Grocery stores were harder to steal from. But in the open market, some merchants could beat people to death for shoplifting. Exhausted, I fell asleep on a park bench the first night, only to wake up a little while later to someone trying to climb on top of me while shoving his hands in my pants. I kicked him off me and ran, then hid in an alley behind a dumpster. I slept with one eye open, in a constant state of readiness to either fight or run."

Dark shapes emerging from the street, like shadows peeling from the night...

I closed my eyes, but it proved harder that way. Seeing Salas's face gave me strength to continue.

"A group of men found me. Someone always found me, no matter how much I tried to hide. They said it was their territory where I hid. They said I had to pay them for sleeping there. They beat me. Broke my ribs and twisted my arm..."

The pain had been excruciating. But blinding, paralyzing fear had dowsed the pain.

"I don't know how many there were, but..." I drew in a breath, resolved to finish telling him what I'd started. "They were all going to rape me. I cried. I said I was only thirteen. That I had no parents or anyone to take care of me. No home. Their leader said they'd let me be if I... sucked him off every time he came by. He put a gun to my head..."

In his mind, the thug must've felt good about himself, noble even, offering me his protection in exchange for blow jobs. It was a shitty choice. But it was the only choice I had.

"I did it, Salas…"

I had not recalled this part in any detail since the night it happened and now, the disgusting images flooded my mind like filth from a backed-up sewer.

Their leader gripped my hair and fucked my mouth until I gagged. Thankfully, he finished before I got sick. Otherwise, I believed he would've shot me. I threw up on the pavement right after. They laughed. That was when the *melicia* showed up.

The local *melicia* conducted raids every now and then. They made it look like they were "cleaning the scum from the city." But what they really did was collect bribes. Those who could pay them off were left alone to do as they pleased. When the sirens of their cars blared, everyone ran, and that was the only time when I did not.

"When the city *melicia* showed up right after," I said, "I walked out of that alley and let them arrest me. I figured jail couldn't be worse than living on the street. When the authorities learned how young I was, they sent me to an orphanage." I cleared my throat again. It felt dry like sandpaper and tight, so tight, I could barely breathe. "And that was my closest experience to having sex with a man, Salas…"

He looked at me, but I wasn't sure what he saw. The expression on his face was as if a bomb had just exploded around us, rearranging our surroundings, and he was still trying to figure out where all the pieces had fallen.

"Ari." He reached for me.

My foot on the couch was the closest part of my body to him. I yanked it away, tucking both my legs under me. His hand ended up landing on the satin upholstery of the seat.

"Ari?"

Ari was a princess. She was confident, powerful, and brave. But she wasn't me. She couldn't be. Because I felt scared, lost, and helpless all over again.

"My name is Ira," I told him.

"Ira is her name. Ira, Irina," Dad's raspy voice shook with need and desperation, sounding as real as on that night.

Everything I'd tried so hard to leave behind followed me into this world where I'd thought I'd be safe.

"Ira was what they called me back in the place where I grew up. It wasn't a happy place, Salas. Everyone drank. Men and women. When sober, they were hurting and angry, so very angry. Fights were common. My parents screamed and fought all the time. One of the first things I learned in life was to hide. I remember always wishing I could turn invisible because if they didn't see me, they couldn't hit me."

"I... I had no idea." His eyes glistened in the dim light of the room.

"For a while, it was better in the orphanage," I kept talking, unable to stop. "I tried to forget about the past. I believed that if I didn't think about it, it would just disappear. Because what is the past but our memories? Without memories, it can't exist. I focused on school because math and grammar filled my mind with things that didn't cause pain. I didn't know what was actually happening in the girls' bedroom at night. I still don't know how many girls had been hurt by the man who was supposed to protect and look after us, before... Before he tried to hurt me." I ran both hands down my face. Why wouldn't the memories stop pounding against my skull? I was purging them. Shouldn't it feel lighter inside me now? Instead, darkness thickened, heavy and suffocating. "That night, I had nowhere to run. I should've been dead, or raped, or both. But instead, I ended up here, in Rorrim. People say it was a miracle, and I don't see how it could've been anything else." I lifted my head to see his face. "Salas, why would men look at a woman and see an object instead of a person? Why do they think she was put on this Earth to be used by them? Why do men feel such an entitlement to a woman's body? And why are there always people, both men and women, who enable that delusion? The more power a man has, the more he gets away with, the less there is a chance for him to be held accountable."

"It's not just men, Princess. And not just where you came from." His voice boomed through the night, but instead of tearing the darkness to shreds, it made it press down heavier.

This wasn't what I wanted to hear.

It couldn't be...

My mind reeled. Reality spun off its axis.

"You have no idea what that world is like," I snapped. "You don't know..."

But deep inside, I had a feeling that he *knew*. From the very first moment I'd laid my eyes on this man, I felt he understood me. Because his past must be similar to mine in some ways. Only how could it be when his past was worlds apart from mine?

The terrible things that happened on the other side of the mirror couldn't possibly happen here.

"It's not true." I shook my head so hard, it was a miracle my neck didn't snap in half. "Not in Rorrim."

This world was supposed to be safe for everyone, ruled by the wise and just queen, my mother.

"Take a look outside of the palace walls, Princess."

"No. You don't understand." I scrambled off the couch. "It's not the same. It just can't be. In Rorrim, crimes are punished. Justice always prevails. Misogyny simply doesn't exist. The system works—"

"Ari, listen to me."

"No..." I kept shaking my head.

Staring at him now was like looking into the dark tunnel inside the mirror. I dreaded what would leap out at me with his next words. My stomach churned, threatening to expel my dinner. With trembling fingers, I gathered the bodice of my dress and yanked it up to cover my chest.

"You should go," I said, avoiding looking at him.

I'd allowed my past into my present, and its darkness soiled my light, filling me with shame and regret. I'd let Salas touch me. He'd seen me naked and at my most vulnerable. And now, he knew my secrets... All of them.

"Please, Salas. Leave."

Moonlight flooded the patio outside, spilling into the bedroom through the open doors. I stepped away from him and could no longer see his expression with my glasses off, but it was better that way. I just prayed he wouldn't talk again. I needed his silence to hide behind.

He got off the couch and collected his cloak. Sorrow gripped my heart. How did he get a hold of me like that in such a short time?

Worry surged next. In my frazzled state, I couldn't focus enough to analyze all the ways my past could be used against me, but if Salas wished to inflict harm, he surely could. This man now knew more about me than anyone else in Rorrim.

Panic pushed me to stop him.

"Wait!"

He glanced at me over his shoulder from the door, ready to leave with his hood on already.

"I... I need you not to speak to anyone about what you heard tonight."

He scoffed softly. "Is that what you think I'll do? Run my mouth about what you told me when we were alone?"

I didn't *think*. I panicked. I no longer had control over my own past. It was now in his possession to do with as he pleased.

"I don't want anyone else to know... Please."

I anxiously swept the room with my gaze. The sparkling mound of diamonds on the side stand caught my attention. The moonlight shimmered in their perfect facets, breaking into a million tiny stars.

"Here." I scooped them all, both earrings and the necklace. "Take these." I shoved them into his hands that were large enough to hide the gems completely.

"Your diamonds for my silence?" he muttered, and I couldn't tell whether he sounded stunned or disappointed. Maybe both?

Before I could figure out what else to offer him, he shoved the bedroom door open with his shoulder. With my clothes in disarray, I leaped away from the light that burst into the room, keeping out of sight of the guards who camped in my sitting room.

"The princess needs her rest," Salas announced, loudly. "Let's go, girls." He kicked the bedroom door closed behind him.

But there was no resting for me that night.

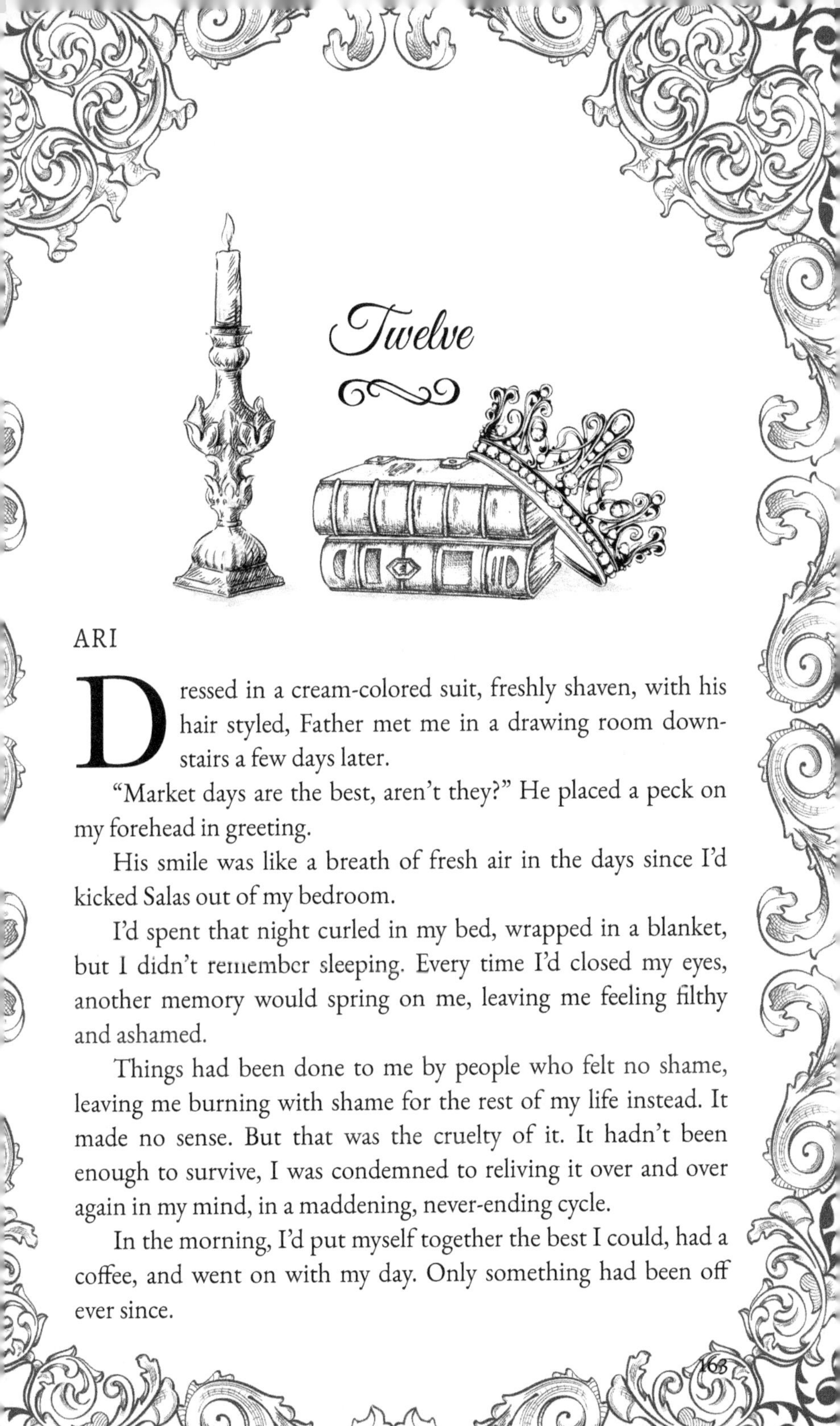

Twelve

ARI

Dressed in a cream-colored suit, freshly shaven, with his hair styled, Father met me in a drawing room downstairs a few days later.

"Market days are the best, aren't they?" He placed a peck on my forehead in greeting.

His smile was like a breath of fresh air in the days since I'd kicked Salas out of my bedroom.

I'd spent that night curled in my bed, wrapped in a blanket, but I didn't remember sleeping. Every time I'd closed my eyes, another memory would spring on me, leaving me feeling filthy and ashamed.

Things had been done to me by people who felt no shame, leaving me burning with shame for the rest of my life instead. It made no sense. But that was the cruelty of it. It hadn't been enough to survive, I was condemned to reliving it over and over again in my mind, in a maddening, never-ending cycle.

In the morning, I'd put myself together the best I could, had a coffee, and went on with my day. Only something had been off ever since.

I used to find solace in the palace library filled with thick scrolls and books on ancient laws that had withstood the test of time. Coming to the council meeting room never failed to reassure me in the wisdom of our foremothers. The many queens, who had come before my mother, passed on the legacy of fairness in justice and intelligence in governance. From the moment I'd arrived here, Rorrim had seemed like the ideal society that others should strive to replicate. It had its problems, of course, but it also had functioning ways to solve them.

Now, the echo of Salas's words never quieted.

"Take a look outside the palace walls, Princess."

What did I miss?

Or maybe it wasn't me? Maybe Salas was mistaken? An isolated case of injustice didn't mean that the whole establishment was flawed.

Salas had gone through some hard times and ended up at the very bottom of society. It had undoubtedly left him feeling bitter. Maybe he didn't get the justice he thought he deserved. In that case, I should've talked to him. Unfortunately damaged and fragile as I felt that night, I couldn't offer him any support at the time. And after the way I'd kicked him out, he might never want to speak with me again.

Gem had returned my diamonds the very same day.

"A palace guard brought them this morning." She stared at me, clearly expecting an explanation. "Your slave gave them to her. Did he steal them, then came to his senses? Royal jewelry wouldn't be easy to sell without risking an arrest for theft."

"I gave them to him. There was no theft." I took the earrings and the necklace from her, then tossed them back on the side stand in my bedroom.

"Why would you give a priceless jewelry set to a slave? What was he supposed to do with it?"

It had been such a stupid thing to do. I had no explanation to give to Gem, other than I'd panicked. I was not in my own mind that night. My life still felt off balance. The entire world did.

But Gem kept staring at me, expecting a logical answer. I gave her the best thing I could come up with.

"I gave it to him as a thank you for his services. He left me very satisfied."

My answer had the expected result. Gem smirked.

"Did he now? He was that good, was he?" She sidled closer for juicy details, but I refused to give her anything more.

Whatever happened between Salas and me belonged to us and no one else. I could only hope he felt the same way too.

"Obviously, it was a useless present for him," I said casually. "I realized that and replaced it with a full payout of his contract, instead."

Just a day after, the queen had successfully petitioned the council for his freedom. Salas was a free man now. He could leave Egami or even Rorrim if he so wished. Maybe he had already done so.

I hid a sigh as Father adjusted the lapels of his suit jacket. He seemed excited about me fulfilling my promise to take him to the market today, and I didn't want my troubled mood to spoil his day.

"We'll have to let Her Majesty know we may be late for lunch," he said, offering me his arm.

"I already did." I threaded my hand through the crook of his elbow. Together, we headed to the carriage that waited for us in the courtyard. "I left a message with the queen's maid. If we're late, I'm sure Mother will forgive us. It's not every day that I get a chance to go shopping with you."

The market was busy that day. It was a good thing that I came with Father. As a man, the king would've been required to bring at least a few of his gentlemen-in-waiting when going out in public, along with an escort of guards. With me, he only needed a couple of royal guards. A female relative, regardless of her age, was believed to be better suited to protect a man's reputation than a whole army of male friends.

As a much smaller group, we moved through crowds more easily, browsing the rows of merchants' stalls.

"Did you want to find some gloves?" I asked, remembering him mentioning that he could use some.

"Not really." He grinned somewhat sheepishly. "Frankly, I have more gloves than I know what to do with. It's just nice to get out of the palace sometimes, isn't it?"

Men, especially high-born men, often ended up house-bound for their own peace and safety since the outside world harbored too many temptations and aggravations. But it also allowed the wives to keep a better eye on their husbands in the world where male reputation could be so easily soiled by just a wrong look or a careless word from someone.

"Oh, these are nice." Father stopped in front of a table with folded linen and stroked a brushed-cotton shirt. "So soft."

"And comfy too, Your Majesty," the merchant rushed to praise her wares.

"They are nice," I agreed, stroking a shirt too. "I have pajamas like that. Perfect for winter."

"You're right, Your Highness." The seller nodded eagerly. "But they're fine enough to wear during the day too. Look at this one." She unfolded the shirt I'd touched.

It was creamy white, with a narrow strip for a collar and small horn buttons halfway down the chest. A simple cross-stitch embroidery on the collar and around the buttons made it look tastefully festive. I could see a farmer's husband wearing it to a fair. He'd give the best hugs, too, wearing something so soft.

Father shook his head, taking his hand off the fabric.

"It's way too plain for me," he said quietly, for only me to hear. "I'd have nowhere to wear it."

"How about to bed? As a nightshirt?" I suggested.

He shook his head again, stepping away from the merchant's stand. "The queen prefers I wear silk to bed."

I opened my mouth to ask what *he* preferred but quickly closed it, realizing he might not know the answer to that question.

Father was betrothed to my mother when he was sixteen and she was thirty. They got married two years later, the day after he turned eighteen. He spent his childhood striving to please his parents by being the perfect son. Since the wedding, he'd been pleasing his wife by being the perfect husband. He'd learned all about *her* preferences, but never really had a chance to figure out his own. He'd been a son, a husband, and a father, but never had a chance to be a man outside of these roles.

We finished our trip through the market with Father acquiring a pair of kid-skin gloves for himself and a silver-tipped writing quill as a gift for Mother.

As he climbed back into the carriage, I paused by the open door.

"I'm so sorry, I almost forgot," I said. "Do you mind waiting for just a minute while I run to get something?"

Leaving my father in the care of the guards, I dashed back to the market stalls. I returned a few minutes later with a fabric bundle in my hands.

"Here, I got something for you," I said, taking my place in the carriage next to Father. "I thought you'd like it." I pulled a book out of the bundle and handed it to him. "It's an illustrated commentary to the eleventh volume of the Complete Political History of Rorrim by Lady Arima. She's lauded as the most insightful historian of the current century. I found her commentary very helpful."

Father stared at me in alarm, as if expecting me to either ridicule him or threaten to expose his reading habits to the world. His skin turned paler than marble. A ripple ran over it, matching the burgundy upholstery inside the carriage, before he all but blended in with it. His body, hair, and clothes appeared transparent, reflecting the panels and cushions of the carriage. Fear prompted him into hiding with the reflex that people in Rorrim had little control over.

My heart ached for him.

"Oh, Father." I lunged forward and grabbed him into a tight

hug. "Please, don't be scared. I promise I'll never tell anyone what you're reading."

I knew my father was content with the way his life had turned out. He even considered himself lucky. Until now, I had wholeheartedly agreed with him. But it no longer felt that way. How lucky could one really be if he had to read in secret?

He released a long breath as I petted his back soothingly. The fabric of his suit slowly returned to its original ivory color. I waited until his *reflection* had passed completely before releasing him from my hug.

"Are you alright?" I asked softly.

He clasped his hands in his lap.

"It's not a crime, dearest. I haven't broken any laws by reading those books." He sounded as if trying to convince himself more than me. "It's simply in bad taste. Some study subjects are just not suitable for men. Learning advanced mathematics, for example, dries the male brain out and makes us bitter and aggressive. History has many difficult topics that may upset us. And politics... Well, it's best for men to stay out of politics—"

I placed a hand on his, stopping his words that parroted what he'd been told probably all his life.

"You're right, it's not a crime wanting to learn the history of the country you've lived in for two decades now. And history is messy. It's filled with wars and political games, with suffering and hatred. If you learn it, you can't pick and choose. You need to know it all—good, bad, and outright disturbing. And if it upsets you... Well, you are a grown man. I've seen you control your emotions in public better than many people I know. I'm pretty sure you're capable of deciding for yourself what you want to read and how much you can handle being upset."

He placed the book onto his lap, running his fingers over the embossed leather. I waited for him to say something, but he just stared at it, seemingly lost for words.

"Look." I opened the cover for him. "It has detailed maps of territories affected by each major treaty, which gives a good visual of the reasoning behind all those agreements."

He gasped, poring over the maps with growing enthusiasm.

"This is wonderful. Thank you so much, Ari."

"You're welcome," I said, hiding the rest of my bundle behind a seat cushion. I had another present there, but it wasn't for my father, it was for someone else.

"Ari?" Father asked, lifting his gaze from the book. "Do you think there is a place anywhere in the universe where boys are allowed to study history and politics freely?"

His question rendered me speechless. Father had never talked to me about the world I'd come from before.

Mother had spotted me on her way from Father's chambers one dark night. She held a candle in her hand to light her way back to her rooms. The candle flame reflected in the large, ancient mirror hanging in the throne room. Only instead of her reflection, she saw my face in it. That happened the night I stared into the mirror corridor, the very same night I ran away from that wretched house I used to call home.

Since then, Mother had stood in front of the ancient mirror often, trying to catch a glimpse of me. She'd seen me in the orphanage from time to time. But I'd never stopped to stare in the mirror long enough to see her again.

She had watched me for years, wishing she could talk to me, wondering who I was and why she could see me but no one else unless they were with me.

The night I was attacked, she heard me scream. She said my pleas for help rolled through the entire palace, instantly raising her from sleep. She ran downstairs and into the throne room just in time to grab me and pull me into the safety of her arms.

She didn't know the details of what happened to me in the first sixteen years of my life. But she gathered enough from what I told her that night while crying and sobbing as she held me, sitting with me on the floor in front of the mirror.

Father knew even less. I didn't meet him until the following morning, and I was too scared to speak to him for weeks. But with time, he won my heart. He'd read children's books to me, without shaming me that I was too old for them. They were light, simple kids' stories that always ended happily, and I liked to hear them at that time. He took me for walks with his dogs and let me teach them tricks. He was the one who made me smile for the first time since that horrible night.

Father had never spoken to me about my past. But one day, not so long ago, he brought me to the royal library and showed me the ancient scrolls he had found. From them, he'd learned that the mirror in the throne room was the only portal between our worlds.

Many centuries ago, a warlock discovered a passage to my old world. He used a forbidden magic to lock the passage in an ancient relic—a mirror created by powerful witches. A group of men paid the warlock a fortune to escape Rorrim. Some were criminals, fleeing the prosecution. But one was a prince of royal blood who left the palace to escape an unwanted marriage. They all succeeded in their crossing through the portal into my old world from which they never returned.

Father believed I was a descendant of the prince. His royal blood connected me to Queen Anna, allowing her to see me through the mirror in the throne room when I used any mirror in my world. The distress from the danger threatening me that night had pushed me through the magical portal, helping me escape. Father also thought it could work in reverse, too, that I could return to that world if I ever wanted to.

Needless to say, I never wished to test his theory. In fact, I avoided the throne room and the mirror as much as I could.

Father never spoke to me about my past before, but he was the one who had found an explanation for what had happened to me by reading books and scrolls the society believed he wasn't supposed to read.

"Yes, Father," I said. "There is a world where boys are allowed to learn whatever they want."

I didn't say that sometimes it applied only to those boys whose parents could afford to pay for their education. I didn't mention that for many girls in that world, an education was still as unattainable as crossing over into the Rorrim Queendom. I didn't say that in that world, many children of every gender were still beaten, abused, and traded like chattel, that they often had no one to turn to and suffered in silence. I didn't say that there were many sores in that society, rotting and ugly.

I didn't say any of it because my father smiled while leafing through his new book, and I didn't want that smile to disappear. So, I said nothing more at all.

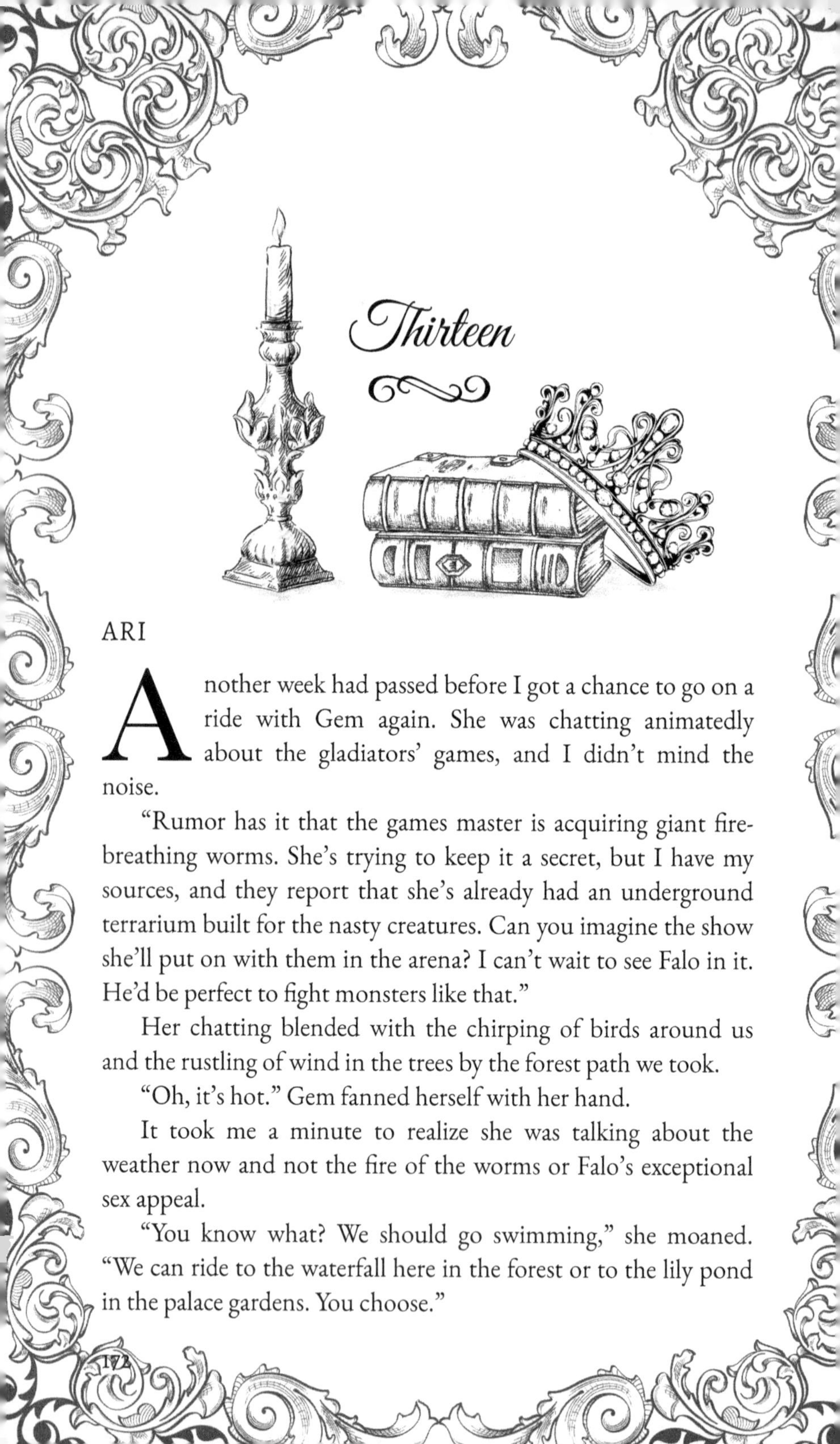

Thirteen

ARI

Another week had passed before I got a chance to go on a ride with Gem again. She was chatting animatedly about the gladiators' games, and I didn't mind the noise.

"Rumor has it that the games master is acquiring giant fire-breathing worms. She's trying to keep it a secret, but I have my sources, and they report that she's already had an underground terrarium built for the nasty creatures. Can you imagine the show she'll put on with them in the arena? I can't wait to see Falo in it. He'd be perfect to fight monsters like that."

Her chatting blended with the chirping of birds around us and the rustling of wind in the trees by the forest path we took.

"Oh, it's hot." Gem fanned herself with her hand.

It took me a minute to realize she was talking about the weather now and not the fire of the worms or Falo's exceptional sex appeal.

"You know what? We should go swimming," she moaned. "We can ride to the waterfall here in the forest or to the lily pond in the palace gardens. You choose."

"I'm not sure I want to go swimming." I eased my dress off my shoulders to let the breeze cool my skin. The heat was bearable here in the shade from the trees.

"Why not?"

I shrugged. "I have things to do."

"You always have things to do. But you need to make time to enjoy life. Before you know it, you'll be a married woman and a queen, running yourself into the ground with work."

I didn't really have that much work to do today. I just preferred to have a nice lunch with my parents, then have some quiet time on the patio with Ria, instead of listening to Gem's idle chatting and nagging for another hour or more while we swam.

Keeping Revlis at a steady pace, I let her walk along the forest path that very few people knew about beside Gem and me. The two of us had traveled here often enough for our horses to become so familiar with the route that they no longer needed our guidance to find the way.

I tipped my head back, letting the sun play with shadows on my face. A bird was singing high in the branches, and I wondered if its song would sound just as lovely everywhere else in Rorrim, specifically in the unknown-to-me place where a former slave lived as a free man now.

I thought about Salas daily. Nightly too, quite often. Sometimes, the thoughts of him hurt, but many were pleasant. I tried to focus on the pleasant ones.

He obviously wasn't afraid of hard work, and I had no doubt he'd found a decent occupation for those skilled hands of his. I imagined he rented a place to live, like a cute little cottage on a farm or in a forest somewhere, where he would come to after a day of honest work to eat dinner in a cozy living room by the fire.

The only thing I could never bring myself to envision was a woman sharing that dinner with him. I wanted Salas to be happy, and that could include him finding the love of his life, settling down, and starting a family. But I just couldn't stomach the thought of his hands that had touched me so tenderly on another woman's body.

In my mind, I often envisioned him wearing the shirt I bought for him at the market, even though I'd never given it to him, of course. It lay folded and wrapped on the bottom of one of the trunks in my dressing room where no maid would ever find it.

I'd bought it on impulse, thinking how perfectly the green and gold embroidery would go with his eyes of many shades of brown. Even as I was paying for the shirt, I knew I'd never give it to him. But I kept it as a memento of him, a souvenir, even though he never wore it.

We'd never see each other again. It was best for both of us. But thinking about the way we parted still filled me with unease and even embarrassment. I hated myself for forcing on him the diamonds he couldn't even sell without putting his freedom and possibly his life in danger. I wished I would've said a proper goodbye instead. I also wished I could take back every single word I'd said to him about my past that night.

However, something good did come out of it. After I'd opened up to Salas, I'd been learning to think about my past without fear. Somehow, spread between two people instead of one, the weight of those memories proved easier to bear now.

"Fine, let's go back to the palace," Gem grumped, following me out of the forest and toward the road to the main gate of the city.

"Maybe we can go swimming tomorrow?" I took pity on her. "That way, I'll have a whole day to prepare myself mentally. You know I'm not very good at being spontaneous."

"Don't I know it," she scoffed, casting her eyes upwards.

We approached a place where the city wall came almost flush with that of the palace grounds. A group of workers were repairing the part where the mortar had crumbled and the massive rocks had fallen out.

"Just look at that asshole." Gem pointed with her riding crop at the man who was sitting on the ground by the wall, smoking a cigarette.

Realizing we'd spotted him, he jumped to his feet, tossed away the cigarette, then pretended to help two other men to haul a rock up the wall for the masons to mortar it into place.

"Who is that?"

"The slave owner's helper." Gem tsked disapprovingly, shaking her head. "He's the only man in that group who is being paid actual wages, but he's been slacking behind the owner's back all along."

"Are the slaves not done yet?"

"They're almost done. Leaving by the end of the next week. Just fixing a few things here and there before our contract with their owner runs out."

The helper and the two other men rolled another huge rock onto the shoulders of a man who'd crouched down. As he straightened, lifting the rock all by himself, thoughts of Salas rushed me again. The man with the rock was of similar height and brawn. He had the same brown shaggy hair, too... and a full beard, just like Salas.

As he rolled the rock onto the wall for the bricklayers, then turned around, all doubts left me. It was Salas.

I gripped my horse's reins tighter.

"What the hell is *he* still doing here?"

While I'd been daydreaming about Salas living in a quaint cottage and making friends with cute forest animals, he'd been here all along. He'd never left. The only thing that changed was that he was now hauling rocks instead of bricks.

"Mother assured me his debt was paid in full over a week ago." I twisted at the waist to face Gem. "Did she lie?"

"Lying is below Queen Anna. The debt has been paid. But you know how it is with some men. They find a way to get in debt again. Once a slave, always a slave, they say."

My shock was replaced by anger. I dug my heels into Revlis's sides and flicked the reins to urge the mare to move faster. Startled by the command she rarely received, the horse eventually sped up a little, but it wasn't fast enough for me.

A short distance from the wall, I slid off from the saddle and proceeded on foot. My anger rose with every step.

He should've been free.

I gave him that chance.

Why did he waste it?

"What the fuck are you still doing here?" I yelled, stomping through the tall grass toward Salas.

He wiped sweat off his forehead with his arm and watched me approach, raking his eyes up and down my frame. His long-sleeved shirt was soaked with sweat. His hair and beard were over-grown and disheveled. He panted in the heat after delivering a boulder that should've taken at least three people to lift.

His beard moved as I came closer. The bastard was smiling, obviously finding my anger amusing.

"Why are you here?" I demanded, out of breath.

"Where else can I be, Princess?" His deep familiar voice trapped me, extinguishing my anger.

No one called me "princess" to my face but Salas. The way he used that word sounded intimate, like a nickname shared only between him and me. It disarmed me.

I stared at him, drinking in every familiar feature, and fought the strong urge to hug him with all his sweat, grime, and the stone dust.

"Why are you here?" I asked with far less fire than before.

"I work here." The light in his expression dimmed. "But we're leaving next week. You won't have to worry about running into me ever again."

"Greetings, Your Highness." One of the masons leaned down from the wall. She was topless, her shirt tied over her head to protect her head and shoulders from the sun. "Is there a problem? Did he do something?"

Gem had caught up with me on foot, holding both our horses' reins in one hand.

"Ari," she said in an urgent whisper, "you're making a scene. And on the verge of your impending marriage, nonetheless."

If there was anything most scandalous at the royal court, it would be "making a scene." Goddess forbid the crown princess made a spectacle out of herself in public by getting into a fight with a slave.

I looked up at the mason and forced my lips to curl into a serene smile.

"It's nothing, good woman. Sorry to disrupt your team's work. I mistook this slave for someone else." I glared at Salas and added with emphasis, "I mistook him for a *free* man."

SALAS WASN'T FREE. And he wasn't gone. He didn't live a happy life somewhere. He still slaved away in the heat all day.

"He is not your responsibility," Gem said as we rode away from the wall with me seething inside.

Gem was right, Salas shouldn't be my problem. But somehow, he had become one. I wished him to be happy. Without even knowing all the wrongs he had endured in his life, I wanted to right them all. If I knew for sure that he was free, well, and happy, then maybe I could stop thinking about him all the fucking time.

"I need to know what happened," I said to Gem. "Why is he still here when he was free to leave days ago? Did he sign another contract with the slave owner?"

"Most likely he did."

"Why? I need more than just 'most likely.'"

I needed to know if Salas had been taken advantage of. Had he been coerced into another contract? Blackmailed maybe? It made no sense to me that a man would give away his freedom that easily, and I knew I wouldn't be able to rest until I had the answers.

"Find out, Gem. Everything."

MY THOUGHTS REMAINED with Salas through the lunch with my parents, then through the entire afternoon and the early evening when I tried to work on a project for the next council meeting.

After dinner, I dug out from the trunk the shirt I'd bought. Then I sat on the floor in my dressing room with the folded shirt on my lap.

To solve a problem, I had to first identify it correctly. The true reason I worried so much about Salas was because I liked him. I had to be honest, at least with myself, about it. I felt a strong attraction for this man.

Some of it was physical. My body tingled with excitement at the phantom memory of his hands on me. But I also admired him as a person.

Also, after spending almost three nights with him, I was still very much a virgin. We had unfinished business, Salas and me. And maybe that was a part of the problem? I hated leaving things unfinished.

Yet sex wasn't on my mind when I finally climbed to my feet a while later, still clutching the shirt in my hands. I took off my crown, draped a dark cloak over my shoulders, pulled the hood over my head, then stuffed the shirt into a satchel to take it with me.

Knowing that all this time Salas had been just a short walk away from me messed with my head and my feelings. Now, I desperately wished to see him again, which presented a huge problem, and like a coward, I hoped that Salas would solve it for me. I hoped he'd use the common sense that I seemed to have lost and send me away when I showed up at the slaves' barracks.

He had plenty of reasons to resent me. I'd barged into his life without an invitation. He was literally dragged in chains to my bedroom. I'd used him. And after all that, I did more to him than had been agreed between us. I'd unloaded the grimy sludge of my past on him, then kicked him out with his hands filled with diamonds as a payment for his silence.

He would have every right to laugh in my face when I showed up with my gift at his door. Maybe he did have a temper like they said. Maybe he would yell at me or even slap me for everything I'd done to him. I almost wished he'd slap me. It might be the only thing that would force me to write him off completely and never think about him again other than with disdain. That kind of humiliation would surely be enough to finally get that man out of my fucking mind.

That was how crazy my thoughts had become.

That was how I knew I had to do something about this before I went completely insane and did something even more unhinged.

I had to resolve this before the council approved Mother's plans for the foreign princes' arrivals. My virginal groom hopefuls would show up in Rorrim soon, with their judgmental handlers in tow. With all of them at the Egami Palace, I needed a clear head and a focused mind. I couldn't possibly keep obsessing over another man while officially courting my future husband.

I couldn't risk plunging the Crown of Rorrim into a scandal it had never faced before.

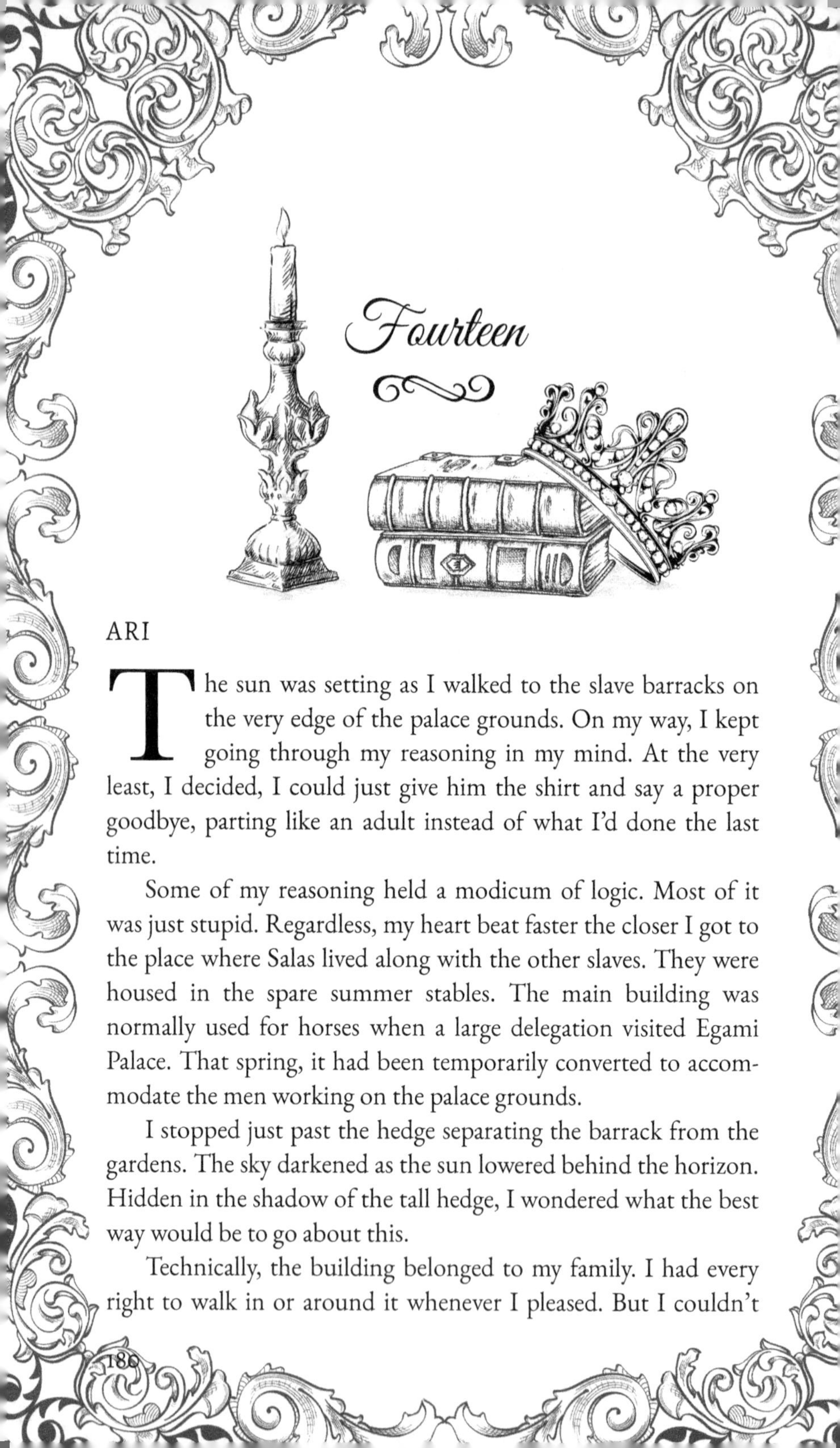

Fourteen

ARI

The sun was setting as I walked to the slave barracks on the very edge of the palace grounds. On my way, I kept going through my reasoning in my mind. At the very least, I decided, I could just give him the shirt and say a proper goodbye, parting like an adult instead of what I'd done the last time.

Some of my reasoning held a modicum of logic. Most of it was just stupid. Regardless, my heart beat faster the closer I got to the place where Salas lived along with the other slaves. They were housed in the spare summer stables. The main building was normally used for horses when a large delegation visited Egami Palace. That spring, it had been temporarily converted to accommodate the men working on the palace grounds.

I stopped just past the hedge separating the barrack from the gardens. The sky darkened as the sun lowered behind the horizon. Hidden in the shadow of the tall hedge, I wondered what the best way would be to go about this.

Technically, the building belonged to my family. I had every right to walk in or around it whenever I pleased. But I couldn't just march into the barracks and search for Salas without raising a million questions from everyone inside and giving grounds for some potentially very harmful rumors.

Maybe I could knock and ask for him? With my hood on and my crown off, whoever opened the door likely wouldn't recognize me. But how could I explain to anyone what I needed from Salas if I couldn't even explain it to myself?

As I stood there, pondering my next step, the door opened, and Salas exited the building. He was alone.

Talk about a lucky break.

I opened my mouth to call him, then realized he was trying not to be seen. Furtively glancing over both his shoulders, he quickly closed the door behind him and rounded the building toward the path that led to the palace gates. He wasn't just going out for a walk. He was sneaking out. Instead of taking the path, he stayed close to the hedge and the bushes, hiding in their shadows.

I realized how much I still didn't know about this man, intentionally so. I hadn't asked him questions or tried to find out anything about his life other than what was absolutely necessary to fulfill our agreement. By now, the unvoiced questions had piled up so high, I could no longer keep collecting them without answers.

Tugging my hood even lower over my face, I headed after him. There was a way to get at least some answers. Like where was he going so late at night when it was highly unusual for young, unmarried men to leave the house, especially unaccompanied like that?

He walked swiftly. I had to jog at times to keep up with his wide stride. When he reached the plaza in front of the palace gates, he paused, hiding in the shadows from the light posts. He waited for a few moments until a large group of servants crossed the plaza on their way to the gates. Then he joined them, keeping his head down and staying about half a step behind the last person.

Smart. I shook my head, impressed by his level of stealth that required extra skill and effort to achieve since his size made him stand out in any crowd.

No one stopped me as I left through the gates. A woman walking alone at night rarely raised any questions or concerns.

Salas turned into the road to the city, and I followed, still without him knowing. By now, I couldn't even let him know that I was behind him even if I tried. He'd gotten way ahead of me. I had to crane my neck, trying not to lose him among the pedestrians taking an evening stroll and the carriages rattling along the road.

It turned out I had good stalking skills, because I managed not to lose him, following him all the way to the large, gray building on the edge of the city center.

Salas used the heavy bronze ring on the front door to knock, then spoke quietly to the woman who opened the door. She let him in, leaving me standing on the corner with even more questions than I'd had before.

Who was this woman? I didn't get a good look at her face, but she appeared to be about my age.

Why did Salas come to see her, secretly, as if committing an illicit act? Were they having an affair?

Their greeting seemed formal, not like between lovers or even between friends. Still, an unpleasant feeling scratched inside me as my feverish imagination ran amok with all the things they might be doing inside right now.

What was this place, anyway?

I stepped back, taking in the gray stone building. Overall, it was low-set and unassuming. Past rainfalls had decorated its walls with dark water stains. I might've passed by here more than once, not paying any attention to its walls hidden behind the pretty cherry trees that grew on the side of the road.

"Excuse me," I stopped two women who were passing by. "Do you happen to know what's inside this building?"

One of them shrugged. "No idea. I walk here a few times a

month, but I never bothered to find out. It's an ugly one, isn't it? Quite an eyesore."

So much was true. The building wasn't an architectural masterpiece by any standards.

"I think they have kids in there," the other woman said.

"Kids?" I stared at her in shock.

She nodded. "I hear them recite out loud on a hot day when they have the windows open."

"What do they recite?"

"I never listened closely, madam."

Another passerby stopped abruptly, having overheard our conversation.

"It's an orphanage for boys," she said. "My sister knows the head mistress. They do an excellent job at disciplining their charges and making sure they grow into obedient, hard-working husbands."

An orphanage?

I thanked all three women, letting them continue on their way, then leaned against the building's wall, trying to process what I'd just learned.

Why would Salas visit an orphanage? Did he come to see somebody? A nephew? Or maybe...a son?

Oh Goddess... My heart beat faster at that assumption. Could that be the reason for him to keep selling his freedom over and over again? Did he have a little boy to support? Was that what he needed the money for?

Stunned by the realization, I missed Salas exiting the building. I only noticed his large figure when he was already way down the road and heading back to the palace. Peeling my back from the cold gray rocks of the wall I'd been leaning on, I promptly followed him again.

He turned into a narrow side street, avoiding the main road this time. As the evening grew into the night, the pedestrian traffic had thinned. Salas would be easy to spot on the main road now.

He obviously wished to attract as little attention as possible, choosing the route away from the light and the people.

We entered the part of the city that respectable folks tried to avoid. It was close to the "fun district" as it was unofficially called. Here, the fun was provided by establishments with questionable reputations, such as gambling halls and brothels, also called "fun houses."

With his legs being longer than mine, Salas had gotten farther and farther ahead. After turning around yet another corner, I lost sight of him completely.

Running at full speed, I approached the narrow street he'd turned into the last I saw him. Several voices reached me from a distance. Salas's deep, low drawl intermingled with a higher feminine pitch.

Carefully peeking from around the corner of a building, I spotted four women dressed in the city guards' uniforms.

"What is such a handsome thing like you doing alone at such a late hour?" one of them asked Salas. "Doesn't your wife want you home by now?"

All four guards were armed with swords and daggers in the sheaths attached to their belts. In addition, two of them also held long spears and had crossbows strapped to their backs.

"I am on my way home, madam," Salas replied calmly.

"And where is home?" the leader of the guards asked.

"There." He waved a hand in the direction of the palace.

"Nothing much is out that way but the queen's palace, boy," a guard pointed out.

The leader snorted a laugh.

"No offense, but you don't look like you belong to the royal court, sweetie." She raked her eyes up and down his body. "Why are you alone and so close to the fun district? Are you one of the working boys, maybe?"

"No," he replied flatly, holding his back as straight as a rod.

Another guard grabbed his arm. "Let's take him in. I have a lot of questions."

He stiffened, squaring his shoulders. But he couldn't possibly fight back. Lifting a finger to a woman, especially to a figure of authority, carried a death penalty.

"I need to get home, madam," he said slowly, his voice strained.

If he didn't make it home on time, I imagined the barrack's door would be locked. Then, he'd have to spend the night outside, risking running into the palace guards and being detained for lurking. Even if the door of the barrack didn't get locked for the night, his absence would surely be noticed and likely reported to his owner. If she deemed it an escape attempt on his part, he'd face a punishment far more severe than another flogging.

There was just no avoiding getting in trouble in this situation for Salas, no matter what he did at this point.

I cleared my throat and stepped out of my hiding spot.

"Oh, there you are!" I threw my hands up into the air dramatically. "Thank you so much for finding him for me, ladies."

They all turned to me. Shock registered on Salas's face for a moment, but he quickly schooled his features into a neutral expression.

It was fairly dark in the narrow street, with only a faint glow of the streetlights from the main road reaching in to lighten the shadows. I kept my hood draped low around my face. The guards didn't know who I was, just that I was a woman who spoke with confidence and that proved enough for them to stand to attention.

"Do you know this man, madam?" the guards' leader asked.

"Yes. He's my cousin. He's big but not very bright." Salas shot me a glare but said nothing, letting me speak for him. "He was supposed to be following me but must've taken a wrong turn back there. Please forgive the dummy, he's not used to walking out here in the dark. I'll take him home now if you don't mind."

The guard let go of Salas's arm.

"It's not the best part of the city for a man to walk on his own," the leader said. "We stop and question every male in these parts."

"Thank you for doing your job, good women." I nodded, placing myself between her and Salas.

The leader slapped his ass at parting.

"Go along now, lad. And don't you get lost again. Men..." She smiled at me, shaking her head. "That's why they need us to take care of them. Can't even make a step anywhere without a woman holding their hand."

I grabbed Salas's hand to demonstrate that I got the situation under control this time.

"Thanks, ladies." I waved at them with my free hand while tagging Salas away.

They laughed and chatted among themselves as we left.

My heart pounded. Perspiration beaded on my brow. I half-expected the guards to call us back once they'd realized they hadn't even asked my name or who I was. I turned into random streets, just to build some distance between us and them.

When the guards' voices quieted behind the buildings, melting into the streets, I stopped and released a breath, allowing the tension to leave my body.

Salas exhaled too.

"Thanks," he said softly.

I lifted my face to him. "How do we get back to the palace from here? I've no idea where we are."

I'd acted confidently in front of the guards. But in reality, it was I who was lost, not Salas.

"This way." He gripped my hand tighter, leading me through a maze of dark narrow streets to the main road.

"You know your way well around the city," I noted. "Do you come this way often?"

"No. I just happened to have a good sense of direction."

I bit my lip before asking my next question. "So, you don't visit that orphanage on a regular basis then?"

He stopped, letting go of my hand, and I immediately missed

the contact with his warm palm. Nothing about us walking through the city together at night was normal, yet holding his hand always felt like the most natural thing to do.

"Have you been following me, Princess?" He sounded incredulous, either having a hard time believing that I would do such a crazy thing or wondering how he hadn't spotted me earlier. "Is that why you're here?"

"Yes," I confessed.

"For how long?"

"Since the palace grounds." I had lots of my own questions that needed answers, however. "I bet you didn't have your owner's permission to leave tonight. Why did you do it? Whom were you visiting in that orphanage, Salas?"

"No one. I don't know anyone there." He lifted a hand to run it through his shaggy hair.

Only now I noticed a worn leather purse clipped to his belt. Reaching for it, I squeezed it to confirm it was empty.

"You gave them the money, didn't you? Was that why you signed the new contract with the slave owner?"

He stared at me for a long moment, as if trying to glimpse through my skull my reasons for all these questions.

"I don't see how it's any of your business, Princess," he finally said.

Pivoting on his heel, he headed toward the palace, clearly trusting me to find my own way back now that we were on the main road again. If he thought he'd be rid of me, however, he was hugely mistaken. I ran, catching up with him.

"I made sure you were free," I panted, barely keeping up with his punishing pace. "Why did you not keep your freedom? How can anyone *choose* to remain a slave? Don't you want to reclaim your life?"

"You don't know anything about my life," he barked out.

"Because you never told me anything. Granted, I tried not to ask much about it either. But I do want to help."

He stopped in his tracks so suddenly, I ran past him a few steps then had to turn back to face him.

"I never asked for your help, Princess." He raked both hands through his messy hair before dropping his arms down. "I have what I have. I made the best I could of my life, and I'm content with it. My allowing you the use of my body for a night or two didn't automatically give you the right to meddle in the way I live. I didn't ask you to fix anything."

Indignity bloomed on my cheeks with heat. It'd been a while since someone had dared to scold me. No one had put me in my place like that. Speechless, I stayed rooted for a few minutes as he continued on his way. He walked a little slower this time, so I didn't have to run once I'd caught up with him again.

We walked quietly for a while. The silence gave the argument a chance to cool off.

"You're right," I spoke first. "I shouldn't have tried to manage your life like that. But normally, paying someone's debt off and setting them free is considered a good thing. I honestly believed I was doing you a favor, Salas. I'm sorry if I was wrong about that."

"No need to apologize," he replied in a far calmer voice too. "I know you were coming from a good place. It's just that..." He rubbed his chin, his fingers lost in his thick beard. "Freedom isn't of much use to me."

I almost tripped over my feet. How could anyone say such a thing?

"So, you'd rather be someone's property? Owned, body and soul?"

He shook his head. "No, Princess. The slave owner doesn't own my body. Or my soul. She owns my time and my labor, nothing more. In exchange, I get a place to live and food three times a day. That's more than I can have as a free man. By paying off my debt, you literally kicked me out on the street, with no money and no place to go."

"I could've given you money," I said, and explained in reply to his glare, "As a loan if you wanted. Until you found a job and got back on track."

He kept on walking, staring straight ahead. "You really don't know much about life outside of the palace walls, do you?"

I sucked in a breath with a new flare of indignation. I knew far more about the Queendom of Rorrim than probably anyone in the world, including Salas. But I sensed that was not what he meant. My knowledge came largely from academic sources, and in that sense, he might be right. I lacked the perspective of an ordinary person living in this country.

"Do you know why slaves are predominantly male, Princess?" he continued. "And why so many of us remain slaves for life? It's because there are so few other options for us out there. Men can't buy a place to live, not even a shack. We can't own a business. We have nothing to offer as a collateral, and the lenders use it to put the most draconian terms on money loans for us. Most of the men I work and live with are illiterate. They can't even read the contracts they sign. After years of trying to work off their debt, many actually owe more now than they did at the beginning of their contracts."

The institution of financial slavery was normally presented to me as something beneficial to both the country and the individual. In theory, it filled the demand for physical labor and provided the means for men to manage their debt. In reality, it seemed there was more to it that no one in the palace knew or cared to share with me.

"I honestly didn't know…"

He heaved a sigh. "I believe you. People are often blind to the injustices done against others if they don't belong to that particular group themselves, no matter how large that group may be."

There was a genuine understanding in his voice, not accusation. But I felt ashamed, nevertheless. And shocked. Shocked to find this level of suffering in the world that I'd considered a perfect place. A part of me didn't want to hear what else he had to say—learning about these things hurt. But I couldn't remain ignorant any longer.

"Thank you for telling me," I said softly.

"Now that you know, will it make any difference?" He glanced at me. Catching my flustered expression, he nodded again. "It is how it is, they say. That's the way it's always been. Women run the world, and men have to find a way to fit in. Those who fail to fit in... Well, there is no second chance for us." He fisted his hands. "I can't change my past. But hopefully, I've made a difference in someone's future. I don't need to be personally acquainted with the boys from that orphanage to know they have nothing going for them. All they're doing right now is reciting rules of conduct and memorizing scriptures. I donated the money in exchange for the written commitment from the head mistress to hire qualified teachers to teach the boys reading, writing, and mathematics for the next three years."

"You did that?"

A hot wave of shame rolled through me. The system failed those children. As the crown princess, I was a part of the system. I failed them. Salas, a slave with nothing to give but his freedom, was single-handedly trying to make a difference. He stepped in where the crown had failed.

"Did you give away the money from your previous contracts like that too?"

He nodded. "To different organizations. In different cities. But under similar conditions."

We walked in silence again until we reached the palace gates. I let Salas go in first while I waited out of sight behind a hedge. After the guards confirmed he was one of the slaves working on the grounds, they let him through.

Once he'd made it far ahead, I took my hood off and approached the gate as well.

"Good evening, Your Highness." The guards let me in without a single question.

Salas waited for me out of sight by the garden path.

"I want you to know that I do appreciate your kind gesture," he said. "Your intention behind paying off my contract was by far the nicest thing anyone has ever done for me. I am grateful, and I'm sorry that the result wasn't what you expected from it."

I rubbed my arms, not feeling any less foolish. But he also had made me think. If a slave could make a real difference in children's lives, surely a princess could do so much more. I had the power, I just had to find a way to apply it.

"I'll speak with my father," I promised. "He's the main patron of all orphanages in Egami City. From what I've learned from him, I thought the children's education was taken care of, that they were taught basic literacy skills along with crafts and trades."

"*Girls* are taught all of that," Salas corrected. "Boys are mostly raised to be husbands and fathers, or general laborers if they fail to find a wife to support them. It's believed that the brain is not required for physical labor. So why teach them anything?"

Everything he'd said to me today resonated in one way or another with words I'd heard often but long ago and in another world.

"It's a man's world. There are few options for women to make it in life on their own."

"You need to find a husband before you're too old to attract a man."

"As a young woman with no connections, if you want a job and a place to live, you'll need a rich man who'd give it to you."

It struck me how similar yet polar opposite these ideas were. How absurd they would sound outside of the world where they came from.

As we reached the slaves' barracks, I stopped uneasily. Sadness curled around my heart as it was time to say goodbye.

Salas turned to me. "Well, thank you for your help with the city guards, Princess. You spared me a lot of explaining I'd rather not do."

"It was no trouble... Oh, I almost forgot." I grabbed the satchel on my side. "I have something for you."

"For me?" He blinked, looking confused.

"It's a present. Kind of…" I pulled out the shirt wrapped in a piece of plain canvas from the market. "Nothing much. I just… well. Just take it, please." I shoved it into his hands.

Who knew that giving presents would feel this awkward?

He smiled into his beard. His cheeks flushed a little.

"It's been a while since anyone gave me a present," he muttered, staring at the package.

"It's just a shirt," I blurted out, not waiting for him to unwrap it. "I thought it'd suit you. I really hope you'll like it." I exhaled a nervous laugh. "Because if you don't, it won't be easy to find someone your size to give it to instead."

"I love it," he said, without even seeing it yet. Holding the package in one hand, he reached for me with the other as if to hug me, then caught himself and dropped his arm without touching me. "Thank you, Your Highness."

Clearly, it was time for me to go. Yet I couldn't bring myself to leave. The shirt just didn't feel like a good enough present for all the things he'd made me feel. On the other hand, no matter how much he'd given me, I wanted more.

"Salas." I took a step toward him, unsure how to say it.

He met me halfway, stepping so close, I could feel the warmth of his body through his clothes. I would've given anything for him to hold me again, but he wouldn't even touch me.

"I'll never forget you," I breathed out. "Wherever you are."

Lifting his hand, he skimmed with the tips of his fingers down the side of my face. His touch was light, like a caress of a breeze.

"You will," he said. "As you should."

He was right, of course. The smart thing would be to forget this man and what his touch had made me feel. But defiance rose in me when he stated it so adamantly.

Rising on my toes, I hugged his neck. He let me guide him down to me, and I pressed my mouth to his. The muscles in his neck stiffened, turning solid like stone. But he parted his lips for me, accepting my kiss. His tongue met mine. He released a soft moan, and I swallowed it in the kiss I never wanted to end. It was tainted with bitterness and desperation, but I devoured it anyway, as long as I still could.

Like always, he pulled back first, his shoulders squared, his chest rising and falling rapidly.

"Princess." His voice was rough, but the word came out soft and tender like a caress.

I forced my fingers to unclench, releasing the hair on the back of his head, then removed my hands from him, hurt by every bit of distance building between us. I pressed my forehead to his chest, unable to let go of him completely.

"I've taken a lot from you already," I whispered.

"You've taken nothing I haven't wished to give you."

I pushed myself away from him. Why was it so hard to do? As if my body was made of metal and he was a powerful, inescapable magnet.

"You and I, Salas, we have unfinished business. And it's only up to you if you want to finish it."

I didn't look up. I didn't want to see his face, scared of the rejection I might read on it. From what I knew, his life had been a series of obstacles on the path of survival, and I'd just selfishly thrown another hurdle in his way.

But I couldn't help it. I wanted him enough to risk it all, including his peace and mine.

As he moved away from me, I turned on my heel and ran. Back to the palace. Back to my room, where my crown waited for me along with a massive load of official obligations, none of which included Salas.

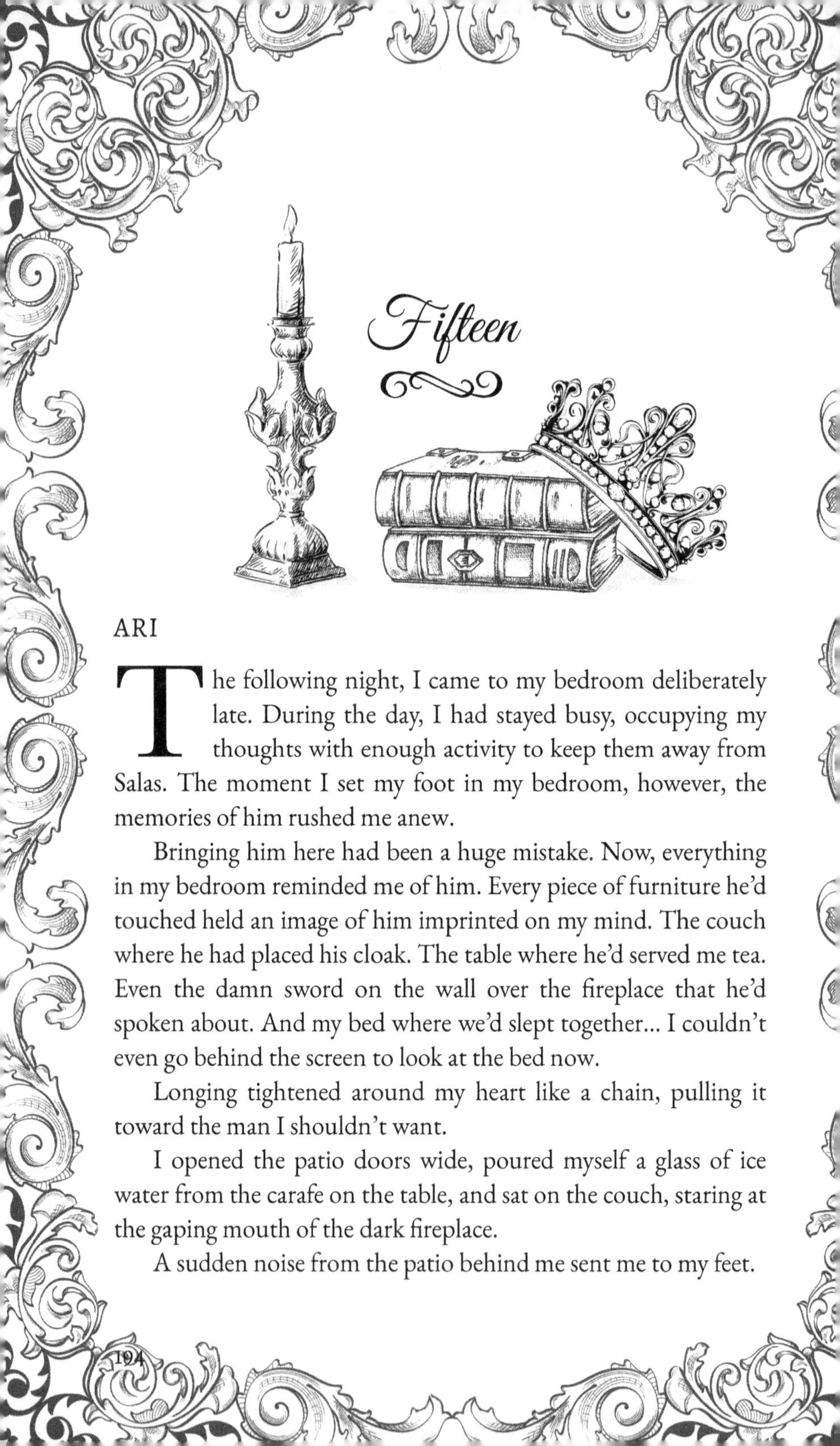

Fifteen

ARI

The following night, I came to my bedroom deliberately late. During the day, I had stayed busy, occupying my thoughts with enough activity to keep them away from Salas. The moment I set my foot in my bedroom, however, the memories of him rushed me anew.

Bringing him here had been a huge mistake. Now, everything in my bedroom reminded me of him. Every piece of furniture he'd touched held an image of him imprinted on my mind. The couch where he had placed his cloak. The table where he'd served me tea. Even the damn sword on the wall over the fireplace that he'd spoken about. And my bed where we'd slept together... I couldn't even go behind the screen to look at the bed now.

Longing tightened around my heart like a chain, pulling it toward the man I shouldn't want.

I opened the patio doors wide, poured myself a glass of ice water from the carafe on the table, and sat on the couch, staring at the gaping mouth of the dark fireplace.

A sudden noise from the patio behind me sent me to my feet.

"Who's there?" I whipped around to face the open glass doors.

"Evening, Princess." Salas stood on the patio, his large frame backlit by the evening sky.

In the sepia light of the dying sunset, he looked like the embodiment of all my thoughts and longing—a wish come true.

Speechless, I carefully set my glass on the table by the couch.

"You need to get someone to remove that lattice from the side there." He gestured at the parapet behind him with the climbing jasmine vines. "It makes it way too easy to climb up."

I exhaled an incredulous laugh, taking him in. He certainly was real, not just an apparition conjured by my lonely mind. He was wearing the shirt I'd given him, and it looked even better on him than I'd imagined.

"You'd mentioned unfinished business between us," he said.

"Is that why you're here?" I finally found my voice, sauntering toward him with a wide grin on my face.

My heart beat faster, my skin flushed. I barely felt my feet carrying me toward him, moving as if I was floating. All because he came to see me again.

It was insane. The effect this man had on me was incredible. It also proved incredibly addictive, and I had no strength and no desire to fight it. I needed his kiss more than I needed my next breath.

He lifted both hands between us, however, halting my advance.

"We do have unfinished business that I'm dying to finish, Princess. But you need to know what kind of a man you allowed into your bed."

"What do you mean?" I kept smiling. "I know who you are."

"No, you don't. I never told you. I never told anyone." He rolled his shoulders back, his broad chest rising with a deep breath as if he was about to jump off a cliff. "I'm a fallen man, Princess. Before I signed my very first slave contract seven years ago, I worked in a fun house. I was a man for hire, Your Highness. Even slaves look down at men like me."

Air rushed out of my lungs. Shock sent me stumbling backwards until my legs hit the back of the couch and I propped my butt on it to stay upright.

I'd never been to a fun house myself. But everything I'd ever heard about "those men" rushed into my mind now.

The men who sold their affections for money were weak, wanton creatures who'd fallen victims to their base instincts, unable to control their physical urges.

They had to work in those places because they had willfully ruined their chances for anything better.

They took their pants off and spilled their seed for every fun-loving playgirl who came along, so no decent woman would marry them now.

They were unintelligent and irresponsible, good-for-nothing drunkards and therefore unable to secure any other form of employment to begin with.

In other words, they were nothing like Salas.

"It's not true." I frowned, waiting for an explanation.

"I wish it wasn't." He folded his arms across his chest and leaned with his shoulder against the frame of the patio doors, not leaving but not entering the room either.

"You're an intelligent man," I argued, folding down a finger for every point I made. "I could tell from the very first words you said to me that you're educated, even though you try to hide it sometimes. You have a stellar self-control. I can personally attest to that. I've had you in my bed more than once, but I'm still very much a virgin. You've kept your clothes on every night we spent together. You're nothing like the men who work in those places."

The look in his eyes hardened.

"How many of the men from 'those places' have you met, *Your Highness?*"

I hated when he used the formal honorific to address me. Right now, he made the respectful "Your Highness' sound like a mockery. It made my blood boil, knocking me off-kilter, which undoubtedly was his intent all along.

"Well, I haven't—"

"Of course, you have not. Princesses don't visit dirty bawdy houses, do they?"

Princesses stay in their pretty palace bedrooms, having men delivered directly to them.

He didn't say that last part out loud. But he probably thought it. Which riled me up even more. Instead of lashing out, however, I did what I normally would during a heated debate in the council. I slowed down my breath and started counting to ten in my mind.

I'd only made it to five before Salas spoke again.

"No boy is born to do what I did." His voice was somber. "I had a good family, born as a son of a blacksmith. My mother owned the shop of course, but my father did most of the work in it. That sword over there," he tipped his chin at my father's present hanging over the fireplace, "it's his work."

"It is?" I spun around to look at the weapon.

"My mother's guild crest is on the blade. But I'd recognize Father's work even without it."

He didn't have to tell me any of it. He didn't need to come here at all tonight, and he could leave anytime. But he stayed, though still not entering the room, just leaning against the doorframe in the threshold.

Maybe Salas needed his story to be heard, and he wanted *me* to be the one to hear it.

"What happened to your parents?" I asked.

He shot me a look from under his thick eyebrows, as if trying to guess the reasons for my asking. I waited, giving him the chance to walk away and take his secrets with him if he wished.

Once again, he stayed.

"Mother died from a sickness when I was twelve," he said. "Her sister inherited the shop and kicked us out."

"Why did she do that?"

"She and Father never got along. She didn't want to have two extra mouths to feed and another dowry to pay in addition to her own sons. Her husband also hated the idea of having another man his age in the house."

"We have charity houses for widowers," I said. "Your father had options."

My father was especially proud of the widower houses in Egami. He said no honorable husband or his children should fall into poverty because of his wife's passing. The crown paid to maintain the houses, and Father personally visited quite a few of them.

Salas gave me a skeptical look.

"I take it you haven't been to one of those either, Princess."

"But I have." I jerked my chin up. "I visited one just last year with my father. The men have spacious, airy rooms for them and their children. They're given options for honest employment while their children go to school. They're fed well and get assistance for clothing and medicine if needed."

His chest rose with a heavy sigh.

"I wish you could visit them all, then. Maybe the conditions in all of them would improve if you did. Either way, a charity house was the last resort for us. The better ones are always full. The others... Well, let's just say they aren't a good place to grow up or to grow old in." He moved his shoulders uncomfortably. "My father could've gotten a job as a blacksmith helper. No one knew his name outside of our village, of course, but Mother's shop did well, and his work was good. This one even made it all the way to the royal palace." He tipped his head at the sword over my fireplace. "But then, the lady who owned the land where we lived offered to take us in. Father got the job of a general laborer on her estate, and I was supposed to be a companion for her son who was only a year younger than me. Father did it for me. He hoped the lady would eventually help me find a good wife and ensure my future."

"That sounds like a great opportunity," I agreed, but he winced. "Was it not?"

"Well, it certainly improved my education. I attended the lessons with the lady's son and learned everything he did. But instead of finding me a wife, the lady set her eyes on me herself. Shortly after I turned fourteen, we became lovers, with little consent on my part."

I gasped in a painful breath. My spine went stiff, my stomach sinking. The darkness of my past brushed over me again with its worn filthy wings. It was a different world, a different life, a different person, yet somehow, I knew exactly how Salas must've felt, and it made me nauseous all the same.

"Did your father know?" I asked, my voice hollow like an echo in an empty cave.

"No. By then, she had sent him away from the estate to work on a distant farm. The hard work ruined his health. He passed away shortly after." His free shoulder jerked once. But he remained in the same casual position, leaning against the frame. "I was seventeen when the lady died too. Her daughter inherited the estate. She knew what was going on between her mother and me and ordered me to leave, afraid that my 'wicked ways' might rub off on her younger brother and ruin his good name along with his chances for an advantageous marriage. As the word about my tattered reputation got out, no one would hire me. I was too young to even sign a contract with a slave owner then." He shrugged, trying to downplay his sufferings. "I knocked on many doors that winter when it got too cold to beg on the street. Few of the doors opened. No one let me in. Except for one establishment."

"The fun house?"

"The fun house," he echoed with a sigh. "I wish I could say my story is unique, Princess, but it isn't. During my years in the brothel, I met men from all walks of life. Actors and musicians down on their luck. Lady's favorites who have fallen out of favor. Widowers. Run-away husbands who'd given up on trying to please their moody, abusive wives and found it easier to please many different women instead. I made friends. I felt safer there than in the lady's manor where I lived before."

"Why did you leave the fun house?" I asked, striving to understand.

He stared past my shoulder, as if peering straight back into his past. "Once again, I had little choice when it happened. As popular as our services were, the town folks hated our establishment. Even those who visited us in private would call the house all kinds of names in public. One fine night, they went even further and set it on fire."

"They burned it? Were there people inside?"

His nod sent chills down my spine.

"We were all inside. A few clients too."

"That's murder," I spat out the accusation, furious at the injustice of it all.

"I'm afraid murder was the point, Princess. They wished us all gone, along with the house."

"Did people die?"

"Thankfully, no. Not that night. The owner woke up. Her husband shook me awake, then woke up many others. Everyone managed to get out. Some got burns and injuries, but all survived that night." He paused, slowly rubbing his right thigh. "The place burned to the ground, however, and the owner chose not to rebuild it."

"Were those who burned it ever held accountable?"

He looked at me as if I'd just said total nonsense.

"For what? For getting rid of a 'sinful place?' They were heralded as heroes by the local folks."

I closed my eyes for a moment. The visions of a roaring fire in the dead of the night assaulted my mind. People running through the flames in panic, screaming, their clothes smoldering. Even imagining it was hard. I couldn't fathom what it'd be like to live through a night like that.

"What did you do then?" I asked softly.

"All I could legally do at that point was to find a similar kind of employment in a different location. But by a stroke of luck, I came into possession of a reference letter that vouched for the bearer's character. It enabled me to enter into a contract with a slave owner, and... well, here I am now."

Salas and I were born and raised worlds apart. His story was different from mine. Yet it resonated with me deeply, reflecting my own experiences in some ways and echoing my emotions.

I remembered what it was like to have no choice. I knew first-hand what a hopeless situation felt like. The feeling of being all alone in the world with no place to go and no one to ask for help was also way too familiar to me.

But my story had a happy ending when his did not.

"Tell me something, please. Did that fight you ended up being flogged for have something to do with your past?"

He frowned, scratching his chest. "I ran into the owner of the fun house that day. The men I worked with insulted her behind her back. So, I threw a punch, and it escalated from there."

"You stood up for the woman who exploited you?"

"Yes. But she was also the one who took me in from the cold when no one else would. She gave me a job that helped me survive until something better came along."

Something better was the slave contract.

"So, you call becoming a slave your lucky strike?"

He nodded firmly. "The meaning of either luck or misfortune is different for everyone. You know what they say? For some, a hardship means their tears are too big, for others it's when their diamonds are too small. In my situation at least, becoming a slave was an improvement. Unlike in a fun house, I don't have to touch or be touched by anyone. I do my work through the day, and I'm left alone at night. My bed is my own even if it's just a bunk with a straw mattress."

What he must've felt when I had the guards drag him to my bedroom, especially after being put through all that invasive grooming and being locked in chains by Gem too.

Guilt gripped me.

"Salas, I..." I got off the couch, clutching my hands together. "I'm so sorry for everything you had to go through because of me. I let others handle our arrangement when I should've just found a way to talk to you first."

He shook his head at that.

"You know as well as I do that there is no chance for a princess and a slave to simply get together and talk." His features softened as he gazed at me. "Unless the slave climbs the wall up to the princess's bedroom."

I kept wringing my hands in front of me, racking my brain about how to right so many wrongs. Where could I even begin? And how could I avoid possibly making it even worse?

"Please, tell me how I can help? What can I do to make it better?"

"For me?" He shook his head. "Don't worry about me, Princess. I've lived a life, and I've made what I have with it. I'm content with what it is now. Hard work has been both my retribution and my salvation. But if you really want to make a difference, don't just free one slave, make changes that would improve life for all. You can do so much more than I ever could. Look outside of the palace and even outside of the Egami City. You are our future queen. Just think about all the good you could do."

"But how? Where do I begin?"

He gazed at me kindly.

"You're the crown princess. I believe you have the brains to figure it out."

Silence stretched between us as I pondered his words. He remained by the door, waiting.

"Forget what I said about the unfinished business, Salas. There is no contract between us anymore. You owe me nothing. You don't have to be here—"

"But what if I want to?"

"Why? After everything that you've been through." I gripped

my hands tighter. "You said you don't like being touched, which I can understand completely."

"Not all touch is the same." His voice dipped with a velvety note running through it. It stroked my hearing, sending a warm shiver down my body. "You have nothing to apologize to me for, Princess. With you, the choice has always been mine. From the very first night."

I released my hands, only for my fingers to immediately clutch my skirts. "Why did you agree to come here that first night?"

"The first time? I just wanted to see if I was right."

"About what?"

"About what I saw in your eyes when you looked at me for the very first time. I was on the scaffold, being whipped. And you arrived on your white horse, wearing your shiny crown—every bit the princess that you are."

I glanced aside, my hand mechanically going up to the crown on my head.

"Except that when our eyes connected," he continued, "I didn't see a princess, or even a woman. I saw someone who noticed the person in me for the first time in many years." His gaze drifted past me, a frown creasing his forehead as he recalled his punishment. "I didn't care about the two lashes that you spared me from that day. Two or twenty—at some point of torture, the number just becomes irrelevant. What shocked me was that you cared enough to intervene. That first night, I came here to make sure I simply imagined things that didn't exist. I had to make sure you were what I always thought you had been—a spoiled little princess, cherished by the queen and worshiped by the entire queendom for coming from another world to save us all."

"You really think that's who I am?"

"That's what many think you are." He moved a hand before resting it on his forearm again with his arms folded across his chest. "I hadn't touched a woman in seven years. I thought I was done with it. I even looked forward to telling it to your face. Such is the freedom of a slave who has nothing to lose. I was going to refuse the princess, consequences be damned. But I couldn't do it outright. Spending time with you proved too enjoyable to end it too quickly. And then, it was too late. I realized it hadn't been just my imagination. You're not just some miracle dropped into the lap of luxury. You're a real person, hiding pain of your own and making it through life the best you can. For a princess and a slave, as it turned out, we have a lot in common."

That we did. I sensed it from the very beginning. And now, he knew it too.

"You've been poignantly honest with me, Princess. All I can do is to be honest with you in return."

"Is that why you're here? To tell me the truth?"

"What else can there be between us now that the truth is out? I want to touch you again. I ache to learn what it feels like to be inside you, and it kills me that I'll never find out now. But you had to know that your first time would've been with a whore, not even a slave."

A "whore" who, by his own admission, hadn't touched a woman for seven years before he touched me. His passion and tenderness had robbed me of breath and stole my peace. It was hard to reconcile all these things into one person. Yet there he was in front of me, with his dark, intense eyes focused on me.

I took another step toward him, which brought me close enough to touch him, but I kept my hands to myself.

"Salas, I'm not going to pay you even a single dented copper coin for tonight. No matter what happens between us, you'll leave this room no better off than when you came here. Am I still your client in any way?"

His beard moved with a smirk.

"No, Princess. You can't hire a working man without paying him for his services."

"Then I'm asking you—not as your client, not as a princess, but as a woman who likes you and appreciates you just the way you are—would you spend another night with me, please?"

He pushed away from the door frame. His arms unfolded and dropped to his sides, exposing his chest to me.

I splayed my hand on it, just over the little horn buttons and the cross-stitch embroidery of his new shirt. His heart thundered under my palm, strong and desperate.

"Knowing your past doesn't change how I feel about you, Salas. You didn't come here just to talk, did you? You want me, and you know I want you too."

Covering my hand with his, he leaned over me. His warm breath fanned over the side of my face, his lips hovering just above my ear.

"I hoped. Yes. I knew I shouldn't, but I did anyway." Finally, he stepped over the threshold. His arms wrapped around me, drawing me to him. I melted into his embrace, as if my body belonged right there, next to his.

"It has to be *me*, Princess," he said in a hot, firm whisper, trailing quick, hungry kisses down the side of my face to my neck. "Sooner or later, you'll marry another, and there is not one fucking thing I can do about it. But I have to be your first. No one else. You came to me. You wanted me. It has to be me."

With his finger under my chin, he lifted my face to him.

"I want it to be you," I echoed, losing myself in the darkness of his eyes.

A soft rumble of approval came from deep inside his throat as he claimed my mouth in a kiss. He held my face between his large hands, and I gripped both of his wrists for support because I needed to hold on to something when he kissed me this deeply, making me weak in my knees.

"Salas..." I exhaled when he let me come up for a breath. His name fluttered from my lips like a gentle puff of breeze. "I'm so glad you climbed that wall tonight."

I fisted the shirt on his chest. Holding me to him with one hand, he undid the buttons of my dress with the other.

"Nothing could keep me away from you, Princess. Not the fear of being discovered. Not even common sense. Goddess knows I've tried." He skimmed the top of my breast with his fingers. My heart thundered so hard, he must've felt it when he pressed his large, warm palm to my chest. "Nothing bad will happen to you when I'm with you, Ari. I promise. If your past starts to haunt you again, I'll be here to help you deal with it. And if you ever want me to stop, just let me know. A word, a look, a gesture from you, is all I need. Give me a sign, remember?"

I nodded, feeling incredibly grateful for this man and his kindness.

My past was still there. I couldn't erase it. I'd tried and failed to bury it for good. I hated to remember it. I cringed when the memories popped into my brain. They still made me sick to my stomach. But their power over me had weakened.

Here, I was safe. And with Salas holding me like this, I felt simply invincible.

"I'm not afraid, just a little nervous. But I trust you."

"Thank you." He kissed the tip of my nose, then placed his hands on my shoulders. "I'm going to take this dress off you now. Ready?"

I nodded, excitement spreading through my body with warm tingles as he slid the dress off my shoulders. Crouching down, he tugged it all the way to the floor, leaving me only in my bra and panties.

"You look gorgeous in the moonlight." He grinned, looking up at me from his crouch.

My face flushed with pleasure. People usually praised things like my speeches, my knowledge, or my decisions. I thought I knew better than to blush at a compliment of my appearance. Yet there I was, with my cheeks warming and my heart fluttering like a preening bird in my chest.

"Come to me, my princess." Salas lifted me into his arms, then carried me to bed behind the screen.

I kissed him as he lowered me onto my silk bedspread. Tomorrow, I would have to find a way to live the rest of my life without his kisses. But tonight... Tonight, he was all mine, to hug and kiss to my heart's content.

"As much as I love seeing this shirt on you," I tugged at the fabric over his chest. "I really want it off right now."

"As you wish, Your Highness." His voice turned light and playful, and I didn't even mind his use of the honorific this time.

Rising on his knees over me, he pulled the shirt off over his head.

"Just to warn you," he said, tossing it aside. "It's been a while since the groomers worked on me last."

"Good," I murmured, sliding a hand up his chest against the slight prickle of the new hair growing there. "I finally get a chance to feel the real you." I pressed my nose to his collarbone, breathing him in. "To learn your true scent."

Through the mild fragrance of the plain soap he'd used before coming here, I smelled salt and earth of his skin, the musk of the male warmed by the sun, and the fresh air of the fields next to the city wall where he'd been working lately.

"You don't miss the fancy perfumes?" He helped me take off my crown, then raked his fingers through my hair, freeing it from the bun.

"Not even a little bit." I nuzzled his chest before sliding a hand down his torso. I stopped my fingers at the waistband of his pants, uncertain. "How are we going to do this?"

"In the most delightful way possible." He chuckled softly, bringing my hand to his mouth to kiss my fingers.

"I heard it hurts the first time," I worried.

"Not with me. It won't," he assured me.

I soaked up his confidence. For once, I was more than happy to relinquish all control and follow someone else's directions. I trusted Salas to know what to do.

Sliding his hand behind my back, he unclipped my bra, then took it off, along with my underwear. I didn't hide my nakedness from him this time. Instead, I welcomed the rush of thrill when he kissed my breasts. He sucked the tip of one into his mouth, gently tugging at the bud of my nipple with his teeth. His rough palms glided up and down my sides.

It was easy to trust him. The last memories of anyone touching me were of Salas, and all of those memories were good.

Anticipation fanned my desire. I parted my legs, needing to feel his touch everywhere. He accepted the invitation, gently cupping me between my thighs.

Massaging me gently with just one finger, he trailed his kisses down my body. The prickle of his beard felt invigorating. Hot flushes of desire burst in my lower belly, making me squirm under the caress of both his lips and his hands. Holding my thighs open, he lowered his head between them, then dipped his tongue inside me.

Warmth spread through me. I gripped his hair, rocking my hips against his mouth. There was no apprehension anymore. Nothing impeded the pleasure rolling through me.

He licked gently at first, but gradually increased the speed and pressure. My pleasure grew like a tightly wound spring, ready to burst. When I thought I couldn't take it anymore, that I might die, lost to this bliss, he pulled back.

"Salas…" I begged in a needy whimper.

"Yes, sweetheart?" His hand replaced his mouth on me.

The change of sensation dropped my arousal from the white-hot melting point to a strong, steady flame.

"I need…" I moaned, lifting my hips into his hand.

"Patience, my darling princess. Patience is everything."

Shifting back a little, he kissed my chest while slipping the tip of his finger inside me. His thumb gently tapped and rubbed the spot where I needed him most. I moaned. Swells of pleasure rolled through me, slowly building higher under his control.

He shifted just a little more down, then dipped his head between my legs again. The glide of his tongue between my thighs added a new thrilling note to the symphony of sensations he played through my body.

He added another finger inside me, massaging and stretching

me. Probing and testing. All the while, his thumb kept playing the tantalizing rhythm on and around my most sensitive spot.

Rising on an outstretched arm, he watched me. I loved seeing him over me like this. His hair framed his face. His eyes glistened in the moonlight. I held his gaze, wishing to remember this moment for as long as I lived. But he pressed his thumb just a little harder, pleasure surged, and my eyelids fluttered closed.

I was only half-aware of his erection pressing against me. The stretch of his invasion synched with the thrill of approaching orgasm that rushed my body. His thumb rubbed harder, and ecstasy flooded me whole.

For a few incredible moments, I was oblivious to the world around me. And when I came back to reality, guided down from the crest of pleasure by Salas's gentle touch, I realized his hips were flush with mine. He was deep inside me.

"It happened?" I marveled.

"It did." He held himself up on his elbows above me.

A huge smile stretched my lips.

"My first time..."

And it didn't even hurt. Or maybe I just was too busy coming to remember any pain?

He kissed my hair with a smile. "You did amazing, sweetheart."

I did nothing. He was the one who did everything while I just writhed in pleasure. But his praise warmed my chest nevertheless, as if I'd just won a medal for running a marathon.

There had been no pain before. But now, I felt flushed and a little achy, trembling slightly. The sensation of having him inside me was exquisite but so new, it felt almost foreign.

Exposed, open, and vulnerable, I could see how terrible, even traumatizing, this entire experience could've been if it happened with the wrong man at the wrong time. Once again, my heart filled with gratitude for Salas.

"How did I get so lucky, finding you?" I wrapped my arms around his neck.

He smiled. "It seems good things can be found on flogging platforms."

I kissed him as if he were mine, my hands sinking into the hair on the back of his head, my body pressed to his. And he kissed me back, like he was claiming me all for himself. For this one night, we fully belonged to each other.

It was such a beautiful lie.

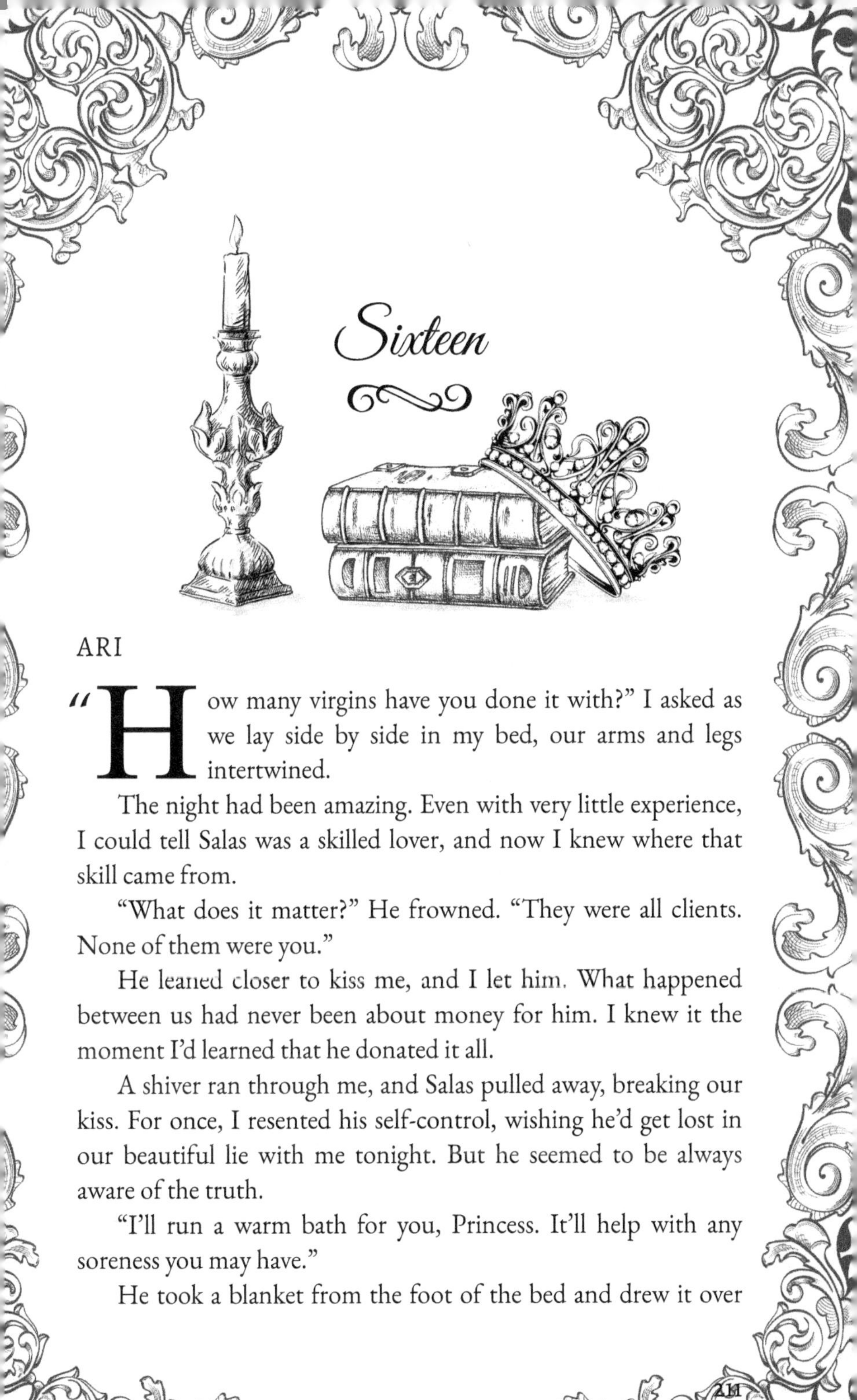

Sixteen

ARI

"How many virgins have you done it with?" I asked as we lay side by side in my bed, our arms and legs intertwined.

The night had been amazing. Even with very little experience, I could tell Salas was a skilled lover, and now I knew where that skill came from.

"What does it matter?" He frowned. "They were all clients. None of them were you."

He leaned closer to kiss me, and I let him. What happened between us had never been about money for him. I knew it the moment I'd learned that he donated it all.

A shiver ran through me, and Salas pulled away, breaking our kiss. For once, I resented his self-control, wishing he'd get lost in our beautiful lie with me tonight. But he seemed to be always aware of the truth.

"I'll run a warm bath for you, Princess. It'll help with any soreness you may have."

He took a blanket from the foot of the bed and drew it over

me before getting out of bed. A moment later, I heard the water rush into the tub through the open door to the bathroom.

I stretched in bed, feeling slightly feverish but elated. It happened. I'd come as close to a man as one could, and it hadn't killed me. On the contrary, I loved it. After dreading sex for so long, I actually enjoyed it.

Did it mean I was now ready to guide my future husband in all bedroom matters?

A sudden grip of sadness seized my heart.

It was over now. There was no reason for Salas to be with me anymore. Yet letting him go was the last thing I wished to do. Even having him out of my sight right now didn't sit well with me.

I tossed the covers aside, ready to go to him when he returned from the bathroom.

"The bath is ready." He scooped me from the bed into his arms.

I hugged him with a soft giggle. The sound felt foreign, even to my own ear. Giggling was unbecoming for a princess, but the giddy feeling Salas caused in me bubbled over, hard to contain.

The tub was filling quickly. No petals floated on the surface this time, but Salas must've added some oils and fragrances from the vials on the stand nearby, turning the water creamy pink.

"Here we go." He gently lowered me into the tub.

The warm water hugged my hips, soothing the ache. For now, it barely reached up to my waist. Kneeling by the tub, Salas scooped the water with his large hand, then poured it over my bent legs to warm them.

I raked my fingers through the water. "Do you want to join me? There is lots of space for two in here."

He hesitated. "I should be going soon."

His words churned with anxiety in my chest. I wasn't ready for him to leave. I never was.

"Stay," I begged. "We have a whole night still."

"Don't you need to get some sleep? There is another busy day of running the country tomorrow."

"I rarely sleep, anyway." I shrugged.

"Why?"

I'd hardly spoken about my insomnia to anyone. What was the point? The one time when I mentioned it to the royal healing witch, she gave me the same sleeping potion that the palace guards used on their crossbow bolts. It knocked me out for the whole night but left me drowsy and aching for two days after. I never took that thing again.

Instead, I managed to do just fine by getting scraps of sleep on the nights after some less stressful days.

"I'm just not a good sleeper, I guess," I said.

"You slept just fine both nights I'd stayed with you. The first night, you even slept in, remember?"

"I did, didn't I?""

Salas proved to be better than a sleeping potion for me. Except that I didn't want to sleep tonight. If this was our last night together, I didn't want to waste a single second.

"Climb in." I splashed the water in the tub in invitation. "It'll fill faster with you in it. Besides, I really enjoy having you close," I confessed, then added quickly, "Of course if you don't feel the same way..."

"Oh Ari." He shook his head in surrender. "The last thing you need to doubt is the joy I feel when I'm with you."

He rose from the floor, then undid the closure of his pants, and I averted my eyes. He'd already been inside me. I'd felt him and loved the sensation. Yet I couldn't bring myself to look at that part of his body. Maybe I feared it'd remind me of the one that'd been forced down my throat long ago. It was the only penis I'd seen so far, and I didn't want any reminders of that memory.

Salas stepped into the bath. Despite being determined to keep my focus on the swirls of water, I failed and jerked my gaze up his muscular legs.

A wide, mangled scar marred his right thigh, stretching from just below his hip all the way down to his knee.

"Is this from the fire?" I asked, looking up at him.

"Yes." He lowered himself into the tub.

Before he settled into the milky water, I caught a glimpse of his erection. To my relief, it looked very different from the dick that I hated to remember. Thicker and longer, Salas's hard length also had a curious ridge and protrusions I'd never seen or even heard of before.

With a deep sigh of relaxation, Salas leaned back against the marble on the opposite end of me. The water instantly rose higher, hiding his peculiar appendage from view.

I turned off the faucet and drew my knees to my chest to give him space, but he found my ankles in the water, then stretched my legs comfortably for me, placing my feet on his thighs.

Every time we got together, it had always been about me. Salas had made my pleasure his mission, but now I wondered how *he* felt. He'd never done anything for himself.

He'd said he was dying to find out what it felt like to be inside me, but he'd slipped out right after that one thrust that had absolved me of virginity. At the time, I was relieved to have him out, ending the invasion. But now, I wished I could make him feel at least a fraction of the pleasure I'd experienced because of him.

"Can you tell me something, please?" I asked, a little hesitantly.

Would he appreciate my attention to the matter? Or would he find it intrusive?

His voice remained light when he gave me permission. "Go ahead, ask."

"Please don't laugh, but I honestly don't know. Does a man's erection always mean he... um, wants to have sex?"

He didn't laugh, didn't even smile, just cleared his throat, shifting a little.

"Not always. But often, yes. It does."

"How about you? Right now? How are you feeling?"

"Does it matter how I feel?"

"Why not? I'd like you to enjoy your time with me as much as I'm enjoying spending it with you. How do you feel when I touch you?"

I placed a hand on his shin under the water but didn't move it any higher, waiting for his reply. He'd known his share of unwanted touches. The last thing I wished was to force more on him.

"How far do you want to go with this, Princess?" His voice dropped to a low rumble.

"All the way." I leaned closer, sliding my hand up to his knee. "If you let me."

He gripped the edges of the tub with both hands. Water splashed and sloshed around us as he sat up straighter.

"May I?" I ran my fingers along a thick corded muscle in his left thigh. "Give me a sign, Salas, say a word, and I'll stop," I echoed his own words to me.

He let my hand travel up his thigh unimpeded, but as my thumb brushed by his shaft, he sucked in a breath.

I halted my advances.

"Don't stop, Princess," he rasped. "Whatever you do, just please don't stop. I can't do anything halfway with you."

"All right then. All the way it is."

I braced against the onslaught of dark memories when curling my fingers around his girth. But the sensation was incomparable to anything I'd ever touched before.

Everything about this man was solid and well-built—from his character, to his heart, to every part of his body, including his cock. Some curious shapes seemed to be inserted just under the delicate skin of his hard length.

He tossed his head back, gripping the edges of the bathtub with both hands as I explored his body.

"What's this?" I tapped with my fingers along the hard ridge at the base of his cock in the front. My thumb slid over a row of round bumps on the underside of his shaft. "Were you born with these? I've never heard of anything like it."

"Of course, you haven't." He groaned softly, either from pleasure or pain.

"Does it hurt?" I jerked my hand away.

He scrubbed a palm down his face before looking at me again. "I wasn't born with these, Princess. A warlock with questionable skill and reputation did it, using fish bladders, liquid onyx, a few magic spells, and goddess-knows-what-else. But the pain is long gone. Now, it's just numb at the base."

"Why did he do this to you? Did you report him? Was he arrested and punished for this?"

He smiled warmly. "My feisty little princess, ready for blood and vengeance. Why would I report him? I paid him to do it."

"You did?" I gaped at him in shock. "But why?"

"For the pleasure of my clients."

"You paid an unskilled warlock to hurt and mutilate you for the pleasure of strangers?"

"Strangers who financed the survival of both me and the establishment I worked for."

I stopped short of arguing, afraid I'd sound judgmental. Instead, I reached out and wrapped my hand around his hard length again.

"How exactly did it give your clients pleasure?"

He covered my hand with his, guiding me.

"This elevation here..." He slid the tip of my pointer finger along the thick vertical ridge at the base in the front. It ran from about halfway up along his cock then up his lower belly for about the length of my finger. "It'll make you come in seconds if I fuck you at just the right angle."

"Oh..." I bit my lip.

"And these here..." He pressed my thumb to the row of rounded bumps on the underside of his shaft. "They would bring you a lot of pleasure if I took you from behind."

Desire surged low in my belly. The mental image of Salas pounding into me with abandon proved incredibly arousing.

"You said it hurt when you had it done?" I asked.

He shrugged. "It is a rather painful procedure, yes."

"But you went through with it, only to feel numb at the end?"

"It never was about what *I* feel, Princess. These things aren't done for the man's pleasure."

"Then tell me what brings *you* pleasure. Where can I touch you to make you feel good?"

He paused for a moment.

"Me?" He guided my hand up his erect cock. "Here—" His breath hitched as he moved my finger in a circle just under the crown of the head.

"Right here?" I rubbed where he showed me.

"Yes..." Salas groaned. "Oh, gods."

His hand fell away, leaving him entirely at my mercy.

I stroked lightly at first, carefully avoiding the magical modifications to his body. Despite his assurance that they were no longer painful, I lost all desire to touch them. They were done for someone else, and right now I wished to pleasure him and only him.

He stretched through his entire body as I played with him, slowly gaining confidence. His low groans and eagerness with which he pushed into my hand were the best encouragement. As he jerked up, the tip of his erection popped out of the water. I bent down and flicked my tongue over the head of his cock.

He moaned, sucking in air in short little breaths.

"Princess..."

I looked up at him.

"What are you doing?" He cupped the side of my face with his large hand.

"The same thing you've done to me." I licked my lips.

"But women don't normally do this."

I arched an eyebrow. "They don't?"

"Not usually. No."

"So, you've never had anyone lick you there?" I stroked with my thumb over his cock's head under water.

"No. Never." The muscles in his belly and thighs strained, turning rock-solid.

A thrill coursed through me. Could it be true? I did something for the first time to the man who had given me so many of my firsts.

"Well, that's just perfect, Salas." I smiled. "My turn to be your first, then. Can you lift him up for me, please? So I can do it again."

I waited for him to lift his hips again for his cock to emerge out of the water, eager to take him in, but Salas kept his body down and his hand under my jaw.

"Are you sure about this, Ari?"

He worried about me because he now knew all the dark parts of my past. But that was exactly why I had to do it. I used Salas's taste, his scent, and the feel of his skin to erase every sensation that had been forced on me by others. I used him because I knew he would let me.

"I'm sure." I nodded. "Please let me taste you again."

He lifted himself out of the water, exposing his cock for me. I wrapped my lips just under his crown, the place where he said he felt the pleasure. He tasted like the rose water of the bath. I sucked then licked, delighted by his tortured groans.

"Ari, I—" He gripped my head, his fingers sinking into my hair.

He lifted me up and off his cock. Then dropped his hips back into the tub, water splashing out. I pumped him with my hand for his climax to erupt. His release spread through the water in tight creamy spurts, and I felt grateful to him for keeping it out of my mouth.

The dark memory churned in my head with a brief swirl of nausea in my throat. Then, it passed, and I knew it would never torture me with the same intensity ever again. Salas proved to be a perfect cure for my sickening past.

I gently stroked up his thigh and over the rugged surface of his scar. His skin suddenly wavered with shimmer, mirroring the mother-of-pearl swirls of the rose oil in the water—a wave of *reflection* ran through Salas.

I'd never seen him *reflect* before, not when he was flogged, not when he faced the guards in the city at night, but he did now while looking at me.

"You'll be my ruin, Ari," he said with a quiet conviction.

The smile slipped from my face. My heart tightened at the foreboding in his words.

A princess and a slave were already a highly unlikely pair. A princess and a man with Salas's past? I couldn't even predict all the repercussions we both might face if it ever came out.

If I was to be his ruin, then he certainly could be my downfall.

AFTER DRAINING the tub and taking a shower together, Salas and I snuggled under the blankets in my bed.

"Have breakfast with me," I said, curling against his wide chest.

He threw an arm around me, holding me close.

"It's way too early for breakfast."

"Tea then? I'll call for it right now." I climbed out of bed and pulled on the ribbon of the bell before he had a chance to object.

He sat up in bed. "Wouldn't the kitchen be closed at this hour?"

"Not in Egami Palace." I found and put on a nightgown. "The Queen's Court is huge. Someone is always hungry, day or night. The cooks rotate in the kitchen."

Salas hid behind the silk screen when a maid came, and I ordered us tea. After my order had arrived, we sat in my bed, shoulder to shoulder, our backs against the headboard, the tea tray on our lap.

"Where did you learn how to serve tea?" I watched him expertly fill the infuser with tea leaves then add just the right amount of dried berries and herbs for extra flavor before submerging it into the porcelain teapot. "You don't need to answer it, by the way," I added promptly, afraid of what kind of memories my question might stir in him. "You don't ever have to answer any of my questions about your past."

"I don't mind," he replied calmly. "My memories hold no power over me. With you, I can talk freely, now that you know everything."

I envied his composure. I could only wish to get to that level of calm and control one day.

"I learned many ways to serve tea in the lady's manor," Salas explained. "Back in our house, Mother kept things simple. We had one fine tea set that came as Father's dowry. But it was mostly displayed in a glass cabinet. I remember taking it out only when Mother's friends came over or when her sister visited, which she didn't do often."

He poured the tea into two cups, then added some cream to one of them before handing it to me.

"Thank you." I accepted it, noticing he remembered how I liked my tea.

"A sandwich?" He offered me the plate with tiny pastries and some meat sandwiches.

"No. I'm good." I waved the food off. "You have some."

I wasn't hungry. I could always get any food I wished. He, however, could use a break from the potato stew served in the slaves' barracks. But Salas didn't seem to be in a hurry to devour such delicacies like doe cheese from the mountains or the sweet fruit from across the sea. Picking up a rye wafer with a thin slice of ham, he took a small bite of it, then placed it back on the edge of the tray.

Salas handled food with the same reservation and control with which he drank fine wine or made love to me, as if afraid to get used to something he knew he couldn't keep.

I set my cup down on the tray, then took his hand in mine. He faced me. His eyes, dark in the pale moonlight, studied my face. I searched for something to say. Something that would express how I felt having him by my side, but no words seemed adequate, so I just smiled.

Leaning closer, he kissed my nose. The tenderness of his gesture spread through me like melted butter. My limbs grew heavy and my resolve to keep it together softened to a mush. He didn't move away from me, pressing another kiss to my cheek.

"Your freckles are hard to see at night," he murmured against my skin. "I need to be very close to spot them."

My glasses fogged up from his breath, and I closed my eyes, using my other senses to feel him.

"Is that what you're doing, Salas? Are you kissing my freckles?"

"Hmm," he hummed, pressing a kiss to the side of my nose. "They're so cute. And extremely kissable."

"I don't remember anyone calling me cute before."

"It's because they don't get to see you like this, with your hair down and your feet up." He pressed his lips to my other cheek next.

Out there, deep behind the horizon, the sun kept moving, bringing the inevitable morning to Rorrim Queendom. Soon, Salas would have to leave. But for now... For now, he was still mine.

I tilted my head back, catching his next kiss on my mouth. He deepened it, letting me taste the sweet tea on his lips. When he pulled away, he panted a little, leaving me out of breath too.

"Have you ever been on a date?" I asked, because this really felt like a date to me, even though I'd never been on one before.

"No," he said. "I was too young for courting when my parents were alive. And then—" He shrugged, not bothering to finish.

But I knew what he didn't say: and then, an adult woman

robbed him of his innocence, his youth, and his future, depriving him of any chance to ever have a date.

"If you were on a date, what would you like it to be?" Salas asked, his voice lifting. Clearly, he refused to be dragged down by memories of his past.

"Oh, I don't know." I tapped my chin with a finger. "I'd go see a play in a theater?" It came out as a question, betraying my uncertainty.

"Is that something nobles do when courting?"

"I'm not sure," I admitted. "I've never really courted anyone. The council and my parents have been doing that part for me so far." I thought about my parents strolling along a garden path, lost in their conversation. "If I had to plan a date, I think I'd go outside. A walk in a garden is something I'd like to do. The palace gardens are a nice, quiet place to talk. Besides, I enjoy being outdoors, even if I don't get out that often."

"How about riding your horse?"

"I like that too, yes," I agreed. "A ride would make an excellent date. Provided of course that my date can ride a horse."

"Or you could teach him."

"I'm a terrible teacher." I laughed, shaking my head. "I could explain a math problem and help find the solution. But to explain things outside of the classroom? That's not in my skill set. I'd be like, 'Alright, Salas, this is the horse. Horse, this is Salas. Now find a way to work together.'"

He grinned, moonlight bouncing in his eyes. "So, it's *our* date you're talking about then? Since it's me you're introducing to that horse."

I didn't argue. What was the harm in letting this fantasy live for a little while? Either way, it was doomed to die with the first light of sunrise.

"Well if so," he continued, "then I'd like for us to go swimming together. Do you swim?"

"I do."

"Great. But I have a condition. The best swimming is at night when no one is around, because it's best to wear no clothes at all, nothing to drag you down. On a calm night, the water is so dark, you can't see the bottom. With the starry sky above and a bottomless abyss below, it really looks like flying. And at that moment, you feel absolutely free."

Free.

I closed my eyes, letting the picture created by his words take me. Of the two of us, it could be assumed I had more freedom than Salas. But I felt more tied up and chained than ever, restrained by so many duties and obligations, sometimes it felt my back would break from their weight.

A kiss landed on the side of my nose, and I opened my eyes to meet Salas's warm gaze.

"I just realized I hadn't kissed that freckle yet," he explained.

He simply wouldn't let me descend into sadness tonight, lifting me up one kiss, one smile at a time. I liked my freckles. But now I wished I had infinitely more of them for Salas to keep kissing them all.

"And after swimming," he continued describing the imaginary date we would never have in real life, "I'd make you the best rabbit pie you've ever had."

"I like rabbit pie. Come to think of it, they don't serve it in the palace often enough."

He huffed in disappointment. "Well, the life of a princess isn't as great as I thought then. In such a case, I most definitely would make you the pie. That's pretty much the only dish I can make, but I can make it exceptionally well."

"I can cook too," I bragged, not to be outdone by his rabbit pie. "I know at least a dozen ways how to cook potatoes. And... well, that's pretty much all I know about cooking." I shook my head, laughing.

"It's a really good thing then that we both have other people to make food for us, Princess."

I had an entire palace kitchen staffed with the world's most renowned chefs. And he had a slave cook. It wasn't quite the same, but I smiled anyway because if I didn't, I'd have to acknowledge the infinite distance between us that could never be crossed.

"*STAY,*" resonated through my mind.

Only this time, I didn't say the word out loud as we stood on the patio, his arms wrapped around me in one last hug.

As much as we'd tried to hide from the sunrise in my bed behind the silk screen, the pale light of the rising sun had found us. Morning slithered through the open patio doors, painting the skies with muddy yellow.

Salas had to leave, and I could no longer hold him. I'd run out of time and out of excuses to keep him with me.

He'd put his shirt back on. I'd smoothed it over his chest, running my fingers over the small, polished buttons. With the shirt now in his possession, I realized there was nothing I'd have of him, not a single memento. Just memories.

My throat tightened. I wished I could do something, say something. But words were void of hope, so I kept them all in.

Salas gently ran his fingers along the side of my face. "I wish you all the happiness in the world, Ari."

I loved the sound of my name from his lips. It pained me to know I'd have to live now without ever hearing it from him again.

Like it had always been, happiness remained unattainable. By now, I believed it simply didn't exist. There was contentment, safety, and peace. I'd felt those. Happiness, however, remained nothing but an illusion, a beautiful but impossible idea. A ghost. Every time I thought I'd come close enough to feel it, it'd flutter away and disappear like an apparition.

"Can you find a way to be happy, too, Salas?"

"I'm content. That's more than I could've hoped for years ago."

I wished I could do something for him, help him somehow. But after my last failed attempt, I feared even an offer of help might come off as an insult to the life he'd built.

"Don't free just one slave..." he'd said.

Mother had told me something similar, though not quite the

same. *"...you can't favor any one person without considering the impact it would have on the rest."*

If I made a change to the benefit of all slaves, then Salas would benefit too. I didn't know exactly how yet, but I was determined to find a way.

"I'll never forget you," I said with a sigh, struggling to keep my tears at bay.

"I will always remember you, too, Princess."

He took my mouth in a kiss that seemed impossibly short when it ended. As he tore himself away from me, I took a step after him, unable to let go. He promptly climbed over the parapet, and by the time I reached it, he'd already made it down the wall, jumping off the lattice onto the ground.

He ripped the lower section of the lattice off the wall, wrested it out of the climbing rose bushes, then tossed it into the nearby hedge with force.

"Don't let them fix this," he growled, before walking away.

Air left me, squeezed out of my lungs by a tight band of sorrow around my chest. My knees gave in, and I sank to the ground. Hugging a stone pillar of the parapet, I watched his large figure shrink into the distance until he stepped off the path and took some hidden passage between the hedges toward the slaves' barracks.

Longing stretched from me to him like a thin but resilient thread. I wished I could break it as easily as he'd broken the lattice to block his way back to me.

A longing could grow into something bigger if I wasn't careful.

But there was no place for Salas in my future.

And I had no place in his.

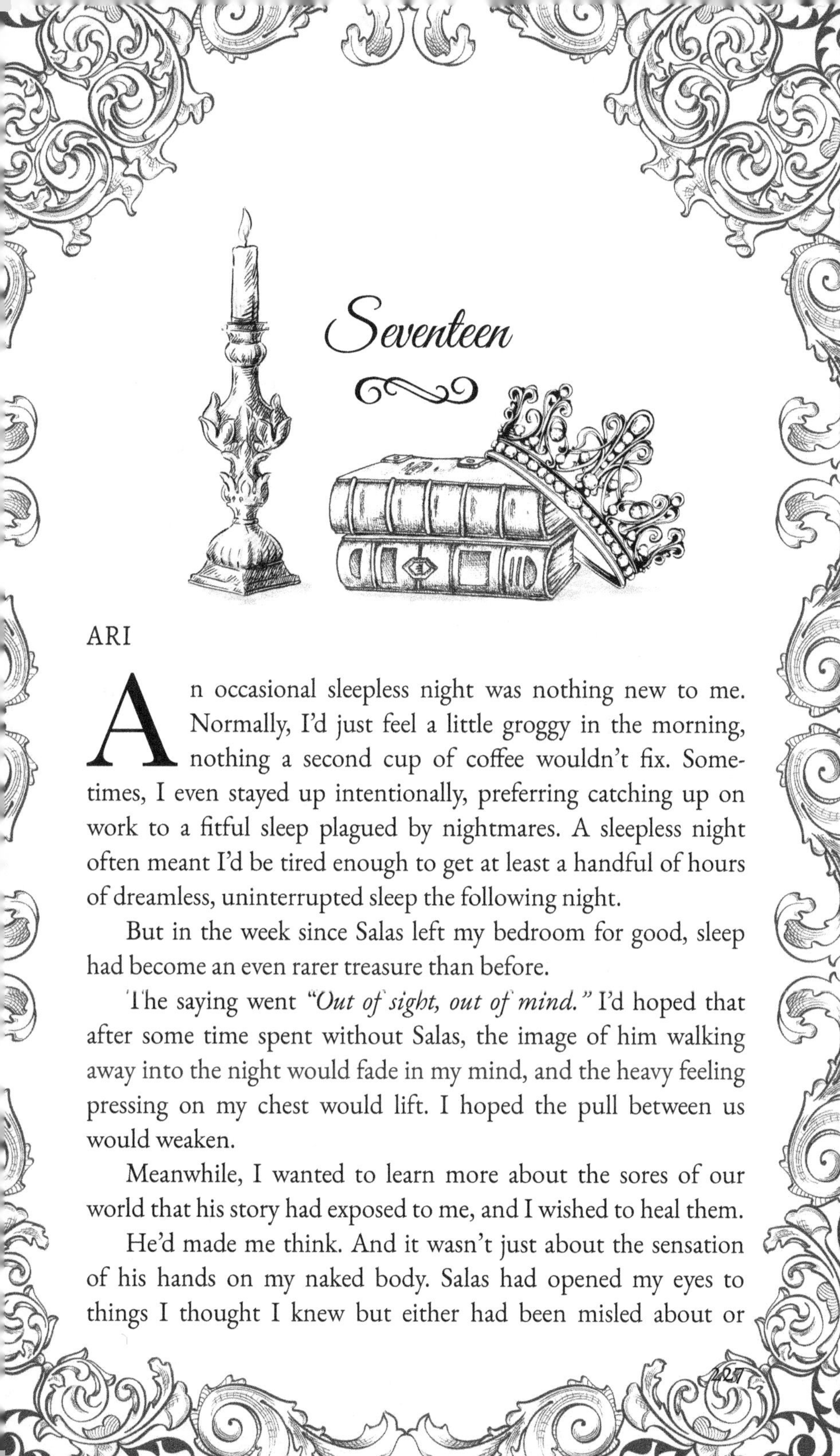

Seventeen

ARI

An occasional sleepless night was nothing new to me. Normally, I'd just feel a little groggy in the morning, nothing a second cup of coffee wouldn't fix. Sometimes, I even stayed up intentionally, preferring catching up on work to a fitful sleep plagued by nightmares. A sleepless night often meant I'd be tired enough to get at least a handful of hours of dreamless, uninterrupted sleep the following night.

But in the week since Salas left my bedroom for good, sleep had become an even rarer treasure than before.

The saying went *"Out of sight, out of mind."* I'd hoped that after some time spent without Salas, the image of him walking away into the night would fade in my mind, and the heavy feeling pressing on my chest would lift. I hoped the pull between us would weaken.

Meanwhile, I wanted to learn more about the sores of our world that his story had exposed to me, and I wished to heal them.

He'd made me think. And it wasn't just about the sensation of his hands on my naked body. Salas had opened my eyes to things I thought I knew but either had been misled about or oblivious to. My new world, my sanctuary, my safe place turned out to be far from safe for men like Salas. It also offered nothing but a bleak future to many children.

The morning before the slaves were supposed to leave Egami Palace, Father and I sat on either side of the cigar display table in his parlor.

An illustrated edition of *Equine Breeds of Western Islands* lay open between Father and me, with neither of us paying any attention to it. The history book that Father had been reading that morning was already securely hidden under the window seat cushion, just in case anyone walked in on us unexpectedly.

"The orphanage funds are set and approved by the council," Father said. "The council also breaks the sum down by location. I have nothing to do with it, dear."

"But you are the main patron," I argued.

"I am." Father nodded. "That means I'm always photographed for newspapers during my official visits to the orphanages. I also give speeches during those visits sometimes, when the council requests it."

"That's not all, though. You organize the fundraisers. Are you not in charge of the funds raised?"

"No, sweetie. I don't actually organize them. I just lend my name and sign the thank-you notes for the donors. I have no say in how the money is distributed. The council decides on that."

I hoped he might at least have some influence on the distribution of charity funds. But it seemed the council firmly held all reins of power in their hands. Just like they held on to all the existing laws on slavery.

I'd managed to put a review of the laws on slavery on the council's agenda, but Lady Etah insisted on limiting the time for my presentation. I had to cut my speech in half, but frankly, I didn't think it would've made any difference had I delivered the entire speech. The vast majority of the councilors voted against the suggested revisions of the existing laws without even seeing my proposal.

They had allowed me to reduce a slave's punishment by two lashes before. They had agreed to increase the number of inspections in the widower houses around the country now. But they vehemently opposed any fundamental changes to the existing laws. The power I thought I had turned out to be not much bigger than that of my father. His name was on all those charities, but he had no influence on their administration.

"The distribution of funds for orphanages is massively skewed for the benefit of the girls." I sighed.

"I know, dearest." Father ran a hand over his neatly styled hair, making sure not to touch the carefully arranged wave over his forehead. "But is it really a bad thing? Think about it, Ari. Education is wasted on boys."

"You're a man, Father. You used to be a boy too. Did you not benefit from education?"

"My main benefit came from marrying your mother. The ability to read helps me combat boredom but not much more. For men of lower classes, education is almost a curse instead of a blessing. You know what they say? Ignorance is bliss. And I'd add, especially when one's destiny is physical labor, one doesn't need to be literate to haul rocks."

Or *bricks*, as it might be in some cases.

Good education didn't help Salas to improve his life. Would he have been better off without it? Or maybe the problems in our society were too deep to be solved by fixing just one issue. If we were to educate the boys, we also had to offer them ways to earn a living with their acquired skills and knowledge in the future.

"Educating a girl," Father continued, "helps her gain employment where she can put her education to good use. She'll earn a living, take a husband, and have the means to support them both. Meanwhile, boys should direct their efforts toward finding a good wife and being a good husband to her. Don't you see? If the funds are split evenly, in the long run both groups will suffer. Boys would do better for themselves if they focus all their energy on attracting a suitable wife."

"What if they fail at that?"

"Then they should try harder," Father replied, undeterred.

"So, as it stands right now, there is no future for an unmarried man."

"An unmarried man is a wasted potential. He's at best useless to our society. At worst, he's dangerous. A man's very purpose is to be a husband and a father. His place is at home, taking care of the house and the children, so his wife can work and provide for them."

"But why is a woman allowed to be so much more than just a mother and a wife when a man is not?" I wouldn't give up. "Does it seem fair to you?"

Father drew in a long breath, looking ready for a lengthy discussion.

"That's how it has always been, Ari," he said, folding his hands on the glass top of the cigar table. "Our society is built through the wisdom of hundreds of generations. Our way of life has withstood the test of time. Look at our gods for guidance. There are only two divine males. Rethaf is the God of Marriage, the husband of the greatest Sun Goddess, and the father of her four children. Her three daughters are the goddesses of War, Peace, and Governance. And her son is Yarnus, the God of Youth and Purity."

A serene expression relaxed Father's features as he spoke about the deities, and I didn't interrupt him.

"Rethaf is a vessel of patience and wisdom," Father said. "He provides a continuous support to his esteemed wife and is revered as the ideal that all our youth should aspire to. The Goddess's son Yarnus represents the starting point of every young man's journey. Looking up to Yarnus, a young boy preserves his purity of both body and soul, saving himself for his future wife. Because only in marriage can he fulfill his life's purpose as a father and a husband. The life of an unmarried man is wasted for both the gods and the society. His seed, if spilled freely, is an insult to his purpose."

"Is procreation life's only goal, Father?" I asked.

"For a man, it is the only one worth achieving. My life was not complete until Goddess sent you to us. I wake up every morning with a prayer of gratitude for her blessing us with a daughter and letting our bloodline continue. Only by becoming a husband and a father, the man earns the highest respect."

Procreation was important in order for a society to go on. A woman's choice to remain unmarried would be frowned upon too. If she was a woman of means, she'd be pestered by fathers of young gentlemen to marry one of their sons. But even if she chose to remain single for life, she would not become a pariah in Rorrim's society. She'd have more options to support herself, too, more chances to avoid the path to poverty that Salas had been pushed onto.

Before I could argue, however, a knock on the door interrupted us.

One of Father's valets entered, "Your Highness, Her Majesty demands your presence for today's city report."

"Now?"

It was too early for the report. Something must've happened if the queen wanted it ahead of schedule.

"Sorry, Father." I gave him a peck on the cheek. "We'll continue this conversation some other time."

"Of course, dearest. It's always a pleasure talking to you."

ON MY WAY to Mother's study, I ran into Gem. Her features were pinched into a frown of concentration.

"What's going on?" I asked.

She darted a cautious look around before speaking quietly, only for me to hear.

"There was a murder in the city last night. A second one. Two murders a week apart."

Crime in Rorrim was mostly reduced to theft or an occasional fist fight, hardly warranting alerting the queen. A murder happened rarely, usually when a brawl got out of hand. Most of those took place between men and were blamed on the nature of their gender that apparently cursed them with a hefty share of aggression.

Gem's expression remained somber as we approached the doors to the queen's study.

"Two women were killed on two separate nights," she whispered quickly as the guards swung the doors open for us. "Possibly by the same man."

I worried my lip, stepping over the threshold. Aggression against women was socially and legally unacceptable and was always punished harshly. A murder of a woman was a grievous crime. It had to be thoroughly investigated. But two murders in one week? That was extraordinary. It certainly demanded immediate action from the crown.

Mother was sitting at her writing desk, half-turned in her high-backed armchair to face Madam Trela, the Head of the City Guards. Madam Trela's social position wasn't high enough to sit in the presence of the queen. She remained standing, her hands in lacy lilac gloves clamped together in front of her. The fitted jacket of the same lilac color as the gloves hugged her voluptuous figure tightly. The jacket's flowery print clashed with the orange polka dots of her long skirt so violently, it proved impossible to look at both pieces at once. I chose to focus on her straw hat, instead, which seemed a safer option.

"Your Highness. Lady Chamberlain." Madam Trela greeted us with a brief bow of her head, the bunch of bright flowers on her hat swayed with the movement.

"It's a pleasure to see you again, Madam Trela," I said. "Sadly, the reason for your visit is far from pleasant, I hear."

The woman sighed. "True, true. I don't usually come here bringing good news, do I?"

"There was a murder in the city last night," Mother went straight to the point, filling us in. "A woman was killed. A second woman in... what?" She glanced at Madam Trela. "In seven days, was it?"

"Yes, yes." The head of the city guards nodded, the flowers on her hat drooping solemnly. "Two murders in seven days. Both victims are women. The first one is Madam Elims, a grocer from the east end of the city. She was murdered not far from the establishment called Sweet Gentlemen."

"It's a brothel," Gem explained.

"Indeed, it is," Madam Trela confirmed. "Madam Elims was one of their long-time customers. She spent the night with one of their new hires. My patrols found her body early in the morning. She died from seventeen stab wounds."

I winced, my chest aching as if being stabbed too. Seventeen? Why? This seemed to be a murder for the sake of brutality.

"Who would do such a thing?" I asked quietly.

Gem leaned her shoulder against a wall panel, folding her arms across her chest. "Was the whore with whom this woman spent the night the last person who saw her alive?"

"Yes, he was," Madam Trela replied. "Unfortunately, he's nowhere to be found. He's now our suspect. I personally questioned everyone at the fun house."

Madam Trela was excellent at her job. Highly intelligent, she possessed an exceptional memory for details. Her reports had always been efficient and on point. If anyone was to get to the root of this crime, it'd be her.

"Has Madam Elims's family been notified?" Mother asked.

"She didn't have a family in Egami City, Your Majesty. Madam Elims was childless and unmarried. Her store is now the property of her sister, who lives on the North Coast. We sent a messenger with the sad news to her." Madam Trela heaved another sigh.

Mother propped an elbow on her desk. "Do you have any ideas on the suspect's whereabouts?"

The head of the guards shifted her weight to another foot, looking uneasy.

"Not yet, Your Majesty. But we're doing everything to find him, and we have a few good leads. Last week, my women saw a man who matched the subject's description. They stopped him near the corner of Green Lane and High Crossing, mere steps from the place where the first body was found just forty minutes later."

"What's his description?" Gem asked.

Madam Trela turned to her. "Tall, large. Brown hair and a full beard."

A chilling tendril of dread slithered down my spine.

"It could be anyone," I said quickly.

"Maybe, Your Highness." Madam Trela nodded thoughtfully. "But isn't it too much of a coincidence for a man with his description to be at that location at that hour? Also, most men in the city are clean shaven nowadays as per the latest fashion."

Gem chewed on her lip, considering something.

"Most," she said, "but not all. Did your women question him, Madam Trela?"

"They were about to bring him in for questioning, but a woman intervened."

"A woman?" Mother exclaimed.

Gem pushed away from the wall, standing to attention in the face of this new information.

My tendril of dread grew to the size of a boa constrictor now, wrapping itself tightly around my chest.

"Yes, Your Majesty. The woman claimed to be his relative, so the guards let him go. Allow me to remind you, it was *before* the first body was discovered. The guards would've been much more vigilant had they known about the murder."

"That woman could've been his accomplice," Gem noted, her frown deepening.

"Or another victim," Mother added with concern.

Madam Trela wrung her hands, the flowers on her hat trembling.

"That's what I fear, Your Majesty. More murders can happen.

Predators like that don't stop on their own. They need to be caught. From what he did to his latest victim…" She winced, tears sparkling in her eyes. "He got a taste for violence, and it's growing."

The emotions on Madam Trela's face were genuine. Though, her anguish and empathy never stopped her from doing her job efficiently and even ruthlessly if required.

Mother rose from her chair. "We need to warn the people of Egami. I'll have to address the city."

"I'll draft the speech for you," I volunteered, grasping at the chance to be useful.

She nodded. "We need to inform and calm the crowd before the panic spreads. The last thing we need is people living in fear. Or even worse, them taking justice in their own hands. I don't want mobs of armed women combing the streets and attacking all bearded men."

"It's probably best not to mention that detail of his description publicly," Madam Trela suggested. "A beard is easy enough to shave off, anyway."

"I know someone who matches that description," Gem announced, and the blood in my veins ran cold. "Someone who, for a fact, did not spend the evening before the first murder where he was supposed to be."

"Who?" Mother's face brightened with hope.

Madam Trela perked up. "Can you give me his name, my lady? We'll investigate."

Gem swept the room with her gaze. When it stopped at me, I gave a barely perceptible shake of my head in a silent plea to keep quiet.

"Give me a few hours to complete my inquiry, just to be sure," Gem spoke to Madam Trela, not releasing my stare from the snare of hers. "I don't want to cause any trouble to an innocent man by mistake."

"Of course." Madam Trela nodded. "We'll follow our leads meanwhile. And, Your Majesty, I will officially petition you to let us issue a public advisory. We need to keep our people safe. A curfew, too, if you deem so necessary."

"I don't think a curfew is desirable at this point," Mother replied. "I'm afraid it may bring more harm than good. We will go with the advisory for now, and I will bring the matter in front of the council today."

I had to do something. But what?

Clearly, it was Salas and me that the guards reported seeing that night. It was exactly a week ago that he'd visited the orphanage, and I tagged along as his stalker. The slaves weren't leaving Egami until tomorrow. After what happened, they would be scrutinized, questioned, and inspected before they're allowed to leave the city.

I had to warn Salas somehow.

"If you'll excuse me. I'll get started on that speech draft." I moved toward the door.

"I'll see you at noon, dear." Mother released me with a wave of her hand. "I'd like for you to come to the city with me today."

"I will," I promised.

As I was slipping out of the room, Gem excused herself too.

"I'll get on with my inquiry right now," she told Mother, then followed me out into the hallway.

"I'll see you later," I quipped and increased my pace, hoping to leave Gem behind.

No such luck. Catching up with me, she seized my arm.

"This way, Your Highness." She slammed her other hand against the door to her study down the hallway.

The door swung open, and Gem dragged me into the relatively small, sparsely furnished room. The atmosphere here was cold and impersonal. However, most people whom lady chamberlain interrogated in here had other things to worry about than the décor.

"Funny how there is a connection to a fun house with these murders." Gem locked the door, then rounded the room, checking under the heavy oak desk, behind the chair, and outside of the window. Satisfied that no one was hiding to eavesdrop on us, she faced me with her hands on her hips. "Just when I discovered that a certain slave used to work in one too."

Dread spread through me, turning my insides to ice. I'd asked her to investigate the possible reasons for Salas signing another slave contract. Lady chamberlain would be terrible at her job if she didn't eventually discover his past too.

"It was long ago," I exhaled.

"So, you knew?" She looked at me with deep disappointment. "Yet I didn't learn about that from *you*."

"He's not doing it anymore."

Gem scoffed.

"Once a whore is always a whore." She hurled the word with force, like a stone.

"Gem," I said in a low voice. "You don't know him."

"But I thought I did." She hid her eyes behind her hand, looking racked by regret. "It was my job to know everything about that man, and I thought I did. I talked to his owner. I verified where his previous contract came from. I checked his history for the past five years. But I didn't discover this little piece of information until today." She groaned. "I should've dug deeper from the beginning. And you should've told me who he was the moment you knew." I inhaled to argue, but she stopped me by raising a hand. "I know, I know. It's not your fault, Ari. It's mine."

"It's no one's fault. There is no need to blame anyone."

But she wasn't listening.

"I made a mistake. I allowed that viper into the palace. But I will fix it."

"What do you mean, Gem? What are you going to do?"

She drew in a breath, standing taller.

"All right. Here is what *we* are going to do. You," she pointed a finger at me, stabbing it through the air energetically, "you will keep your mouth shut. You know nothing. No one will be able to identify him for certain as the man who came to your bedroom a few times. I made sure of that."

"But what are *you* going to do meanwhile?"

"Me..." She gripped her upper arms, pacing the room. "I have a report from the night guards. They saw him returning to the palace that night, just before the body was found. The report is evidence."

"But he didn't do it. He didn't kill anyone."

"He could have," she spoke as if thinking out loud. "I'll just have to present it to Madam Trela in a way that she'd agree with me. The two murders don't have to be related. Let her hunt down the killer responsible for the last one. Meanwhile, we'll execute Salas for the first."

Her words sliced through my heart like a knife. Gem had the power and the ability to do anything she put her mind to, and her mind was clearly set on annihilating Salas.

"Gem, listen to me!" I yelled, finally getting her attention. "Salas didn't do it."

"He's a fallen man, Ari. His physical urges got the best of him. Clearly, he has no control over them since he used to sell sex for money. He's aggressive. He's injured a man already, remember?"

"There were six men, Gem. Six men provoked him by insulting someone he—" I cut myself short, afraid to reveal more than was necessary and make the matters worse.

Thankfully, Gem was too preoccupied with developing her plan to notice my misstep or to push for explanation.

"The point is, he's violent, as it has been proven," she continued, "and sexually insatiable, as all whores are. It won't take much to convince everyone that he's capable of both rape and murder. Especially since we have witnesses. The guards will recognize him. He wasn't in his barrack at the time of the murder. I need to talk to the slave owner's helper. He will be another witness for the crown."

She spun on her heel, heading for the door in a spur of energy.

"Salas didn't do it, Gem," I repeated resolutely.

"You don't know that for sure," she dismissed.

"But I do." I stepped between her and the door, blocking her exit. "I am a witness too. I was the woman who led Salas away from the guards. That night, I went to the city with him. We came back to the palace together, though we walked through the gate separately. I'm in the gate guards' report, too, if you look closely."

"Ari." She shook her head, backing away from me. "You're not helping here."

"I'm not going to help you execute an innocent man. Salas is not a murderer, and you knew it before you even started cooking this whole thing up in your head."

She sighed. "Oh, sweetie. For you and me, it's not about the murder. Or about the truth. Don't you understand? He's a brothel boy, a whore—"

"*Was*," I corrected, my cheeks burning hot as if she'd slapped me by insulting him.

She waved my correction away. "Regardless, he's a fallen man, a ruined man. Legally, his only place is in the brothel. But that's not where he has spent the past seven years, is it? However he obtained that first slave contract, he did so by fraud. Whores can't leave the fun district without a permit, not even for a night. And he's been away for seven years now. Do you understand? Either way, he's a criminal. Every day he's lived for the past seven years has been a crime. That's the law."

"But why?"

I knew that men working in fun houses had to be registered. I was not aware that it was the only occupation they could ever have for the rest of their lives. None of my professors ever mentioned the laws on prostitution. It simply was not a priority of the crown to focus on them or work on improving the lives of those men. Even speaking about them was considered improper. This was another thing about my new world that made sense on the surface but stank with injustice when one poked deeper.

"For public safety," Gem snapped. "Whores belong to brothels, under the penalty of death if they leave. They're certainly not allowed anywhere near the palace, not to mention into the bedroom of the crown princess. By not disclosing who he was, he deceived everyone, including you and me. He deserves to be executed, Ari." She grabbed my shoulders. "Either way, he's a dead man, rightfully so. The only way we can protect ourselves now is to keep both our names out of it. Which means, he needs to be executed for murder, rather than for vice and treason."

She said it as if Salas's death was a decided thing already. All that remained was figuring out the details.

How eager Gem had been to bring Salas into my bedroom earlier, and how much she wished him dead now.

"I can't let him die," I said firmly.

"But it is the only way, sweetie. We can't have our reputation connected to a man like that. He's committed a crime against the crown. You are the crown. You're supposed to uphold our laws, not fornicate with a criminal. Think about what would happen if it all came out? If we let him live, sooner or later, the truth about his past will come out. Someone will recognize him. He's so beneath you, even mentioning his name next to yours will mean your downfall, Ari, can't you see? Your perfect reputation up until now, your miracle status, your stellar performance in the government, nothing will save you."

Unbeknownst to him, a noose was tightening around Salas's throat, and there was nothing I could do to stop it.

"There is no one to recognize him," I said in desperation. "He left his village when he was twelve. His looks have changed since."

"He became a criminal, Ari, and a whore. He couldn't keep it in his pants. He has no one to blame but himself for his poor life choices."

"He was fourteen!" I exclaimed in anguish. "Fourteen, Gem. He was just a boy when he was ruined by an older woman. How much do you think it was his choice at that age? He started working at the fun house at seventeen because he had nowhere else to go. How long is he supposed to carry that stigma and be punished for a decision he made when he wasn't even an adult?"

She pursed her lips. The look in her eyes remained hard.

"Don't believe everything he told you. Men like him are

usually very good liars, skilled at telling sob stories to milk sympathy and money out of women. Tell me why did he take you to the city that night? What did he force you to do for him?"

He didn't "take" me. I followed him. But that wasn't the point. The reason for Salas's visit to the orphanage was his business, not mine. I had no right to reveal all his life to Gem. But if I didn't, would he get to keep his life at all?

"Nothing, Gem. Salas never asked me for anything, not for one fucking thing for himself." I heaved a breath, running a trembling hand through my hair. "He is a good man. He deserves a chance at happiness, even if he did step off that straight, perfect path that men are expected to follow. Why wouldn't society give men like him even the slightest chance at redemption?"

"It isn't hard to stay in line." Gem flipped her ponytail over her shoulder, then crossed her arms over her chest again. "There are plenty of men who do just fine following that path, but some choose debauchery and self-destruction instead. And no, you can't blame society for their bad choices. Rorrim's laws are the most lenient toward men. In many other countries, men are treated much worse. They're not allowed to leave the house unchaperoned. In some, they can't show their faces to anyone but their wives. Some countries' laws demand their genitals be caged or mutilated or both. They get married off before they even hit puberty to women many times their age, sold on open markets like livestock." She pinched the bridge of her nose. "Trust me, men in Rorrim have it much better than anywhere else in the world. Yet look at how many still take it for granted. Spoiled, ungrateful brats."

My mind was racing, fervently searching for a solution. My plan to improve life for all slaves had encountered serious obstacles from the council. I hadn't abandoned it, but it was a long-term solution that required time.

Meanwhile, Salas's life was in immediate danger. To save him, I had to act now. I couldn't think about the millions of others. I just had to save this one man.

"There has to be a way," I muttered to myself.

Gem dropped her hand away from her face.

"I'll take care of it. All you have to do is keep quiet about everything."

Gem wasn't my ally in this case. She couldn't be because we had different things to protect. I worried about Salas's life. She feared for her reputation.

"No one can ever know anything about him and you," she instructed me. "It'd be like he never existed. We won't even have to pay compensation to the slave owner if he's charged with murder. The owner knows nothing about you. I was the one who dealt with her. Ugh."

She gripped her hair. Shiny, brown lines of *reflection* ran through her skin and dress, mirroring the dark wood of the desk and the wall panels behind her. Lady chamberlain rarely lost composure to *reflect* like that. I couldn't remember ever seeing her do it before. But she was clearly distraught now.

"How could I have allowed this to happen?" she lamented. "That cunning bastard had been at it for years. He managed to deceive even me. I'm risking everything here, Ari. If word about it gets out, I'll lose it all—my position, my place at court, probably even my title. You and I are the only two people who know the whole truth." She snapped her eyes to mine again, splaying both hands in the air to emphasize each word. "Just. Keep. Quiet. Please."

"I will not." I held her stare as a solution began to form in my head. "Not unless you promise me that Salas won't get hurt."

She gasped for air, as if being pulled under by a current stronger than herself.

"Ari. There is nothing I can do for him. I don't care how good of a fuck he was for you. There will be others just as good or even better. You have to let this one go."

But I stood my ground.

"I won't let you throw him to the wolves."

She smirked. "Well, 'the wolves' have to be fed, sweetie. And I'd rather it's him than you or me. There is no other way."

"Yes, there is." I took a step forward, my idea taking shape as I spoke. "You will pay off his debt to the slave owner."

She laughed. "Haven't we tried that already? It didn't work out that well last time, did it?"

"It will this time if you carefully explain to Salas the risks of staying a slave in this current situation."

Salas couldn't remain at the mercy of the slave owner who might eventually take him to the parts of the country where he risked being recognized. His situation was much worse than I ever knew. He'd been in mortal risk for years.

Many things made more sense now. How he avoided me at the beginning, trying to remain invisible despite being intrigued by my attention. How adamantly he refused all my offers of help.

Meeting new people while looking for a job as a free man carried a risk of exposure. As a slave, few paid attention to him, making his current occupation a better hiding place. But it was not good enough. If anyone recognized him, he'd be executed. On his own, he stood no chance to defend himself from the law. To protect him, I had to keep him close.

"The queen will never agree to freeing him again," Gem pointed out.

"She won't. But we don't really need her permission. We'll find the money."

I had a generous allowance from the crown, and every piece of jewelry I owned could feed a man for months. But my expenses were carefully monitored. Selling royal jewelry would not go unnoticed. A large withdrawal of funds would raise questions and might bring unwanted attention to Salas.

"Where will we find the money?" Gem demanded.

"I'll give you as much as I can without attracting scrutiny or speculations. You will come up with the rest."

"Me?" She almost choked on the word.

"Yes, Gem. You have an annual allowance from your family.

In addition, the crown pays you handsomely for all the work you do for us. I'm sure you can work out an arrangement to free a slave, and I will repay you in time. Unlike me, you can do all this far more discreetly."

"Why the fuck would I free him?" she yelled.

"To keep him quiet about where your people brought him for three nights. To keep me quiet about it too."

Her eyes opened wide with shock. "You wouldn't dare, Ari. This is blackmail. One that won't work. You can't speak about it without exposing yourself along with me."

"But was any of it my fault?" I said in an exaggeratedly sweet voice and batted my eyelashes at her. "I am just an innocent princess who did what her mother told her to do. The queen trusted you to make the arrangements. And you failed us both, putting my life in danger."

Gem glared at me, her stare burrowing through me like a spear.

"Sometimes, I really wish you stopped being a princess just long enough for me to slap you," she gritted through her teeth. "What do you want me to do with him after I free him? Hide him somewhere? You know he won't be able to support himself. The moment we free him, he'll sign another contract and end up where he started." She moaned as if being tortured. "He really should just go back to a fun house where he belongs. With any luck, he'd get killed in a brawl or something."

Salas had made it clear he preferred the back-breaking labor of a slave to the work in a fun house. He'd been risking his life daily to stay away from his former occupation. Forcing him back would be a huge betrayal of his trust.

But I needed to keep him in Egami. I had to watch over him from now on.

"I want him to stay in the city."

Gem blew out a laugh. "Are you going to rent him a place? Because sooner or later, someone will discover who pays for his accommodation. And no," she stomped her foot, "I'm not financing that shit for you indefinitely."

"No. Salas will never agree to being a kept man."

As kind and agreeable as Salas was with me, he had a stubborn streak. Unshakable pride was at his core, the inner dignity that no punches of fate had managed to crack or weaken. He wouldn't accept handouts. I'd learned that already.

"Well, then he has more sense than you do." Gem walked away from me and propped her butt on the desk behind her.

"He needs a chance to make his own living," I said.

"And how do you propose he'd do it, other than taking his pants off for everyone who pays?"

I let that insult slide, holding on to the idea that churned and evolved inside my brain.

"Here is what I want you to do, Gem." I headed toward her. "I want you to talk to the games master. You'll tell her that you want to put a word in for a new gladiator you've found."

"I... what?" she squeaked, making a move to jump up from the desk, but I pressed down on her shoulders, keeping her butt on the edge.

In my desperation to save Salas, my thoughts on this might be flawed. But Mother's gladiators were well taken care of. They got paid well, ate good food, had free access to the queendom's best healing witches if needed. They lived in their own apartments in the gladiators' quarters, away from the city crowds. At Salas's age, he wouldn't perform in the arena for long. In a few years, he'd have a full pension from the crown that would allow him to live the rest of his life in dignity and peace.

Also, he'd be right here, in Egami, a short carriage ride away from the palace.

I held Gem down, making her listen to every word I said. "You'll tell the games master that Salas fought alone against six men and won. You'll tell her you've made inquiries into his background, and his past is clean."

"But—"

"You'll tell her," I wouldn't let her squeeze a word of protest in, "that you personally vouch for him and give him your recommendation to become one of Her Majesty's royal gladiators."

Gem released a long, tortured moan as if I was slowly twisting her arm out of its socket.

"You are insane, Ari." She dropped her face into her hands.

I didn't argue with that. It was insane. A crazy, daring plan based on lies. And if the lies were exposed, none of us would get out of it unscathed. But the queen's gladiators enjoyed care, protection, and respect no other group of unmarried men in Rorrim had. And I wanted Salas to have it all.

"There are only three people who know the truth—you, me, and Salas. All three of us have very good reasons to keep it to ourselves. It will work," I assured her.

She lifted her head, looking at me like I'd completely lost my mind.

"The men who become Her Majesty's royal gladiators have impeccable reputations."

"Do they really?" I arched an eyebrow. "Or are their reputations only as good as the references they receive from powerful women?"

She made a face, as if I was feeding her the sourest lemons straight up. "Think about it, Ari. You want me to pass a whore for a warrior. It's impossible. The games master will see right through it the moment she meets him."

I shook my head at that.

"Salas *is* a warrior. He's fought more battles in his life than you could ever imagine. He's a survivor, and he's gotten through it all while keeping his kindness and integrity intact, which is more than I can say about many people here in the royal palace. What he needs is a chance. A word in his favor from the powerful lady chamberlain, the favorite niece of Her Majesty, would surely convince the games master to give him that chance."

Gem tilted her head, squinting at me from her perch on the desk.

"And if he refuses to take this chance?"

I rubbed my chest against a stab of worry. "He certainly has the right to refuse."

"Well, there you go!" She tossed her hands in the air. "I'll stick my neck out for him, and it'll be all for nothing. He'd be stupid to miss out on such an opportunity, but we established already that man isn't bright. When we paid off his last debt, he was dumb enough to trip and fall right back into another one. He clearly has no clue what's best for him. They say he doesn't even *reflect*. Ever. Clearly, he feels no shame and no fear, like an animal."

But Salas did *reflect*. I'd seen it. Only it wasn't pain or humiliation that scared him. It was me and what I made him feel.

"He has to have a choice," I insisted. "Ultimately, it needs to be his decision. I want you to explain what's going on, without pushing or coercing him either way. Do you understand?"

"Ah so," she said slyly. "You don't want me to do to him what you're doing to me? It's fine to coerce me, but not the slave."

I felt a slight pinch of guilt about forcing Gem into compliance, but it remained just slight.

"It's not the same, Gem. You're only risking your status. In Salas's case, his life is at stake. You will lay it out to him as is. Then, you'll give him a choice. If he doesn't accept our offer, you'll let him go. Either way, we'll have Madam Trela hunt the real killer without distractions. But if Salas refuses your help, I'd like to speak with him before he leaves Egami."

"No, you won't!" Gem jumped to her feet. "If I do this, Ari, if I put my wealth and status on the line for a worthless whore, there is one thing I absolutely demand of you. You will never speak to that man ever again."

"But if he refuses, I need to hear his reasons why."

If I were completely honest with myself, I wished to see Salas just one more time if he chose to leave the city and my life for good.

But I'd already broken my promise to Mother not to see him after the last night Gem had arranged for him to come to my room. I'd promised her not to associate with him anymore, but then went to the slaves' barracks anyway.

Gem was right to doubt me. When it came to Salas, I had no willpower to resist his pull, even if my honor was at stake.

Gem gave me a knowing look. "There is absolutely no need for you to know the reasons for his refusal. If you're giving him a choice, it's not up to you what he chooses. If he wants to slave his life away, let him. Respect his decision and let him go. And if he takes this chance," she lifted a finger for emphasis, "then you won't search out his company either. I don't give a fuck about how much you care about him or how much you may miss him."

"But I'm not—"

She huffed, cutting off my protests. "You made a huge mistake, Ari. He was supposed to be a nobody, a fleck in your memories, a toy for you to use for a night or two. And look where we are now. You're blackmailing me and lying for him. And all for what? A whore is not a gladiator, even if you dress him up as one. He'll get himself killed during his first fight in the arena. Which will probably be the best outcome for all of us." Looking bitter and disappointed, she demanded, "Swear you're not going to see him one on one ever again. No talking. No fucking. From now on, you don't know him at all."

I wasn't doing this for me. It wasn't my intention to keep Salas close as a lover. I simply wished to save his life and give him a chance at a better future.

"All right," I said. "I won't seek him out."

Gem didn't appear pacified, however. The bitterness in her eyes shifted to pity.

"Do you realize what you've condemned yourself to, Ari? You obviously care about this man. Now, you risk seeing him regularly during the Games. If he becomes a gladiator, you won't be able to avoid it. You'll watch him in the arena, but you'll be married to someone else. Do you think you have what it takes to keep your promise?"

'Out of sight, out of mind' would no longer protect me in that case. But it wasn't about me.

I stepped aside, leaning with my hip against the desk that Gem had vacated.

"I don't have a choice, do I? As long as Salas is safe, I'll manage."

She heaved a sigh, heading to the door.

"Let yourself out whenever you will, Your Highness. Now please excuse me, I have to sweet-talk the games master into accepting into her team someone she absolutely should not."

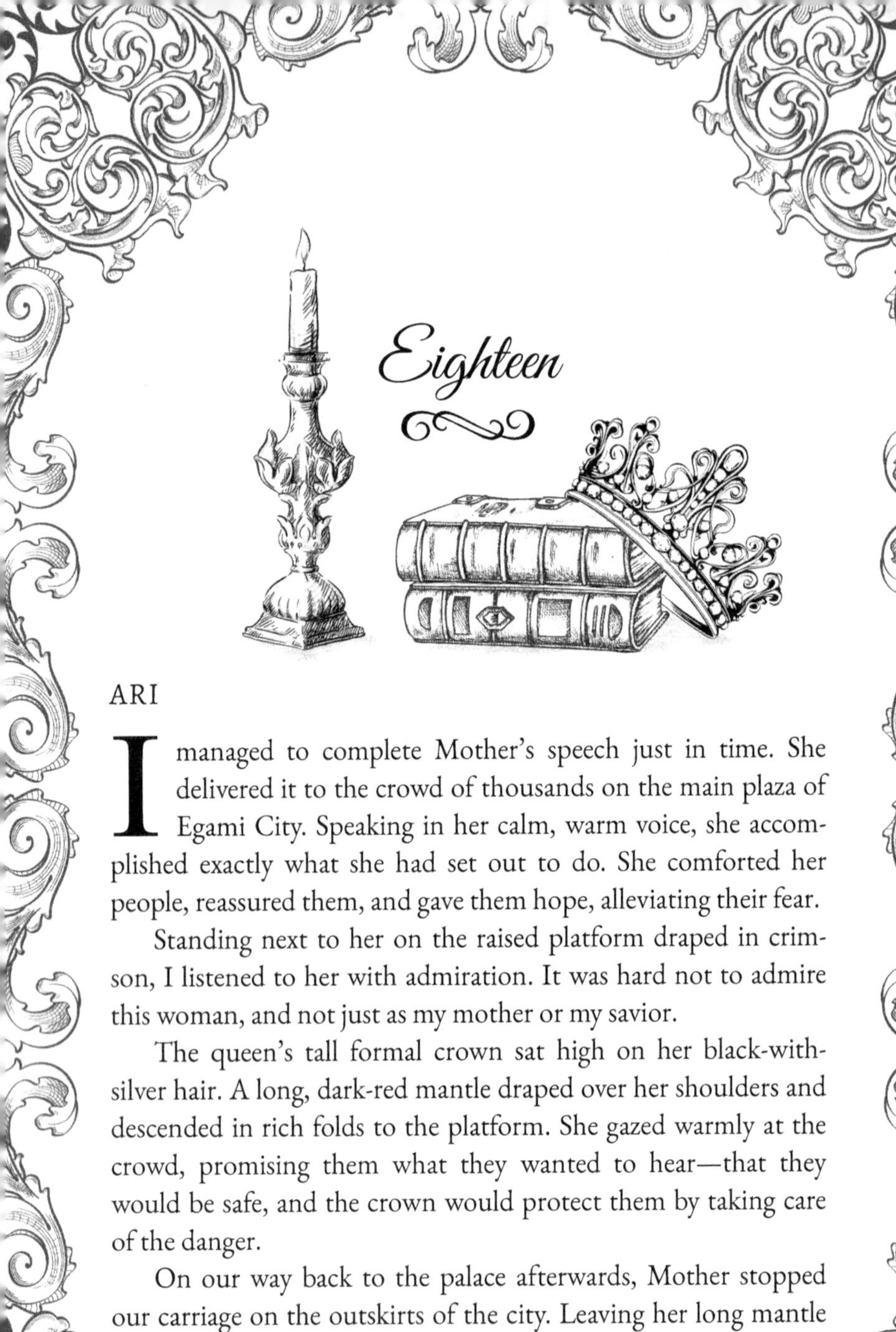

Eighteen

ARI

I managed to complete Mother's speech just in time. She delivered it to the crowd of thousands on the main plaza of Egami City. Speaking in her calm, warm voice, she accomplished exactly what she had set out to do. She comforted her people, reassured them, and gave them hope, alleviating their fear.

Standing next to her on the raised platform draped in crimson, I listened to her with admiration. It was hard not to admire this woman, and not just as my mother or my savior.

The queen's tall formal crown sat high on her black-with-silver hair. A long, dark-red mantle draped over her shoulders and descended in rich folds to the platform. She gazed warmly at the crowd, promising them what they wanted to hear—that they would be safe, and the crown would protect them by taking care of the danger.

On our way back to the palace afterwards, Mother stopped our carriage on the outskirts of the city. Leaving her long mantle in the carriage, she asked me to follow her out. She took me to a low set building in a narrow street off the main road.

An older woman in a long rubber apron opened the door when we knocked.

"Your Majesty," she gasped at the sight of the queen, sinking into a deep curtsy. "Your Highness." She bowed, holding the door open for us. "Madam Trela is not here. She went to the plaza..."

"I know," the queen assured her with an elegant wave of her hand. "We're not here to see Madam Trela. Can you take us to your work room please?"

The woman's eyes darted between me and Mother. She seemed uncertain about the request but didn't dare question the queen. Bowing her head, she led us down a narrow corridor and into a wide room with a low ceiling and metal grating on the floor.

The windows on both ends of the room were wide open, sending a breeze through. Yet the outside air could not completely banish the stench of rotten flesh as Mother led me to a covered narrow table in the middle.

I yanked a handkerchief from my pocket and pressed it to my mouth and nose, breathing through the fabric.

"Forgive me for what I'm about to show you, Ari. But I want you to know what a man is capable of doing to a woman." Mother lifted a corner of the gray soiled sheet that covered the table, moving the fabric aside.

I held my breath, forcing my eyes not to stray from the body of the dead woman on the table. Blood had been washed off her skin. Her flaxen blonde hair had been brushed and braided. But there was nothing anyone could do about the dark bruises covering her skin or the gruesome wounds torn in her flesh.

"Look at her, Ari, and remember what you see. There have been a number of murders in Egami over the years of my reign, but none quite as brutal as this one. Look at her wounds and note their location." Mother pointed at the ragged tears that looked like they had been left by teeth and claws of a wild animal. "These weren't made by a rabid beast but by a man driven mad by lust."

The bites, scratches, and bruises covered the woman's breasts and upper thighs more thickly than the rest of her body.

"She was killed violently," Mother said. "The reason for her murder was to satisfy the man's unquenchable thirst for sex and blood."

"He must've gone mad." My voice came out strained from the horror gripping my throat. "But not all men are like that, Mother. You know it."

She shook her head somberly. "Some may control it better than others. But all have the thirst for violence and dominance by nature. It's up to us, Ari, to control it when they fail to do so themselves."

Another sleepless night.

I'd had quite a few of those lately.

The preparations for the arrival of the princes had been on the way for weeks. By now, almost everything was ready. The increased activity in the palace had the air buzzing with anticipation, which didn't help with settling my nerves down enough to fall and stay asleep.

It took me just a few minutes of tossing and turning in bed to know I wouldn't fall asleep tonight either.

With my nose pressed into the pillow, I realized I was breathing deeply, hunting for the traces of the familiar male scent that had long gone. I tossed the pillow aside and sat up.

Everything in here still reminded me of him. Subconsciously, I kept to one side of the bed, as if leaving space for him on the other. When having tea, I thought about his long, strong fingers crumbling the tea leaves to press them into the infuser. When getting into the bath, I thought about the creamy pink water sluicing around his hips, the tip of his hard cock bobbing over the surface, his body turning momentarily transparent with *reflection* as I'd made him go undone.

On the sleepless nights like tonight, I also remembered how comforting the warmth of his body felt and how easy it'd been for me to fall asleep with him by my side, as if my soul had sensed the safety in his closeness and trusted him to keep nightmares at bay.

I climbed out of bed and threw on my cherry blossom robe over my nightgown. The patio doors were open, but the mid-summer night was too warm to cool off the room after the heat of the day. I caught myself sifting through the sounds from the garden, subconsciously waiting for the noise of a man climbing up the palace wall.

That sound could never come again. The lattice was no longer there, and the man might not even be in Egami anymore. The slaves had finished their work and left almost two weeks ago. Their barracks had regained their purpose as horse stables to accommodate the mounts of all the people arriving with the foreign princes' extensive escorts.

I didn't know if Salas had departed with the slaves or if he had accepted my offer and was now in the gladiators' quarters. Gem had been sulking ever since I twisted her arm and forced my plan on her. She wouldn't talk to me. But that was only a part of the reason why I hadn't asked her about her conversation with the games master or how Salas took our proposition.

Either way, I had no control over his decision. I had to trust he would do what was right for him. Meanwhile, I had to do what was best for the queendom.

Drawing the ends of my robe together over my chest, I opened the door to my bedroom, crossed the sitting room, then slipped out into the hallway.

The guards by the door stood to attention, briefly bowing their heads in greeting. I walked past them toward the grand marble staircase with gold railings that led down to the main floor.

There was always someone awake in the palace. Someone rushed up or down the stairs somewhere. Servants were bringing late night snacks for courtiers suffering from insomnia like me or just staying awake on purpose. Wives might be visiting their husbands' bedrooms. Courtiers would be sneaking in with their lovers. Or just a lonely princess wandering the halls aimlessly, with the sole purpose of killing night hours while running away from her worries and thoughts.

The night guards opened the doors to the throne room as I approached, and I walked in. This enormous room was the epitome of governance for me. The royal throne stood on the platform with three wide steps leading up to it. The three steps represented the foundation of support for the monarch of Rorrim Queendom—the people, the Temple of the Great Goddess, and the Royal Council.

A wide, floor-to-ceiling banner stretched on the wall behind the throne. The crest of Rorrim Queendom on it had been embroidered by the ladies of the council, the queen, and me. It had been divided into twenty-six parts. Each of us embroidered one. Then, the parts were assembled together as a symbol of unity in our government.

I found the section I'd worked on for several months while trying to lay every stitch perfectly straight. It depicted a ray of the golden crown in the middle and a white rose of peace over it.

Peace was treasured above all in Rorrim. But now, I wondered what peace really meant for my people. The mere absence of war clearly did not guarantee a peaceful life for everyone. Some waged inner battles more brutal than any war.

The mood in Egami City remained turbulent. The killer was still on the loose. Also, with so many foreign dignitaries arriving soon, peace would be hard to find anywhere in the capital.

The ancient mirror hung to the left of the queen's throne. Since the night I'd fallen through it and into my mother's arms, it had been covered by a long sheet of black velvet.

For the first time since that night, I approached it and splayed my hand on the soft material. My palm pressed against the hard mirror surface underneath. I hadn't looked into this mirror since the day I arrived at Rorrim Queendom. I had no need to do so, no desire to come anywhere close to the world I'd left behind and feared to remember.

The fear had eased now. Looking back still felt unpleasant. I believed it always would be. But it no longer terrorized me with paralyzing horror. I have looked back, remembered, and I survived. The more I thought about the past, the less power it held over me. Little by little, I chipped away at the chains that bound my mind.

I was not afraid.

Taking the edge of the velvet shroud, I pulled it aside. The hard, glossy surface offered me nothing but the reflection of the throne room behind me and the face of the princess staring back at me.

She was older and far more confident than when I had stared into this mirror from the opposite side ten years ago. There was no fear in her eyes behind her glasses that looked like a piece of fine jewelry compared to the cheap, outdated plastic frame of the girl from the orphanage.

But there was no peace in the eyes of the princess, just as there hadn't been in the eyes of the orphan girl. The sleepless nights had left shadows under my eyes. I looked tired and worn out by worry. I'd found safety and family in Rorrim, but happiness remained forever elusive.

"Ari!" The soft gasp came as a crack of a whip in the stillness of the night because Mother's voice was powered by a sharp note of concern.

I turned around, letting the velvet shroud fall back in place.

Holding a candle lantern in one hand and the hem of her long robe in the other, Mother rushed to me from the doors left open by the guards.

"What are you doing up so late?" She smoothed the velvet over the mirror, making sure there were no gaps left between the fabric and the frame.

"Just couldn't sleep." I shrugged. "You?"

"I was on my way to the king's wing and saw you in here." She gently stroked my unbound hair. "Something is bothering you, my child."

Without her crown, in the soft light from her candle, she looked more like just a woman and a mother and less like a mighty queen.

"What is it, dearest?"

I sighed, disarmed by the warmth in her eyes.

Mother had not supported my last initiative in the council. The queen believed the current laws on slavery worked as intended, with no reform needed. But she didn't impede my efforts either, allowing me to do what I felt was right.

"Will I make a good queen, Mother?"

She smiled, cupping the side of my face. "Why would you ever doubt that?"

"You know I question things. Sometimes, I still feel like an outsider. I wonder if that makes me see things differently than you. What if I can't follow in your footsteps the way I should?"

"As proud as we all are of Rorrim, no establishment is perfect. A part of the queen's duties is finding and fixing its flaws. There is no harm in questioning and improving, my dear." She hugged my shoulders, leading me away from the mirror. "I'm proud of the woman you have become, Ari. I can't wait to see the queen you will be one day. You have been handling every task I've passed on to you well. I have no doubt you will handle the crown with dignity and skill whenever I decide to pass it on to you."

"Thank you, Mother." As always, her words alleviated my worries, making it easier to breathe.

"It's the anticipation of all the upcoming nuptials that must be rattling your nerves lately. A marriage is a big event in everyone's life, but the wedding of the future queen has a state-level importance. It carries a lot of weight, and you're undoubtedly feeling the pressure. The unknown is always rife with anxiety, but it will pass soon."

"I hope you're right," I said, wishing for some of her optimism.

"Trust me on this, darling. The moment you choose your future husband, the anxiety will settle. A man's attention is always sweet, and a woman's desire often grows with age. A marriage is to be enjoyed. There is no need to worry."

I longed to believe her with all my heart, pushing away the doubt. I wished to be the queen now more than ever. I believed I could make Rorrim a better place for everyone, but I needed more to succeed. More knowledge, more experience, and more power to stand up to the council. Getting married, giving birth to an heiress, and eventually acquiring the queen's crown would make my position that much stronger.

And for that, choosing my husband should be my next step.

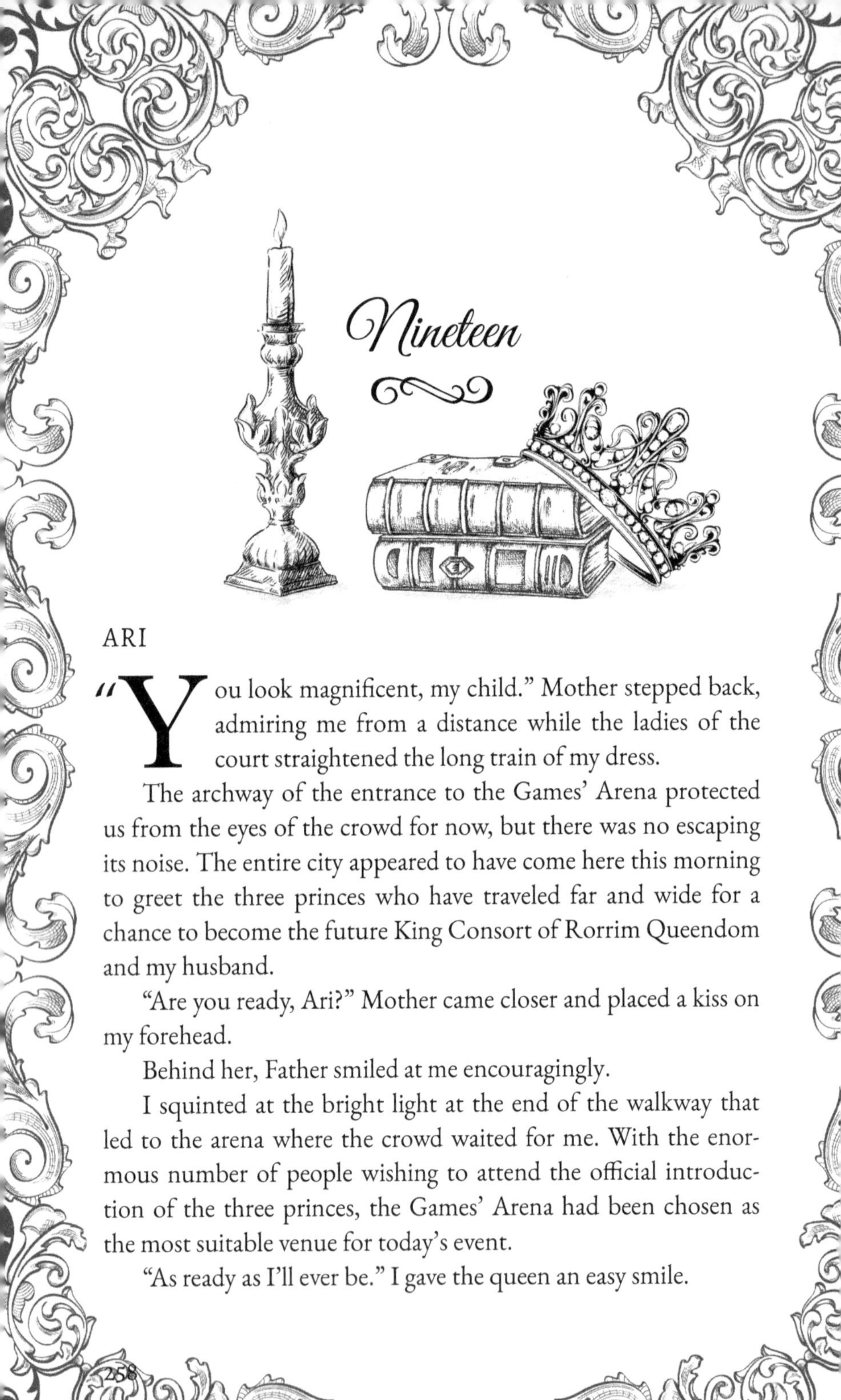

Nineteen

ARI

"You look magnificent, my child." Mother stepped back, admiring me from a distance while the ladies of the court straightened the long train of my dress.

The archway of the entrance to the Games' Arena protected us from the eyes of the crowd for now, but there was no escaping its noise. The entire city appeared to have come here this morning to greet the three princes who have traveled far and wide for a chance to become the future King Consort of Rorrim Queendom and my husband.

"Are you ready, Ari?" Mother came closer and placed a kiss on my forehead.

Behind her, Father smiled at me encouragingly.

I squinted at the bright light at the end of the walkway that led to the arena where the crowd waited for me. With the enormous number of people wishing to attend the official introduction of the three princes, the Games' Arena had been chosen as the most suitable venue for today's event.

"As ready as I'll ever be." I gave the queen an easy smile.

My nerves were under control. I might not have been born into this, but fate had brought me here for a reason. I'd studied and worked for years to be worthy of my place. Regardless of what I felt in my heart, in my mind I knew I could do it.

I'd earned my crown. I was the crown princess.

The queen took the hand of her king before going ahead of me down the walkway. Heralds announced the arrival of the royal couple. The crowd erupted in cheers. Music exploded, signaling the beginning of the festivities and my cue to head out too.

I straightened my back against the ribbed seams of the stiff bodice of my formal gown, rolled back my shoulders topped with a standing collar of golden lace, and walked toward the exit from the archway.

The sun blinded me as I left the shadows of the archway and stepped onto the crimson rug laid over the pristine white sand of the arena. The wave of cheers surged higher, and I lifted my face toward it, basking in sunshine and people's admiration.

These were my people. My destiny was to lead them. It was that simple and that complex at the same time.

Holding my head up high, I walked along the rug across the arena toward the stairs on the other side. Stopping halfway, right in the middle of the sand-covered oval of the arena framed by the queen's soldiers and royal gladiators, I raised my hand in a wave and slowly turned around to greet the crowd. From the left to the right, I twisted mostly only at the torso so as not to displace the carefully arranged train of silk and precious stones laid out behind me that stretched all the way back to the archway.

People shouted and clapped, waving back. From this distance, I couldn't make out individual faces, but I was taking them all in, all the rows upon rows of people cheering and waving at me.

I vowed right then and there that I would never let them down. I'd live to be their queen and their champion.

I crossed the arena and ascended the stairs to the royal platform to take my seat next to my mother.

The circle of soldiers and gladiators moved, forming a procession. They filled the arena in neat rows. The soldiers wore the Royal Army uniforms with shiny buttons and wide epaulets. Their swords hung in sheaths over wide silk sashes crossing their chests. The high general, a proud, well-built woman, headed the procession on a tall black stallion.

The gladiators presented a less uniformed and more colorful sight. Their clothes represented the characters they assumed in the arena during the Games. Led by the games master, an energetic woman with shoulder-length dark curls held by a bright red hairband, the gladiators marched across the arena, holding up their weapons toward the royal platform in salutation.

My gaze slid along the long line of muscular men and stopped, caught on a tall figure that towered over the rest.

The top half of his face was concealed behind the lowered visor of his helmet, but I would recognize his beard out of a million. A thrill rushed along my skin at the memory of that beard gliding down my body to settle between my thighs.

Salas had accepted the offer. He had become one of the queen's gladiators. Relief washed over me. He was here. He was safe. No longer did I have to stay awake at night wondering where he might be and whether he was well, fed, and rested.

As the procession of gladiators marched across the arena, displaying various formations for the amusement of the spectators, I couldn't tear my attention from that one man.

It appeared the games master had already chosen a persona for him to play in the arena. She didn't miss the opportunity provided by his exceptional height and size, dressing him in fur and leather like a wild man from the highest ridge of the Drazil Mountains. A full-size bear hide was draped over his wide shoulders, which must be torture to wear in this heat.

The rules on male modesty applied only loosely to the gladiators. Salas was wearing no shirt. His broad torso was covered only by the layer of his chest hair, which was uncannily almost the identical color as the bear hide on his shoulders. His crudely made helmet fit in with the overall savage look of his outfit. The helmet had been chosen wisely—with the visor over his face that kept him safe from being recognized by anyone from his past even if they happened to attend the Games.

With his visor down, I had no way of telling whether he saw me. He appeared to be looking straight ahead, focusing on executing the formations along with the others. But it didn't matter. Right now, it was enough for me to see him safe and sound.

I watched him furtively, hoping my glasses hid my eyes enough for no one to notice. I saw his hand gripping the handle of the massive ax he carried on his shoulder, and I remembered those thick, strong fingers dancing on my body while I writhed in pleasure under him. I saw his biceps bulge under the bear hide and remembered how he carried me in his arms, the press of his body against mine so gentle and warm.

Salas might be safe. But I could never be safe from my feelings for him.

There he was.

The keeper of my secrets.

The giver of all my first.

The fallen man who made me fall too.

He made me question this world that before him I'd accepted with no reservations.

His soul had linked with mine in a connection I didn't know how to break. My body ached for him. Ahead of me lay the torture of having him close without a chance of ever calling him mine.

Despite the heat of the late morning, chills ran down my arms as the gladiators left the area.

The heralds brought their long trumpets to their mouths, sounding the fanfare before the princes were finally announced.

I sat straighter. The dreams about hugs, and kisses, and caresses of a beard had to remain in the past. My future was with one of the three men entering the arena now.

The colorful crowd of richly dressed courtiers spilled into the arena. It had been decided to do the introduction of all three princes simultaneously, so as not to wound the pride of any one Queendom by arranging them into a line with the first and the last.

The three courts filled the arena, dividing it into three sectors. Three young men ascended the stairs to the platform where I sat with my parents. They greeted us before taking a knee in front of me.

The princes were young—still boys who'd barely crossed into manhood. I stared at the three heads bowed to me and wondered how I could build a connection with any one of them.

I decided to start from left to right.

"I trust your journey here was pleasant, Prince Leafar," I addressed the blond head.

At the sound of his name, the prince looked up.

"It was filled with peril, Your Highness. But every bit of danger was worth seeing you now."

I wondered what perils the prince could've encountered while traveling in his cushioned carriage across the border. Of the three of them, Prince Leafar's journey was the shortest, since Olakrez Queendom was the closest to Rorrim. But I said nothing to question his claim.

"And you, Prince Nevar? Did you find your accommodations in Egami Palace to your liking?"

The head with long straight tresses lifted next. Sweat beaded on Prince Nevar's pale brow. His outfit consisted of several layers, including the floor-length jacquard coat. The poor prince must be boiling alive in this heat, all for the sake of fashion and propriety.

Despite the heat, Prince Nevar's voice rang strong when he replied, "The rooms assigned to me and my court stun us with their splendor, Your Highness, just like the rest of the magnificent palace of your highly esteemed mother, Queen Anna."

With a nod and a smile, I rummaged through my endless

collection of small talk topics to use next. All of them were safe and boring, meant to fill the air with sound and nothing more.

"How do you find the weather in Rorrim Queendom, Prince Elbon? We're having one of the hottest summers of late."

The prince on my right jerked his head up, too, flicking his numerous shoulder-length braids.

"The heat is often unbearable back in Tresed Queendom, Your Highness. It is a reprieve to escape it for a while. The weather in Rorrim is lovely in comparison."

I nodded, acknowledging his reply.

Mother smiled warmly at them. "We have many festivities planned for the entire duration of your visits, dear princes. I trust you'll enjoy your time in Rorrim."

Her smile remained while the princes bowed and retreated to their respective handlers.

"So?" she asked the moment they were out of earshot. "What do you think? How are you feeling about them?"

I pondered her question.

My heart beat steadily. My breath remained even. There was no pull to any of the princes, no particular interest either, other than the normal curiosity about them as representatives of foreign lands.

I felt nothing. But Mother was looking at me, expecting an answer.

"They are... um, well-schooled."

She nodded eagerly, as if I'd said a compliment.

"Yes, so well behaved. Excellent upbringing." She patted my hand optimistically. "You'll have plenty of time to get to know them better before making your decision."

I had a few weeks before the princes' scheduled departure. One of them would stay, and everyone expected me to decide which one that would be.

Were a few weeks enough time to make an important decision like that?

I didn't know.

But I'd vowed to dedicate my life to Rorrim. The duty of the crown princess was to get married and ensure a direct succession, which in turn would ensure stability and prosperity in the country. So, marry I must.

As for the feelings...

They weren't necessary, were they?

Patreon

For more illustrations to this and other books by Marina Simcoe, including NSFW art, please visit the author's Patreon:

Rise of a Fallen Man

CHAPTER 1

SALAS

"This way, son. In the bucket it goes." Father directed the heavy sword blade that required two pairs of tongs to hold toward the barrel of water.

Gripping the handles of my tongs with both hands, I strained my muscles and bared my teeth from the effort. The water bubbled and hissed as we plunged the hot metal in it.

"Well done, Salas," Father said after we had finished for today.

He wiped his sweaty brow with his thick forearm. And I mimicked his gesture, wiping my forehead with my sleeve. The pounding of horse's hooves against the packed dirt road came from behind the workshop.

"Mother is back." Father took my leather apron from me. "Go check on the pie and see if she needs help to unload. I'll close up the shop for the night."

"Yes, Father." I took off my work gloves and placed them on the shelf by the door before leaving.

"And fetch some wine from the cellar, boy," Father shouted after me. "She likes a glass of wine after a long day at the market."

I dashed into the main room of our log house. With a large

hearth in the center, this space served as a kitchen, a dining room, and a living room all at once. A square wooden table took most of the space in front of the river-rock hearth. I'd already set it up with the earthenware bowls and carved wood spoons for our dinner.

There were just three people in our family. I was the only child. Mother said there had been a time when she wished to have more children, but the gods decided otherwise. Sometimes, I wished to have a brother who'd share the chores with me. But when I worked with Father at the forge, I loved having his undivided attention.

After taking the rabbit pie out, I set it on the table. The thudding of hooves and clanking of metal grew louder in the yard.

"Stand still, you demon!" Mother yelled at the horse.

She sounded frustrated, clearly needing help out there. Leaving the wine in the cellar, I ran into the yard to help before her frustration would blow into anger. She wasn't a cruel woman, but got angry and snappy at times, especially when she was tired.

"Greetings, Mother."

I grabbed the reins of our horse. He shook his head, impatient to get the harness and the collar off.

"Oh, there you are, Salas." Mother looked exhausted but relieved to have help.

Children' laughter came from the road on the other side of the house. My ears almost twitched with excitement resonating through my chest. A year ago, I'd be running out there, too, to play tug or hide-and-sick with the neighbors' kids.

But once I'd turned twelve, Mother decided I was too old to go outside unchaperoned, especially since some families on our street had girls my age.

"Girls are nothing but temptation and trouble," she'd said. "You better stay home, my boy, keep your father company, and learn the trade. People like to wag their tongues and make stories out of nothing. If you're home, no one can say a single bad word about you. This way, it'd be easier for you to find a good woman to marry when the time comes."

There were a few boys my age on our street who were still allowed to play outside. None of them were as tall as me, though.

The last time I had gone to the market with Mother, a customer ran her gaze up and down my body and smacked her lips.

"Are you looking for a wife for that one already?" she asked.

"No. He's way too young," Mother snapped before sending me to sit in the wagon, out of sight.

"Couldn't be that young." The woman laughed. "He's as tall as me."

"He's barely twelve. Hey, how about this sword for your husband?" Mother grabbed a weapon, turning the blade to reflect the sunshine.

The woman ignored her, staring at me as I tried to hide in the wagon by folding my legs under me. All my limbs seemed to have grown way too long lately. Mother often complained about how fast I was growing out of my clothes.

"Twelve, you say? What are you feeding him to grow that big? My husband is twenty-seven. But I bet your boy would wrestle him to the ground before we could even blink. Look at those arms of his!"

Mother huffed, losing her patience.

"Here." She grabbed another sword. "This one is nice and light. Perfect for your puny husband, who can be so easily over-powered by a twelve-year-old boy."

Ever since that day, she'd stopped bringing me to the market or letting me play outside. As much as I loved spending time with Father, sitting at home got boring sometimes. It didn't help that I didn't even understand the reasons for Mother's worries. How could girls mean trouble for me? Boys were more likely to start a fight.

A peal of girly laughter trickled from the road into the yard. It tugged at something inside me. I wished I could be playing with the others out there, but the pull was deeper than that, like a twist of longing for something I couldn't name.

"How was the market?" I tied the horse to a hitching post.

"Good, good." Mother ran a hand over her face. "I sold a lot. There isn't much left to unload. Leave it for your father to deal with." She waved a dismissive hand at the horse and the wagon. "Make me some tea instead, will you?"

"Sure." I ran back into the house ahead of her.

As she entered with slow, heavy steps, I filled a metal pot with water and set it on the fire to boil, then grabbed a porcelain tea set from the glass cabinet. The set was a part of Father's dowry and had Mother's favorite teacup that we didn't take out very often. I hoped it'd cheer her up to drink from it tonight.

"Father told me to fetch some wine too." I made a move toward the trapdoor to the cellar dug under the floor, but she stopped me.

"Leave the wine for now, my boy. Tea is great." She folded her tall frame into the armchair at the head of the table.

Mother was a large woman—tall, strong, and solid. She lifted the crates with heavy swords as easily as any man I knew. I once saw her stop a running horse in its tracks.

The last time she'd slapped me, it was for dropping a pot on her foot. My hands were covered in flour after kneading the dough. The pot slipped from my fingers and hit her foot. She swore and swatted me aside as if I were a fly. Propelled by the impact of her blow, I'd hit our kitchen table and shoved it all the way to the wall.

"Watch it, boy," she'd growled, limping out into the yard.

That limp was gone the next day. Mother was strong as a bear and healthy as an ox. Until just a few weeks ago, she'd unload the wagon and tend to the horse all by herself after spending the entire day at the market. Today, she slumped in her chair, waiting for me to get her tea ready. She breathed heavily, as if lifting an anvil, even as she just sat there, not moving a limb.

Father came in, wiping his hands on a clean cloth.

He hugged Mother's shoulders and kissed her cheek. "How did it go?"

"Good." She patted his hand before reaching into the pocket of her skirt. "Here." She dropped a leather purse on the table. It landed heavily, thick with coins clinking inside. "They really liked those hunting knives you made. The arrow heads sold well, too, like always. There isn't much to unload, but the horse needs to be tended to."

"I'll do it," he said, heading out into the yard.

"Your tea, Mother." I filled her cup. "The meat pie is ready if you're hungry. Or do you want some sweets and cookies with your tea instead?"

Her asking for tea at dinnertime confused me. She usually had it after work in the afternoon, often when other women from the village came to visit or her friends from the Blacksmith Guild dropped by. Then I served them tea with cookies, jams, and meat sandwiches. For dinner, we usually had a stew, a roast, or a meat pie. Now, I wasn't sure what to serve her.

"No. Just tea for now, Salas. Tea is good." She leaned back in the chair and stretched her legs in front of her. "Help me take these boots off, will you? My head spins when I bend down."

I kneeled by her feet and pulled her short, worn boots off one by one.

"Ahh," she exhaled, as I gave her feet a quick rub to relax her a little. "You're a good boy, Salas. Strong. Hardworking. Kind. All you need is a good woman who would appreciate everything you have to offer." She sighed heavily. "If only—" A rough, coarse cough cut off her words.

She bent over, coughing so hard, as if trying to hack a passage in her throat for her next breath. Her shaking hand rummaged in the pocket of her skirt before pulling out a handkerchief and pressing it to her lips.

"Mother..." My voice came out small. I wasn't used to seeing her weak like this.

Fear wormed its way into my chest. Mother had always been the epitome of strength to me. Father might be slightly taller and considerably wider in shoulders than her, but he was softer at heart. He would often keep quiet, while Mother was never afraid to speak up.

"Mother?" I placed a hand on her shoulder, wishing I could stop her body from shaking from her chest-ripping cough. "What can I do to help? More tea?"

I moved the cup a little closer to her.

She waved a hand at me between the bouts of convulsions.

"Go—" she squeezed out in an altered, strangled voice. "Go, boy... Help your father outside."

I took a step toward the door, thorn between the instilled in me the need to obey her and the fear of leaving her alone like that.

"I..."

"Go, I said," she snarled, wiping her lips with her handkerchief.

Bright red stains bloomed on the beige linen of the handkerchief. My fear turned into a lead-heavy ball of dread in my chest.

"Go, Salas." She waved a hand at me, looking deadly tired. "Just go, will you? I don't want you to see me like this."

Her voice turned soft. Pleading. I'd never heard her speak like this before, and it terrified me even more.

I turned on my heel and ran.

* * *

During the long months of Mother's sickness, her body lost most of its bulk. The strong, solid woman I knew most of my life had melted down to just a wick of her former self. She'd turned thin and frail. With her skin paled, she'd look like a ghost if it weren't for the feverishly bright red spots on her cheeks.

As the village's healing witch shook her head, talking to my father in a subdued voice, I gathered the bloodied pieces of cloth from around Mother's bed, then gave her a clean one.

"Salas," she said, her voice sounding like a rustle of a breeze in fallen leaves. I had to lean closer and strain my hearing to catch her words. "Bring me a piece of paper and a quill. I need to write a letter," she explained, answering my questioning stare. "I'll be gone soon—"

"No, Mother," I interrupted her. She was weak. She might look like a corpse already, but my childish optimism still made me believe my parents were invincible. They had to be. She and Father were my world. What was life supposed to be without one of them? "You'll get better."

She lifted a hand, stopping me while fighting another bout of a body-shaking cough.

"I will be gone soon," she repeated after the coughing fit had finally subsided. Every word was a struggle for her, and I didn't interrupt her this time, not wishing to force her to repeat. "I've been trying to make sure that you're taken care of. You and your father will be all right. I promise."

My wishes and prayers for Mother's life proved useless. She died, no matter how well father and I took care of her.

It was a sunny but frigid day when she passed. The weather remained freezing the day of her funeral too. The villagers had to burn bonfires for the entire night prior to thaw the ground enough to dig a shallow grave.

The priestess of the Great Goddess Nus said a few words over the casket. She spoke about Mother being a well-respected woman, an honorable business owner, a long-standing member of the Blacksmith Guild, a wife, and a mother, survived by her loyal husband and son.

Father stood by the gaping hole of the grave, silent and grim. His eyes remained dry. He didn't cry. But a ripple of *reflection* ran over his large body with a shudder now and then.

I'd cried so much in the past few days, I had no tears left either. They just burned now in my chest like a ball of inextinguishable fire.

I held Father's hand in mine, watching the *reflection* momentarily discolor them both into the grays and browns of the surrounding landscape.

Father was scared, and so was I. What would happen to us with Mother gone?

Her younger sister came down from the mountains for Mother's funeral. She glared at Father and me from across the open grave.

My aunt was a tall, broad woman, just like my mother. The similarity between them was so strong, it made my heart ache.

While the priestess spoke, the aunt sobbed, dabbing at her eyes with a lacy handkerchief. After the priestess had finished and the first shovelfuls of dirt hit the pinewood lid of Mother's casket, the aunt left, not sparing me or Father another glance.

People came by to offer us their condolences and to shake Father's hand. Eventually, everyone left. Only Father and I still stood over the freshly filled grave. Frost in the air bit my face. Cold wind seeped through my coat and woolen pants.

"Let's go home, Father." I tugged at his hand.

He squeezed my fingers in his. "That house is no longer ours, Salas."

With a shiver running through his body, his skin and clothes changed their color, *reflecting* the frozen hill and the black stones of the cemetery. He turned nearly invisible, blending into our surroundings to hide from the world. Now that it was just me and him, he no longer had to keep his fear at bay, and the fear urged him to hide.

I'd rarely seen Father *reflect* before. Granted, when Mother was alive, he had fewer reasons to feel fear or shame that caused *reflection*. But I also *reflected* far less than other children did. Mother had wondered if I was less sensitive than most. But Father had told her that the men in his family generally *reflected* less than normal, even when they were genuinely scared.

Now Father must be terrified, turning practically invisible against the bright winter day.

"Why can't we keep the house, Father?" I asked, squeezing his hand tighter.

His broad chest expanded with a deep breath as he took control of his emotions once again. The *reflection* passed, allowing his image to solidify again.

"Your aunt owns both the shop and the house now. Like the law says, 'the next living female relative...'" He rubbed the back of his neck. "She's always hated me. Their whole family does. Your mother came from a well-to-do family up in the mountains, Salas. And I was a nobody when she met me, the fifth son of a goat shepherd with nothing to my name. My parents couldn't even scrape enough for a dowry. But your mother married me anyway."

"That's not true. You had a dowry," I objected. "Our tea set is a part of it."

He huffed a laugh. It was a sad, miserable laugh, but it was still better than tears.

"That tea set was all my parents had of value. A family heirloom, you see?" Father pulled his hat lower over his head and hiked up his collar to hide from the bitter wind. "The set is your aunt's now, like everything else. But she didn't want to keep you. She has three boys of her own. All will need a dowry at some point, and you'd be just another mouth to feed. Her husband also said he'd hate to have more men in the house, so..." He waved a hand in the direction of the village as if rejecting that entire place after they had rejected us.

A heavy feeling pressed on my chest. The house where I'd spent all my life was no longer my home. We had no shelter to get out of this cold.

"What are we going to do?"

Father patted my shoulder reassuringly.

"We'll go to Lady Lana's manor, son. She owns everything around here." He swept with his arm toward the frozen fields that surrounded the cemetery and the dark strip of the forest in the distance. "Surely, she'll find a place for you and me." He took my hand again, tugging me along the path toward the road. "Your mother wrote to Lady Lana, asking for her kindness. The lady agreed to take you in as a companion for her son. He's about the same age as you."

I'd never been to a lady's manor. Living in one seemed exciting.

"What does it mean to be his companion? What will I have to do?"

"It's kind of like being his friend," Father explained. "You'll play with the little lord, sit in the lessons with him, learn everything they teach him."

"Like what?"

He shrugged. "To read the right books, to dance, and to fence with a sword like a gentleman."

"I know my way with a sword already. You taught me."

"It's not the same." Father shook his head, huddling into his coat against the wind as we left the cemetery behind. "Noble folks have their own ways of doing things. When they teach you, you'll learn how to act just like them."

"What for?"

"For your future, boy. You'll have a chance of a better marriage if you speak and act like a highborn. If you gain Lady Lana's favor, she'll find you a good wife and may even offer a dowry for you. You'll have a chance at a much better life than any men in our family ever had, son."

I hadn't met a noble lady before. I had no way of knowing whether marrying one would be a good thing, but Father seemed to think it was. His face lit up with hope, and I didn't question it.

"And you, Father? What will you do when I get married? Will you stay with me and my new family?"

He grunted uncertainly, then tugged his coat closer around him.

"I'll be around," he replied evasively. "But you're getting way ahead of yourself, boy. Let's just get there first."

The road ran down the hill. My boots slid on the hard, frozen dirt mixed with ice and snow. Freezing wind pelted my cheeks and nose, no matter how hard I tried to hide my face in my coat. But Father's hope proved contagious. Huddling into the coat I'd already outgrown since the last winter, I hurried along, lured by the promise of a better life.

A Look in the Mirror

TRILOGY

Downfall of a Princess
Rise of a Fallen Man
War of Smoke and Mirrors

Seven Horny Sins

Let Me Claim You
Let Me Win You, coming 2025

The World of the River of Mists

Joyless Kingdom

Somber Prince

Joy Guardian, coming 2025

Wingless Crow Duet

Wingless Crow

Crownless King

Fire in Stone Duet

Fire in Stone

Hearts of Fire

Serpent's Touch Duet

Serpent's Touch

Serpent's Claim

More by Marina Simcoe

PARANORMAL ROMANCE

<u>Demons (Complete Series)</u>

Demon Mine

The Forgotten

Grand Master

The Last Unforgiven - Cursed

The Last Unforgiven - Freed

<u>Stand Alone Novels</u>

The Real Thing

To Love A Monster

<u>*Midnight Coven Author Group*</u>

Wicked Warlock (Cursed Coven)

About the Author

Marina Simcoe likes to write love stories with human heroines and non-human heroes who just can't live without them. She firmly believes that our contemporary world could always use a little bit of the extraordinary.

She has lots of fun exploring how her out-of-this-world characters with their own beliefs, values, and aspirations fit into our every-day life.

She lives in Canada with her very own extraordinary hero, their three little offspring, and a cat who is definitely out of this world.

facebook.com/MarinaSimcoeAuthor

instagram.com/marinasimcoeauthor

amazon.com/author/marinasimcoe

bookbub.com/profile/marina-simcoe

goodreads.com/MarinaSimcoe